Jackie
by Josie

Caroline Preston

Scribner

SCRIBNER
1230 Avenue of the Americas
New York, NY 10020

This book is a work of fiction. Names, characters, places, and
incidents either are products of the author's imagination or are
used fictitiously. Any resemblance to actual events or locales or
persons, living or dead, is entirely coincidental.

SCRIBNER and design are trademarks of Simon & Schuster Inc.

Designed by Brooke Zimmer
Set in Electra
Manufactured in the United States of America

1 3 5 7 9 10 8 6 4 2

Library of Congress Cataloging-in-Publication Data
Preston, Caroline.
Jackie by Josie / Caroline Preston.
p. cm.
1. Onassis, Jacqueline Kennedy, date. —Fiction. I. Title.
PS3566.R397J33   1997
813.54—dc20   96-42177
CIP

ISBN 0-684-83077-9

To Chris

Acknowledgments

My deepest thanks to:

Elinor Lipman, the best friend a fledgling writer ever had; all the members of my Tuesday night writing group for their support, candor, and friendship; my agent, Lizzie Grossman, and my editor, Jane Rosenman, for their enthusiasm and guidance; and my dear husband, Chris, for his faith in me.

Sources Note

ALL THE QUOTATIONS by and about Jacqueline Bouvier Kennedy Onassis are authentic, and are from published and manuscript sources. This is not to say that they are necessarily true. The number of contradictory and ridiculous things that have been written about JBKO is remarkable, including what the Kennedys have written about themselves.

All the quotes from Teddy White's Camelot interview with JBKO are also accurate and are taken from the notes and transcripts of the Camelot interview released by the John F. Kennedy Library in May 1995. White's letter to JBKO, in which he writes that he did not transcribe some of her comments because they were too personal, is also authentic. The only exceptions are the "lost Camelot notes," which I fabricated. The Theodore H. White Papers at Harvard University do not contain any copies of the Camelot interview, cataloged or otherwise.

The primary sources I used were the oral histories and periodical files at the John F. Kennedy Library, as well as biographies and memoirs by Kennedy family associates and employees. The following publications were particularly useful: John Davis, *The Bouviers, Portrait of an American Family*; Diana Dubois, *In Her Sister's Shadow*; Mary Gallagher, *My Life with Jacqueline Kennedy*; C. David Heymann, *A Woman Named Jackie: An Intimate Biography of Jacqueline Bouvier Kennedy Onassis*; Rose Kennedy, *Times to Remember*; Ed Klein, "The Other Jackie O" (*Vanity Fair*, August 1989); Frank Saunders, *Torn Lace Curtain*; Maud Shaw, *White House Nannie: My Years with Caroline and John Kennedy, Jr.*; Theodore H. White, *In Search of History: A Personal Adventure*. I am also grateful to Sarah Sherman and to Megan Desnoyers, Supervisory Archivist of the John F. Kennedy Library, for their help with my research; and to Ed Klein for inadvertently providing me with the inspiration for this book.

Jackie by Josie

chapter |

Josie Trask is sitting in her car in the parking lot of Almac's Supermarket, waiting for the cigarette lighter to heat, when she hears on the radio that Jacqueline Kennedy Onassis is dead. "At ten-thirty yesterday evening . . . at her Fifth Avenue apartment . . . her two children . . . of non-Hodgkin's lymphoma." The lighter pops out and Josie presses the red coils against the end of a True menthol, the only brand she allows herself to buy now that she has secretly taken up smoking. She turns off the car, shutting off Jackie like a switch, climbs out, and leans against the dented hood. Part of her smoking ritual is that she only does it standing up in parking lots so she won't leave any telltale signs in the house or in the car.

She inhales vigorously (these Trues are hard work) and studies a clump of trees along the edge of the lot, covered with a green shimmering of new leaves. May won't look like this in California, Josie thinks glumly. I will never see this green again. She stares hard to memorize the color of a tardy New England spring—not neon green, not apple, not emerald, but a combination of the three.

Through the lattice of gray branches, she can make out the Custom House observation tower perched like a jaunty hat above the great stone building. She's never noticed this rather dramatic view from the Almac's parking lot before—down a steep hill at the spires and cupolas of Providence. If I'd been standing here two hundred years ago, she thinks, I might have seen the masts of the *Ann and Hope* gliding up the Providence River, its holds heavy with sacks of souchong, and Canton platters buried in sawdust.

Josie Trask is good at stripping away the twentieth century. With the blink of an eye, she can eliminate a Wal-Mart and an interstate, and restore a tavern that once stood at the four corners of the New-port coach road. This ability had impressed her husband, Peter, when they first met as graduate students six years ago. "You were born in the wrong century," he'd said, probably when they were in bed together. "I know," she'd said almost proudly, forgetting that some of her behavior was distinctly twentieth century.

"What doing, Mommy?" Henry yells out from his car seat.

Josie hides the cigarette behind her back and pokes her head through the open car door. "Hi, buddy," she says guiltily. "I'm just putting the grocery bags in the trunk. Want to get going?"

Henry pulls another cookie from the animal cracker box she bought him at the grocery store and holds it up for her. "Giraffe," he announces and bites off its head. He's gotten used to these cigarette breaks by now.

She turns her back to him and takes one last furtive drag, catching a reflection of herself in the windshield. A lot of unruly blond hair hanging past her shoulders Woodstock-style, and a wide-eyed, angelic face, which looks at least ten years younger than her twenty-eight and particularly grotesque with a butt. She stubs it out on the pavement and wonders why she bothers to hide her smoking from Peter; surely he's noticed the smell on her hair and clothes, although he's never commented. He must not care, even about the effects of secondhand smoke on Henry. He probably doesn't care that she was born in the wrong century anymore, either.

Before she pulls out of the parking lot onto Olney Street, she adjusts the rearview mirror so she can see Henry's face. He's looking out the window, bouncing his chubby legs up and down in his car seat, holding the box of crackers in one hand and his yellow school bus in the other. "Truck," he says, pointing out the window. "'Nother truck. Bus." He holds the *s* in "bus," making it hiss like a snake. Josie watches his face, how he smiles in wonder each time he sees a truck. Life is always a surprise when you're three. A car behind her honks twice, and she readjusts the mirror so she can see out the rear window. A woman in a big van behind seems to be making angry faces at her. Josie frequently drives around Providence with the mirror turned on Henry, and she's had a few near fender benders as a result. This is another one of her bad habits that she hopes Peter doesn't know about.

She turns the radio back on. NPR is now having an earnest panel discussion about the contributions of Jacqueline Kennedy Onassis. Josie reminds herself to pay attention; some aspects of the twentieth century cannot be ignored. Jackie's sense of style, a woman says— those sleeveless dresses and brioche hairdos. Inviting Pablo Casals to the White House, her transformation of the White House from Eisenhower Grand Rapids to a showcase of American history. Her perfect, accentless French, which was more than you could say about her English. "But, of course, her greatest achievement was as a mother," another woman concludes solemnly, making it sound as if Jackie had invented motherhood along with the pillbox hat.

Josie flips through a mental file of Jackie images—surrounded by two dozen adoring ushers at her wedding, swinging Caroline in the waves of Hyannis Port, smiling beguilingly into Khrushchev's warty face. Josie has seen more recent photographs, of course, but the only way she can remember Jackie is as a thirty-year-old. Just about my age, Josie thinks with a start. She wonders if Peter has heard the news about Jackie Kennedy. Probably. He's in his office right now figuring out an angle for an article, on the phone making a pitch to one of those editors he courts. Not some sappy personal tribute. He would analyze Jackie as an icon of popular culture, sort of like the Super Bowl.

Josie pulls up in front of a brown shingle two-family with a peeling porch on Charity Place. Peter is from California and has never gotten over the Puritan overtones of New England. "When I moved to Providence," he says, "first I lived on Hope, but now I live on Charity." Their apartment is on the second floor, and unloading the car with Henry is a chore because she would never leave him alone, even with the doors locked, even for a minute. She unsnaps the car-seat strap and pulls him out. As she lifts him onto her left hip, she bends over and kisses him twice in the velvety indented spot between his eye and the edge of his curly dark hair. She does this every time she picks him up; a reflex, like blinking. One time she tried to count how many times she kissed him there in a single day, but she was kissing him as she counted.

"See Daddy?" Henry asks.

"He's not home yet. He's still teaching at school."

"Daddy gone away," he sings, swinging his box of cookies around by the string handle. She kisses him again, picks up a bag of groceries in the other arm, and trudges up the stairs. When she opens the apartment door, she's greeted by the red message light on their answering machine blinking in the dark hallway. Back in January (about the same time she took up smoking), when Peter had signed a contract to turn his dissertation into a book and was considering two job offers, he had moved the answering machine from their bed-room into the hallway. His career was on such a meteoric rise that he couldn't wait the twenty seconds that it took to walk into the bedroom.

She dumps Henry and the groceries simultaneously onto the saggy futon couch in the living room. "Want to watch TT?" she asks. He called the television TT when he was a baby, and she still says it even though Henry mastered "TV" a long time ago. "Look, it's Big Bird and Grover!" she says brightly.

She pushes the Play button on the answering machine. The first message is from Peter's publisher. What did Mr. Stadler think about Eva Gabor in her "Green Acres" getup for the cover? The second message is from Berkeley summer school. They need Peter's course descriptions ASAP for the course catalog. The third is from Stedman Rollins, the chair of the graduate program and Peter's thesis adviser. Did Peter want to get together later in the afternoon for a beer? The messages are always for Peter, and Josie wonders if she should bother with the last one, but she does anyway.

"Fiona Jones here, for Josie Trask. It's Friday at ten. I got your name from Stedman Rollins. Please call back."

The voice is British, and the tone is impatient. She says her name as if Josie should know who she is. Josie replays the message and jots down the number with one of Henry's thick markers, feeling a surge of gratitude that Stedman Rollins has actually recommended her for something. He used to invite Peter to come along with him to conferences and even helped him get the book contract for his dissertation on the popular culture of 1966 (*From the Valley of the Dolls to the Ballad of the Green Berets*). Whenever Stedman ran into Josie, he mostly asked her how Henry was.

Maybe Stedman has recommended her for a job; Fiona Jones sounds imperious enough to be a department head. Josie hasn't applied for any teaching jobs yet because she still hasn't finished her dissertation. Now that Peter has gotten a job at Berkeley, they decided her unemployment was all for the best. "You can finish your dissertation," Peter said, "no distractions" (although she suspected what he really meant was no excuses). Josie looks at the New York area code and considers whether she could possibly take a job in New York. Maybe she could—for a year—and they could have one of those academic commuter marriages. She stops; this speculation is absurd. Fiona Jones probably sells life insurance and Stedman gave her name out as some kind of joke.

She glances over at Henry and wonders if she can trust him not to bother her while she calls Fiona Jones. He's stretched out on the couch sucking his thumb and seems about to nod off. She decides she'd better not risk it. Usually when she's on the phone, he starts pounding the buttons and wrapping himself up in the cord, or, even worse, begs to say "hello." She opens a kitchen cabinet and gropes around the top shelf until she finds the baby bottle she's hidden there. At the pediatrician's insistence, she and Peter made a big show a couple of weeks ago of saying good-bye forever to his bottle. "Bottles are just for babies," they had said, "and you're a big boy."

She fills the bottle with milk and offers it to him. "Time for night-night," she says, tucking his teddy bear quilt around his legs. He yanks his thumb out of his mouth and grabs the bottle with both hands, smiling as if he's seeing a long-lost friend. He starts sucking furiously, his eyes already shut, only the crescents of his eyelashes visible.

She tiptoes into her bedroom, shuts the door, and dials New York. A woman, not British, answers. "Fiona Jones?" Josie asks.

"What? I can't hear you." Josie realizes that she's been whispering, so she asks again, slightly louder. She can still hear Henry rustling on the couch.

"Miss Jones is in a meeting," says the woman, but when she hears that Josie Trask is returning Miss Jones's call, her voice warms slightly. "Let me see if she's available."

"Josie!" says the Fiona Jones voice, clicking on the line so quickly that Josie wonders if she had been eavesdropping. "Good of you to call back. I bet you're curious why I called."

"Well, yes," says Josie slowly, playing for time. Where can she have met this woman?

"I'm starting a new book, and I was wondering if you'd be interested in doing research for me."

Josie twists the cord around her index finger and watches the flesh bulge red. What if this woman asks if Josie's read her other books, and she has to admit she doesn't even know what they are? She slips into her serious-scholar persona—using clear enunciation, pitching her voice lower. "Tell me what your new book is about."

"Can't you guess?" Fiona sounds cozy and confidential, as if they were having a chat over tea. "About Jackie O. I just finalized the deal this morning."

Josie looks at her watch. "Jackie Kennedy's been dead for barely twelve hours, and you already have a book deal?"

"Well, let's just say we anticipated that event."

"Ah," says Josie. Just what the world needs—another book of regurgitated Jackie gossip. She sees no reason to be deferential to Fiona Jones any longer. "I'm sorry, but I have no idea who you are. Have you written any other books?"

There's a long pause. "Well, yes. I thought you probably had heard of them. Most people have," she adds pointedly. "They've been on the best-seller list; Book-of-the-Month club selections. *Picasso—The Magnificent Monster; Queen Elizabeth—The Regal Burden.* My last one was *Vivien Leigh—The Winds of Madness.*"

Can Stedman have seriously given her name to this person? "How do you know Stedman Rollins?"

"We have the same agent. In fact, I was just having dinner with him last night at her apartment."

Schmoozing with some celebrity biographer at a New York dinner party is the sort of thing Stedman would do. The new Stedman, that is. Five years ago, when Peter and Josie started at Brown, Stedman was just another poorly dressed academic. But then he wrote a deconstructionist treatise on rock and roll lyrics, which had become such a cult hit that he now did a rock music column for GQ. He'd even posed for a Gap ad, his wild hair and bushy beard making him look like Rasputin in a pocket-T.

"I was discussing this book, and how I needed a researcher who could do a lot of work in a few months and he told me about you, and how you're an expert on presidential wives."

"He did?" says Josie, trying not to sound astonished. "What did he tell you?"

"That you've been a research assistant in one of the premier archives of presidential papers. That you've published scholarly articles on several presidential wives."

A classic Stedman half-truth. One semester, Josie had worked part-time in the Brown rare book library cataloging memorabilia in the Lincoln Collection. It was a "premier collection" — of campaign buttons, walking sticks, whiskey bottles, and other oddball stuff with Lincoln's picture on it. And she had written an article, only one, about Mary Todd Lincoln in *Brown Library Notes*. A pair of her net gloves had recently been donated to the Lincoln Collection, and legend had it that the russet stain on three fingers was Lincoln's blood. Josie was able to prove positively that Mrs. Lincoln had *not* worn her net gloves to Ford's Theater that evening.

"And that your father was a congressman during Camelot."

Once again, true — technically. Her father, Griffin Trask, was a congressman for three terms, but by the time Josie was born in 1965, he'd been kicked out of office, and the Trasks were back in Crowley, Massachusetts, for good. As far as Josie was concerned, Camelot was like a good party she missed, one she hadn't even been invited to.

"So, are you interested?" Fiona Jones has dropped the cozy, confidential act. Now she sounds impatient, as if she doesn't have any more time to waste on Josie, who is clearly not what she was cracked up to be.

"Tell me what kind of research you had in mind."

"I want you to start at the Kennedy Library and see what you can turn up. Diaries, love letters, that kind of thing. I'll do the interviews myself. All the research has to be done by the end of the summer."

Josie wonders what there could be at the Kennedy Library that hadn't been pawed over by a hundred muckrakers searching for scandal in every laundry list. She imagines piles of thank-you notes with loopy handwriting that looked like her mother's, all smudged with greasy thumbprints. "That's not much time," she says, hedging. They're moving to California in a month, and she's planning to spend the entire summer finishing her dissertation. "How much were you thinking of paying?"

"If you could do it by the end of August? Oh, I don't know." Fiona's voice becomes bored at the mention of money, the way only the British can sound bored. "Ten thousand, might we say?"

Ten thousand—enough to pay for their move, an overhaul on their car so it could make it across the country in one piece, a deposit on an apartment in Berkeley, and then some. "Sounds tempting. Let me think about it."

"You have twenty-four hours," says Fiona Jones.

Josie tiptoes back to the living room. Henry is asleep on his back, an arm hanging limply over the couch, the bottle fallen on the floor. She walks down the hall to her office, or the space that Josie thinks about as her "office." Office, without quotations, seems too grandiose for what used to be an oversized closet with a window. When she was eight months pregnant, they finally admitted that they needed something bigger than Peter's dirt-cheap one-bedroom apartment on Hope Street. Four bedrooms was the minimum—one for them, one for the baby, and offices for both of them—even if it meant moving to Pawtucket. But eventually they'd settled on a three-bedroom with a big closet, around the corner from their old apartment. Peter took out the clothing rod and hooks and painted it mauve as a surprise for Josie when she was in the hospital having Henry. He'd set the whole room up for her— a student's desk which just fit her computer and printer, a one-drawer filing cabinet, a low bookshelf, even a Dundee marmalade jar filled with pencils.

When she came home from the hospital and peered into her "office" for the first time, she burst into tears. Peter beamed, thinking she was overcome by his thoughtfulness. But she really started crying because the room reminded her of a game she used to play with her best friend, Sarah. They'd hung blankets to cordon off a corner of one of their bedrooms, and then set up a little office where they banged away on an old manual typewriter, pretending they were secretaries. Standing there with Henry clutched against her engorged breasts, she realized that her own childhood was over for good.

Josie hasn't worked on her dissertation for over a month, and now she sits down at a desk piled high with junk mail and catalogs. The bundles of note cards stacked on the windowsill have started to yellow and curl. Josie is doing her dissertation on Ada Silsbee, the so-called Songbird of Crowley, a little-known poetess in the Whittier tradition. "Little-known" is putting a good face on Ada Silsbee (who, judging from the vulture nose and heavy jaw captured in the one surviving tintype, might have welcomed a good face). "Obscure" is more like it. Josie decided to do her dissertation on Ada in a flush of excitement when she unearthed a cache of long-forgotten letters and books in the basement of the Crowley library. No one, it seems, had ever heard of Ada's four volumes of poetry; Josie had made a literary discovery, the new Emily Dickinson. But she has since come to suspect that Ada deserves to remain undiscovered. Her diary contains mostly lengthy descriptions about her wardrobe; her correspondence was primarily with her dressmaker in Boston about the latest fashions. Even Whittier admitted in a letter that although he admired her poetry, he found his protégée "sometimes frivolous."

Josie takes down a bundle of note cards, peels off the dried rubber band, and fans it out. "A.S. Library" says the top card, and then a list of every book in Ada's library—Sir Walter Scott, Tennyson, Longfellow—which Josie compiled so she could chart Ada's literary influences. She puts the note cards back, feeling slightly sick. This summer she plans to write the last four chapters of *Ada Silsbee: The Poet and Her Muse*, while Peter teaches summer school at Berkeley. His mother, Ruth, has offered to stay with them and baby-sit so Josie can get some writing done.

The specter of spending the summer under the judgmental eye of her mother-in-law makes Josie's mouth feel dry. Ruth Stadler is a retired college professor who never seems to take Josie's academic aspirations seriously, maybe because she heedlessly had a baby while she was still in graduate school. Ruth has a knack for making comments that set Josie seething, and sometimes when she has trouble falling asleep, she recites them like a catechism.

> *"What's your dissertation topic again? I keep forgetting."*
> *"With that hair, you look like one of those Pre-Raphaelite mistresses."*
> *"I don't mind that you're not Jewish. Really."*
> *"Have you considered becoming a textbook editor?"*
> *"It's uncanny. Henry looks just like Peter, not a trace of you anywhere."*

Josie leans back in her chair, closes her eyes, and indulges in another one of her bad habits—daydreaming. More time has been spent in this office with her eyes shut than she would care to admit. She fantasizes about spending the summer in the East as a researcher for Fiona Jones. So sorry, Ruth, I won't need you as a baby-sitter after all. So sorry, Ada, I'm busy, but I'll get back to you later. The fantasy lurches to a halt; Josie has no place to stay in Providence—they have to move out of this apartment in four weeks. Oh, yes, she could stay with her mother in Crowley. She shuts her eyes and imagines playing the dutiful daughter for a couple of months.

Eleanor Trask is one of those uncomplaining women who deserved the best and got the worst, as if fate has singled her out for some lifelong practical joke. Twenty years ago, her husband ran off with the snappy divorcée who had run the unsuccessful "Reelect Trask" campaign and, as a final insult, he left her the Trask homestead, the tumbledown Federal mansion on the Crowley common where they lived, as a divorce settlement.

But Eleanor made do. She managed to get Josie and her sister, Leslie, through college on a pittance of child support, and cobbled together a life in Crowley Center with her garden and her ancient Boston terrier, Rascal. She collected cans for the church food pantry and visited inmates at the local prison; walked two miles every day and read all the new mysteries at the library. "Her life isn't *that* bad, is it?" Josie sometimes asked Peter.

A few months ago Leslie, a psychologist, reported to Josie that their mother was a secret drinker. Leslie lived in Phoenix and hardly ever came back east to visit, but she felt competent to psychoanalyze her family telephonically.

"I called Mother at five o'clock, and I'm sure she'd been drinking."

"Did she sound drunk?"

"No, that's just the point. She sounded very, very clear, like she was trying to sound sober."

Leslie implied darkly that this was somehow Josie's fault for not being "proactive" enough, whatever the hell that meant. "Moving to California is a form of denial," Leslie said. "You and Peter just don't want to see anything that would inconvenience your life." In a way, Leslie was right; it was inconvenient to think about her mother too much, spending winter evenings alone in that freezing wreck of a house. Who could blame her for hitting the martini shaker? Josie rubs her forehead as she considers a summer spent shoring her mother up, like sandbagging a levee threatened by flash floods.

Suddenly the front door slams, followed by two sets of footsteps pounding up the stairs, and she jolts upright. It's Thursday, of course; Peter and Monica play tennis every Thursday. Monica Glass entered the Ph.D. program the same year they did. Now the three of them are the only ones left; everyone else from their year dropped out to go to law school or enroll in a bank-management program. Practically anything was more promising than a Ph.D. in American Civilization. Monica refers to the three of them as the "Am. Civ. ménage à trois," bound together by poverty and gallows humor. She's even managed to get a teaching job in California too—a one-year fill-in at Mills.

Josie creeps out of her office to intercept them at the top of the stairs.

"Shhh. Henry's sleeping."

"Hi," Peter whispers, waving his tennis racket at her. He has on his usual tennis getup—jogging shorts, an old Stanford T-shirt, and a Giants baseball cap on backward. He was wearing his Giants hat the first time she met him at the American Civilization Department cookout six years ago, and she still thinks he looks particularly cute in it, like a stringy wise-guy twelve-year-old.

"Hi," Monica says, not whispering.

"Shhh," say Peter and Josie in unison. The three of them tiptoe single file down the long hallway, past the living room, toward the cubicle kitchen at the back of the apartment. They wedge in past Henry's high chair, a basket of laundry on the floor, a stack of newspapers waiting to be recycled. Josie can hear Henry start to thrash around, but hopes he'll settle down again if they can keep Monica quiet. Monica sits down at a table that barely accommodates three folding chairs and moves Henry's cereal bowl, left over from breakfast, to one side. She blots up the milk spills with a folded napkin.

Peter rummages through the refrigerator. "Is there any beer left?" He takes plastic containers out of the refrigerator and stacks them on the floor. "We should clean this out sometime. Christ, here's some bean dip from the New Year's party."

"What's the rush?" Josie asks. "We're moving in a month. We don't want to have to clean it twice."

"Yeah, you're right." He pulls out a beer bottle from the rear and puts back the plastic tubs, including the bean dip. They both love to parade all their sloppy habits under Monica's fastidious nose. Then he sits down between Monica and Josie, and picks up the list Josie has made of his phone messages. "Eva Gabor in 'Green Acres' for the cover? I don't know." His brow furrows with concern.

"Eva Gabor seems a little marginal to me," says Monica. "How about Sharon Tate?"

"Interesting," says Peter, taking a brooding sip of his beer. "But the movie of *Valley of the Dolls* wasn't made until '67. And then she was murdered in 1969. So I think she would confuse the 1966 metaphor. What do you think, Josie?"

He's just asking her to be polite; all she knows about either Eva Gabor or Sharon Tate is what she read in his dissertation. "How about Anne Sexton?" They both stare at her. "She won the Pulitzer Prize in 1966. It could be a poet instead of a television star, right?"

"Maybe," he says neutrally.

"How was tennis?" If Josie doesn't change the subject, they'll talk about Peter's book cover all evening.

"Well, Monica *humiliated* me, six–one, six–zip. There she was bounding around like a *gazelle*, sending me staggering all over the court. The women's varsity was practicing at the same time, and they all stood there *laughing*." He takes off his sneakers and starts rubbing his feet in a pitiful way.

Monica smiles smugly and leans back in her chair, stretching out her long legs. She's dressed in one of her hip stonewashed, garment-dyed outfits—khaki shorts and tank top with a black bra peeking through the armholes. Josie scrutinizes Monica's tanned legs, which look good even in running shoes and anklets. Josie's legs are short, and she hasn't allowed ankle socks anywhere near them since she was on the field hockey team in high school.

Monica throws one bony knee over the other. "Sorry, Pete. You're just a wimp."

Peter swings his feet into Monica's lap, wiggling his toes under damp sweat socks. "You can give me a foot massage as penance."

Monica shoves them to the floor with a thud. "Gross! Josie, how can you stand this guy?" She gives her ponytail a swing of disgust.

"I think sweaty feet are kind of a turn-on," says Josie. She can hear Henry stirring; Monica has succeeded in waking him up.

He comes padding down the hall into the room, clutching his blanket and bottle. He waves the bottle in Peter's face. "More milk, Daddy."

Peter scoops him up into his lap and kisses him on the temple—he's got the habit too. "Where'd you find this? You don't need a bottle anymore, remember, big guy?" He gently pries the bottle out of Henry's hand and puts it on the table.

Henry gives Josie a pleading look. He's not used to parents acting capriciously, one giving him something, the other taking it away. He waits for Mommy to make it right.

"I had to give him a bottle so he would go down for his nap," Josie says with a shrug. She bends over and drops her voice so only Peter can hear, "I'll explain later." She makes it sound portentous, and he gives her a curious look. She rinses the bottle, refills it with milk, and places it between Henry's outstretched hands.

"So, Henry. How was school today?" Monica asks in the same tone she uses to speak to adults. Henry pops the bottle out of his mouth and eyes her suspiciously.

"He doesn't go to school yet, just a baby-sitter, and he didn't go today," says Josie. Monica doesn't even pretend to be interested in Henry, and Josie suspects she actually dislikes him. In a way, she has cause; Henry was indirectly responsible for Stedman's dumping her. Monica was involved with Stedman for years; in fact they met at the same cookout where Josie met Peter. The four of them were inseparable, until Josie got pregnant and Stedman became so terrified that Monica might get the same idea that he bolted. Josie looks over at Henry leaning back in Peter's lap, sucking his bottle and stroking Peter's arm, and wonders how Monica can resist him.

Monica stands up and stretches her arms over her head. Now Josie can see the black bra is made of lace. "Well, I better go. I've got fifteen blue books to grade by tomorrow." Monica usually stays for dinner on Thursday, but she seems to realize she's not going to get an invitation tonight. She squeezes Peter's shoulder. "Think you can face me again next Thursday?"

"Don't get cocky." Peter and Josie sit listening to Monica's steps retreat down the stairs, the bang of the front door. Monica always slams the door. Probably a sign of her innate hostility toward babies, Josie thinks.

"What's up?" he asks.

"Someone named Fiona Jones called today . . ."

"Fiona Jones? Called *you?*" He is staring at her.

"You've heard of her?"

"Of course. Who hasn't?"

"She wants me to be her research assistant on her new book. A biography on—you'll never guess." She waits for him to try.

"Jackie Kennedy. Am I right?"

"Right," she says, deflated. "She got my name from Stedman."

"Stedman!" Peter hoots. Henry turns around to look at his father's funny face and jumps down. "Good old Stedman. He would know Fiona Jones."

Josie feels the way she usually does around Peter and Stedman— left out. Left out of the joke, left out of the banter about rock songs and sitcoms. "So, what do you know about Fiona Jones?"

"Just the scandal about her Queen Elizabeth book."

"Oh, yeah, right," she says. "I sort of forget. What happened?"

"She hired a male prostitute to seduce Queen Elizabeth's footman. Who then spilled the dirt on life behind closed doors at Buckingham Palace."

Josie remembers reading something about this a long time ago, maybe in the obstetrician's waiting room. "What dirt could there possibly be on Queen Elizabeth?"

"Mmm." He looks pensive. "Something about how she sleeps with all those corgis, and Prince Philip's bedroom is on the other side of the castle."

"Fiona Jones wants me to do all the research at the Kennedy Library, and she says she'll pay me ten thousand if I do it by the end of the summer."

He gives a low whistle.

"But I know it's out of the question," she adds.

Peter puts down his beer, wraps his big peasant hands around one knee, and studies her face as if this were the first time he's seen it in a long time. "Why is it out of the question?" he asks quietly.

"Because I'm going to finish my dissertation this summer, right? I thought that's what we agreed I should do." A defensive tone creeps into her voice, the way it usually does whenever they discuss her stalled dissertation.

"Maybe you should consider taking a job instead." He drops his eyes and starts to peel the foil label off his beer bottle.

"What are you saying?" She can hear Henry pushing his fire truck up and down the hall, humming an alarm sound. It crashes into the wall.

"Uh-oh," Henry croons.

"What I'm saying is you haven't worked on your dissertation in months. Even when Henry's at day care and you have time to work, you're either moping around here or outside sneaking cigarettes. I don't think you're going to get motivated all of a sudden when we move to California. Maybe taking a job for a while will help you climb out of your rut." The speech comes out with the pacing and polish of something that's been practiced for weeks.

Josie sinks back in the spindly folding chair and has a momentary attack of vertigo—the dishes piled high in the sink bob back and forth, the stacks of newspapers start to list toward the back door. She shuts her eyes and rubs them, trying to figure out how this conversation took such an ugly turn from Fiona Jones to the future direction of Josie's life. Her eyes snap open. "You think being a research assistant for a celebrity biographer is a good career move?" she says unpleasantly. He probably does think that, the man who did his dissertation on Jacqueline Susann. She glares over at him, noticing unwillingly how handsome he looks—already tan in May, the straight dark hair tucked behind one ear, the eyes which always seem greener when they're focusing in on something. In this case, her shortcomings.

"I'm only saying that it might feel good to do something different for a while, and earn some money. In this case, a lot of money." The tone of his voice has shifted from strident to coaxing, which Josie finds even more unnerving. "And I think it might feel good to get away from me," he adds.

"Is that what you think? That I want to get away from you?"

He shrugs and drops his head sheepishly. "Maybe."

"Why?"

"You always say we only talk about me—my job, my book. So maybe if you got away from me for a while, you could figure out what you want to do."

She wants to say that's ridiculous, but then realizes that he has spoken the truth. Peter is like a one-man band she once saw performing on the sidewalk in Harvard Square—he'd played the glockenspiel and accordion while simultaneously blowing into a kazoo and thumping on a tambourine and a bongo drum with his feet. The only thing a bystander could do was smile and applaud. She stands up and busies herself rinsing off dishes. "But wouldn't you miss me?" she says with her back turned so he won't see the doubt in her eyes. "And Henry," she adds, realizing that Henry would have to stay with her. She might agree to be apart from Peter, but never Henry—not for a month, or a week, or a day.

"Of course I would. But would it be such a bad thing to miss one another?" He walks over to her, wraps his arms around her waist, and kisses the back of her hair. With a soapy hand, she reaches down and feels the ropes of muscle in his arm, his knobby elbow.

That night, when Peter slides his hands under her T-shirt, traces the line of her spine, the slope of her shoulders, up the hollow of her throat and along the ridge of her jaw, combs his fingers through her hair, and then moves down over her breasts and across the flat of her stomach, along her hips, and between her legs, Josie feels transformed, as if he is touching a different woman. Her skin feels milky, her face finely honed, her torso long and wiry. She wonders if a job offer from Fiona Jones has made her more alluring. If he is missing her already.

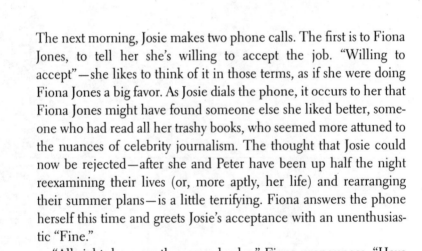

chapter 2

JFK was in and out of a motel room with several women and under the influence of prescription drugs during much of the Cuban Missile Crisis and Jackie stood in for him. She not only ordered the blockade of Cuba, but personally called Khrushchev to warn him that the U.S. meant business.

— "Jackie's Secret Diaries," *Weekly World News,* July 12, 1994

The next morning, Josie makes two phone calls. The first is to Fiona Jones, to tell her she's willing to accept the job. "Willing to accept"—she likes to think of it in those terms, as if she were doing Fiona Jones a big favor. As Josie dials the phone, it occurs to her that Fiona Jones might have found someone else she liked better, some-one who had read all her trashy books, who seemed more attuned to the nuances of celebrity journalism. The thought that Josie could now be rejected—after she and Peter have been up half the night reexamining their lives (or, more aptly, her life) and rearranging their summer plans—is a little terrifying. Fiona answers the phone herself this time and greets Josie's acceptance with an unenthusias-tic "Fine."

"All right, here are the ground rules," Fiona pronounces. "Have you got a pencil? You're going to need to write this down."

Josie obediently gropes around for a pencil and a scrap of paper and positions herself to take notes, feeling as if she's back in third grade taking spelling dictation from Mrs. Shroeder.

"My cardinal rule is *secrecy.* You may not tell anyone you are working for me. Maybe your husband, but no one else. *Particularly* all those flunkies at the Kennedy Library. You tell them you're just plain old Josephine Trask working on your dissertation."

Josie is not taking notes. Instead, she is making a doodle of Fiona Jones with Elizabeth Taylor eyebrows, a helmet of black hair, a cigarette dangling from bee-stung lips. How old is this woman? Fifty-five with a face-lift, she decides.

"You're not at university anymore doing research on some tiresome suffragette no one cares about," Fiona continues. Josie adds a V-necked blouse sprouting cleavage and is only listening in snippets. "I want to know what the servants saw . . . what Jackie was wearing . . . how many times a week Jack and Jackie did it . . . make friends with the librarians . . . get them to leak . . . two thousand now . . ."

At the mention of money, Josie snaps to attention. "Say that again?"

"I'll send you two thousand now, and then more later, according to your progress."

"I'm not sure I understand. How are you going to judge my progress?" Josie makes her voice go cold, so Fiona will understand that she is not to be trifled with.

"You'll send me a memo every week describing what you're doing. When I think you've gotten far enough, I'll send you another check."

"I get it. Sort of a reward system."

"Well, I suppose you could call it that." Josie tries to place Fiona's accent, which yelps like a dog getting its tail stepped on. From the Midlands, she guesses, knowing nothing about English accents. She imagines a semi-attached with a privy behind, sallow-faced children playing on a soot-covered stoop. Fiona Jones clawed her way up from somewhere.

"And what if I don't find what you want?" Josie says testily. "I don't think there's going to be a letter at the Kennedy Library from Jack to Jackie saying how many times a week they did it. Then what? I don't get paid?"

"Don't be silly." Fiona's voice thaws to a friendly purr. "I just need to know you're moving fast enough, not getting bogged down. It's all quite simple."

"I'll look for your check," Josie says, fearing that it's not going to be simple at all.

Next, Josie calls her mother.

"Stay with me for the whole summer?" says Eleanor, sounding about as pleased as Fiona Jones. "But why? You and Peter aren't having problems, are you?"

"I have a job in Boston, that's why," says Josie, feeling slightly miffed. She had expected joy, gratitude, maybe even a few tears.

"Well, I'm not sure where I can put you and Henry," Eleanor muses.

"Mom, I don't get it. Our house has five bedrooms. What's the problem?"

"But now Fred's in Leslie's old room. I told you Fred was moving in, didn't I?"

"Fred?"

"Fred Rizzo. One of my friends that I used to visit at MCI Crowley. He got out last month."

"An ex-convict is living in Leslie's room?"

"We don't use the term 'ex-convict.' We say formerly incarcerated."

"Okay, have it your way. A formerly incarcerated person is living in Leslie's room?"

"It's working out splendidly. He's got a job at the McDonald's Distribution Center in Ayer, and I find I very much enjoy his company."

Josie ponders what "enjoy his company" could possibly mean. She imagines her mother and a burly man in denim and tattoos sitting side by side on the screened porch, both reading cellophane-bound mysteries from the Crowley library. "So what did he do?"

"Do?"

"To get locked up."

"Incarcerated. I don't think that's any of your business, Josie. He's paid his debt to society."

"Mom," she says, exasperated, "it *is* my business. What if he molested little kids? How can I let Henry be around someone like that?"

"All right," Eleanor says, the righteous indignation waning. "He didn't molest anyone, he didn't murder anyone, he didn't rape anyone. Nothing violent. That's all I'm going to say."

Josie decides to be a good sport about Fred, at least for now. "Okay. But I'm not going to share my bathroom with him."

Eleanor doesn't seem to think this is funny. "And I expect you to be polite to Fred. He is a guest in my house."

"You're making me feel really welcome."

"Oh, dearie, I'm sorry. Of course you're welcome. I just get on my high horse sometimes. These men are treated so unfairly."

"Uh-huh," says Josie, wondering what Fred Rizzo's victims would say.

THREE WEEKS later, they are loading a jumbo U-Haul truck. The three of them—Josie, Peter, and Monica. They start at Monica's apartment in the attic of a big Victorian on Olney Street. Monica has packed up all her things into regulation moving boxes she bought from U-Haul, making a pyramid in the center of the room. Each one is labeled in big block letters: "Juice Glasses, Coffee Mugs, Dinner Plates—Kitchen"; "Books—Fiction, A–H." Josie looks around the tiny angled rooms and realizes how few times she has been here in six years. The floor is already swept, no dust bunnies where the bed used to be. She speculates whether there were ever piles of dust under Monica's bed—probably not. The only piece of furniture that Monica is taking with her is a queen-sized brass bed, now disassembled and leaning against the wall like ornate garden fencing. The three of them coax the bed sections down the winding stairs, Peter at one end, Josie and Monica on the other. Every time they lift the brass bar, Josie and Monica's upper arms rubs together, and Josie can look straight through the neck hole of Monica's T-shirt at her pointy tan breasts. This time Monica is not wearing a bra.

Somehow it has been decided that Peter and Monica will drive the U-Haul to California. The Thursday after the Fiona Jones offer, Monica mentioned that Mills wanted her to teach summer school as well. It seemed serendipitous (Monica's word) that they were moving to California at the same time. Why not coordinate (another one of Monica's words)? "Great idea," said Peter. "If I drive out with you, Josie can keep our car in Crowley for the summer."

That night in bed Josie did her best to sabotage this plan. Why didn't they just store all their things in her mother's barn for the summer, and then caravan to California in September? Henry and Josie would go in the Honda and Peter in the U-Haul. They could make a family vacation out of it, see the Grand Canyon, Yellowstone Park. Monica could make her own travel arrangements.

"But I need my books in California this summer," said Peter, "and so does Monica." He offered Josie a compromise which didn't seem like a compromise at all—he'd fly back east in September and they would drive the Honda to California and have their family vacation.

Josie lay there in the dark, her knees propped against his, and imagined Peter and Monica sitting side by side in a truck. A map spread out in Monica's lap as she navigated, Peter steering with one hand and balancing a cup of coffee in the other. She heard their voices, not any words but just the sound of them enclosed in the little truck cab, talking, talking, talking. They could discuss ideas for Peter's book cover all the way through Pennsylvania, Ohio, Indiana, Illinois, Iowa. Then maybe the conversation would switch to Monica's dissertation and the revisions she was making to turn it into a book. "I'm so glad you didn't get bogged down the way Josie did," he would say. "I really admire you."

As if he could hear Josie's thoughts, Peter turned toward her and leaned his head up on one arm. He studied her expression in the murky glow of the streetlight outside their window. "What are you stewing about?" he asked. "It's not like I'm going to sleep with Monica. She wouldn't even want to. It might mess up her makeup."

What could she say—I'm not worried that you're going to sleep together, I'm worried that you're going to have fun together? She looked up at his thin face, green in the vapor light. "Ralph Nader says those U-Haul trucks are dangerous."

After they finish with Monica's apartment, they drive over to Peter and Josie's apartment. Peter takes the U-Haul, and Josie gets a lift with Monica. Josie sits in the passenger seat and scrutinizes Monica as she drives. The operative word for Monica, she decides, is sleek. Her straight black hair is pulled back in an expensive-looking tortoiseshell clip, trendy red sunglasses sit perched halfway down her thin nose. The perfect tan rim of her ear, her long tan fingers resting lightly on the steering wheel so as not to damage clearly polished nails. This is the view that Peter will have as they drive side by side all the way to California. Will Peter think Monica is sleek?

Josie looks down at her own thigh flattened against the seat like a slab of punched-down bread dough. Not that her body is bad; far from it. She has always thought she could have been a 1950s pinup girl—the type in the cutoff blue jeans, a bandanna shirt tied under grapefruit breasts, honey braids, a pushed-back straw hat, a piece of hay dangling from moist red lips. Short and sexy rather than sleek. But sleek looks good forever, and she knew from watching her mother age that sexy is only fifteen pounds away from dumpy.

Peter once said Josie was one of those people who look better with clothes off rather than on. He meant it as a compliment, but it didn't feel like one. Her occasional attempts to dress sleekly—like Monica—were usually a failure. She bought a navy-blue suit for her first academic conference, the type with an oversized jacket and short skirt. She even bought accessories to go with it—a silk tank top and pumps with spiky heels. When she modeled her outfit for Peter, her hair pinned up in a French twist, he burst out laughing. "You look . . . just . . . awful."

"Well, what am I going to do?" she wailed. "I want them to take me seriously."

He opened the door of their closet and pawed through Josie's few dresses hanging droopily off wire hangers. He pulled out the Laura Ashley dress she'd bought during a semester at the University of London when she was a junior. It was made of a quaint fabric sprigged with thistle flowers and had leg-of-mutton sleeves and a wide sash. "I always thought you looked really nice in this," he said. Josie wasn't sure. She always thought it made her look like someone's bridesmaid—all she needed was a bunch of flowers in her hair and linen shoes dyed to match. But she'd worn it anyway, with the spiky pumps. In January, in Chicago, hobbling down the carpeted hotel hallways, Monica scissoring ahead in a black miniskirt and flats.

Monica makes a smooth turn onto Charity Place, parks, and turns to Josie. Monica slides off the red sunglasses and sets them on the dash. "Listen, I wanted a chance to talk to you privately. I don't want you to feel uncomfortable about us driving across the country together or stopping in motels. Nothing is going to happen."

The mention of the word "motel" makes Josie's stomach lurch. She pictures the neon-red motel sign at dusk, the subterranean glow of the swimming pool out front. The few times Peter and Josie stayed in a motel, the vibrating bed and pay-per-view adult movies seemed to inspire all sorts of primitive sexual behavior. She wonders if Peter remembers. Really, how could he forget? "I never thought anything was going to happen," she says, feeling patronized. "I trust Peter, I trust his commitment to me and Henry . . . And I trust you too," she adds as if it were an afterthought.

Now it's Monica's turn to feel patronized. "I never said you were jealous, Josie. All I said is you might feel weird about Peter and me driving across the country together. I probably would if I were in your shoes."

Monica slips her sunglasses on and steps out of the car. She bends down and sticks her head back through the rolled-down window. "And besides. I was your maid of honor. Didn't I promise to uphold your marriage vows?" Her lips peel back from a row of perfect teeth, and with that she strides ahead into their house.

Josie watches Monica's tawny calves retreating and repeats to herself, as if it were some hazy memory, "That's right, she *was* my maid of honor." It had seemed like a good idea at the time. Josie's best friend, Louise, wasn't available because she was in Chicago having a baby. And Leslie wasn't available either because her husband, Simon, had come down with a painful case of shingles. (He always fell ill whenever a Trask family get-together loomed.) So Josie had chosen . . . Monica.

Josie and Peter's apartment looks as if it's been ransacked by the police—closets and cabinets open, drawers pulled out. Cartons and crates from the liquor store are littered through the rooms, half-filled and unlabeled. The closets are bulging, the bed is unmade but still together, Henry's room and Josie's office are untouched. A sitter, one of Peter's female students who has a crush on him, is stretched out with Henry on the futon couch watching television.

Monica stands in the center of the living room, swiveling. "You're not going to be ready for hours. No way are we going to make Ohio by ten." Monica has planned a daily itinerary that will get them to California in exactly three days—no sightseeing, no dawdling. For once, Josie is grateful for Monica's compulsive, impatient ways.

"Hey, Monica, lighten up! We'll be ready to go in an hour," says

Peter, heading into the bedroom with a huge carton that once held a dishwasher. He takes all his clothes out of the closet, wads them into a giant lump, hangers and all, and deposits them in the box. Then he walks over to his bureau, pulls out each drawer, and dumps in the contents. Finally, he takes an armful of his shoes from under the bed and sprinkles them on top like bread crumbs on a casserole. He tapes the box shut and writes on the side with a big black marker, "Pete's Duds." "Well, I'm all packed," he says.

Monica leans on the door frame, watching. "Great, Peter. What are you going to wear for the next three days?"

He shrugs and points down toward his baggy shorts and Nathaniel Hawthorne T-shirt. He smells his armpit. "Not too bad yet." Josie smiles. She's pretty sure he's doing this for her benefit. See, he's saying, Monica thinks I'm repulsive. Monica grimaces and starts tapping her foot in spasms. He holds up a knapsack stuffed with clothes. "Just kidding, okay?"

Peter flies through the rest of the apartment, emptying cabinets and bookshelves willy-nilly into boxes. Then he starts filling up the truck at maniac speed, thundering down the stairs carrying cartons three at a time, a nest of chairs, stacks of bureau drawers. On his final trip, he wrestles the futon, flopping and folding like a tentacled sea monster. Henry tags along after him with a shoe box which he's filled with Matchbox trucks. He has the same outfit on as Peter—baggy shorts and a T-shirt—only his T-shirt has a cow on it. He stands on the pavement, his bare feet splayed like a duck's, and holds his box up to Peter. "Here, Daddy."

Peter reaches down for Henry's offering. "Thanks, buddy. But you're going to need these this summer. Let's put them in the car."

"Okay," he says, still convinced he's going somewhere fun with Daddy in the big truck.

Peter hitches Monica's car to the back of the truck. Monica climbs in the truck's passenger side, places her tote bag of travel essentials at her feet. Peter picks up Henry and says, "Give me a big hug. It's got to last for three months." Henry obligingly wraps his soft arms around Peter's neck, Peter rubbing his hand round and round on his tiny back. Josie watches Peter's face furrow, sees the shine of tears in his eyes, and thinks, good. Then he hands Henry to her and climbs into the driver's side. He rolls down the window and bends down to them. "This feels lousy. I wish I hadn't talked you into taking that stupid job." He cranes out and gives her a crooked, sweaty kiss on the lips. "Have fun with Jackie."

"Have fun with Monica," she says. She stands on the stoop, Henry straddling her hips, and watches the truck drive away, Monica's car fishtailing back and forth behind. They both have their windows rolled down and are waving extravagantly, like a bride and groom off on their honeymoon.

"Bye, truck," Henry calls.

AT MIDNIGHT Josie flops down next to Henry on the air mattress, the only piece of furniture left in the apartment. She's spent the last four hours scrubbing out the refrigerator, the oven, the kitchen cabinets, the baby-blue tile above the tub. This was the first time she'd done any of these chores since they moved in three years ago, and she went at it with a kind of scientific fascination. When she scraped the hardened grease above the stove with a knife, it curled off in ridged spirals like fancy butter. Almost pretty, really. The variety of dead insect and moth carcasses in the corners of the kitchen cabinets was quite remarkable. Hard to imagine what they'd found to eat in there.

Henry is asleep, of course, has been asleep for hours. She wraps her arms around his little barrel chest and pulls him close, his hair rubbing the bottom of her chin. This is the way Peter usually holds her, curling his long body around hers, keeping her spine warm all night, his breath in her hair soothing her to sleep. Now her back starts to feel achy and chilled; Henry's raspy snores are as calming as a sump pump.

One eye opens a slit, just wide enough to take in the two cartons of her Jackie Kennedy research sitting in the corner, with a stack of twenty cardboard Federal Express envelopes perched on top. In the bare shadowy room, they look almost like a person crouching in the corner, getting ready to pounce. In a way, it is—Fiona Jones.

In the last three weeks, Fiona (as Josie now calls her) has been sending daily FedExes. The first time Josie opened the door to find one of those official-looking envelopes with the bar codes and the address enclosed in a plastic pouch, she felt a novel rush of self-importance. Fiona Jones was willing to spend ten bucks to tell her something, something that couldn't be trusted to the U.S. mail or the phone. The stiff envelope contained a single sheet of paper—a memo with a one-sentence command.

To: *Josephine Trask*
From: *Fiona Jones*
Re: *JBKO Project*

Prepare annotated bibliography of ALL printed material with references to JBKO

Deadline: September 1, 1994

On and on they came, day after day. *Prepare clip file with annotations of significant periodical articles pertaining to JBKO. Prepare daily chronology of JBKO life. Read all Fiona Jones books.* All with the same deadline—September 1. After the third one, Josie figured out why people use Federal Express—it announced that the sender was too important to dial a phone or stick on a stamp.

The first dozen memos gave Josie enough chores to keep her toiling through the summer. After that, she stopped opening them and tossed them in the bottom of Henry's closet along with piles of his soggy laundry. The moment the two-thousand-dollar check was spent (exactly two days after she'd gotten it), Josie grasped her true relationship to Fiona Jones—indentured servant.

Sleep is hopeless. Might as well do her master's bidding. She flicks on the overhead (the lamps are on their way to California), props the pillow against the wall, puts on Peter's flannel shirt which serves as her bathrobe, and picks up *Vivien Leigh—The Winds of Madness.* So far, this is her favorite. She'd started with *Queen Elizabeth—The Regal Burden*, thinking there might be some first lady parallels with Jackie, but even Fiona Jones couldn't make Queen Elizabeth interesting. *Picasso—The Magnificent Monster* outlined the dozens of ways there were to mistreat and humiliate women, and all by the same man in a single lifetime (even though he did live to be ninety-two)—quite an accomplishment.

What she likes about this one are the descriptions of Vivien

Leigh's clothing; the outfits she wore when she landed the part of Scarlett O'Hara (a navy gabardine suit cut on the bias with a flared peplum), when she had her first breakdown (a Christian Dior peignoir set in ecru satin), caught Larry Olivier in bed with her best friend (a trim riding habit with buff-colored jodhpurs and mud-splattered boots). One of Fiona's memos was *Make detailed descriptions of outfits worn by JBKO*, and Josie is trying to pay more attention to people's clothing. But, as Monica once observed, Josie hardly has a lot of "fashion sense"; she had to look up "peplum" in the dictionary. She's not even sure how one goes about getting fashion sense. It's probably innate, passed along like high cheekbones from a fashionable mother. Monica's mother was a buyer at Neiman Marcus who kept her constantly supplied with free samples; Eleanor still wore the sweater set she'd had during her freshman year at Smith.

After Vivien is dumped by Larry, the book loses steam, limping toward her tragic end in and out of sanitariums. Even her wardrobe went downhill. Josie turns off the light, locks her arms around Henry, wedges her hip into the air mattress, and wills herself to sleep. She thinks of the skirt of Jackie's wedding dress, a complicated thing with huge silk flowers made of something like fifty yards of silk brocade. What are those folds all over the skirt called—pleats, ruching, tucks, shirring? Mostly they remind Josie of the antimacassars her grandmother pinned to the armchairs, but she suspects this is hardly what Fiona, or Jackie, had in mind.

Her father used to call Eleanor's mother and her antimacassars (along with all the rest of the things in her house) pure Grand Rapids. Jackie said that too. She banished the Eisenhowers' furniture to the White House cellar, labeling it "Grand Rapids." What's so bad about Grand Rapids? Josie wonders. Could it be any worse than Flint? Or Kalamazoo?

When Elizabeth saw the dashing young naval officer, resplendent in his dress uniform with gold braid and ribbons, she began to toy nervously with her neck-lace. It was a five-strand choker of baroque pearls with an exquisite platinum clasp holding a four-carat cabochon sapphire. The necklace had belonged to her great-great-grandmother Queen Victoria, and had been appraised by Harry Winston at over a million pounds. But right now, Elizabeth was too absorbed by the mysterious stranger to think about her necklace. She bent over to her lady-in-waiting and whispered, "Who is he?"

— FIONA JONES, *Queen Elizabeth — The Regal Burden*

The next morning Josie is heading home to Crowley Center. The Honda station wagon, loaded to the ceiling with boxes, leans on the cloverleaf turn off Route 495. She looks in the rearview mirror and nervously eyes the stack of cartons wobbling behind Henry's sleeping head. Peter lashed them together so they wouldn't avalanche, and she checks to see if the ribs of twine have shifted. She taps on the brake, the car lurching up to the stop sign like a stubborn horse. "Whoa," she says. She points out the window toward the green road sign. "Look. Just five more miles to Grammy's," she says loudly, but Henry sleeps on.

The car lumbers onto 2A, a two-lane that strings Ayer, Crowley, Leominster, and Fitchburg together like a necklace of tarnished beads — all of them ghost towns left over from the glory days of industrial New England. The road loops down through the center of Ayer, past the commercial block with half of its storefronts vacant and black. The hairdo posters in the beauty parlor window are faded blue; the liquor store has a handwritten sign in the window announcing an inventory reduction sale. Only Tiny's Diner at the edge of town looks prosperous, its parking lot almost full in the middle of the afternoon. Josie drives past a trailer park, an abandoned car dealership beached in acres of empty asphalt, the military base slated for closure in 1995.

At the Bull Run Restaurant, where her father used to hobnob with the local big shots, she turns left on a narrow road ribboning through shadowy woods, along a fenced paddock with a grazing horse and an old farmhouse chipped clean of paint. Ahead Josie can see the white buildings of Crowley Center and feels a familiar sense of dread—she spent too many summers there with nothing to do and nowhere to go.

She circles slowly around the town green with its Civil War soldier facing pensively south. The old town hall and Unitarian church stand side by side—their white clapboard sides stained and warped, the gravel parking lots in front empty. There are no cars anywhere, the only sound Josie can hear through the rolled-down window is the distant buzz of a lawn mower.

She drives past the Morrows', the Foxes', the Lansings'—all white Federals with a hodgepodge of additions: cupolas, porches, back ells, barns. Right after the Spragues', she turns into the dirt driveway of the most imposing house in Crowley Center, perched on a knoll above the common as if it were claiming superiority to everything in its view. Josie parks at the bottom of the driveway so she won't block her mother's car in front of the carriage barn. A walkway of marble slabs winds up from the road to a fluted, fanlighted front door. The path is edged with spiky, overblown flower beds—lupine, daylilies, delphiniums, foxglove. Josie wonders for the first time who planted these flowers—her mother, or some long-forgotten Trask? The white paint under the gables is peeling, but her mother will probably postpone a paint job for another two or three years.

Josie unbuckles Henry. "Come on. Wake up. We're at Grammy's." He doesn't budge, his head slumped to one side, mouth open, a string of drool down his velvety chin. He was up late last night watching her clean the apartment. She slings his arms and head over her shoulder and carries him up the path, kicking the screen door open. "Mom? We're here." No answer. She steps in the front hall and is assailed by the smell of moldy basement seeping through the floorboards. Their house always smells like this, even with the windows open. Josie used to find it comforting until one of her high school friends said, "Phew, who died in here?" Then she began to notice that other people's houses didn't smell decayed and abandoned.

She lugs Henry, still asleep and forty pounds of deadweight, down the long hallway toward the kitchen in the back ell. Rascal's porcine body is stretched out underneath the hall table, shuddering slightly with every snore. She's gotten so deaf she doesn't budge for intruders, friendly or otherwise. "Mom?"

"She's not here," a man answers.

Fred Rizzo. Josie stops and hugs Henry tighter. She had expected her mother to provide a formal introduction to Fred Rizzo, like a referee explaining the ground rules for fair play. She considers for an instant backing out the front door and waiting in her car, but then decides that's paranoid. It's the middle of the day, what can possibly happen? I can always scream, she thinks. Someone will hear me.

Josie has already decided how she's going to treat Fred Rizzo — polite but wary. She plans to let him know that she doesn't trust him and is keeping an eye open, even if her mother isn't. "Who is that?" she yells.

She hears footsteps coming from the kitchen and readjusts her grip on Henry, taking a few steps backward, toward the open screen door. Maybe she could nudge Rascal with her foot and try to rouse some of her old watchdog behavior.

"Hi, Josie. I'm Fred Rizzo, your mom's boarder," the voice says, and then Fred Rizzo looms into view out of the shadowy hall. He is, of course, not at all what she expected. He is older, in his early sixties, she guesses, and shorter, almost as small as Josie. Instead of a denim work shirt, he's wearing an alligator polo shirt. No tattoos, no menacing facial hair. He has thick gray hair parted on the side, his smile reveals benevolent dentures. He has a dish towel tucked in his pants as an apron. He wipes his hands. "I'd shake, but I've been cooking. Come in the kitchen. I just brewed some iced tea."

She follows Fred into the kitchen and sits down at the chipped enamel table, Henry cradled in her lap. A saucepan and a stew pot are steaming on the old Garland eight-burner. Strips of dough rolled out on wax paper run the length of the linoleum-covered counters. "What are you making?" she asks.

"Cannelloni stuffed with veal. Sort of a welcome-home meal for you." He moves over to the stove and stirs the pots with a wooden spoon. Then he picks up a large glass pitcher on the counter and fishes out a cheesecloth bag filled with loose tea and orange peels. "Ever since I moved in here, I've gotten into cooking."

Prison food will do that, she thinks. Or my mother's food. Eleanor's idea of dinner is opening the freezer and running her hand down a row of orange Stouffer's boxes. If she has a guest for dinner, the guest gets to pick. "What'll it be, Josie? Chicken tetrazzini, chipped beef, or tuna noodle?"

"I'm sure that makes my mother happy," says Josie. "She doesn't like to cook much."

Fred pours tea from the pitcher into an ice-filled glass and sets it down in front of her. "Yeah, I noticed." His tone is neutral. "Let me know if that needs more sugar."

Henry arches his back and rubs his eyes with a fist. "We're here," she whispers. "We're at Grammy's."

Fred opens a dented cookie tin and offers it to Henry. It's filled with homemade, brown-edged sugar cookies, nested in wax paper. "Want a cookie, Henry?" he says.

Josie shoots Fred a warning look, takes a cookie, and then pushes the tin away. "I'll give it to him," she says. "I'm not supposed to let him take food from strangers. You know, all this stuff about abducting children." She hands it to Henry. "See, Mommy's got a surprise for you."

Unoffended, Fred puts the tin back on the counter and starts cutting the cannelloni dough. "You've got to be so careful with kids these days. I've got five grandchildren of my own, and I worry about them all the time. My little girl must be about your son's age. She's a real sweetheart."

She gives a disinterested "Mmm." She's not about to get enmeshed in Fred Rizzo's personal life, not like her mother. Eleanor knows every detail about her MCI "friends." Their divorces, their children's medical problems, their unfair treatment by the prison system. She buys them cigarettes, lends their girlfriends money for bus fare, writes letters on their behalf to the parole board.

Henry jumps down and starts prowling around the kitchen. He opens the cupboards under the counter and starts pulling out pots and pans, flipping over a roasting pan and banging on it with a wooden mallet. "Where's my mother?" Josie says, wondering why she hadn't asked sooner. She pictures Eleanor bound and gagged in an upstairs closet.

"Over at the church. Tagging clothes for the rummage sale."

Fred wraps dough around veal and béchamel sauce and sets the cannelloni in tidy rows in a glass baking dish. Josie watches his hands expertly tucking and rolling. Maybe he was a professional cook. Or did KP duty in jail.

She stands up and puts the pots and pans back. "Come on, Henry. Let's go find Grammy at the church." She takes his hand and heads down the hall. At the screen door, she yells, "See you, Fred. Thanks for the tea."

They walk down the path and across the road to the Civil War Monument on the green. Henry climbs up the granite base and tries to shimmy up the soldier's legs toward the bronze rifle in his hands. "Me get the gun, Mommy." He grabs the bronze pant leg, his navy sneakers scrambling for purchase, and then slowly slides down until he falls on the grass. He jumps to his feet and starts climbing back up.

Josie sits on the grass and watches. This is a game they play whenever they visit Grammy. "You can't get the gun," she says. "It's not a real gun. It's attached to the man's hands." She's explained this before. The clock on the town hall chimes five, and she wonders where Peter is. They made it to Pennsylvania last night, and plan to make Kansas City today. She decides they must be crossing Illinois now, and pictures the wheat fields and telephone poles flying by. What are they talking about? Probably Monica's love life—old complaints about Stedman, speculations about whatever new man she's interested in. For some reason, women always confess their men problems to Peter. Josie's not sure if he actually dispenses advice, or just looks sympathetic. Later they say to Josie, "You're so lucky. I wish I could find someone like Peter." He said he'd call at ten; only five more hours. Last night, he called from a pay phone next to the check-in desk at an Econo Lodge. Twice he said, "I wish I wasn't here all by myself," which made her feel better.

There still aren't any cars on the road, even the lawn mower has stopped. Josie remembers this hot, airless silence. She'd spend her days during summer vacation stretched across her bed reading books bound in faded green cloth from the library—*Daddy Longlegs, The Grapes of Wrath, Rebecca.* When she couldn't stand the silence anymore, she'd walk the two miles to the package store in Crowley Depot, change rattling in the pocket of her shorts for penny candy when she got there. Sometimes she'd find someone along the road—a younger kid, an adult, anyone—to talk to.

Josie stands up and brushes grass clippings off her shorts. She looks across at the Trask homestead in all its shabby grandeur and decides to convince her mother to sell it. Her mother could move away from this stillness, maybe buy a condo on Beacon Hill, hear cars and neighbors shouting at each other all night long. A red car comes darting down Longley Road like a prophecy, honks twice at Henry and Josie, and heads left toward Crowley Depot.

She tugs on Henry's shirtsleeve. "Let's go see Grammy." She expects him to protest, but he slides obediently to the ground and reaches up to grab her thumb. They cross over to the church and walk around the back to the parish-hall door. The parish hall smells moldy too. Her mother sits all alone at a long worktable on the stage with her back to the door, and she doesn't look up. A heap of clothes lies at her feet, and she's writing something with a thick black marker. She's wearing a shirtwaist dress with navy pinstripes that she's had as long as Josie can remember. Her white hair, which used to be so blond and curly, is cut straight at the chin line and pulled back by a hair band. Josie quietly crosses the room until she's standing by the stage. "Hi, Mom," she says.

Her mother whirls around, her pale eyes wide in alarm behind her reading glasses, her hand at her throat. "God, you startled me."

Josie steps onto the stage, bends down, kisses her mother's cheek. Her skin seems thinner and looser than the last time Josie kissed her, at Easter. Josie can now see that her mother is marking white paper tags—.50, .25, $1. Nothing more expensive than a dollar. A

Pendleton suit smelling of mothballs lies on the table. "Well, we made it."

Eleanor turns around to Henry, who has found a big fire truck in the pile of church-school toys, which he is pushing across the floor at top speed. "Hello, Henry."

Josie looks over at the heap of tagged clothing: a blouse with a pointy collar, a bright green dress with gold buttons up the front. "Who buys this stuff?" As she says this, a sour taste comes to her mouth. After Grif left them when Josie was seven, Eleanor started buying their clothes at church rummage sales. Josie wonders if Eleanor will think she's making a pointed comment, but she seems oblivious.

"You'd be surprised. Lots of teenagers come to our sales. I think they buy the clothes for Halloween costumes."

Josie picks up the jacket of a herringbone tweed suit. Without the pleated skirt, it's not so bad. It's the kind of thing Monica would buy from one of the trendy secondhand clothing stores near the Rhode Island School of Design, and accessorize with leggings and a black camisole.

Eleanor puts the marker and tags back into an ancient cigar box. "Let's head back. Fred will have dinner ready." They walk out, and she pulls a large brass ring of church keys out of her pocketbook to lock up. In June, she was elected church deacon in addition to serving as secretary of the vestry, chairwoman of the altar guild, and assistant director of the choir. The First Unitarian Church of Crowley only has thirty-five members, and Eleanor seems to be the youngest and fittest of the lot. "Did you get a chance to meet Fred?" she says.

"Yup," says Josie noncommittally. Eleanor is watching her face, waiting for her to admit that he's not so bad, but Josie is not ready to concede anything yet.

They stop in front of the Civil War Statue and watch Henry make a couple of futile climbs. "Oh, and guess what? I found you a baby-sitter," says Eleanor, looking quite proud of herself. "One of Allen's nieces is living with him for the summer. She's twenty and saving money to go back to college. I told her to come tomorrow at eight for an interview." Allen Railsback, the Unitarian minister, usually had a wayward relative or two staying with him.

Josie gives her mother a hug of gratitude, feels Eleanor's soft bosom and middle press into her. Now Josie can start her research tomorrow. With luck, she can be done at the Kennedy Library and on her way to California by the end of July. She wonders if Peter is out of Illinois yet.

Fred has set the table in the dining room—linen tablecloth, silver, a vase of snapdragons cut from the garden. Eleanor stands at the doorway smiling, fingering her pearls nervously. "Fred, you spoil me."

"You and Josie go sit on the porch, while I do the finishing touches," he says, heading back into the kitchen.

Eleanor turns to Josie. "Cocktail? I'm having a martini."

Josie hesitates. Leslie has warned her not to collude with their mother's drinking. Josie watches Eleanor briskly measuring jiggers of gin and decides that Leslie is simply being hysterical. How could an alcoholic find a baby-sitter? "I'll have white wine," she says. "Does Fred want something?"

Eleanor shakes her head violently and silently mouths, "AA."

They settle on the screened porch off the living room—Josie stretched out on a wicker couch, Eleanor sitting on a wicker armchair with her feet propped on a hassock, Henry cross-legged on the floor spoiling his appetite with a bowl of Pepperidge Farm goldfish. The screened porch hasn't changed since the days when the house was only used during the summers forty years ago—the cushions covered in faded linen flowers, Chinese urns filled with straggly geraniums. Eleanor takes a hearty sip of her drink. "Ah, that hits the spot." She folds her hands contentedly in her lap and leans her head back. "It's hard to believe you're doing a book on Jackie. I first met her when she was pregnant with Caroline."

"You knew her back then?" Josie asks. She has a hard time remembering that this woman in the thirty-year-old shirtwaist dress ever knew Jackie Kennedy.

"A little. Both of our husbands were in the Massachusetts delegation, so I used to see her at functions. I think I even sent her a present when Caroline was born. That's the kind of thing I was supposed to do as a congressman's wife."

"So what was she like?"

Her mother takes another long sip and gives a self-deprecating smile. That strip of white teeth—a reminder of the porcelain-doll beauty she used to have, back when she knew Jackie. "Well, believe it or not, I don't remember her very well. She was very young, so pretty with all that short dark hair, reserved. If I'd known she was going to become the most famous woman in the world, I would have paid more attention." Her mother stares over Josie's head toward the back field that runs behind the house. "Strange, isn't it? Strange what happened to her, strange what happened to me."

Josie tries to think what her mother could possibly mean. Jackie Kennedy's life had strange twists of fate, but her mother's life seemed pathetically ordinary. Married a handsome man, got dumped by a handsome man, and then, after that, a succession of days filled with volunteer jobs no one else would do. What was so strange about that? Just as Josie opens her mouth to ask for an explanation, Eleanor stands up and heads toward the kitchen. "Want a dividend before dinner?"

Cocktail talk—dividends, jiggers, fingers. A bar stocked with three different kinds of gin, liqueurs in oddly shaped bottles, glasses in a dozen sizes, ice buckets, little napkins printed with roosters. Back when they were married, her parents observed the cocktail hour religiously. From six to seven, on the porch in summer, in the living room in winter, no kids allowed. After the divorce, her mother observed the cocktail hour alone, reading one of her mysteries. When Josie and Peter got married, her father urged them to establish a cocktail hour. "A time to describe the events of the day, to reflect upon your lives," he said majestically.

Fred steps onto the porch. He's taken off the towel and combed his hair. "Dinner is served," he says, and gives a courtly bow in Josie's direction. He picks up Henry, carries him into the dining room, and sets him down on a booster seat he's fashioned out of a *Columbia Encyclopedia.* Josie watches Henry link his arms around Fred's neck and decides she will have a talk with him about trusting strangers later. Then Fred scoots around to her place and pulls out her chair. She plunks down ungraciously. "Thanks, Fred. That's hardly necessary."

Fred stands behind Eleanor's chair and waits for her to come back with her drink. Eleanor seats herself, tilts her head up toward

Fred, and gives her beautiful, bashful smile. "Thank you. I can't remember the last time a man pulled my chair out for me." Fred serves them each three cannelloni neatly placed in the middle of her mother's best Spode plates, then sits down at the head of the table, puts his napkin in his lap, and waits. "Please start, Fred," says Eleanor.

"You take the first bite."

"All right," says Eleanor, picking up her fork and delicately taking a bite. "Mmm, delicious. You're a culinary artist."

Josie keeps her hands folded in her lap, her irritation mounting. She's not sure she can stand a whole summer of watching her mother act like a love-struck schoolgirl, especially with Fred Rizzo as the object of her affection. He's trying to inveigle his way into her mother's life, but why? Maybe he mistakes this shabbiness for Yankee frugality; maybe he thinks she's rich.

Henry pushes the pieces of cut-up cannelloni around his plate. "This is yuck," he announces.

Josie gives him an indulgent smile. "That's okay. You don't have to eat it. I'll make you something else later." Henry hops down, heads back to the porch, and comes back with the bowl of goldfish crackers. She turns to Fred and waits for some disapproving comment, but he doesn't seem to have noticed. He is staring at her attentively.

"Now that I've met you, Josie, I can just picture your mother at your age. What a knockout. I wish I'd met you thirty years ago, Eleanor. My life might have turned out differently." Eleanor is stroking her pearls again. He turns to Josie. "Has anyone ever told you how much you two look alike?"

"Nope," says Josie, daring her mother to contradict her. "You look so much like your mother" was the refrain of Josie's childhood. Eleanor's baby pictures have always given Josie a chill, as if she were seeing herself in a former life.

Fred is undaunted. "Your mom tells me you're doing a book on Mrs. Onassis. I used to know Jack Kennedy."

"Oh, really," Josie says without looking up from her food. She prepares herself for some self-aggrandizing tale—how he procured prostitutes for JFK, helped buy votes in Chicago, shared a cell with the Mafia hit man who really killed JFK.

"Not very well, of course. I was a driver for him during the '56 campaign. Used to take him to Chelsea and Brighton and Cambridge. Churches, the Rotary. Never saw her, though. I always thought she was kind of snooty."

Josie feels a little prickle of interest. This is just the kind of lead she's supposed to be sniffing out for Fiona Jones. Maybe Fred drove JFK around while he necked in the backseat with some eager campaign volunteer. That's what her father had done, with Terry Mascone, the divorcée who had run his reelection campaign. Who fucked him at lunch hour at the Olde Fitch Motel across the street from the campaign office, who persuaded him to leave his wife and daughters for her and her two bratty kids. Josie decides not to ask more about Fred's days as Kennedy's chauffeur, at least not now. "How interesting," she murmurs. Her mother gives her a sharp look, which makes her instantly repentant. "This is great. May I have a little more?" she says, reaching for the platter of cannelloni in the center of the table.

Fred mercifully drops the Kennedys and moves on to his job at the McDonald's Distribution Center. "Oh, tell her, Fred," her mother says in a girlish voice that makes Josie sit rigid. "It's fascinating."

Josie looks over at her mother's martini glass, which is filled. Leslie has instructed her to monitor Eleanor's drinking, but she's not sure if this is the dividend from before dinner or a refill. Her mother's cheeks are flushed with cheer, and she's waving her hands in front of her face as if she's swatting flies.

"I do inventory control," says Fred. "Guess how many packages of ketchup we send out of there in a single week. Just guess."

"Oh, I don't know. A million?"

"Well, no. Not that many. Two hundred thousand. That's still a lot."

"Isn't that something?" says Eleanor, laughing.

Josie tries to look impressed. Fred clears the table, refusing any offers to help. "No, no. Tonight's my treat." He comes back with dessert—frozen lemon mousse in white ramekins decorated with fresh mint leaves.

Josie takes a single bite of mousse and then has a thought that is so horrifying she loses her appetite. Could her mother possibly be sleeping with Fred? Josie glances from her mother to Fred and back again. They are chuckling over another funny story from the distribution center—the time two tons of frozen french fries got misplaced. Could her mother know about the HIV rates in prisoners? About how to practice safe sex? Josie thinks how she could tactfully bring this up—a bedtime chat? During the cocktail hour? She decides this is a job for Leslie, who would arrive with condom samples and demonstrate proper usage on a banana.

Josie stands up and carries her uneaten dessert toward the kitchen. "This is delicious, but I'm on a diet."

"You, on a diet?" says Fred. "Your figure is perfect." He kisses his fingertips.

Josie scrapes the plates and stacks them so violently that one of the gilt edges chips. Eleanor follows her. "We'll do that, Josie. Fred and I always have so much fun doing the dishes together. You go upstairs and get Henry settled." Her eyes are bright, her face is even redder from laughing.

"All right." Josie's had enough of Fred and Eleanor's fun for one evening. "I'll get my stuff out of the car."

"Oh, I emptied the car for you," says Fred. "I put the boxes and suitcases in your old room."

Josie picks up Henry and is halfway up the stairs before she can bring herself to call out, feebly, "Thanks."

chapter 4

Meanwhile in Massachusetts Jack Kennedy dreamed
Walking the shore by the Cape Cod Sea
Of all the things he was going to be.
He breathed in the tang of the New England fall
And back in his mind he pictured it all
The burnished New England countryside
Names that a patriot says with pride
Concord and Lexington, Bunker Hill
Plymouth and Falmouth and Marstons Mill.
— JACQUELINE KENNEDY, October 1953

❦

At ten o'clock, just after Josie has gotten Henry tucked in the trundle bed in her old bedroom, the phone rings. She goes to the top of the stairs and yells down, "That's for me, Mom. It's Peter. I'll take it in your room." Loud music, Benny Goodman, is blaring from the living room, and she's not sure Eleanor has heard her. She walks down the hall to her mother's bedroom and picks up the phone on the bedside table. Eleanor and Peter are talking.

"Well, we miss you, dearie," her mother is saying. "Josie seems so gloomy without you. And Henry's been talking about you nonstop."

"I've got it, Mother," Josie says, an edge in her voice.

"Now, you be careful, Peter," Eleanor continues. "I'm going to worry until I've heard you've made it to California." And then a click as she hangs up.

"I'm not gloomy," says Josie.

"I never said you were," says Peter. "How about hello, how are you?"

"Hello, how are you?" She hears a burst of laughter in the background. "And where are you?"

"You'll never guess. We started having trouble with the truck just as we hit Illinois, so we detoured to Chicago. We're at Doug and Louise's."

"Oh," says Josie, trying not to sound wounded. Louise was in their class at Brown for a year and Josie's best friend until she transferred to business school at Northwestern. "So how are they?" Louise married an investment banker around the same time that Josie married Peter, and they live in suburban splendor in Winnetka.

"Rich as Croesus. This house looks like Fontainebleau. An au pair, a lawn care service, a BMW, and a Jeep Cherokee. They have sold out *big-time*." Then she hears Peter yelling, "I'm telling her, Louise. Now she knows your dirty little secret." More laughter.

"So what's wrong with your truck?"

"Transmission is shot. It sounded like a dentist's drill. They say it will take two days to get another truck that size. Monica was freaking out, but I convinced her that we could have some fun sightseeing in Chicago for a couple of days. Doug has actually agreed to lend us his sable-brown BMW tomorrow, and we're going to see all the Frank Lloyd Wright houses in Oak Park." Peter is talking in what Josie calls his enthusing voice. Just the way he says "sable-brown" and "Oak Park," going so high with excitement that it cracks, makes her sick with yearning. And she doesn't even like Frank Lloyd Wright. It was the enthusing voice that made him such a seductive teacher, made his students tag along behind him after class, following him all around campus and back to their apartment, inviting themselves for dinner. Just to hear that voice talk about baseball or Whitman or reruns of "The Mary Tyler Moore Show."

"And then on Wednesday, we're going on to Wrigley Field. Doug's company has season tickets in the sky box," he says and then shouts to the other room, "Now I'm telling her about the sky box, Doug." Laughter.

This is the trip Josie and Peter have talked about taking for the last two years. Louise said they could leave Henry with her au pair for a few days, see the sights in Chicago, maybe drive up to Mackinaw Island. The trip they kept postponing so Peter could finish his dissertation, and then his book. Josie's throat feels tight, as if she might start to cry, and she takes a drink from the water glass on her mother's bedside table. She spits it on the floor; it's gin.

"Josie?"

"Sorry. Something went down the wrong way. It sounds like you're having a lot of fun. I'm jealous." She says this as blandly as possible.

"I know," he says, dropping his voice. "I know how much you miss Louise. We'll stop here when we drive out in September. I promise."

"Okay," she exhales, sounding pathetic. She looks down at the little spot of gin on the hooked rug. It will probably dry without making a stain.

"How's our baby?" he asks. When it's just the two of them, they sometimes revert back to calling three-year-old Henry the baby. He makes her describe everything Henry has done—what toys he is playing with, what books he looked at, how toilet training is coming.

She answers, "The red fire truck with the broken ladder," and "*Mike Mulligan and His Steam Shovel*," and "Just one poop today, but it was a big one," and "He spent twenty minutes trying to get that gun on the Civil War Statue."

"*Really?*" says Peter, his voice going high and squawky again. "Has he really asked about me?"

"Constantly," Josie lies.

"So how's your mother? How's Fred Rizzo?"

"He's . . ." she starts. What can she say? He made cannelloni for me, carried my suitcases, is nice to my mother, and I don't trust him? "I think she might be sleeping with him," she says. Peter starts laughing in a way that makes her wonder if he's drunk. "It's not funny."

"Oh, come on. Yes, it is."

"It's not. Can I talk to Louise?"

"Sure. Don't be mad at me." He sounds eager to please, just like—Fred Rizzo. While Peter goes to get Louise, Josie listens to the lapping waves of distant conversation. She tries to imagine where they are sitting in that Winnetka mansion—a fancy dining room with chintz curtains, a family room with rounded couches in burgundy leather? She can hear Monica, not any words, just the animated rise and fall of her voice. Monica has always been good at parties.

"Hey, kiddo. I wish you were here." Louise sounds drunk too.

Josie has been without a real best friend ever since Louise left, and she feels five years of friendlessness in a single pang. She hasn't seen Louise's little girl since she was a baby. "How's Zoe?" she says.

"The usual pressured-child scene—swimming lessons, gymnastics, Suzuki violin starting in the fall. So what's Henry up to?"

"We're working on more basic things, like toilet training."

"Ah, men."

"So, should I be worried?" Josie says.

"About?"

"Peter and Monica." There's a pause. Josie licks her lips and wishes she hadn't asked.

Louise yells, "You guys are making too much noise. I'm going to close the door." The sound of laughter snaps off like a switch. She comes back on the phone. "Okay, I'm here. Why are you worried?"

"That's what I'm asking you."

Louise makes a small, impatient sigh. It's the kind of sound Josie makes with Henry when she finds him climbing up on the kitchen counter or doing something else she's told him not to a dozen times. "You and your inferiority complex about Monica. When are you going to realize that Monica is not such a hot ticket?"

"You think so?"

"Josie, how many times have we had this conversation?" Louise stops to take a loud drink of something. "Let's look at this rationally." This was Louise's classic response, which Josie sometimes found offensive. It seemed to imply that her approach to life was irrational. "You know I used to have my doubts about Peter, but he's not such a bad husband after all. He even showed me some snapshots of you and Henry. And if he *was* having an affair with Monica, do you think he'd visit me—his wife's best friend? Think about it." She says the word "affair" matter-of-factly, probably the way she says Dow-Jones Industrial Average when she's being an investment banker.

"I guess you're right," says Josie, not feeling particularly reassured. She glances at the silver picture frames on her mother's dresser—a studio portrait of Congressman Trask in an oval frame, her mother as a bride. Divorced for twenty-five years and still defining herself as Griffin Trask's wife. Jackie didn't do that; she married some old Greek satyr just so people wouldn't think of her as John F. Kennedy's wife anymore. Would Josie spend two decades mourning for Peter if her marriage ended? She feels the answer in the pit of her stomach— Maybe.

"Nope, I think you're safe," Louise concludes. "But I'll keep an eye on Monica. Make sure there's no creeping around after lights-out." Louise always thought Monica was sneaky.

Josie hangs up and glances around her mother's room looking for more signs of covert drinking. She kneels down next to the four-poster and peers under the bed skirt. A pair of pink corduroy slippers and dust, but no hidden bottles. She carries the gin glass into the bathroom, rinses it, and leaves it next to the faucet for her mother to find. Would Leslie think this was being proactive enough? She walks back down the hall to her bedroom. The music from downstairs is still playing—Ella Fitzgerald now. She imagines Fred and Eleanor dancing slowly, Fred crooning "That's Why the Lady Is a Tramp" softly in her ear.

Henry has struggled free of his covers. He lies on his back, his rounded stomach showing between Power Rangers underpants and a Ben & Jerry's T-shirt which has worked its way up to his armpits. Josie kneels down by his bed, smoothes the dark hair off his forehead, rubs her cheek lightly on his belly. His fingers weave themselves into her hair, but he doesn't wake. "You miss Daddy, don't you?" she whispers.

THE FIRST TIME Josie met Peter Stadler, at the get-acquainted barbecue on the patch of dirt behind the American Civilization Building, he didn't bother to speak to her. Later she teased him; "You didn't even notice me," she said. "That's ridiculous," he protested, "I spotted you right away." But she knew that wasn't true, because she had been watching him like a private detective.

There was something about Peter that seemed to make women home in on him—with his skinny body that was sexy rather than scrawny, big square teeth under that baseball cap, a mouth that was always moving. She watched how he joined the cluster of other first-year graduate students for a while, but kept glancing over their heads toward the group of faculty standing over by the barbecue. And then excused himself to get another beer and never came back. Josie, still stuck in the circle with all the other first-years, furtively scanned around until she found him sitting cross-legged on the dirt with the wild man on the faculty, Stedman Rollins. After a while, Josie noticed Monica Glass, another first-year, also tall and self-assured, slip away from their group and wedge herself between Peter and Stedman.

The next time Josie saw him was at their graduate seminar, a kind of gladiator blood sport for the first-year students, with Stedman Rollins awarding the spoils—fellowships for next year. So far, it had brought out the worst in everyone. Peter and Monica predictably did most of the talking, but Josie scored a few unexpected points when Stedman tried to quote Emerson's "The Sphinx." He got the first line, "The Sphinx is drowsy," but then blanked. His eyes swept around the table for help.

Without missing a beat, Josie provided the rest of the stanza.

> Her wings are furled:
> Her ear is heavy,
>> She broods on the world.
> "Who'll tell my secret,
>> The ages have kept?—
> I awaited the seer
>> While they slumbered and slept.—

She looked up at a circle of dumbstruck faces. What they didn't know was that she could have recited the next sixteen stanzas, or practically any other poem by Emerson. Or Dickinson, or Whitman; or Blake, or Donne. Josie was a properly educated New England girl—from a hundred years ago. She knew the Latin names of plants, could diagram the pantheon of Greek gods, could identify the constellations. What she didn't know was anything about popular culture or current academic trends. The Trasks hadn't had a television (her father had taken it with him when he left in 1972), and her mother even disapproved of magazines. When Josie heard the other graduate students spouting off about modern media and deconstruction, she actually started to sweat. All she had to do was make one terrible slip—admit that she had never seen a single episode of "Charlie's Angels"—for them to discover she was a fraud.

After a few moments of respectful silence, Peter said, "What I think is so interesting about 'The Sphinx' is the way Emerson experiments with gender bending." "Right," said Stedman, and that got everyone going on gendered voices in Emerson.

Josie sat fuming over the arrogance of these people—slapping the latest critical label on anyone they felt like. "Certainly identity was a major theme of Emerson's writing in the 1840s," she said at last. "But I think one should be careful when one uses a facile term like 'gender bending.' " She did not direct her comment toward Peter, but the scolding tone in her voice was unmistakable. All right, she thought, so what if they think I'm a wet blanket.

At the end of class, he was standing by her side, inviting her back to his apartment for espresso. Somehow his attention felt almost insulting, as if she had passed a test and proved herself, but she said yes anyway. She had to jog slightly to keep up with his long strides as they walked down Hope Street, and she kept glancing up at his big nose, his dark hair, which was parted on the side and kept needing to be pushed back, and how his mouth looked when he laughed, which was frequently. His apartment was on the third floor of a Victorian with sagging porches—three angled rooms with tiny dormer windows strung together by a long hallway. He gave her the tour—a living room with a couch and books stacked on the floor, a bedroom with a box spring and mattress propped up on cinder blocks, a kitchen with a two-burner stove and a half-sized refrigerator. The espresso machine, a real Italian one with brass valves and copper tubes, took up all of the counter space.

They settled on the long couch with espresso cups made of thick white china. She lay at one end reading *The House of the Seven Gables*, and Peter was at the other end reading Wallace Stevens for his Modern American Poetry seminar. She stretched out her legs so her stocking feet bumped his knees; he rested a hand on her foot as if by accident. She tried to read but he kept interrupting her. Finally she put down her book, and they dissected the members of their class: Bruce Feldman—class suck-up; Vincent Covello—class dummy; Marcia Wagner—suspicious lesbian; Louise—too sensible to stick with it. Peter pronounced Monica "scary."

"She's got her sights set on Stedman," he predicted. Josie hadn't noticed but was glad to hear it. She had pictured Monica with Peter because they were both tall and tan and from California. She certainly seemed a more logical fit than short Josie with her frizzy blond hair and milky, untannable skin.

He invited her to stay for dinner and made Kung-Pao chicken (a Chinese student at Stanford had given him cooking lessons). She cut up the vegetables while he rolled chicken pieces in cornstarch and made a sauce of fresh gingerroot and garlic. Josie, the daughter of Eleanor, didn't even know ginger was a root. He ate with chopsticks, she ate with a fork. She watched him pick up squares of chicken, delicately, one at a time; his arms were strong and smooth, with hairs as fine as hers. She pushed the peanuts and peppers around on her plate, too nervous to eat, and thought how different he was from the boys she'd been subjected to at Dartmouth, whose idea of cooking was boiling dehydrated food on the top of Mount Washington.

Over dinner, they recited their life histories. Peter described his parents as "your basic lefty Jewish intellectuals." His mother was a professor of Romance Languages at Pomona, who had prevailed as a woman in academics back in the dark ages. She only allowed herself to have a single child (when she was forty, during a sabbatical year), so she wouldn't fall behind on her publications. His father had been a labor lawyer, a champion of oppressed workers. Peter was twelve when Harry Stadler dropped dead in the middle of a lettuce field, where he was trying to organize migrant workers, a Pall Mall still hanging from the corner of his mouth.

Josie felt envious. She'd always wanted to be from someplace normal like California, always wished she had a professional mother who *did* things, instead of Eleanor who passively accepted whatever life dished out. At least Peter's father had the decency to die. How much simpler her life would have been if her father had merely been dead. She gave him the comic version of her childhood—the Gothic horrors of the Trask family homestead, her father the defrocked-congressman-turned-Florida-real-estate-developer.

When Peter asked her what she planned to do her dissertation on, she shamefully admitted Emily Dickinson, or maybe Emerson. In the first week of graduate school, she'd already figured out that transcendentalists were hopelessly passé, unless they were black or gay or had some other multicultural angle. He said breezily that he was planning to do his dissertation on TV. She'd also figured out during the first week that you could actually do a dissertation on television, that it was, in fact, cutting edge. She gazed over at Peter, who was doing a drumroll on his plate with his chopsticks, and realized that she was confronting her true opposite (or as opposite as someone could be who was in the same Ph.D. program). Her hormones surged the way they sometimes did around inappropriate men.

After dinner, they ended up back on the couch with their books and more espresso, his hand resting on her foot again. After a while a finger started tracing down the top of her foot, and up along the arch. She was having trouble concentrating on Hepzibah's penny shop in Chapter Three, and glanced up to find Peter staring at her.

"That was pretty great, you know. How you rattled off that poem," he said.

"What can I say. I was such a weird kid I didn't know memorizing poetry was abnormal." She shrugged.

He stood up, walked over to the bookshelf along the wall, and pulled out a thick poetry anthology. "Okay, I'm going to give you a test. I'll give you a line, and you give me the next one." It was Untermeyer's anthology, the same one she had; this was going to be easy. He thumbed through the pages, considering choices. "*We talked between the rooms—*"

Emily Dickinson was almost too easy. "*Until the Moss had reached our lips—/And covered up—our names—*"

He looked up at her over the tops of his reading glasses and grinned. "Don't get overconfident. That was just a warm-up." He flipped to the back of the book, his long fingers crawling over the pages like a walking stick. "All right, now I've got you. *The bridle-post an old man sat/With loose-flung coat and a high cocked hat.*"

"*The well-curb had a Chinese roof;/And even the long sweep, high aloof,/In its slant splendor, seemed to tell/of Pisa's leaning miracle,*" she answered back.

"Whittier? 'Snowbound'? You *were* a weird kid." He tried a few more—Longfellow, Whitman, Vachel Lindsay. "You're tough. How about *To be my own Messiah to the burning end."*

She considered for a few moments. "Beats me," she said.

"Yvor Winters!" he crowed.

She straightened out her leg and knocked a foot against his knee. "No fair. That's cheating."

"Here, let me show you," he said, wedging in on her side of the couch. He held the book up to her face, but before she could see anything, he jerked it away, slammed it shut, and dumped it on the floor. He raised himself up on one elbow, stared at her for a moment to see if she was going to object, inhaled, and kissed her hard. She closed her eyes, turned toward him, and wrapped her arms around his neck. The couch was too narrow for them to lie side by side, and she started to roll onto the floor. They sat up and started kissing again. She could feel his teeth with her tongue, the crooked incisor that made his smile lopsided, and tasted the residue of peanuts in his mouth.

After a while, Peter's lips left her mouth and moved toward her ear, and then headed south. He fumbled open the top three buttons of her shirt. She untucked her shirt and unbuttoned the rest herself. She was wearing an old underwire number that Leslie had discarded, which was a size too small. When he touched one of her breasts, it came sprawling out. He bent down and kissed it with his tongue. It had been five months since she'd been kissed by anyone, and that had been by her soon-to-be-ex-boyfriend Stu on her closed mouth while standing on the steps of the Dartmouth library. Josie unbuttoned the cuffs of her sleeves and got ready to strip off the rest of her clothes.

Suddenly Peter sat up straight, closed the flap of her shirt discreetly over her drooping breast, combed his hair back with his fingers. "You know, maybe we shouldn't be doing this," he said. "We're going to be in school together for a long time. We might be sorry later."

Josie glared over at him and felt a flash flood of indignation. Granted he looked a little disappointed as he said this, but at least his clothing was still buttoned. He didn't have body parts hanging out, wasn't getting ready to chuck graduate school etiquette out the window. What was she supposed to do? Tuck her breast back in and find where she'd left off in *The House of the Seven Gables*?

She thought she should at least level the playing field. "You're probably right," she said and noted that he seemed surprised. "I'm glad you brought it up." Without moving her eyes from his face, she slowly stretched and dropped her hand softly in his lap. She waited a moment, then unbuckled his belt, unzipped his fly, fishtailed her hand past the elastic of his boxer shorts, and watched as the resolve melted from his eyes (green, with those curly eyelashes that only men seem to get). He started breathing through his mouth, sharply, his teeth clenched.

"We should think this through carefully," she said.

They managed to make it onto the bed. It was only eight when they turned the lights back on, both put on white T-shirts from Peter's dresser, and sat side by side in bed reading. Josie managed to read twenty pages to the end of Chapter Four by nine-thirty, but mostly she was stealing glances over at Peter in his reading glasses (who seemed to be having no problems concentrating on Wallace Stevens), and wondering what in God's name she was doing here.

Admittedly, she had behaved in a bold and ill-considered way, but that could probably be blamed on four years of Dartmouth boyfriends. First there had been Jamie, the Patagonia-clad leader of her freshman hiking trip, who taught her how to identify animals from their droppings and cook flapjacks on a campfire. He had been taciturn; when he enjoyed his food, he said "Good," when he watched the sun rise over the White Mountains, he said "Nice." Their sexual encounters mostly took place inside a mummy bag on frozen earth. Then there was Stu, a computer science major who had read books on how to be a considerate lover. By the time he put on New Age music, lit candles, and gave her a back rub with scented oil, she had frequently fallen asleep. During her last semester, she gave up on boys and had a crush on her thesis adviser, who wrote sonnets, carried a pocket watch on a brass chain, and looked as if he was unhappily married. They worked side by side editing her thesis on the erotic imagery in Emily Dickinson's poetry, and sometimes his hand accidentally brushed against her breast. No wonder the first time she got around a normal, intelligent, available male, she lost control of herself.

She decided that Peter was right, this was a bad idea. She tried to imagine all the awkwardness that lay ahead. In an hour or so, they would have to confront the issue of whether she would spend the night or not. He probably wouldn't want her to, would make some excuse about early classes and needing sleep, and then she wouldn't see him again until their seminar in two days. Maybe he would really behave like a jerk, sit on the other side of the room, avoid her eyes, conspicuously ask someone else, that Monica perhaps, over for espresso after class.

Josie replayed the evening in her head so she could figure out where she'd gone wrong, and not only was she not remorseful, but she started wanting it to happen all over again. Why was sex so contrary and undignified? Better a preemptive strike. She climbed out of bed and picked up her shirt.

"Where are you going?" he said, closing his book.

"I need to get back home." It was the first time she'd ever referred to her depressing room at graduate student housing as home.

"You can stay here, you know."

"I've got to get some books."

"Well, at least say good-bye." He reached over, grabbed her wrist, and pulled her back to the bed. She climbed up, and he slipped the T-shirt over her head. She woke up at seven the next morning, crept out of bed while he slept, showered and got dressed. Just as she was about to leave, she poked her head back in the bedroom. He was sitting in bed with his glasses on, reading Wallace Stevens.

"Thanks for the espresso. I've got to go."

"Well, at least say good-bye." She was ten minutes late to her eleven-o'-clock seminar. He invited her back that afternoon for more espresso. She stopped at her dorm room first and picked up clean underwear, a toothbrush, and her diaphragm. He made Szechuan beef with red peppers for dinner, and when they were almost done, she swung her bare foot into his lap. He put down his chopsticks, dropped his hand under the table, and said, "Let's leave the dishes." They arrived twenty minutes late to their seminar the next day with wet hair.

For two weeks, she walked around looking tired and disheveled. Louise, who lived down the hall in the graduate dorm, asked her if she was getting the flu. She took Josie out to lunch at a natural-food restaurant and insisted she eat a trough of bulgur stew. "I'm worried about you," Louise announced.

Josie's mouth was too full of roughage to answer, so she waved a piece of sprouted bread like a question mark.

Louise had met a medical student in their dorm who had gone to Stanford with Peter. "She says he's bad news," Louise warned. Every few months he took up with a different female, wooed her ardently until she decided he was her soulmate, and then he moved on. One jilted girl was checked into the infirmary for two weeks on a suicide watch until the antidepressants kicked in.

Josie thought she might gag on a lump of turnip, and dropped her wooden spoon. Her darkest suspicions were correct; he was nothing but a serial seducer. All that passion was generic, nonspecific; her charm, her ability to recite obscure nineteenth-century poetry had nothing to do with it.

"Okay, you don't have to stop sleeping with him," Louise conceded, probably realizing that Josie would never do anything that drastic. "Just try to create a little emotional distance. Besides, aren't you behind in your work?"

For the next week, Josie made an inept stab at emotional distance. Each morning, she resolved to spend the night in her dorm room, do her laundry, catch up with her reading. But every afternoon after class, she was heading back to Peter's, her legs getting rubbery with lust by the time she reached the corner of Hope and Angel. Slowly, her clothing and books migrated over to his apartment and sat in messy piles on the floor. One afternoon she arrived to find that he had emptied out the top two bureau drawers, set up another computer table in the living room, and had an extra key made.

That's when Josie decided to go home for the weekend to visit her mother. She needed a break. She wanted to sleep alone in her lumpy spool bed, do her laundry in the thirty-year-old Maytag in the basement, eat creamed chipped beef on toast at the kitchen table. In two days maybe she could figure out why she was jumping into the bed and bureau drawers of a man who would surely break her heart.

Peter overheard her on the telephone making travel arrangements with her mother. It was complicated getting from Providence to Crowley. She would have to take a train into Boston, and another one out to Crowley.

"I'll drive you if you want," he said. "I'd like to meet your mother."

"That's okay. The train is fine." It wasn't just that she wanted to be alone. She wasn't ready to expose her mother and the Trask homestead to Peter's scrutiny. The out-of-date clothes, the peeling wallpaper, the Stouffer's frozen dinners, the Boston terrier with runny eyes. To make matters worse, Josie's mother had fallen under the sway of the new minister, Allen Railsback, and had become something of a Unitarian zealot. She had taken to linking hands with Josie and praying over the tuna noodle casserole. Allen Railsback sometimes came for dinner with his guitar and would serenade them on the porch with folk songs, including "Michael, Row Your Boat Ashore." Last summer her mother had spent an evening reading the essays of Robert Fulghum aloud to her. Her mother hadn't read to her since she was a child. Josie sat curled up in an armchair and found the reflections on life in kindergarten so sweet and wise that she almost started weeping. She wouldn't let her mother be treated as a joke.

"Don't worry. I'll wear clothes. I'm good with people's mothers," Peter said. By people she assumed he meant his suicidal former girlfriends. So, she thought, he stuck around long enough to meet their mothers. Her mouth tightened. "Then let me drop you off," he coaxed. "There's no sense in you spending half the day on the train."

On Saturday morning (almost noon, actually; they were off to another late start) they climbed into Peter's dented Honda for the sixty-mile drive to Crowley. The inside was ankle-deep in junk left over from his drive across the country—used coffee cups, crumpled maps, a half-sucked Tootsie Pop stuck on the dashboard. He fished a pair of sunglasses missing a side piece off the car floor. In a single swing of the steering wheel, he backed out and made a U-turn across

Hope Street. Josie gripped the door handle. "Don't worry," he said, laying a patch on Hope Street. "I'm from California. The freeway is in my veins."

Fifty minutes later they were looping around the Crowley common. Peter slowed the car to a crawl and peered out over the steering wheel. The white meetinghouse, flanked by bronze and golden oaks, was right off the "Fall in New England" calendar shot. "Wow," he said. "Ethan Frome land. Where's your house?" Josie pointed up the hill to the Trask homestead, which was looking particularly majestic—slates gleaming, a litter of autumn leaves chasing across the lawn, twin chimneys brilliant against a cobalt sky. He turned to her and took off his glasses. "I'm impressed."

"Don't be," she said. "It's a dump inside." He pulled into the driveway, and Josie grabbed her backpack, ready to leap out as soon as he stopped the car. Suddenly Eleanor popped up out of the daylily bed, a work-gloved hand waving. She squinted at Peter and the car and started down the path toward them. Josie leaped out and slammed the door. "Thanks," she said, "see you tomorrow."

He turned off the engine, rolled down the window, and leaned his head out like an eager cocker spaniel. Eleanor walked over and pulled off her work gloves. She was wearing a pair of khaki pants that Josie's father had left behind, one of Josie's Dartmouth T-shirts, and navy Keds. Her white hair was pulled back in a stubby ponytail. The effect was younger and hipper than her usual vintage shirtwaist dress and Belgian loafers. "Hello. I'm Josie's mother. And you are . . . ?" She looked over at Josie, who hadn't told her mother about Peter yet.

"Would your friend like to stay for dinner?" Eleanor asked.

"Why not," Josie sighed, defeated.

Peter yanked up the emergency brake, slipped an oxford-cloth shirt over his ratty T-shirt, and bounded out of the car. As Eleanor ushered them back up the path for some iced tea on the porch, he glanced back at Josie and slid her a theatrical wink.

On their way through the living room toward the porch door, he paused in the center of the room and pivoted slowly, his hands in his pockets. She tried to see it through his eyes—the portraits of glowering Trask ancestors in oval gilt frames, an oriental rug worn down to threads, a couch with arms sprouting tufts of stuffing. Did he think it was charming or pathetic?

They settled on the porch, Peter in an armchair with his long legs stretched out in front of him. He had his hands folded in his lap and stared out across the back field dotted with milkweed. For once, he wasn't saying anything. *Now he knows why I didn't want him to come,* she thought.

"Well, Peter," said her mother, "it's a funny old place, isn't it? I expect it's quite different from California, although I've never been there." Eleanor prided herself on never having been anywhere—the American West, Europe. The farthest she had been was Bermuda on her honeymoon.

"Yes," he said inscrutably.

A snuffling sound like from a pig came from under the couch, and Rascal, the Boston terrier, clambered out. Peter smiled, his pensive mood vaporizing. "Who's this, Mrs. Trask?" Rascal's black toenails clicked across the floor toward him, then scrabbled against his pant legs. He bent down, scooped her up, and held her like a baby on its back. He stared into her face; it was not a pretty sight. Rascal had some condition that made her eyes water constantly, a river of dried tears running down both sides of her pug nose. He bent down and planted a loud smack on top of her bony head.

"I can see you're an animal lover, Peter," her mother said pointedly. She sometimes accused Josie of not being sufficiently affectionate with Rascal.

When Eleanor left to get iced tea, Josie turned to him and narrowed her eyes to slits. "You kiss that dog again," she said, "and we're leaving."

"I guess I got a little carried away," he said, sheepishly depositing Rascal on her toothpick legs. She clicked off down the hall.

Josie carried her bulging knapsack down to the basement and dumped the contents into the washing machine. Three weeks of round-the-clock sex had generated a lot of laundry. Every time she got dressed in some clean clothes, they were being peeled off again and pitched into the corner. She took her time, measured out exact amounts of detergent and bleach, carefully selected the rinse cycle, all the while trying to figure out why Peter had insinuated himself into her house. Not out of love, she guessed, or even horniness; he could live without her body for one day. He was just plain nosy, she decided. She'd told him enough about her bizarre New England upbringing to make him curious (that had been her intention, after all), and he'd come to check it out for himself. The question was: What would happen after a visit to Crowley? Would he move her clothes out of his bureau and back onto the floor?

She climbed back upstairs and found Peter standing on a stepladder in the front hallway. Her mother was holding his ankles. "What's going on?" she said.

"I asked Peter to change the lightbulb over the front door. I'm too short to reach it," Eleanor said. Josie watched as he unscrewed the globe around the fixture, handed it down to her mother, and then stood on tiptoes to screw in the bulb. Josie had never studied the vaulted ceiling above the fanlight before. The arc was crisscrossed with cobwebs; a large mustard-colored water stain oozed down one side.

He jumped down, brushing his hands against his pants. "Okay, Mrs. Trask."

"Please call me Eleanor."

"Anything else you want me to do, Eleanor?"

Her mother paused, a finger thoughtfully rubbing her upper lip. "It's a lot to ask," she mused.

"What?" said Peter, sounding like a Boy Scout going for his Eagle badge. He had admitted to Josie that he'd been number one in his class in high school, editor of the newspaper, junior Phi Beta Kappa at Stanford—always the eager beaver.

"Well, it's this lilac bush I want to move. It's this big." She held a hand two feet above her head.

"Show me," he said, and they walked out the front door toward the side of the house.

Josie settled back on the porch and conspicuously buried her nose in *Tanglewood Tales*. She refused to bear witness to Peter's snow job. Out of the corner of her eye, she could see them opening the toolshed door, then Peter pushing a wheelbarrow past the porch, Eleanor tagging along behind with a shovel propped on her shoulder. Despite her efforts to tune them out, their voices and her mother's laughter echoed across the lawn. He dragged the bush across the lawn like a corpse and dug a new hole over by the barn while Eleanor supervised. Josie overheard her mother say, "Careful, dear." Next he was dispatched to move the compost heap and careened by with the wheelbarrow mounded high. The final chore was to nail down a row of loose shingles on the toolshed roof. They walked back to the porch, Peter wet and splotched with dirt.

"Well, Josie, I'm afraid I gave your Peter quite a workout. Too bad you don't have some clean clothes to change into."

"I think I have some clothes in my car," he said. Eleanor went upstairs to run a bath while he loped down the driveway.

When he came back swinging a gym bag, Josie slammed her book down on the table. "A bag of clothes. Well, that's a stroke of luck."

He leaned against the screen door, exasperated. "I'm trying to be nice to your mother. So what's your problem, Josie?"

Lines of sweat streaked his grimy face. It's because I love you, she thought, and I'm already worried that you're going to leave me. She heard the water running upstairs and felt the urge to climb into the claw-footed bathtub with him and soap his back. And then, still wet, make love with him on her spool bed. "Problem?" she said. "I don't know."

After he had taken a bath and changed, she took him on a tour of Crowley Center, starting with the Civil War Monument on the common. "And here we commemorate seventeen of Crowley's finest who perished at Bull Run, Shiloh, and Chancellorsville. Fondly do we hope, fervently do we pray, that this mighty scourge of war may speedily pass away." It sounded as if she were reading an inscription, but the granite pedestal was blank. Peter was looking at her strangely. She walked ahead down the sloping green and across the road to the meetinghouse. The gravel parking lot was empty; one of the treads on the back stairs had rotted through. "And here, in 1739, the Reverend William Phipps was physically removed from the pulpit and escorted, along with his wife and five children, to the town line and warned never to return for espousing the New Light heresy of George Whitefield," she intoned and followed a dirt path that circled behind the meetinghouse to the cemetery.

The path ran between a pair of listing granite posts and snaked around clusters of family gravestones. The grass was ankle-high, with leaves piling against the headstones and fence posts. The Trask plot perched on a rise—a macabre echo of the Trask homestead—encircled by an ornate iron fence. Josie swung a heavy gate open and stepped in. She pointed to the obelisk in the center, the base carved to form the word "Trask" in relief. "Here is our family founder, Elisha Trask, who made the family fortune with an excelsior mill. And the little stones are lesser Trasks. William, the suicide; Susannah and her three children, who died in a single week from diphtheria; my great-grandfather, George, the dipsomaniac. Here the spaces for all the rest of us when we croak."

Peter stood outside the fence, gripping two of the iron fence posts as if they were jail bars. He had the same curious expression. "You really hate this place, don't you?"

"You got it."

"Why?"

She looked at the hulking tamarack behind him, its needles hanging like funeral crepe, and wondered how he could be so dense. "Does Crowley seem like a fun place to grow up?" she said fiercely. He shook his head.

"Let me tell you about my childhood. When it rained, we used every pot and pan in the house to catch the leaks. Each summer we got to spend one day at the ocean, where we'd eat fried clams, and another day at the amusement park over in Lunenburg. And that was it." Josie didn't care that she sounded self-pitying. "By the time I was in eighth grade, I had read every single book in the children's room at the Crowley library. After that, my mother took me to the Fitchburg library once a week. That's how I know about Crowley. I was so desperate I read books on local history."

"Well, what about your father? Didn't you ever go to Florida?"

Oh yeah, she thought, him. She never considered her father as someone who could be counted on to do parental things. He was more like a madcap uncle who popped in once in a while. "Leslie and I got to go to Coral Gables every couple of years for spring vacation. When we got there, he'd take us on a shopping spree for Florida clothes—bikinis and sundresses. And then nothing for two years." She didn't bother to mention her stepmother, Terry, who always sent such sweet birthday and valentine cards but never included them on family vacations. Or her stepbrother, who used to try to feel her up.

"Well, my childhood wasn't exactly a barrel of laughs either," he said.

"I thought you had a lot of fun." He'd told her stories about sand-lot baseball, smoking dope in his bedroom while his mother was teaching, getting laid for the first time when he was fifteen by the National Merit scholar his mother had hired to supervise his home-work. (She was really very conscientious, he had said. We couldn't start fooling around until after I'd done my homework and she'd checked it. My grades really improved.)

"You might say my mother was a little overinvested in my success."

"Then she must be pleased. You've done her proud."

"Lucky thing, isn't it?" He held out his hand. "Let's get out of here."

She slipped her arm around his waist and started thinking about the spool bed again.

Over dinner (one of Eleanor's better efforts—creamed chicken in Pepperidge Farm puff-pastry shells) at the kitchen table, Peter asked her mother questions about growing up in Elgin, Illinois. Usually, Eleanor was so uncomfortable talking about herself that people gave up after a while and started talking about themselves. But tonight, lubricated by a couple of martinis and flattered by Peter's attention, she grew expansive. In the three weeks she'd known him, Josie had seen Peter have this effect on people several times. He tilted his head inquisitively, asked some probing question, and then sat back. Suddenly a mousy department secretary or some taciturn eighth-year graduate student who was writing a nine-hundred-page dissertation on Cotton Mather would burst forth with some private story that he or she had never told anyone before. And instead of feeling violated, they adored Peter because he made them feel clever and interesting.

Eleanor's father had been the engineer in charge of quality con-trol at the Elgin Watch Company. "A very important job at a watch factory," said Eleanor respectfully. The family had lived a mile down the road in Elgin Estates, a neighborhood of Tudor and Norman mansions built in the 1920s for Elgin Watch executives. "We had a sweet house with lead-casement windows and a walled garden. My mother used to win prizes at the Elgin Garden Club for her Mary Baldwin roses."

And then, in 1938, calamity struck. Eleanor's father, Howard Fahnstock, was driving home from work one February evening. It had started snowing lightly an hour before, and his Buick V-8 hit a patch of new-fallen snow and skidded into a massive oak. Howard Fahnstock, age thirty-three, was pronounced dead at the scene. "Later, they said the oak was much too close to the road but attempts to remove it had been blocked by the Elgin Garden Club. And my mother was the vice president. Ironic, isn't it?"

Josie watched Peter listening soberly to Eleanor's childhood trauma and felt guilty. She and Leslie had always thought the story of their grandfather's death was hilarious. It seemed typical of Eleanor's bad luck that he had been done in by half an inch of snow—not even the drama of a multicar pileup or a ten-wheeler with failed brakes. What really cracked them up was how Eleanor would end her story by rolling up her sleeve and displaying her Lady Elgin watch like a battle scar.

Peter leaned back in his chair and brought his hands together, the fingertips bouncing against each other aerobically. "Must have been hard to lose your father when you were only six." He said this as if he considered himself lucky to have reached the ripe age of twelve when his father keeled over with a fatal coronary. Josie had never thought to ask this before. She had asked what her grandfather was like, but not if it had been hard to lose a father—maybe because she already knew.

Eleanor put down her fork and gazed pensively toward a portrait of the doomed Susannah Trask. "For a long time, I would sit by the living room window in the evening and wait to see his headlights turn into the driveway. I didn't believe that he was dead, you see. I can't remember when I stopped waiting for him to come home again." She pushed up the sleeve of her cardigan and showed Peter the platinum watch with the black cord band. "Here's the Lady Elgin the president of the company gave me when I graduated from high school, in memory of my father. I've worn it every day for forty-five years."

Eleanor stood up to clear the table. "May I ask if you two are dating?"

Josie pondered the word "dating" and how she should answer. Not that her mother would be particularly shocked by the truth. Eleanor had a progressive Unitarian attitude toward her daughters' sexuality. When they brought boys home to visit from college, she waved them toward the bedrooms in the back of the house, saying, "I'm sure you can find enough beds for everyone down there," and then tactfully retired to her bedroom in the front of the house.

"Josie came over to my apartment for coffee once," said Peter. He had started drinking martinis with Eleanor during the cocktail hour, and now sat with his arm propping up one side of his face as he polished off his third helping of creamed chicken.

"That's nice," Eleanor mused. "I had to quit drinking coffee. Too overstimulating." After dinner she decided that Peter should spend the night. "I think I wore you out with that lilac bush." By this time, he was stretched out flat on the living room couch with his hands folded across his chest. He swung his legs onto the floor, shook his head, and followed Eleanor up the stairs. She opened the guest room door for Peter, gestured him in, and then retreated down the hall, her Belgian loafers as silent as Indian moccasins on the wide floorboards.

Josie propped her back against the knobby headboard of her spool bed and tried to read *Tanglewood Tales*, but the print danced across the page. She'd skipped the martinis but had made up for them with the white-wine jug. Peter probably thought they were a family of drunks. He had told her that his mother (who more and more sounded like someone Josie didn't want to meet) never drank because she always had papers to grade after dinner. She saw the light go on under the bathroom door and heard the toilet flush. The door swung open silently and Peter crept in.

She considered whispering, but decided not to bother. "Recovering from the martinis?"

"Barely. I don't think Jews are supposed to drink gin." He studied the hanging shelf by the door with its china horses that Josie had collected when she was eight. Then he bent down to a low bookcase which still held the *Little House* books and the blue spines of a complete run of Nancy Drews.

"Girls' bedrooms are so weird," he said. Josie always had the same feeling about boys' bedrooms with their bunk beds and heaps of baseball cards and disemboweled model airplanes. Not that she had seen very many. Occasionally one of her friends had had a brother, and she would peek in his room from the hallway, feeling a little alarmed that she might see something dangerous or unhygienic.

He opened the closet door, pulled the light chain, and peered at the shoebag nailed to the door, the Samsonite suitcases on the floor. He reached in and pulled out what looked like a very short, pleated jumper. "What's this?

"My field hockey tunic. I was the star left wing in high school."

He held it up in front of his body. "What did you wear underneath?"

She walked over, reached under the tunic and pulled out a pair of matching navy bloomers hooked over the hanger.

"Girls in California don't dress like this," he said.

She gave him a secretive smile.

"I think I need to see you in this," he said. She slipped the tunic and bloomers out of his hands. "Without the pants," he added.

The next day as they walked down the marble path to Peter's car, Eleanor slipped her arm around Josie's waist and whispered, "If I were you, I'd set my cap for him." Her eyelids lowered sphinxlike to indicate she knew about such things. "He's a keeper."

chapter 5

MR. KARITAS: *So she would ask Sister Parish or any other decorators around what their ideas were about certain things. We'd go ahead and do it and then if she didn't like it after it was all completed, she would change it to suit her own preference.*

MISS TURNURE: *I see. Was she apt to change quite a bit?*

MR. KARITAS: *Well, she was always changing things.*
— Oral history with Joseph Karitas, White House painter

As Josie threads her car across the six lanes of Morrissey Boulevard toward a tiny "Kennedy Library/Columbia Point" sign, she can hear Eleanor's voice in her head. Her mother had stood outside the kitchen door, holding Henry's hand, and shouted warnings at Josie while she snapped on her seat belt. "Keep your doors locked and windows rolled up. Just follow the signs for the Kennedy Library. Remember the library is in Dorchester, but don't go *to* Dorchester. Go to Columbia Point."

Josie heads off on a peninsula that she hopes is Columbia Point. By now, her hands are so slick with sweat that she can hardly steer. A baby-blue sign with a federal crest reassures her that this is indeed the way, and then the road appears to veer straight into Boston Harbor. At the next turn, the Kennedy Library, vertical slabs of white aluminum and blue glass, looms up in the distance like a postmodern Emerald City in a field of poppies, but the poppies are pink beach roses fluttering like tissue paper. As she approaches, the roses give way to acres of parking lots filled with tour buses. Josie cruises through the parking lots until she finds a clump of beat-up Japanese cars, and noses the Honda in between two others. This must be where the scholars park.

She gathers up her research supplies, which consist of two pencils and a package of index cards, and wishes she had at least brought Peter's laptop, which she's borrowing for the summer. But two pencils and index cards were the best she could come up with on short notice. She hadn't exactly been planning to come to the Kennedy Library today.

Allison Railsback, Allen's allegedly wayward niece, had shown up at the dot of eight. Josie had forgotten she was coming and was still in her nightshirt, brooding over a cup of coffee about Peter and the Oak Park tour. Josie didn't even hear her come in. She just happened to look up, having visualized for the third time Peter and Monica admiring the underbelly of cantilevered eaves, and found Allison standing there, hands folded patiently, waiting. Neat as a pin, that's how Eleanor had described her. And so she was—straight brown hair pulled back with matching barrettes, oxford-cloth shirt tucked into pressed jeans, the same kind of brown loafers that Josie wore when she was ten. Allison held a big tote bag that seemed to be filled with baby-sitting supplies—children's books, toys, a portable intercom.

"Mrs. Stadler?" she said, sounding slightly intimidated.

No one ever called Josie that, and for a moment she thought the girl was asking for Peter's mother. Josie jumped up and tried to hide her unshaved legs and bare feet behind the chair. Now that she was standing, she realized that Allison was a good six inches taller. "Allison, right? I've been expecting you."

Allison presented her with two typed pages. "Here's a résumé."

Josie sat back down and made a show of scrutinizing Allison's résumé, as if her baby-sitters routinely provided résumés. Her eyes flitted over *Wellesley, B.A. expected 1996, concentration in Biology, vice president glee club, National Merit finalist, fluent in French and Spanish.* "This certainly looks impressive." Josie fixed her let's-get-serious look on Allison's slightly pimply chin. "You sure you want a job as a baby-sitter?"

"Oh," said Allison, smiling for the first time. "I really love kids.

I'm getting certified to be a teacher." As if on cue, Henry came in from the porch and made a beeline for the bag of toys. She stooped down and fixed him with a brown-eyed stare. "Are you Henry? I brought you something." Without dropping her gaze, she reached into the tote and pulled out a small yellow box.

Henry cradled it for a moment in both hands before he pried it open and brought forth a lime-green road grader. He held it up to Josie, his eyes moist with adoration. "Green truck," he blurted.

"When do you think you could start?" Josie asked.

"Right away, if you want," said Allison with a modest shrug.

By this time, Eleanor had appeared. "I told you Allison was a great girl!" Actually, her mother had not told Josie that Allison was a great girl. What she said was that Allison had taken a year off from college because of "some emotional upset," but that now she was "right as rain."

Eleanor, Allison, and Henry stood in a conspiratorial huddle, all smiles and cheer. Henry was holding Allison's hand. "Run along," Eleanor coaxed. "We'll be fine." Josie dawdled for another ten minutes explaining approved activities (library and playground), appropriate television programs (anything on Channel 2 except "Barney"), and potential household hazards (loose screens on windows, electric sockets without child protector caps, chipping lead paint) until Eleanor said, impatiently this time, "Just go."

And so here she is, an hour and a half later in the parking lot of the Kennedy Library. She joins the line waiting to get in through the revolving front doors and finds herself in the middle of a herd of Japanese tourists. The uniformed guards act as cowpunchers funneling them into what looks like a marbled mall of Kennedy memorabilia staffed by a bank of ticket takers. Josie had the not unreasonable expectation that the Kennedy Library would look like a library. She pictured leather-bound copies of *Profiles in Courage* in floor-to-ceiling shelves and a proper Brahmin lady dispensing library cards and stamping book slips.

The Japanese obediently fork over seven dollars apiece to a uniformed black woman with complicated earrings that encase the rims of her ears like brass hearing aids. She recites for each one, "The introductory film will begin in ten minutes. Please wait in the theater lobby."

"I'd like a ticket to use the library, please," says Josie, scanning for a mention of a library in the list of shows and exhibits on the wall. The woman looks up toward a spot behind Josie's shoulder and faintly seems to register this interloper among the Japanese. "The library is only open to serious researchers," she says.

"Well, I *am* doing research. On . . ." says Josie and then trails off unconvincingly. What's she going to say—on Jackie, on Mrs. Kennedy, on Jacqueline Kennedy Onassis? They all sound equally nonserious. The woman's eyes sweep over Josie's black rubber sandals, jean shorts, measly pencils, and she raises a single skeptical eyebrow. Josie imagines having to tell Fiona Jones that she couldn't get past the front desk.

"On the Nuclear Test Ban Treaty," she says, snapping her Brown graduate student I.D. down on the polished granite counter. Without even bothering to inspect it, the woman waves her toward an elevator.

Josie crosses the marbled lobby, strides past the souvenir busts of John and Robert to the security guard nursing a Kennedy mug filled with coffee. "I'm looking for the library," she says. "I'm a serious researcher," she adds, feeling foolish.

He picks up the phone and says, almost apologetically, "I've got to get clearance from upstairs. What are you researching?"

This time, Josie is a little quicker on her feet. "The media's portrayal of women in politics," she says, feeling quite pleased that it sounds both plausible and boring.

"There's a woman who says she's researching something to do with . . ." He looks back at Josie, and she repeats it loud enough so this faceless gatekeeper on the other end can hear. He hangs up. "She says you can go up."

Josie steps off the elevator, half expecting to find the door blocked by a phalanx of archivists with their arms linked, but the only greeters are a person-sized philodendron and a wall of lockers. A rather timid sign says, "Researchers Are Requested to Check Handbags and Briefcases." Unmollified, she strides around the corner, her purse and index cards unchecked, into the reading room. A librarian, with "Laura Steinberg" stitched on a lab coat, looks up with a start. She seems to be in the midst of sorting a two-foot stack of reprints into two one-foot stacks.

Josie places both palms flat on the desk, hovers over the reprints, and glares straight into the woman's admittedly pleasant face. "I'm a serious researcher. All right?" The word "right" comes out like a challenge and seems to hang in the air, suspended by the supersonic hum of the climate-control system.

She looks past the librarian into the reading room. It's tiny, barely the size of Eleanor's living room. Instead of the usual long tables lined with chairs, there are rows of oak desks, one for each researcher, lined up like a schoolroom. A bespectacled man peeks out above a wall of gray manuscript boxes; an archivist sorting another stack of reprints puts down his pencil and stares. It doesn't take much to cause a ruckus in an archive.

Laura the librarian gives her a dreamy smile. "What can I do for you?" Her round face and thick hair hanging down her back eerily remind Josie of herself. Maybe this is what happens to people who don't finish their dissertations.

Josie gives her spiel about the media's portrayal of women in politics. It sounds even better the second time around; maybe she should consider switching her dissertation topic, that is, if she ever *does* a dissertation. "I think I would like to start with any secondary sources you might have on Jacqueline Kennedy Onassis."

"Secondary sources? On Mrs. Onassis?" the librarian says as if she can scarcely believe her ears.

"Don't you have any?"

The woman points toward two shelves of books. "The books pertaining solely to Mrs. Onassis are over there." Josie is thinking this doesn't look too bad when the librarian pulls out a thick computer printout and flips it open to the middle. "This is a subject guide to the books and periodicals. The entries for Mrs. Onassis run from page 32 to 75."

Josie's mouth slackens as she scans over the hundreds of entries, envisioning one of those scenes from old movies of calendar pages flying off past July, August, September. "All right," she says resolutely. "How about manuscript sources pertaining to Mrs. Onassis?"

"Oh, we don't have any of her private papers," Laura says.

Thank God, Josie thinks.

"Just the White House correspondence files."

"What's in those?"

"Mrs. Kennedy's letters when she was in the White House. About the White House renovation, guest lists for her parties, things like that."

In other words, the sorts of odds and ends that Fiona Jones expects her to check out. "I don't suppose the files are very big, are they?" Josie's voice lifts with hope. "I mean, she only lived in the White House for three years, right?"

"Just a few hundred boxes," Laura says, and plunks down a finding aid on top of the computer printout. "And then there are the oral histories. Many of them mention Mrs. Onassis." She sets a card index on top of the finding aid. "Let me know if there's anything you want."

Josie carries her load over to a desk, the one nearest a monstrous window looking out over Boston Harbor. She aligns the computer printout, the White House correspondence guide, and the card index neatly along the top edge of the desk. Then she places the package of index cards in front of her, and the pencils at right angles to the left. Perfect order. Arranging the top of her desk before starting to work was a little ritual she established back in elementary school. Peter called it, somewhat derisively, a "girl thing." He could sit down at his computer table littered with week-old coffee mugs and gum wrappers, sweep everything to one side, and work unperturbed. Maybe mental order out of physical chaos was a "guy thing." She should probably discourage Henry when he insisted on sorting his trucks by color.

She stares out the window. No land in sight, just a panorama of murky sea and cirrus clouds, the kind of view that people pay big money for. Here it's wasted; nothing but one more distraction for that untenured professor, that A.B.D. graduate student working against the clock. Or me, she thinks. With two months to plow through a mountain of papers, or else. Or else what? Or else Peter might spend the summer going to baseball games with Monica.

The white wedge of a sailboat appears on the horizon, so far away it barely seems to move. She watches as it glides imperceptibly across the window and out the left-hand side. When she looks back to the wall clock, it's exactly ten minutes later, eleven-thirty already. Should she call to check on Henry and Allison? Her spirits soar at the idea of escape to a pay phone until she remembers that they're still at Story Hour at the library. She'll call at twelve-thirty; that way she'll know they made it back safely.

I will work for one hour, she resolves. I won't look out the window. I won't think about Henry . . . or Peter. She takes off her Lady Elgin (a high school graduation present from her mother, but gold-tone rather than platinum) and sets it next to her pencils. Not even an excuse to glance up at the clock.

She decides to start with the books and rummages through the two shelves of biographies strictly on Jackie. She passes over the respectful *A Tribute to Mrs. Kennedy,* then pulls out *I Was Jacqueline Kennedy's Dressmaker* and *White House Nannie.* Then she makes a pile of all the biographies with the words "unauthorized" or "shocking" on the cover. These are the words that always appear on Fiona Jones's books, after all.

She makes a three-foot stack next to the desk and sets a blank index card in front of her, pencil poised. She opens *White House Nannie,* checks the index for topics that Fiona might find interesting ("Kennedy, Caroline, birthday parties of," and "Kennedy, Jacqueline, personality of"), and starts making notes for the Jackie timeline.

Nov. 25, 1960—*John F. Kennedy Jr. born. Maude Shaw, Caroline's nanny for three years, tries to prepare Caroline for arrival of little brother. They go shopping so Caroline can buy a present for the baby—a silver comb and brush. Caroline allowed to feed the baby water in a bottle, even though Auchincloss nanny disapproves.*

Dec. 1960—*Maude Shaw goes with Jackie, Caroline, baby, and baby nurse (Mrs. Elsie Phillips) to Kennedy estate in Palm Beach so Jackie can rest up for inauguration. Hardly ever see President-elect.*

Jan. 1961—*Kennedys and Maude Shaw move into White House. Margaret Truman's apartment transformed into kitchen so children will have hot, freshly cooked meals. John still somewhat*

*underweight and restless. Shaw switches his beef extract to
lunchtime, which helps settle him. Joseph Kennedy says John-John
is now "twice the fellow he was." John's room has blue-and-white
wallpaper, and a crib decorated with blue bows. Caroline's room
has pink-and-white wallpaper and a canopy bed. Her favorite toys
are Raggedy Ann doll, dollhouse from Madame de Gaulle, and
stuffed donkey on wheels, which is eventually appropriated by
John.*

Mar. 1961—*Maude Shaw settles children into routine: 6:00 children
wake; 7:00 Caroline washes and dresses herself while Miss Shaw
feeds John; children and Miss Shaw have breakfast in dinette
(Caroline has big breakfast—cereal, eggs, bacon—and is not a
fussy eater); 8:30 Children visit father in his office; 9:00 Caroline
to school and John has bath; 10:30 John has nap (in pram on
Truman balcony if weather is fair); 11:30 Mrs. Kennedy comes to
nursery to feed John and discuss children's progress with Miss
Shaw. (Mrs. Kennedy was content to let me have full charge of the
children and bring them up the way I felt sure she wanted me to
do.) In afternoons children play on White House lawn or see
movie in White House cinema. Miss Shaw insists that Caroline
call Secret Service men Mister Foster and Mister Meredith and
not by their first names. Caroline also not allowed to use baby
talk. 7:30 after dinner, children go back to father's office. Play
with Mrs. Lincoln's typewriter and swivel chair. Then go with
father for swim in White House indoor pool. 9:00 bedtime and
stories. The President and Mrs. Kennedy come up for good-night
kiss at prayer time. After children asleep, Miss Shaw does some
knitting or mends one of Caroline's doll dresses.*

Apr. 1961—*Mrs. Kennedy starts private kindergarten for Caroline on
third-floor solarium. School attended by fifteen other children from
family friends of Kennedys and embassies in Washington. Caroline is "among the brightest pupils." Miss Shaw confronts White
House chef when liver is served to children three times in four
days, backed up by Mrs. Kennedy.*

Josie is somewhat disappointed that *White House Nannie* contains nothing but accolades for her boss. Jackie was a loving and

levelheaded mother who sensibly agreed with all of Miss Shaw's British notions of child rearing. But the memoirs by other White House staff and Miss Shaw's oral history at the Kennedy Library reveal a darker side of Jackie's relationship with Miss Shaw. When *Life* magazine did a profile of Jackie in 1958, Miss Shaw was hidden away. A photo caption reads, *Tucking her daughter in for an afternoon nap. Jackie does not have a nurse for Caroline.* In a memo to the White House usher, Jackie wrote, "Miss Shaw won't need much in her room. Just find a wicker wastebasket for her banana peels and a little table for her false teeth at night." After the President's assassination, Mrs. Kennedy presented each of the White House servants with one of his possessions as a keepsake. His valet was given the President's rocking chair, but Miss Shaw was handed one of the President's old shirts ("I couldn't believe it, but what could I say?"). Four years later, when Miss Shaw wrote her memoirs, Mrs. Kennedy hired a lawyer to block publication so a terrible secret would not be revealed—that Miss Shaw, rather than Jackie, had told Caroline of her father's death. ("I said, 'Your father has gone to look after Patrick. Patrick was so lonely in heaven.' And the child started to cry so violently that I was afraid she might choke.")

They didn't tell John-John because they thought he was too young to understand; he turned three the day of his father's funeral. Josie finds it almost shocking that little John-John, who sat through a state funeral without squirming and without getting his suit dirty, who saluted smartly when his mother told him to, was just three. She doesn't even want to consider what Henry might do at a televised funeral (when he got nervous, he tended to clutch his penis). Josie stares out the window again and wonders how much Henry would notice if Peter never came back again, if that person who played "car crash" and sang "Yellow Submarine" was gone one day. Would he think to ask where Daddy went? Or would he simply accept Eleanor and Allison and maybe even Fred as the new parents in his life, all infinitely replaceable?

She covers two index cards in her small, tidy script (also a girl thing, according to Peter) with descriptions of Halloween costumes (actually the store-bought kind that Josie used to have, with the slippery rayon suits and plastic masks), favorite meals (hot dogs, candy, and Cokes allowed only when they were on holiday), the books read at bedtime (Beatrix Potter, which Caroline could read when she was four because she had "a high IQ."). Josie looks over at her watch— one-fifteen—and smacks the pencil down. On her way to the elevator, she stops at the reference desk. Laura has almost finished sorting reprints into two piles.

"I'm just going to make a phone call," Josie says apologetically. "I'll be right back." Laura glances up, puzzled that Josie is bothering to tell her this. "Do whatever you want," she says.

Josie steps in the elevator, already starting to feel nervous about Henry. How can she help it, after reading about the Kennedy children with their phalanx of nannies and Secret Service agents, their French classes and private kindergartens, being paraded around in their Halloween costumes for the press. Last Halloween, Henry had gone as a pirate with one of Josie's scarves tied around his head. Peter had drawn a stubbly beard and a scar on his face with a black Magic Marker. Henry had stood on a chair so he could see himself in the bathroom mirror, turning his face slowly from right to left so he could get the full effect. But after he went trick-or-treating, they couldn't wash the beard and scar off even though the marker was theoretically washable, and he'd gone off to day care the next day looking bruised. Nothing like that ever happened to the Kennedy kids.

"Sound asleep on the couch," Eleanor says. "He was so tired after story hour, he just lay down and boom, off to the Land of Nod."

Maybe he's sick, Josie thinks. Maybe Eleanor should feel his forehead to see if he's got a temperature. "How's Allison?"

"Guess what she's doing? Unpacking all of Henry's clothes and toys." She hangs up saying, "Don't give us a second thought."

Josie walks into the snack bar and inspects the sandwiches in a glass-fronted refrigerator. Gourmet sandwiches—ham and Boursin, tarragon-chicken salad; Jackie would approve. But after Eleanor's vaguely reproachful phone call, Josie doesn't have the stomach for lunch. She should have unpacked Henry's things last night, of course, but she was distracted by Oak Park and the Cubs. She yawns. This place is as air-locked as Biosphere II; no fresh air, just recycled tourist breath. That's probably why she's feeling anxious—lack of oxygen. She buys an extra-large coffee and heads out the revolving doors toward the glitter of Boston Harbor.

The breeze off the water is sharp, and Josie's bare arms goose-bump in the bright sunlight. She circles around the building toward the water in search of shelter, but the only windbreak is an improbable wooden sloop propped on blocks in the middle of the back lawn. For a moment, she wonders if it's some fancy yacht club boat broken loose from its mooring and washed up in the last hurricane, but then sees a brass plaque: "John F. Kennedy's sailboat, the *Victura*."

She heads toward a lush tuft of grass by the prow of the boat, but stops short. It's occupied by the bespectacled man from the reading room, the one who was hiding behind the wall of manuscript boxes. He's lying on his side toward the water, holding a cigarette Jean-Paul Belmondo–style between finger and thumb. He glances over his shoulder with a start, and then scrambles up to a sitting position. He stubs out the cigarette, squints up at her, and pats the indented spot he's left in the grass. "Please. Have a seat."

She had been looking forward to a solitary brood over the choppy waves of the harbor. There were a lot of possible topics to mull over—Caroline and John-John in their little blue coats (Daddy's gone to heaven to take care of Patrick), or maybe, probably, something closer to home.

The man is watching for an answer, smiling bashfully. He's handsome in a fine-boned way, with the pale, prematurely aged look of someone who has spent too much time in libraries. His sandy-colored hair, thinning across the crown, undulates softly in the breeze. This is the kind of library insider that Fiona Jones has instructed her to make friends with. Josie sits down in the center of his indentation, rests her coffee against her thigh, and takes his now-outstretched hand. It's thin but warm.

"Roger Denby."

"What are you doing with all those boxes?"

"A book on McGeorge Bundy and national security policy in the 1960s." He says this with a sheepish shrug, as if to say, "I know I'm boring."

"McGeorge Bundy, huh?" She thinks of a man with slicked-back hair and pink-rimmed glasses, but then realizes she's thinking of

Robert McNamara. "I always liked those Kennedy eggheads." Her best friend growing up in Crowley, Sarah, had a father like that— with the glasses and stooped posture and threadbare tweed jacket; he taught classics at Holy Cross. Whenever someone asked the simplest question (Where's the bicycle pump?), he ruminated and then answered so deliberately that Sarah would yell, "Dad, *spit it out!*" But to Josie, he seemed far preferable to her own father with his good looks and quick answers.

"Yeah, me too," says Roger, brightening. "Those were the glory days for eggheads. Now poor Clinton has to apologize for being a Rhodes scholar." He shakes his head sadly.

It dawns on Josie that Roger is talking about his own, underappreciated egghead self. "Were you a Rhodes scholar?"

"Well . . . sort of." He's actually blushing. "But I don't usually spread that around." He opens a brown paper bag and peers in. "Do you want a sandwich? I always make two, and then I only eat one." He pulls out a sandwich Baggie.

Through the plastic, Josie can see green and red flecks of olives in cream cheese, and her mouth starts to salivate. When she was little, this was Eleanor's special treat. Usually lunch was egg salad or tuna fish (she didn't believe in peanut butter), but when Josie was home sick or especially good, Eleanor made olives and cream cheese on Pepperidge Farm white. "Sure. Thanks." She can't help feeling slightly wistful that this one's on pumpernickel. She takes a bite and suddenly recalls the best part of olives and cream cheese—the texture. Those hard, slippery, salty olives buried in soft mush.

She leans against the varnished warmth of the *Victura*, tilts her face toward the sun, and shuts her eyes. "So tell me about McGeorge Bundy."

In a deep professorial baritone, he describes the rise and fall of Mac Bundy—brightest boy at Groton, at Yale, youngest dean at Harvard. "Considered the most glittering star in Kennedy's constellation." Along the way, Roger reveals that he is indeed a professor—of modern politics at Rutgers—but is on something called the Emily Smith DeForest Fellowship for a year to do his book. His words come out in an eager gush, as if he hasn't talked to anyone about Mac Bundy, or maybe anything else, in a while.

With the honeyed heat on her back and face and Roger's drone mixing with the lapping of the water, Josie starts to drift off, leaving Mac at the Gulf of Tonkin. The scratch of a match jolts her awake. She pushes herself up on her elbow, blinks, and wonders what she's missed.

Roger is cupping his hands around a flickering match, trying to light a cigarette. He takes a long drag, and the end glows red. "I quit smoking fifteen years ago, but there's something about the air in there. Too many ion filters. I walk outside, and my lungs start craving pollution. Want one?" He points a package of Merits toward her and shakes it.

Why not, she thinks. She hasn't had a cigarette since the day Fiona Jones called (employment seemed reason enough to quit), but suddenly she's tempted. Smoking might put her in the right frame of mind to understand Jackie. Maude Shaw described the pains Jackie took to hide her chain-smoking from the public—ashtrays cleaned four times a day, cigarette boxes tucked behind the plants. It might even help her create a rapport with Fiona (who probably despises antismoking Yanks). Inhaling and exhaling at one another over the phone, they could swap Jackie gossip. She lights one and takes a hungry puff.

Roger winds up Mac Bundy, apparently unaware that she dozed off during the Vietnam crisis. "Well, enough about me," he says unconvincingly. He links his arms around his blue-jeaned legs and turns toward her politely. She decides that he's older than she originally thought—more of a boyish forty-two than a middle-aged twenty-eight. "Media portrayal of women in politics, eh? Never really thought about that one before. Of course, most of them were just politicians' wives."

"That's the point," she says testily, stubbing her cigarette out in the gravel underneath the *Victura*.

"Eleanor, Mamie; Jackie, of course," he says.

"Don't forget Bess, and Happy."

"Lady Bird and Pat. Who was Mrs. Goldwater?"

"Jane. How about Mrs. Humphrey?"

"Muriel, I think. Mrs. McGovern was another Eleanor. Betty, Rosalyn, Nancy, Barbara."

"Kitty, Marilyn, and then . . . "

"Hillary and Tipper," they say in unison. He grins wolfishly, almost like Peter, and she considers for an instant telling him about her true mission for Fiona Jones, but decides not to risk it. These academic types stick together; he might feel honor-bound to turn her in.

"You think I'm going to find anything about Jackie here?"

"Oh, sure. They seem to pride themselves on collecting every screed written against the Kennedys. I think there's a whole wing of the library filled with nothing but assassination books." He stands up, collects their butts in his lunch bag, and neatly folds it in quarters. "And then there's all the secret stuff they don't let anyone see." One of the rather blue, rather long-lashed eyes behind his horn-rims winks.

"Really?"

"Yup."

"Like what?"

"Oh, lots of stuff. Kennedy's medical records. Jackie's interviews with William Manchester and Teddy White. I think most of them are closed until 2063."

Josie stops. "A century? You're kidding." Not that a closed collection would daunt Fiona. She'll expect Josie to inveigle her way into the closed stacks somehow—disguise herself as an archivist in a gray lab coat; hide in one of those lockers and creep out after dark.

"These Kennedys are a paranoid lot. At least about things that haven't been published yet. No amount of pleading will help. Nigel Hamilton got in such a lather that he finally quit."

By the end of the afternoon, Josie has made her way through *I Was Jackie Kennedy's Dressmaker*, *The Kennedy White House Parties*, *Upstairs at the White House: My Life with the First Ladies*, and *My Life with Jacqueline Kennedy*—the last by a disgruntled former secretary. A portrait emerges of Jackie as charming to those she wanted to impress (usually men), and mean-spirited and stingy to those she didn't (usually women). The servant's-eye view—the celebrity biographer's mother lode. At four-fifty, Josie stands up and stretches, feeling deeply gratified by the two-inch stack of cards she's covered with notes. She can type up her first research memo tonight, and maybe get another check by the end of next week. Until then, she'll have to borrow from Eleanor to pay Allison.

Roger Denby rides down the elevator with her, she holding her cards and pencils, he clutching the kind of oversized briefcase that salesmen carry. They walk side by side to the parking lot, and he climbs into a dented Honda next to hers.

"So, you're going to be a regular?" he says, leaning out his car window.

She peers in his side window and sees a collapsible black umbrella reclining along a spotless backseat. She props her body protectively against the side of her car to block his view of spilled Chee•tos and juice boxes—a sight that single, childless people seem to find so revolting. She assumes Roger is single and childless, although he hasn't said; she can't imagine those tidy sandwiches being made by a married man. "At least through August."

"Well, then. I'll keep making two sandwiches."

She wonders if this is a mild come-on. She didn't mention Peter or Henry, but how could he miss her wedding ring? Was he that much of an egghead? "We'll take turns," she says affably. "I always have to make extras for my son. But I'm afraid mine might be peanut butter and jelly."

He gives her a puzzled look, the kind she's gotten before when people learn she has a child. Sometimes she's mistaken for a baby-sitter or even a teenage mother. He rolls up his window and locks the car door (maybe he has a mother like Eleanor). "See you Monday," he calls out through the glass, sounding as if he's underwater.

She pulls onto Morrissey Boulevard, composing the first lines of her memo to Fiona in her head. *To understand JBKO, one must understand how she organized a dinner party for eight. "First," she said, "you must start with the flowers."* All right! Josie thinks. She turns off NPR, pops in one of Peter's Ten Thousand Maniacs tapes, and accelerates. Out of the corner of her eye, she sees the interstate entrance ramp fly by. The roadway dissolves into potholes, sunlight fading as she drives under the interstate. Uh-oh. She has just gone *to* Dorchester. She bumps onto Dorchester Avenue and pulls over to check if everything is locked and rolled up—feeling ridiculous and paranoid, but she did promise Eleanor.

She's parked in front of something called Raoul's Package Store. The gutter along the curb is littered with tiny one-shot liquor bottles; the windows and doors are covered with narrow-meshed grilles. But there aren't any menacing gang types around; in fact she doesn't see anyone. Perfectly safe, she decides, peeling off the two dollars she's saved by not buying lunch. She hides the index cards under the seat so they won't be stolen, unlocks the car, and ventures forth into Raoul's. The store clerk is enclosed in a small booth that seems to be constructed of bulletproof plastic. She feeds the bills through a pull-out drawer, and he feeds out a package of menthol Trues.

My life revolves around my husband. His life is my life. It is up to me to make his home a haven, a refuge, to arrange it so that he can see as much of me and his children as possible — but never let the arrangements ruffle him, never let him see that it is work.

— JACQUELINE KENNEDY, 1960

Do you think a wife should let her husband think he's smarter than she is?

— JACQUELINE BOUVIER

Question asked as Inquiring Photographer for the *Times-Herald*

⁂

On Saturday morning, Josie and Eleanor are facing one another in the bay window of Eleanor's bedroom. They sit in matching "boudoir" chairs covered in tufted blue satin, hand-me-downs from Eleanor's mother and hopelessly Grand Rapids.

"You? Smoking?" says Eleanor.

"Only when I'm working," says Josie, taking a final guilty drag and stubbing the cigarette out in the Wedgwood saucer on Eleanor's bureau. Josie is conducting an interview about Eleanor's experience as a congressman's wife in the 1950s for her Jackie research—at least that's what she's told Eleanor. Leslie dreamed up this subterfuge during one of their phone consultations about Eleanor. "Establish a dialogue. Get her to open up. Then you can go after her about the drinking."

Go after her—their sibling relationship summed up in three words. Leslie's Omar Bradley to Josie's private in the first wave at Omaha Beach. Just follow orders, soldier. It reminded Josie of the time Leslie instructed her to pat their neighbor's rottweiler to see if he was friendly. He wasn't; Josie ended up with stitches and a tetanus shot. But then she decided that Leslie had a point; deceit was

the only way to pin their mother down. Eleanor was slippery. Whenever they asked a personal question, she demurred and shrugged
until, before they knew it, she had segued to Rascal or her Bible
study group.

Josie steadies a writing pad with a list of questions on her knees.
"Okay. Ready?"

Eleanor's face is turned toward the window, watching Henry
chase Allison around the back lawn with a garden hose. His piping
voice floats through the half-opened window. "Got you! Got you!"
She leans back with the resigned expression of an eight-year-old
stuck in school on a beautiful summer day. "Shoot."

"Tell me what Washington was like when Dad was first elected."
To nudge her mother along, Josie taps her pencil point on the top
line of the page.

"Well now, let me think." Eleanor twists her platinum wedding
and engagement rings, which, inexplicably, she still wears. "Grif and
I moved there in December of 1958. We drove to Washington from
Crowley in that Plymouth station wagon we used to have. You probably remember it."

Josie writes "Plymouth station wagon" with such force that the
pencil makes a deep, shiny groove in the paper. As if she could forget the Plymouth. Her mother drove it for twelve years, long after
they moved back to Crowley, even though her father bought a new
sedan for himself every three years. ("It's what they expect of me," he
said, never explaining who "they" were. His constituents, his law
clients, his mistresses?) Josie can still remember every place on
Route 2A where the Plymouth broke down. Her embarrassment
when the sea-foam-green monster with fins lumbered into the parking lot at school.

Josie follows Eleanor's eyes as they wander toward the window
again. Henry is naked now, standing swaybacked so his potbelly juts
out over his feet, filling up a bright blue wading pool with the hose.
"There had been a big blizzard two days before we came. As we
came down Pennsylvania Avenue, the White House was surrounded
by snowdrifts like a fairy-tale castle. I said to Leslie, even though she
was only a baby, 'Look, there's where our President lives.' And then
your father said, 'Maybe we'll live there someday.' "

Josie lifts her pencil, her face feeling hot with embarrassment for both of her parents. Her father, who couldn't even hang on to his seat in Congress, for saying it. And her mother for repeating it now.

Eleanor's brow furrows. "I can't believe this is really helpful."

"You're doing great, Mom. Keep going. Tell me about your house."

"All right. We sublet a house on Thirty-fifth Street from someone in the German Embassy. Your father got it into his head that we had to live in Georgetown because he said that's where all the movers and shakers—that's what he called them—lived."

"Like who?"

"The Kennedys, of course. Tony and Ben Bradlee."

"You were friends with the Bradlees?"

"Well, no. They lived over on N Street, where the bigger houses were. But Thirty-fifth Street was the most we could afford. It would have been more sensible to live out in Arlington or Bethesda, where all the other freshman congressmen were. But that was Grif—it had to be Georgetown." She turns her palms up helplessly, probably the same way she did back when her life was rearranged to suit Grif's whims. (Leslie once pointed out that their father's name was just one letter away from "grief.")

"It was really big, right? A mansion?" A hostile edge has crept into Josie's voice. When she was little, Leslie used to tell her all about the wonderful house they had lived in when Grif was a congressman. All the furniture was gold, she had said: the chairs, the mirrors, everything. Leslie was eight years older and loved to regale Josie with stories about the Washington years she had missed—the kids' pet show at Hickory Hill, the Easter egg hunt on the White House lawn, being among the special group of mourners allowed to pass by Kennedy's casket.

"No," says Eleanor, puzzled. "Who told you that? It was a horrible place with tiny rooms crammed full of this awful gilt furniture."

"Oh." Josie's voice trails off. "But you all did a lot of fun things." Eleanor still looks puzzled. "The pet show at Hickory Hill? The Easter egg hunt on the White House lawn?" She doesn't include being in the group of special mourners, because that was technically not fun, although Leslie always made it sound like fun.

"Maybe," says Eleanor uncertainly. "I don't really remember doing any of those things, but I could have forgotten. It was a long time ago."

Josie clears her throat. "Well, what did you do? You must have gone to a lot of parties." Leslie had told Josie about the parties that happened practically every night, Eleanor's sequined evening dresses, how handsome Grif looked in his tuxedo.

"As a congressman, your father went to cocktail parties and receptions at night, but you know me. I hate those kinds of things, so I stayed home with Leslie. Mostly I went to concerts and museums with Phoebe Converse, my Smith roommate. She was a cataloger at the Library of Congress." She brightens as if she's reliving those jaunts to the National Gallery with her old pal Phoebe.

All these years Josie had felt so envious about missing out on Camelot—the halcyon years of her family, all over before she was born. She should be furious with Leslie, but instead she feels almost disappointed. Back when Grif was trying to restart his law practice in Fitchburg and had no income, or later, when he left and moved to Florida, it had been sustaining to think that her parents had once been glamorous, had once hobnobbed with the Kennedys. That her dreary childhood was a fluke, a mere setback, like those children in Victorian novels who are temporarily sent to an almshouse because their parents (of noble birth, although no one knows it) have been captured by Barbary pirates. "So what *did* you do as a congressman's wife?" It comes out like an accusation.

Eleanor seems relieved that they've moved on from her Washington social life. "Oh, I had a lot to do. Back in those days, they didn't give congressmen any money to hire a staff. So I ran his office with a part-time secretary. When people came to town from our district, I got them tickets to tour the White House. And then I arranged to have their pictures taken with Grif on the steps of the Capitol. I stuffed envelopes, made coffee." In other words, the kinds of jobs she still does, only now for the Unitarian church.

Eleanor looks modestly toward the floor. Josie studies how the scalp where her thick white hair is parted glows rosy-pink in the sunlight. "I even wrote a few speeches. Sometimes I wrote summaries of bills Grif was too busy to read."

I bet, Josie thinks. Twenty years after her divorce, Eleanor still takes pains to conceal how much smarter she was than her husband. How she wrote papers for him so he could squeak through Dartmouth with a C average. How she tutored him for the Massachusetts Bar exam until he passed on his third try.

"And then there was the Congressional Wives Club. All the wives were expected to participate in that."

Josie has heard about the Congressional Wives Club before. Mostly, the wives put on skits for one another; something to keep them busy while their husbands were off running the country.

"There were lots of committees, and your position was determined by your husband's rank in Congress. So I had a very low post on the costume committee."

"But you can't sew." Growing up in Elgin with an equally impractical mother, Eleanor had never learned a single domestic art besides gardening.

"Well, I was expected to, and I did," Eleanor says grimly. "I was in charge of the costumes for the spring revels, our big annual production before summer recess. It was *Antigone*, and I managed to make thirty togas." Somewhere, probably at Smith, she had learned that women do what they are told without complaint, no matter how onerous or ridiculous.

"So what about Jackie? Was she in any skits?"

"Of course not. She was a senator's wife; they had their own club. But I don't think she went in for that kind of thing. She had her own set of friends."

Like the Bradlees, Josie thinks. "Okay, let's go back. I want to know about you and Dad before you got married." Now that she knows the truth about the Washington years, she might as well find out the rest. Eleanor never said much about her courtship with Grif, and it always seemed tactless to ask, considering how it all turned out.

Eleanor's hand darts up to her face and slides a piece of hair behind one ear, the rim as delicate as a seashell. Then the hand drops back to her lap and starts twisting the rings again. Still the perfect Smith girl, posture erect, ankles crossed. And still beautiful in her own soft way; those placid blue eyes, skin as fine as Henry's, just a little looser down around the chin. "What's that got to do with Jackie?"

"You and Jackie had a lot in common. You both got married in '53. You had children at roughly the same time." You both had handsome husbands who cheated on you, she adds silently.

Eleanor looks unconvinced. She's dressed in her gardening clothes and she's antsy to get back to the vegetable patch. She readjusts herself on the blue satin, starts tapping one of her navy Keds. "Well, I met Grif through Aunt Sally, who lived on my hallway. He had gotten her a date for Winter Carnival weekend, and asked her to bring someone along for him. You know all this."

Her parents' first date at Winter Carnival is a familiar story, but Josie doesn't mind hearing it again. It seems to be the only part of their relationship that evoked any nostalgia; they were happy and in love so briefly. Just the words "Winter Carnival" conjured up romantic images of rosy-cheeked girls and boys in reindeer sweaters having a snowball fight in front of a thirty-foot ice sculpture of Jack Frost.

Eleanor, with her fuzzy twin sets and long blond pageboy hanging over one eye like Veronica Lake's, was positively seductive. Grif, president of his fraternity and campus big shot, wore his hair parted in the middle and brushed back like F. Scott Fitzgerald, even though this was 1950, the age of the buzz cut. To impress his date, he had the fraternity house decorated from top to bottom with hothouse flowers, orchids and lilies, trucked up from Boston.

"Of course, when the bill came later for four hundred dollars, the frat had no way to pay it, and everyone was furious." Eleanor smiles indulgently—the first of Grif's unpaid bills.

The temperature was subzero all weekend, and the Hanover police had issued a frostbite warning. But on Saturday night, after the big dance, Grif and Eleanor threw caution to the wind.

"We bundled up like Eskimos, so we could neck in the backseat of Grif's car," Eleanor says, bringing her hand to her lips as if she can still taste his kisses. Josie wonders if he told her then, with his overcoat wrapped around her, his whispered breath a white cloud, that he planned to become President.

Eleanor is hazy about the rest of their courtship. After that weekend, they had an "understanding," but they couldn't get married until Eleanor finished college and Grif graduated (barely) from Suffolk Law School. Four years later, they were married in the walled garden of her family's house at Elgin Estates, surrounded by Mary Baldwin roses.

"So tell me, Mom. Did you sleep with Dad before you got married?" Josie lifts her pencil expectantly and tries to make her voice sound clinical—just doing research on gender roles and sexuality in the 1950s, nothing personal. In fact, she and Leslie have speculated about this for years. Definitely not, says Leslie. Eleanor was a virgin all the way, not even a technical virgin.

"Don't tell me that has anything to do with Jackie Kennedy."

"All right. I admit it, I'm just curious." Josie shrugs defensively. She suddenly realizes how much she hopes it is true. Please let her have had some passion, some pleasure with him. Something more than false hopes.

Eleanor sits still for a moment, cogitating. She has always prided herself on having enlightened attitudes about sexual matters: advocating abortion rights, birth-control education, breast-cancer awareness. She dutifully makes a fifty-dollar donation to Planned Parenthood every year. She inhales sharply as if she's about to plunge into an icy lake. "Yes, we did. After we were engaged, we started having intercourse." She says this with an air of finality. That's that, now let's change the subject. She stares out the window toward her vegetable garden. Even from this distance, she can probably see the weeds sprouting up around the tomatoes, the carrots and lettuces crying out for thinning.

The image of her parents making love illicitly, hungrily, strikes Josie as surprisingly erotic, like Deborah Kerr and Burt Lancaster rolling around in the surf in *From Here to Eternity*. She speculates where they did it. In the backseat of his car (again), in his apartment near Suffolk Law School while his roommate was at class? A quickie, wherever it was. Josie and Peter have made a specialty of quickies over the years; the half hour between classes, Henry's nap time. And frankly, she prefers them to the clothes-off, in-bed, all-the-time-in-the-world variety, when she can get sleepy. Back then, it was probably nothing but quickies, for the married and unmarried alike. "Weren't you afraid of getting pregnant?"

Eleanor glances back over her shoulder, smiling slyly. "Things weren't that uncivilized, Josie. We had rubbers."

Josie considers what would have happened if Eleanor had gotten pregnant, a definite possibility in the days of low-tech condoms. Maybe things would have turned out differently, better, she thinks, and then stops herself, repelled. That seems to imply her relationship with Peter turned out for the best because she got pregnant. That's hardly what Josie believes, although she can't say what would have happened if she hadn't gotten pregnant. No matter how it happened, her marriage is obviously sounder than her parents' ever was. She didn't have romantic delusions; she didn't fall for the frat president on Winter Carnival weekend. She chose her partner wisely. Despite being good-looking and charming, Peter was nothing like her father. For starters, he wasn't dumb.

Josie stands up and searches out the window for any sign of Allison and Henry, but the lawn is deserted. His clothes still lie in a tangled heap next to the wading pool, its surface rippling turquoise in the sunlight. Somewhere from behind the carriage barn, she can hear his high voice laughing. One summer, she and Leslie built a clubhouse behind the barn out of plywood scraps and an old door. They furnished it with stuff they found at the Crowley dump: a bookshelf, an armchair, a three-legged table they propped up with a rake handle. Leslie, who was the president, got to sit in the armchair and give orders to Josie, the only other member. She hopes Allison isn't letting Henry play in the ruins. A rusty nail could go right through his foot.

From the window, Josie gazes down the driveway into the barn. A line of ancient lawn mowers and garden rakes slumbers against one wall, a plank shelf holds at least fifty cans of dried-out paint. She resolves to help Eleanor clean it out this summer. Suddenly it occurs to her that the parking space in front of the barn door is empty. "Hey Mom, where's your car?"

Eleanor answers briskly, as if she's been expecting this question. "Fred has it. He uses it to get to work."

Josie steps back, so she can look her mother square in the face. "Doesn't he have a car?"

"Not yet. He's just getting on his feet." She sounds unconcerned. "I don't mind. I don't need it."

"Oh, come on. You can't get anywhere around here without a car. What if you need to go to the grocery store or the bank?"

"Fred does the shopping on his way home from work."

"Well, good," says Josie. "I think that he should at least buy groceries." Last night he served up thick pork chops in crème fraîche, and she started to wonder who was paying for all this extravagance. She suspects Eleanor doesn't charge Fred any rent, because she had steadfastly refused to accept any from Josie.

Eleanor leans back against the windowsill and crosses her arms. "I didn't say he paid for the food. I said he picks it up. I've told Fred I want him to save his money for a car. I give him my bank card, and he withdraws money to pay for groceries." She is speaking with deliberate slowness, her eyes bright with defiance.

Josie settles back down on one of the boudoir chairs. "You let Fred use your bank card? Do you realize what could happen?" Her voice is actually trembling.

"I'm not stupid. Of course I realize what could happen. He could take my car and all my money and disappear. But I have faith that he won't."

"But why tempt him? You're tempting him to rob you. It's like leaving booze out for an alcoholic." As she says this, it occurs to her that booze is the real problem here. Drinking has impaired Eleanor's judgment.

"You and I have no idea what it's like to be in prison," says Eleanor soberly. "Every minute of your life is regulated—when you eat, when you sleep, when you go to the bathroom. No wonder these men get out of prison and they fall apart. Every shred of their humanity has been stripped away."

"So explain to me how letting Fred use your car and your bank card is going to restore his humanity."

Eleanor stoops down and retrieves her work gloves off the floor. "Because he knows that I trust him. What could be more empowering than another person's trust?" she says simply, slapping the gloves across her palm. With that, she walks purposefully across the room and out the door. Her soft step retreats down the stairs; the screen door groans open and then bangs back.

Josie leans her forehead against the windowpane and watches her mother circle along the side of the house—the same purposeful strides—and into the vegetable garden, with Rascal trotting loyally behind. Eleanor gingerly kneels down into the soft, black earth and bends over her tiny lettuce plants. One ear is tilted toward them, as if they are whispering secrets.

THAT NIGHT Fred outdoes himself—stuffed jumbo shrimp on a bed of saffron rice with marinated asparagus spears from Eleanor's garden. The shrimp catches in Josie's throat like hardened lumps of Play-Doh; all she can think about is her poor mother's shrinking savings account. She studies Eleanor in the candlelight, how her eyes close halfway when she's taking a drink of her martini. Tonight, like every night since Josie's been back, Eleanor has observed the cocktail hour with a martini plus a dividend. By the time they sit down to dinner, the sensible Smith woman who talked so nobly of empowering men with her trust has disappeared. What's left is an old woman with streaks of garden dirt on her elbows and uncombed hair who laughs too much. "What's this yellow rice called again?" she says, squinting down at her fork.

"You should open a restaurant, Fred," Josie says. She's now decided her mission is to find out what Fred is up to and get rid of him. She'll get help from the police, the parole board, whatever. If Fred has to go back to jail, so be it.

"Actually, I used to own one of those big restaurants on Route 1. But that was a long time ago." For once, the gregarious Fred seems subdued, and Eleanor shoots Josie a warning look to drop the subject.

Josie's heart quickens at this nugget of information. Before, she had speculated that Fred might be some two-bit criminal like a bookie, if there was still such a thing as a bookie. But a restaurant sounds like big-time fraud: cooked books, embezzling, a possible Mafia connection.

After dinner, Josie and Henry are once again shooed upstairs. She tucks him into his trundle bed and then stretches herself out on Eleanor's bed waiting for Peter to call. He is supposed to reach Berkeley today.

Their last two conversations had been strained. He called from Doug and Louise's to report that the truck was fixed and that the

Cubs game had been rained out. This time he sounded sober, and there was no laughter in the background. His tone implied that this news should make Josie happy (which it did), and she wondered if Louise had given Peter a lecture on marital fidelity. It was the kind of thing she might do, unfortunately; she took her job as Josie's protector seriously.

The next night, Peter called from a Ramada Inn outside of Denver. Josie described in detail her two days of research at the Kennedy Library, but the revelations by Maude Shaw and Jackie's dressmaker came out sounding trivial. He said, "You mean, some guy is already making you *sandwiches?*" Peter always insisted that Josie was irresistible to men, and his tone was slightly accusatory, as if she was using her feminine wiles to inveigle a free lunch. When Peter asked if Henry was still missing him, Josie said, "He seems to have gotten over it." Both of them had been careful not to mention Monica's name.

She can hear Eleanor and Fred still doing the dishes, their voices raised so they can talk over the running water. A pot lid clatters to the floor, and Eleanor lets out that girlish giggle she makes only for Fred. Josie rolls over on her side, wraps her arms around her knees, and vows to be nicer to Peter when he calls, no matter what. She misses him too much, she needs him too much.

The phone rings nearly two hours later, waking her up. "Josie? Well, I made it. I dropped Monica and her stuff at her apartment in Oakland, and I'm at Berkeley." He sounds relieved.

The words "dropped Monica" give Josie a surge of evil pleasure. She imagines Monica standing on the sidewalk with a stack of U-Haul boxes and her brass bed.

Then he says in his enthusing voice, "And *guess what?*"

"What?" she says warily. She's learned over the years that the enthusing voice can mean trouble; Peter is getting carried away again by some new person or project or passion. The night air has turned chilly, and she starts to shiver in her shorts and T-shirt. She folds down the bedspread and crawls under the covers of Eleanor's bed.

"I found this *incredible* house for us in the Berkeley Hills. A medievalist in my department is subletting it for two years because he's got a Guggenheim to study Gregorian chants in Tuscany. So—" His words are coming out in a rush. "It's perfect for us. It's got three bed-rooms, and a backyard filled with all these hanging orange flowers. I don't know what they are, but they're unbelievable. *And* you can even see the ocean. Think of that, Josie. Henry can see the ocean."

She doesn't point out to him that Henry could see the ocean in Rhode Island too. For some reason, Peter never thought that the Atlantic quite counted.

"And it has a swing set and a sandbox, because they have a five-year-old boy. And his room has a bunk bed and *helicopter* wallpaper. Henry will *flip out*."

"Sounds great," she says, and it does. They had resigned them-selves to living in some two-bedroom dive off Telegraph; a whole house had seemed out of the question. "But it must be expensive."

"Well, that's just it," he says, the enthusing voice evaporating like morning mist. "It's fifteen hundred dollars, and I would have to take it now."

"That seems pretty high," she says, feeling like a killjoy. They had figured that $1,200 was the most they could do, and would be able to swing that only by having Peter live in the dorms all summer.

"But there's the extra money from your job. And Mom could probably help us out."

She is sitting up in Eleanor's bed now. From this angle, she can see herself in the mirror hanging over the bureau, her hair falling over one side of her face like Eleanor's in her Veronica Lake days. A house of their own. At last they can be a real family, not just graduate students with a kid. "Let's do it," she says.

"*Really?*" he exhales.

She hangs up saying, "I want Henry to see the ocean too, you know."

She slides down under Eleanor's cover and closes her eyes, trying to picture this house in the Berkeley Hills. A trumpet vine climbing up an arched trellis, orange petals curled back, stamen as long and curved as a hummingbird's bill. Tiny square rooms with white walls and floors the color of syrup. A bay window with a round table just big enough for three, the windows half open, sheer white curtains undulating in the breeze. Far away, past the hills dotted with red-wood houses, a silver ribbon slicing across the sky—the Pacific.

chapter 7

Women are all the victors in my generation.

—JACK V. BOUVIER III

Each party will refrain from commenting to either child, on the character or con-
duct of the other party, save and except, if at all, to speak in words of praise cal-
culated to increase the love and respect of the child toward the parent
mentioned.

—Divorce agreement of John V. Bouvier and Janet Bouvier, 1940

This time, Fiona Jones calls. "Soo-per," she says about Josie's research memo. "Love the part about the nanny. I'm popping a check to you FedEx." She gives Josie her next instructions: complete chronology of Jackie's childhood, with particular emphasis on her father, Black Jack Bouvier.

"Jackie had a father fixation," she pronounces. "Black Jack was handsome and fun, Janet was nothing but a social-climbing bore. Jackie's life fell apart when her parents got divorced." There is a pause as Fiona lights a cigarette. "That's the key to my book— Jackie's lifelong search for a father figure. First it was Jack, then Ari, then Maurice." This strikes Josie as pretty unoriginal; Jackie's biographers have always made a fuss about Black Jack. Surely Fiona is going to come up with something better than that. "So here's what I need to know." Fiona pauses again, exhaling loudly, presumably so Josie can fetch her steno pad to take notes.

Josie climbs off Eleanor's bed and ambles over to her slant-top desk, poking through the pigeonholes for paper. The best she can do are two sheets of buff stationery with "Mrs. Griffon Trask, Trask Homestead, Crowley Center." No street address, no zip, not even the state. Left over from the days when everyone knew who you were and where you lived. Back when her mother was someone, if being Mrs. Griffon Trask could be considered being someone. "Okay," says Josie, "I'm ready."

"I want a time line with the usual stuff—their financial problems, who Black Jack was screwing." Fiona sounds tired. After a while, all those infidelities must be exhausting—Pablo's, Prince Philip's, JFK's. Who can keep it all straight? "Also, he apparently had some strange condition that made his skin a funny color. JFK said he had blue balls. Check it out in a dermatology textbook and see if you can identify a disease. Maybe it was an undiagnosed venereal disease." Her voice lifts with anticipation. "So how's little What's-his-name?"

Things with Fiona have evolved to the point where they now have an obligatory conversation about personal matters. Josie has learned that Fiona is on her third husband; that she has a summer rental in Sagaponack, an irritable colon, and a grown son in the "fashion industry," whatever that means.

"You mean Henry?"

"I suppose he's away at camp by now."

"He's only three."

"Oh, my brother was sent to boarding school when he was three. Up in Scotland. Had to swim across a freezing loch every morning. Then again, maybe he was older." There is a pause. "And things in California are status quo, I hope?" Fiona has somehow managed to ferret out the particulars of Josie's summer living arrangements. That's her profession, after all—getting people to confess things they wouldn't tell their psychiatrist.

"Just fine," says Josie, trying to sound blasé. "Nothing to worry about except earthquakes. And brush fires."

The next day, Josie is back at her desk at the library with Peter's laptop and a stack of Bouvier books, most of them by disgruntled Bouvier relatives Jackie snubbed after her rise to fame. She squints at a photograph of Black Jack with four-year-old Jackie in East Hampton in the thirties. Hard to tell in a black-and-white what color his skin was, but it looks more tan than blue. His dark hair is parted in the middle and slicked back with something so viscous that the comb marks show. The pencil-thin mustache leaves a band of skin above his thick lips, making them even wider. When *Gone With the Wind* came out, women mistook him for Clark Gable and asked for his autograph. He is wearing a pale linen suit with a long silky scarf drooping out of the breast pocket and two-toned shoes—white with tan tips. Black Jack was famous for his elegant wardrobe, even when he was flat broke. He leans toward the camera, head tilted to one side, as if to say I know I am irresistible.

What a vain, silly man, Josie thinks. He reminds her of Grif—not many brains, not much talent, but plenty of charm. Tried to squeak by on bluster and the right club memberships, and it almost worked.

July 7, 1928—*John Vernou Bouvier, a 38-year-old stockbroker, marries Janet Lee, 21-year-old daughter of self-made financier, James Lee. Fellow stockbrokers give him nickname "Black Jack" because of skin which he keeps tan year round with a sunlamp. On honeymoon on SS* Aquitania, *Black Jack has flirtation with Doris Duke. Janet breaks mirror in jealous rage.*

July 28, 1929—*Jacqueline Lee Bouvier born six weeks overdue at Southampton hospital.*

Oct. 24, 1929—*Stock market crash. Black Jack initially makes money selling short, then takes huge losses reentering market too soon.*

1930—*Moves family into Park Avenue apartment owned by "Old Man Lee." James Lee demands that Black Jack cut living expenses; he responds by having apartment remodeled with gold-plated fixtures, taking European vacation, hiring a trainer, a masseuse, a cook, two maids, two grooms, and an English nanny.*

March 3, 1933—*Caroline Lee Bouvier born.*

1933—*Makes $2 million investing in liquor stocks right before repeal of Prohibition. Then speculates and loses all but $106,000.*

1934—*Earned $7,000, had trading losses of $43,000. Living expenses for New York duplex, East Hampton cottage, servants and 7 horses—$39,000. Blames new SEC head appointed by Roosevelt for losses—Joseph P. Kennedy. His womanizing so flagrant that Janet refuses to attend social functions with him anymore.*

1936—*Has 6-month trial separation from Janet. Moves into West-bury Hotel. Pays $1,050 in monthly child support. Has right to visit children "Saturday afternoons and Sunday mornings as he*

*may wish." Takes children to Bronx Zoo, on buggy rides in Central
Park. Sometimes borrows dogs from pet stores for children to walk
because all family pets are on Long Island.*

1937—*At Black Jack's urging, Janet agrees to try a reconciliation.
Family spends summer together in East Hampton. In September,
Black Jack and Janet separate permanently. Jackie is described by
servants and relatives as sad and withdrawn. James Lee, Janet's
father, detests Black Jack so much that he requests his cabana at
the Maidstone Club be moved as far as possible from the
Bouviers'.*

1938—*Janet rents summer house in Belle Porte, forty miles from East
Hampton. Tells servants that Black Jack is never to be allowed in
house, and that Jackie and Lee should be spanked if they ask for
their father.*

1939—*Janet hires private detective to gather evidence of Black Jack's
adultery.*

1940—*Janet and children spend six weeks at Lazy-A-Bar Ranch in
Reno, Nevada. Granted a divorce on July 22 on the grounds of
mental cruelty.*

This is a Jackie that Josie never knew existed—the dark-eyed,
somber girl who retreated into her own world after her parents'
divorce, who holed up in a third-floor bedroom memorizing poetry,
pasting pictures in a scrapbook, writing stories about her pets. She
produced plays with her cousins and always cast herself in the same
role—the Queen of the Circus. I know this girl, thinks Josie.

After they divorced, the Bouviers' lives diverged like the final
chapter of a John O'Hara novel. Janet married an Auchincloss,
while Jack's life spiraled downward into booze and increasingly
shabby digs. All the while, the two squabbled over their daughters—
where they would spend their vacations, who would pay their dental
bills. A Bouvier relative called it "the fight for Jackie." Gradually,
Janet was victorious. Josie can't cram them both into a single time
line, so she tries two columns.

Janet

1942—Marries Hugh Auchincloss and moves into his estates in Newport and Virginia—Hammersmith Farm and Merrywood.

1943—Jackie and Lee spend Christmas at Merrywood. First Christmas not spent with Bouviers at Lasata, East Hampton.

1947—Jackie makes debut at Hammersmith Farm, declared Deb of Year by Cholly Knickerbocker.

1950—Jackie spends summer in Europe. Turns down offer to live with Black Jack in New York. Instead transfers to George Washington and lives at Merrywood.

1953—Jackie's wedding to JFK held at Hammersmith Farm. Janet insists that Black Jack not be invited to bridal dinner.

1955—Kennedys buy Hickory Hill, two miles from Merrywood.

1957—Jackie pregnant again but neglects to tell father, who reads about it in the newspaper. At father's funeral, has baskets of flowers to look like the garden of Lasata. Only two dozen people attend.

Jack

1942—Moves into four-bedroom apartment in east 70s overlooking an air shaft. Has affair with wife of British officer. Nine months later she has twins after she has returned to England.

1944—Commits himself to Silver Hill to dry out.

1947—Not invited to Jackie's debut.

1948—Father dies but leaves most of estate to his other children. Lasata sold two years later.

1950—Has cataract operation, spends summer recuperating in East Hampton by himself. Insists that Danseuse, Jackie's horse, be boarded at East Hampton rather than Newport so she will be forced to visit him.

1953—Black Jack has special cutaway made. Gets so drunk morning of wedding, Janet forbids him to attend. Hugh Auchincloss gives Jackie away instead.

1955—Sells seat on Stock Exchange and retires. Becomes recluse, drinking alone in his apartment. Only companion his maid Esther, who lends him money.

1957—Dies of liver cancer so suddenly, Jackie can't get to the hospital in time. Last word allegedly "Jackie." Leaves Jackie painting of horse in will, which she sells because it doesn't fit decor of new house in Georgetown.

Two columns—really a very tidy way to describe a marriage, Josie thinks. Of course the columns for her parents' marriage would be the mirror image of Jack and Janet's—Grif ascending, Eleanor descending. She skips down a few lines and types:

Grif	*Eleanor*
1972—*Joins Coral Gables Country Club. Builds five-bedroom Mediterranean-style house overlooking 12th hole. Trades in Mustang for Mercedes SL.*	1972—*Takes out second mortgage on Trask homestead. Shuts off and drains back wing of house. Has engine rebuilt on 1967 Plymouth station wagon. Gets part-time job*
1973—*Sends stepchildren to Coral Gables Country Day School. Over spring vacation, charters sailboat in St. Martin and takes new wife and family on two-week cruise. Not enough room for Leslie and Josie.*	*as filing clerk in Fitchburg insurance office.*
	1973—*Leslie transfers from Concord Academy to Ayer High School. Over spring vacation, Leslie and Josie visit Museum of Fine Arts and the Paul Revere House.*

Josie lets out a snort. Pretty funny, really. She'll print it off and send it to Peter, who is always amused by Grif's disgraceful behavior and Eleanor's martyrdom. She scrolls back up to where she left off— *The fight for Jackie.* "The fight for Jackie," she whispers. Without warning, she feels heat rush into her face and her nose start to fill. Oh Christ, she thinks, cupping her hands around her face, I'm going to start crying in the Kennedy Library reading room. Suppressing a sniffle, she stands up with her back carefully turned to Roger and stumbles toward the elevator. Outside, she jogs around the building, past the *Victura*, and then scrambles down the rocky embankment to the strip of mud where the harbor water washes in. Staring down at her feet, she wipes at her nose with the back of her hand.

Her black rubber sandals start sinking, but stop just as the gray muck is about to rise up over the top toward her toes. She studies the line of litter bobbing in the lapping waves—the red husk of a disposable lighter, the remains of a small, flat fish. Not very much, really. A library grounds person probably cleans it up every day—as spotless as Disneyland. With her feet still mired, she twists around toward the spire of plate glass and white concrete looming above her. The silver profile of a jet on takeoff from Logan glides across its mirrored surface. It's not fair, Josie thinks, her mouth pulling to one side. He didn't fight for me. He didn't care where I spent my vacations.

GRIF LEFT THEM for good on Labor Day, 1972; two days after the Crowley Players' final performance of *Meet Me in Saint Louis*.

He founded the Crowley Players in 1964, the year he lost his seat in Congress. "I'm better at plays than politics," he said airily—he'd been head of the Dartmouth Drama Club, after all. But his defeat had been humiliating, and everyone in Crowley knew it. George Vaskian, a jeweler from Fitchburg, had challenged his seat saying no rich guy from Crowley was going to tell him what to do. He had made a big deal out of Grif's attendance record, which admittedly had been poor in recent years. George Vaskian's campaign poster showed a photograph of Grif at some embassy party dressed in a tuxedo, a cocktail in one hand and a cigarette in the other, with the caption *Does Griffon Trask represent you?* printed in angry, slanted letters underneath.

Now Grif was back in Crowley Center, among people he had known all his life, and they rallied around his plan for starting an amateur theatrical group. The Derbys, who had lived in the Center as long as the Trasks, donated the unused dairy barn behind their house for a theater. They didn't have the funds to remodel it, but Grif reassured them he could easily handle the expenses himself. He diverted the money he had borrowed for redoing the septic system and bathrooms in the Trask homestead to build the Crowley Playhouse—a stage, a curtain made of green velvet, a lighting system that would have done the Schubert proud, built-in seats for two hundred (not, as Eleanor suggested, folding chairs borrowed from the high school), a new Steinway upright, two ticket windows, a paved parking lot. Nothing amateur about it.

As artistic director, Grif was in charge of casting, and no one seemed to mind that he always cast himself as the lead. "Griffon Trask's voice," Frances Derby was fond of saying, "is better than that Robert Goulet." If he'd had his way, he would have given all his family members lead roles, but only Leslie lusted for center stage.

Eleanor insisted on staying in the background with the props and scenery, and Josie couldn't be persuaded out of the back row of the children's chorus.

Meet Me in Saint Louis was to be the Crowley Players' most spectacular production yet. Grif drew sketches for the scenery, which he unrolled with a flourish every night across the dining room table for Leslie's and Josie's inspection—the Smiths' parlor with Victorian settees and an old-fashioned telephone, a front porch with a swing, and a *real* streetcar that everyone could sit on, not just a cardboard cutout. Grif dismissed Eleanor's concern about expenses with the wave of one of his finely tapered hands. "I'll handle the overruns myself," he said. "Trust me."

At fifteen, Leslie decided she was ready for the romantic lead, Esther. She paraded around in one of Marian the Librarian's dresses left over from *The Music Man*, pinned her hair up in a pompadour, stuffed her bra with tissue paper. "Can't I get my braces off just for the summer?" she pleaded, examining her profile in the hall mirror. If she couldn't be Esther, she wanted to be Tootie, Esther's five-year-old sister, who got all the best lines. "I can act five," said Leslie.

On the first day of rehearsal, Grif stood up on the stage and read off the parts to the assembled Crowley Players. He would play the father, Alonzo Smith. The oldest daughter, Esther, would be played by Terry Mascone, Grif's old campaign volunteer, who had recently gotten divorced and was renting a house in Crowley for the summer. Leslie would play the middle sister, Agnes, and the role of Tootie would be played by Josie. Then he jumped off the stage and handed out the scripts before anyone could raise a word of protest. Leslie slumped into one of the back-row seats and thumbed through the script, counting her lines. "Seventeen," she muttered.

That night, Josie sat on the porch and overheard her complaining bitterly to Eleanor in the kitchen. "How can Mrs. Mascone play Esther? She's as old as you."

"No, she's not. She's not even thirty." Eleanor's voice had the brisk, efficient tone she used to explain hard truths. Things which had to be accepted because they couldn't be changed—like homework and limp hair.

Even Josie could tell that Mrs. Mascone looked a lot younger than Eleanor. For starters, Mrs. Mascone didn't have a sensible mother haircut or wear shirtwaist dresses and loafers. Her dark hair hung to the middle of her back like a teenager's, and it was glossy and swung when she walked. And she dressed like a teenager too, in short Indian print dresses and silver earrings, and sat as they did in the theater seats, sideways, with her bare legs dangling over the arm. And she treated her two sons as if she were their baby-sitter rather than their mother. When they acted like brats at the theater, screaming and running up and down the aisles, she simply watched them, not even embarrassed, waiting for Grif to holler at them, which he eventually did.

"How about Josie? She can't play Tootie."

Now Eleanor sounded angry. "Why not? She's seven. Your father says she's got the best voice in the whole chorus."

Tootie was supposed to be funny, Leslie explained, and they both knew that Josie didn't know how to be funny. She'd wreck the play, and then everyone would be sorry.

Josie sat rigid on the shadowy porch, listening hard. When Grif had read out that she was going to be Tootie, she had felt ashamed, as if she'd been standing in front of the class and had said something stupid. Leslie was right, she couldn't be funny and bratty at the same time like that Margaret O'Brien. She made up her mind. When Grif came in to kiss her good night, she would beg him to give the part to Leslie.

Then something metallic slammed on the counter. "No one asked for your opinion, Leslie," Eleanor said. "Josie is going to be a wonderful Tootie." Her voice rang with such conviction that Josie believed her. That night, she sat in bed and neatly underlined her part in red ballpoint. One hundred eighteen lines, she counted. In the dark, she whispered them out loud. "I am queen of the banshees." Then louder, brattier, with her face twisted in a scowl. "*I am queen of the banshees.*"

At the first read-through, it seemed as if Leslie might have been right after all. Standing up on the stage, Josie felt even smaller than a second grader. She said her lines slowly and carefully, just as she did in reading circle so she didn't mispronounce any of the words, and she had to keep her arms pressed tight against her sides so they wouldn't shake.

"Look up when you're speaking, Josie, or we can't hear you," Grif said in that slow, deep voice he used when he directed the Crowley Players. Standing next to him on the stage, it sounded as if he were yelling. "Look up!" he said again, impatiently this time.

At the end of rehearsal Grif dismissed everyone except Josie. "I want you to stay with me a while longer." As she stepped off the stage, Leslie turned and gave Josie a delighted smirk, as if to say, "Told you so." Josie dropped her eyes to the rubber caps of her Keds, hugged her script, and waited for Grif to deliver the bad news. She was too young after all, he would say; one of the bigger kids could handle Tootie better.

"Okay," he said, his voice sounding distant, "let's go through it again." She looked up. Grif had left the stage and was now sitting in the middle seat of the fourth row. He had his Top-Siders propped on the seat in front of him, one bare ankle thrown over the other. His face was already a ruddy brown, and his polo shirt was unbuttoned so she could see the hairs on his chest. Lately, he'd started wearing his graying brown hair longer and tucked behind his ears, curling where it touched his collar. He flipped open his script. "Well, Tootie, what did you do today?"

Josie had already memorized her first few lines, so she was able to keep her eyes fixed on his face. "One of my dolls died today. I buried her in the backyard." She tried to make her voice loud like his, but it came out sounding like a cry for help.

"Don't scream your lines. Just talk in a regular voice, but loud enough so I can hear you back here. And remember to open your mouth."

This struck her as stupid advice. How could she talk *without* opening her mouth? She tried again, stretching her mouth wide like a hippo at feeding time. The voice that came was foreign, but she thought it was almost as bossy as Margaret O'Brien's.

"Better," he said, standing up and moving back four more rows. They repeated their lines back and forth until Grif had made his way to the back row. By now it was dusk, and she couldn't make out his face anymore, or even his pale eyes. His voice called out to her from the shadows, sharp and clear like a voice across a lake, and she answered back. *One of my dolls died today.*

Josie and Mrs. Mascone had extra rehearsals with Grif to practice their opening duet of "Meet Me in Saint Louis." He played the piano and shouted his directions up at them. "Hold that final note. Good. Now step, step, turn toward each other. Terry, take Josie's hands. Look at each other and smile. A big smile."

Terry's hands were small and warm, and on the final note she always gave Josie a squeeze, as if to say, "See, we did it." If they did particularly well, she wrapped her arms around Josie's neck and kissed the top of her head. Josie liked to nestle under Terry's neck and smell her dense, spicy perfume. She had come to admire everything about Terry. (Mrs. Mascone said she should call her Terry now "Because you're my little sister.") Her frosty-pink lipstick; those woven Indian sandals, which showed off her long toes; how she pulled her hair back with a clasp made of hammered silver.

Usually after their rehearsals, Grif gave Terry an extra coaching session, and made Josie walk home alone. Terry's voice did occasionally wobble and needed work, but Josie still felt left out. Once at dinner, Eleanor waved her hand in front of her face and said, "Whew! Terry's perfume is all over you two."

Grif didn't look up, as if he hadn't heard. Josie felt that one of them should stick up for Terry. "I like it."

"It stinks," said Leslie, who still hadn't forgiven Terry for getting to play Esther.

That summer, Josie had morning swimming lessons at the pond and then spent the rest of the day hanging around the theater. She picked up programs that had fallen under the seats and straightened the racks of candy-striped costumes. If she couldn't think of any chores, she sat on the trolley car and daydreamed about the next production of the Crowley Players. Maybe *The Sound of Music*, with Grif as Colonel Von Trapp, Terry as Maria, and she could be one of the Von Trapp kids with blond braids and a dirndl. She hoped she would still see Terry every day after the play closed. Maybe they could go on a family outing with the Mascones over Labor Day to

Crane's Beach, and she could show Terry the roadside stand where they always bought fried clams.

It seemed as if she hardly ever saw Eleanor, who hadn't been to the theater since opening night. When Leslie and Josie came home after a show, they'd find her in the big armchair in the living room, having waited so long, the house had grown dark around her. "How did it go, girls?" she'd ask, but when Josie told her, she didn't seem to be listening. She followed them upstairs to the bathroom, then lathered up a washcloth with Ivory soap to scrub off their makeup. She did it fiercely, attacked their eyes and lips until every trace of blue shadow and red lipstick was erased. Once Josie grabbed the washcloth out of her hands and threw it on the floor. When Eleanor stooped to pick it up, Josie saw that her hair hung in greasy clumps, as if she hadn't washed it in a long, long time.

At the closing night party, Grif and Terry sang "Meet Me in Saint Louis" with funny lyrics about all the cast members. Leslie and Josie found Eleanor asleep in the chair that night, her head tipped back and her mouth hanging open. When they shook her shoulder, her head flopped forward but she didn't wake up. They didn't know what else to do, so they left her there for Grif to find when he got home. In the middle of the night, Josie woke up to the sounds of Grif and Eleanor talking in their bedroom, and fell back to sleep, relieved that her mother had made it safely to bed.

The next morning, Grif had his suitcases spread out on the bed and across the floor, packing. It was a fancy set of matching luggage from his days in Congress—trimmed in leather, with his initials stamped in gold. She felt a rush of hope—maybe they were going on a family vacation with the Mascones after all. No, Grif said, kneeling on the floor so that he was just as short as she was. He explained that he was going away to Florida to start a new business, that he would miss her, that he would call her every week so she could tell him about third grade, that she would see him at Christmas or even sooner.

Okay, she said happily, thinking how her friend Sarah went to Tampa over spring vacation and found whole sand dollars. A few days later, Josie noticed that the house the Mascones had been renting was empty, and that they were gone too.

Weeks later, when Josie said something about spending Christmas in Florida, Leslie told her the truth. "You're so stupid," Leslie said. "Don't you get it?" Grif wasn't ever coming back; he was going to divorce their mother so he could marry Mrs. Mascone. At first, Josie thought Leslie was making up one of her mean stories, like the time she told Josie she was adopted. He couldn't marry Terry anyway; she was his daughter, she was Josie's big sister.

That year Josie read every animal book in the Crowley library—*Black Beauty, Misty of Chincoteague, Old Yeller*—and won the lower-school reading prize. She liked the sad books best and was proud that they never made her cry, even when the animal died. Her teacher told Eleanor that she was doing extremely well, but wished she would talk more in class. Her voice was so soft that Mrs. Shroeder finally moved her desk into the front row. The Crowley Playhouse was boarded up, and a couple of summers later teenagers broke in and burned it to the ground.

The main thing for me was to do whatever my husband wanted. He couldn't—and wouldn't—be married to a woman who tried to share the spotlight. I thought the best thing I could do was to be a distraction.

—JACQUELINE KENNEDY

I brought a certain amount of order to his life. I can be helpful packing suitcases, laying out clothes, rescuing lost coats and luggage. It's those little things that make you tired.

—JACQUELINE KENNEDY

Fiona sounds urgent—complete chronology of Jackie's courtship with Jack ASAP. "I'm writing 'The Wedding of Guinevere' chapter next week, and my dates are hazy," she says.

"You've already started to write?" says Josie, feeling annoyed. Could her research memos be nothing more than footnotes?

"I'm writing my version, and then I use your memos and my interviews to fill in the details later," Fiona says breezily. "It's important not to get bogged down in too much research. Any biographer will tell you that."

There seems to be an important distinction between too much research and no research, but she has to admire Fiona's cockiness. Maybe Josie should try that approach with Ada Silsbee—create an inspirational feminist tale from whole cloth, fabricate a romance or two, a little artistic angst, throw in a few quotes from diaries and letters to support her thesis. The astonishing life of an unjustly forgotten woman poet, the new Emily Dickinson. So much more interesting, more readable, than the truth. Josie wonders what Fiona's thesis is for Jackie—a rehash of the ever-popular Jackie-as-spoiled-celebrity, or a revisionist history. Jackie at peace with herself at last—

the mother, the grandmother, the competent book editor, satisfied in the arms of portly old Maurice, taken away too soon by cancer. Sounds a little tame for Fiona.

On Monday, Josie is back at the Kennedy Library reading room at five past nine and finds Roger Denby already slouched down behind a phalanx of manuscript boxes. His head pops up, he waves a yellow pencil at her, and then dives for cover again behind acid-free cardboard. Josie settles down at her usual desk by the window, assembles various memoirs by the Kennedy faithful, and starts to patch together a chronology of a romance that even Jackie described as "spasmodic."

Aug. 1950—*Transfers from Vassar to George Washington University. After year in Paris at Sorbonne, refuses to be "a schoolgirl among schoolgirls" any longer. Wins 1951* Vogue *Prix de Paris essay contest, beating out 1,280 entrants, and then turns down prize (working in Paris as junior editor for a year) because her mother felt "terrifically strong about keeping me at home."*

May 1951—*Introduced to Congressman Kennedy at Georgetown dinner party given by Charles and Mary Bartlett. Impresses JFK by being better at "The Game" than he is.*

Aug. 1951—*As part of deal with mother to turn down* Vogue *job, gets to spend summer in Europe with Lee. Decides, over father's objections, to settle in Washington. Describes period in life as "pure frustration," that parents' only expectation is for her to "marry well."*

Dec. 1951—*Through connection of her stepfather, Uncle "Hughie" Auchincloss, gets hired by* Times-Herald. *Later, promoted from city room receptionist to Inquiring Photographer. Interviewed people and snapped their pictures. Earns $42.50 per week. Lives at Merrywood, Auchincloss mansion in Virginia, to save on rent.*

Jan. 1952—*Becomes engaged to John Husted, a New York stockbroker. He gives her sapphire-and-diamond engagement ring that belonged to his mother, which looks poor because her fingernails have turned green from photo-developing chemicals she has used at work.*

March 1952—*Relationship with Husted cools when Janet Auchincloss discovers he is only earning only $17,000 a year. Jackie starts to date other men even though still engaged and writes Husted, "Don't pay any attention to drivel you hear about me and Jack Kennedy." After weekend with Husted at Merrywood, drives him to airport and drops engagement ring in suit pocket.*

April 1952—*Starts erratic courtship with JFK. Uses newspaper column to woo him. Asks group of tourists at Lincoln Monument, "Can you give any reasons why a contented bachelor should marry?" and "Are the Irish deficient in the art of love?" Occasionally drops by JFK's office with hot boxed lunches for two. Spends weekend at the Kennedys' Palm Beach estate.*

Jan. 1953—*Attends Eisenhower's inaugural ball as JFK's date. Helps JFK write position paper on Southeast Asia, writes art history term paper for his younger brother Ted, a Harvard student.*

Feb. 1953—*JFK meets Black Jack for the first time. They discuss sports, politics, and women. Black Jack reports that JFK is "a decent chap, not like his old man."*

May 1953—*JFK proposes. Formal announcement postponed because the* Saturday Evening Post *had just published a story: "Jack Kennedy—The Senate's Gay Young Bachelor." Jackie goes to England to attend Queen Elizabeth's coronation, and also reportedly to think over prospect of marrying into overbearing Kennedy clan.*

June 24, 1953—*Engagement announced.* Life *magazine publishes cover story about couple: "Senator Kennedy Goes Acourting."*

July 1953—*Janet Auchincloss and Joe Kennedy bicker over wedding plans. She wants small wedding, no photographs, no press.*

Sept. 10, 1953—*Wedding at Hammersmith Farm, Newport. Twelve hundred guests, including entire U.S. Senate. Jackie memorizes Alan Seeger's "I Have a Rendezvous with Death" for JFK as wedding present.*

At noon Josie stops typing, discouraged. She's done nothing but assemble the old chestnuts—the Inquiring Photographer's coy questions, JFK's sisters' making fun of Jackie's big feet and "babykins" voice, the one letter JFK sent Jackie during the courtship—a post-card from Bermuda saying, "Wish you were here." Josie sifts back through for eyewitness accounts, but everyone seemed baffled, even in retrospect, why Jack and Jackie got married. JFK's cronies agreed that he didn't want to get married but was badgered into it by old Joe, who thought he needed a "classy" wife to advance his political career. Evelyn Lincoln, who usually called JFK's girlfriends to make his dates, wrote that "the senator had never mentioned her to me and never asked me to call her." When they were engaged, Mrs. Lincoln said, "Who is this Jackie?"

Josie gazes out the window at the white light flickering off the steel-gray waves. She stands up, almost giddy, and before she knows it is through the revolving doors and leaning against the *Victura*, eyes shut, sunbathing. Jackie is more inscrutable than Ada Silsbee. An old friend of Jackie's speculated that JFK was a logical choice for a woman who identified with Madame Récamier. Why would any-one aspire to be Madame Récamier, Josie wonders crossly, a woman whose primary achievement was directing conversation so that griz-zled old politician, that shy young poet, would spring to life and daz-zle? Did Madame Récamier really lounge around on one of those curly-ended sofas? Josie makes a mental note to look that up.

"Is it that bad?" a voice asks.

Josie lifts herself up onto her elbows, squinting at the backlit fig-ure of Roger Denby. She must have on one of her tortured faces again, the type she makes when she's cogitating about something. "I was thinking about Madame Récamier."

"I do that all the time," he says, dropping into the grassy spot next to her. "Madame Récamier's a bad habit to get into."

She has to study his face, a silly lopsided smile that makes his glasses sit crooked, before she realizes he's joking. He unpacks a large paper bag. "Egg salad, Snapple iced tea, Cape Cod potato chips. Is that okay?"

She feels embarrassed; this is all starting to feel a little excessive. The sandwich Baggies lie nestled in a lush tuft of grass, the oozing yellow against the green making her suddenly hungry. "Great," she says, unwrapping a sandwich. "But next week it's my turn."

"But really. You looked as if you were in pain." The silly smile slides into a worried expression, his pale forehead furrowed. Roger needs to spend more time in the sun, Josie thinks.

"I'm supposed to make this time line of Jackie's courtship with JFK. And none of it makes any sense. I can't figure out why they got married."

He looks at her oddly. "What's that got to do with the portrayal of presidential wives in the media?"

She turns away fast, and stares out over the water. How could she have made such a stupid slip? Then she glances back to Roger, who now seems to be having problems tearing open his potato-chip bag, and decides she can trust him. She inhales sharply and then tells him everything—about Fiona Jones and the ten thousand dollars, about Peter and the house in the Berkeley Hills, about Ada Silsbee and the bogged-down dissertation. When she finishes, he's knocking the residue of potato-chip crumbs into his palm. He looks a little undone, as if he's not used to strange women unburdening themselves. "I didn't tell you before because Fiona Jones made me take a vow of secrecy. She thinks the Kennedy Library might expel me if they knew the truth." This comes out sounding ridiculously self-aggrandizing, and she wishes she hadn't tried to explain anything.

Roger puts a finger up to his lips. "Your secret is safe with me." He pulls out his cigarettes and lights up. "Most people get married for stupid reasons. I decided to marry this girl because she knew how to drive a Deux Chevaux." He sees Josie's puzzled expression. "Really. I was in graduate school at Harvard, and there was this girl, Gretchen, who lived upstairs and one day she asked to borrow my Deux Chevaux, with a stick shift you pulled out of the dashboard. My old girlfriend wouldn't even try it. But Gretchen hopped in, and before I could even explain how it worked, she took off down Mass. Ave. I said to myself, that's the girl I'm going to marry."

"Did you?" She sits up alertly, and lights one of Roger's cigarettes. This is much more interesting than Jackie and Jack.

"Uh-huh," he says glumly.

"Did it work?"

He makes a derisive snort. "No. In fact, it was probably a good reason *not* to get married. Gretchen was this MIT dropout who was a mechanical whiz. She plumbed our bathtub for a shower, she wired in the phone lines. Finally, after we'd been married for eight years, she left me because she said I was too hapless." He still sounds wounded.

"I don't think so," says Josie loyally. In truth, Roger does look a little hapless; a drop of egg salad has fallen onto his khaki pants and left a grease spot.

"Well, she did. She went out to California and started this software company called Galactic Software that designs these strange fantasy games. Out of the blue, she sent me one called *The Castle of Zoroaster*, with this note that said, 'Call me if you can't figure this out.' Well, that really *pissed* me off. I spent about a hundred hours trying to solve it, but there was this part in the castle basement where I kept getting stomped to death by trolls. I finally spent twenty-five bucks calling their nine hundred hint line. You have to stop at the Pizza Hut outside the castle and take the shaker of red pepper flakes to throw in the trolls' eyes."

Josie nods her head sympathetically. Her computer came with a game about lemmings which she sometimes played when she was feeling discouraged about Ada. The sight of row after row of lemmings leaping off a cliff, their bodies mounding higher and higher at the bottom, was oddly restful.

"I could picture Gretchen laughing at me. But I got back at her. I took every cent of my IRA and bought Galactic Software stock, and I've made a bundle." Roger leans back, grinning triumphantly. This story seems to have brought him to life—his eyes are snapping, patches of color have flooded into his cheeks. All it took was a little attention, a few probing questions from Josie—just like Madame Récamier.

"So why did you get married?" Roger asks.

She shades her eyes with a cupped hand and squints over at him. "I was pregnant."

"Oh!" He jumps to his feet, embarrassed, and busies himself collecting their crusts and chip bags. "Really a very . . . traditional reason," he says haplessly.

JOSIE ALWAYS thought her shotgun wedding to Peter could be blamed on writer's block. After two years of graduate seminars and one year preparing for orals, they were on the final lap. All they had to do was write their dissertations. "And I'm out of here," said Peter, shooting his arm up like a rocket. "Eighteen months max, and I'm gone." When he talked like that, all Josie could hear was the "I." He was going away, by himself, as soon as possible. She was content to stay a graduate student forever, spending lazy afternoons in their apartment doing research. Potluck suppers with some other graduate students, cheap movies downtown at the Cable Car on Tuesdays, sweet bread from the Portuguese bakery at Fox Point for Sunday brunch. What more could Peter want? What was this compulsion to get on with a life that didn't seem to include her?

If anything, it seemed as if Josie might get her dissertation done first—she was off to an inspired start. Ever since she had started graduate school, she had been casting around for a dissertation topic, but all those titan nineteenth-century poets seemed a little shopworn. Then, the week after her orals, over Memorial Day weekend, when she had stopped by the Crowley Library to return some mysteries for Eleanor, she had made a momentous discovery.

Out of habit, she found herself wandering down to the local history alcove in the library basement, one of her favorite haunts during those childhood summers when she'd run out of things to read. The local-history closet, which had always been locked (she usually gave the big brass knob an experimental turn), stood tantalizingly ajar, and Josie peeked inside. Several shoe boxes of discarded catalog cards, a stack of spare metal library shelves, and a canvas-covered trunk with "Rev. Edward Silsbee" stenciled in black ink on the lid. After a furtive look around for any scolding librarians, Josie shoved the shelves and boxes to one side, unfastened a corroded hasp, and hefted up the lid to reveal a mound of musty papers—a few slim books bound in green morocco, a long volume that looked like a ledger, and bundles of letters tied up with red string like Christmas presents. She pulled out a thick letter from the top bundle and unfolded several sheets of stationery covered on both sides with fervent, slanted handwriting.

My Dear Miss Silsbee,
 I have spent a good part of a morning looking over the sheaf of poems you were so kind to send me. I am flattered that you

have such a high regard of my critical faculties to seek out my
opinion. As you may know, I am frequently asked for encour-
agement by verse writers of your sex, and I must gently dash
their hopes. However, this is not the case with the work of Miss
Ada Silsbee. I feel you have a powerful and original poetic
voice, and I would like to offer my assistance in obtaining a
publisher . . .

Josie flipped the letter over to the signature—*J. G. Whittier*—
then opened one of the thin volumes, *New England Narcissa*, by
Miss A. Silsbee, and read the first line of "At Derby's Dam":

> *The mill hand's back, a wet muscled ridge,*
> *He straightens, ridges smooth . . .*

Josie was able to convince the librarian to let her borrow the book
and a few letters, which she presented to the tiny but formidable
Irene Horton, Early American poetry expert, on Monday morning.
Professor Horton adjusted the two bobby pins holding tufts of
mouse-gray hair in place and congratulated Josie. "You have made,"
she pronounced, "certainly a quite, and possibly a very, important
discovery."

Josie turned one corner of their apartment living room into a
miniature archive of the life and works of Ada Silsbee. A copy of
Ada's tintype hung above a filing cabinet stuffed with photocopies of
Ada's diaries and letters. At first, Josie's task seemed quite simple—
read through the Ada archives, cover a few thousand index cards
with notes, and then bang out a cogent, insightful life of a minor
woman poet. Steps one and two went quite smoothly; in six months,
stacks of index cards, each bound up with a rubber band and labeled
with a yellow Post-it note, had sprouted up like mushrooms over the
windowsills and tabletops. She outlined Ada's life neatly into eight
chapters, sat down at the computer with the note cards gathered
around her like doting relatives at Thanksgiving dinner, typed Chapter One: "A Yankee Girlhood," and then stared at the black screen,
the neon-green cursor throbbing impatiently.

Somehow, the essence of Ada Silsbee was proving elusive—the

woman and her work did not fit together. On one hand, her poetry was powerful and frankly erotic. "Narcissa," the description of a woman at her toilette, was a glorious description of the female body—the swelling of a breast and the tapering of a waist, the soft flesh at the fold of an elbow, the indentation behind an earlobe, the sound of a brush pulling through long, tangled hair. And Ada's men were boldly drawn, such as the mill worker in "At Derby's Dam," with his shirtless back slick with sweat. Josie stared at Ada's portrait and couldn't imagine this homely woman, dressed from head to toe in frills and lace, writing such things. Josie tried to find some clues in her biography, but as far as the world was concerned, Ada Silsbee had hardly existed. Josie couldn't find a birth record or where she was buried, and the only biographical tidbits came from Ada's own letters.

> *My Dear Mr. Whittier,*
>
>   *You ask me about myself, and I will tell you as best I can, although I am not comfortable with self-scrutiny. I was raised in the western part of this state, and educated at home by my beloved mother. I moved to Crowley ten years ago, when my dear brother became the minister of the first church. He is unmarried, and I run his household. These duties and my writing keep me so occupied that I have no acquaintances in this town and never receive visitors. I have what might be called a reclusive temperament.*

And yet this misanthrope with no social life corresponded with dressmakers in Boston and New York, and in the year 1862 spent the monstrous sum of $223.53 on new clothing.

At first Josie tried to portray Ada's life as a tale of female oppression. Living under the thumb of her minister brother, she had been forced to repress her sexuality and exuberant femininity, which could only find expression in poetry and dresses. But as Ada said herself in her letters, the Reverend Silsbee was generous with money for new clothes and highly complimentary about her verse. Josie could only conclude that, for all her earnest correspondence with poets across the country, her lengthy diary entries about every homely detail of her daily habits, Ada Silsbee's life seemed . . . unlived.

Peter deconstructing 1966, the year of his birth, in the bedroom didn't help Josie's concentration. Quietly burrowing through a stack of books and taking notes on index cards was hardly Peter's style. To get in the mood for his dissertation, he liked to play period music— loudly. Some of it was all right—*Rubber Soul*—but most of it wasn't—Tijuana Brass, the Monkees. He would sing his favorite, "The Ballad of the Green Berets," and drum along with a pencil on the desktop. At intervals, he would lean back in his desk chair and wing a tennis ball against the wall so it ricocheted around the room and then dribbled along the floor.

Whap-Whap-Whap-dadadada. He practiced this for weeks before he could do it without knocking anything over. He scrawled lists in red Magic Marker and taped them to the wall.

1966 BEST-SELLERS—Valley of the Dolls, The Secret of Santa
   Vittoria, Human Sexual Response
1966 TV—"Bonanza," "Green Acres," "Bewitched," "The Beverly Hill-
   billies," "Gomer Pyle, U.S.M.C."
1966 INVENTIONS—*toaster ovens, stereo cassette decks, Taster's
   Choice, Rare and Endangered Species List.*

When two walls were covered, he started writing, five pages a day. Then things quieted down, nothing but the clickety-click of his keyboard and an occasional *whap-whap-whap-dadadada.*

For hours, Josie stared at the blinking cursor. Slowly, painfully, she tried to paint Ada's New England—the walks along the roiling spring freshets, the oily froth at the bottom of the milldam, the cellar holes sprouting birches, the black slate tombstones carved with skulls, and then realized she had described nothing more than her own childhood rambles around Crowley. She hit Delete and returned to the blank screen. Then she heard *whap-whap* from the bedroom and a lamp clattering to the floor. "Oh, shit," said Peter. She turned off her computer, walked into the bedroom, and found him leaning back in his chair, studying the shards of broken lightbulb arcing across the floor. She tipped his chair up straight, bent down, took his narrow face in her hands, and kissed him on the lips. He reached around her and clicked the mouse on Save. Afterward, they fell asleep, and when they woke up it was dark and time for dinner.

This set a pattern. She spent the morning writing some desultory stuff about Ada, read it over at lunch, hit Delete, and headed for the bedroom. And then they would settle down for an afternoon nap, the windows open now because it was early spring, the air heavy with green smells and birdsong. She would dream about Ada, who appeared different from the homely woman in the tintype—she was a girl with a thick plait down her back, bushwhacking up Mount Wachusett with a staff fashioned from a rock-maple branch. Sometimes Ada spoke to her, her lips parted in a secret smile, her voice low and strong, mixing with the splash of rushing water. Josie could see Ada in sentences and paragraphs; all she needed to do was push herself awake, walk over to the computer, and write it down. It all seemed so easy. And Peter was right there, next to her, sighing into her hair.

After about three weeks of this, Peter started awake one day and groped for the clock on the floor next to the bed. "Six-fifteen! Christ!" His bare feet thumped onto the floor. "I was supposed to be done with Chapter Two by now. That's it. I'm getting a carrel in the library."

But it was already too late; Josie was pregnant. She waited two weeks for her period, every day more convinced that it would never come. Her body felt different, as if something foreign had insinuated itself inside, and her tissue was softening to receive it.

This was the way Louise had described the first moments of her pregnancy. Louise was now six months along, but properly so, married to an investment banker, with a house in the Chicago suburbs. Since Christmas, she had been calling every few weeks with an update. "I heard the heartbeat." "We saw it moving in an ultrasound." "I felt the baby kick."

Josie's first impulse when she decided she must be pregnant was to call Louise and announce, "Guess what!" She felt an illogical thrill of sisterhood, the urge to share every pregnancy symptom in detail. But if she called, Louise would of course ask impossible, unanswerable questions. Have you had a pregnancy test yet? Have you told Peter? How can you have a baby when you're still in graduate school? What are you going to do about this, Josie?

So, for two weeks, Josie kept her possible pregnancy a secret—both delicious and horrible. She stared at the pregnant women in the grocery store with their looming girths and ugly maternity smocks and felt wistful. She studied Peter and dreamily imagined how their genes would combine. She didn't care that there were some disastrous possibilities—a short, round-faced boy or a lanky girl with a bumpy nose and canoe feet. Even Peter's prehensile toes sprouting tufts of black hair did not give her pause. She tried to figure how they could incorporate a baby into their lives without too much bother. Josie could give up her dissertation for a while and work full-time as a cataloger in the Lincoln Collection. That way, Peter could keep going on his dissertation, and then, when he was finished and got a teaching job, she could get back to Ada. They wouldn't even have to move out of their one-bedroom apartment. She figured they could fit a crib and a bureau in the hallway, where Peter kept his bicycle. How much space could a little baby take up, anyway?

Finally, she decided it was time for a home pregnancy test. She camped out in the bathroom, filled the vial, and sat on the edge of the tub reading *The Golden Bowl* for half an hour without so much as looking up. Then she glanced over, could see the telltale circle nestling at the bottom of the tube from across the room, and ferried it gently toward the bedroom, where Peter was typing up lecture notes for his class. When she walked in, he didn't even look up from his computer. "Nope. I'm not interested," he said, holding his hand up like a traffic cop. "Don't even try to distract me."

She set the vial in its little mirrored holder carefully on the desk next to his mouse. "What's this?" he said. She handed him the instructional pamphlet. He put on his glasses, unfolded it, and read carefully, examining each of the diagrams. Then he stood up, peered down at the fatal circle, and settled weakly back into his chair. He put his palms together and held them up in front of his face. "Well, I guess we shouldn't be surprised," he said at last. "I've produced something like six hundred trillion sperm in the last month. Spermicidal jelly probably has some theoretical limit, like six hundred trillion minus one. So next time we could use condoms, but that could get expensive. I wonder if they're reusable?"

Josie sat on the bed listening to this performance. "Do you think," she said, "that we could have a serious discussion about this?"

He looked chastened. "I'm sorry," he said. "I'm really sorry this happened." She waited, and he searched her face for clues of what she expected him to say. "I'm sorry you have to go through this." Still she said nothing. "I'll go with you, and pay for it, and whatever else you want." Now there was almost a pleading look in his eyes. "Okay?"

She looked down at her pale hands, which were folded patiently in her lap. Her fingers were stubby, and she wondered why she didn't at least grow her fingernails long. "Well, that's just it. I was thinking that I wouldn't have an abortion."

Now he sat up straight and his eyes darted back and forth over her head; she realized he was reading the red notes taped to the wall. And then his eyes wandered around the rest of the room, over the pile of his laundry on the floor, the stacks of books, the dirty coffee cups. "I don't think," he said, "that you and I are ready to have a baby. Look at this place." He was speaking slowly, more slowly than she had ever heard him speak before.

"It's not that I want to have a baby, Peter," she said, realizing how rarely she called him by his name. "It's that I don't want to abort *our* baby."

He checked his watch. "My seminar is starting in fifteen minutes," he said. He turned his back to her and shuffled through the papers on his desk, being careful not to knock over the vial. He grabbed a jumbled handful of lecture notes and said, "I have to let this sink in for a while. We'll talk about it more over dinner." He headed toward the door, stopped as if he'd forgotten something, then bent down stiffly and kissed her on the cheek. A mere brushing of his lips, the kind of kiss her father gave.

Josie stood by the window and watched him shuffle slowly down the path with his head hung low. Peter usually walked with a bouncy step, like Tigger, Louise had once observed. Josie turned away from the window and sat down at her worktable. Perversely, inexplicably, she put every thought of the pregnancy and Peter's reaction and what would happen next right out of her head, and did an inspired rewrite of Chapter Five: "A Poetic Awakening."

Later that evening Peter sat silently at the kitchen table drinking beer and reading every section of the *New York Times* while Josie cooked dinner. (Meat loaf made with Lipton onion-soup mix—her one dish that people seemed to like.) She was silent too; she wasn't going to be the one to mention what she'd come to think of as "it" again. Finally, he folded up the business page and smiled at her in a way that was almost painful, the skin stretching tight over his cheeks. "Maybe we can borrow some baby things from the Herberts," he said.

Mentioning the Herberts was a bad sign. Dave and Debbie Herbert were graduate students a year ahead of Josie and Peter, who had a daughter whom everyone referred to as "little baby Hannah." As far as anyone could tell, Debbie Herbert had not lost a pound since the day she gave birth and was still wearing maternity dresses two years later. She had taken to camping out with little baby Hannah in the department lounge, with her diaper bag and playpen and Snugli and stroller. While she breast-fed, or stretched Hannah out on the floor to change a poopy diaper, she would regale any passerby with child-care advice—how to get a newborn to sleep through the night, how to introduce solid foods, where to buy disposable diapers by the case. After a while, the other graduate students stopped going to the department lounge and started congregating at the Penguin Café on Thayer Street. Peter perfected an impersonation of Debbie Herbert, which he did on a daily basis, and they all laughed until tears streamed down their cheeks.

And that was it; they never had another serious discussion about whether or not to have the baby. If Peter had pushed for an abortion, Josie suspected she would have caved in. But he was reluctant to be decisive in any way, seemed to prefer sitting back and letting it happen. She wondered if his ambivalence stemmed from a story he had once told her about his mother. Ten years before Peter was born, when Ruth was thirty and newly married to Harry Stadler, she had gotten pregnant accidentally. She had just been hired as an instructor at Pomona, and, apparently without too much agonizing, had an abortion rather than derail her career. It was late enough so she knew the sex—a girl. "And so I've always felt that I should have had a big sister," he had said, looking for a moment like someone's baby brother.

For two weeks, Josie's pregnancy went mostly unmentioned. Sometimes when she went to the bathroom and threw up, he brought her a glass of ice water and handed it to her, wordlessly. Then one day at the Penguin Café, Peter said to Stedman and Monica, "Hey, guess what? Josie and I are going to have a little baby Hannah." Every day he added a new detail. They would call the baby "Little Hannah—The Sequel." Josie and Debbie would hold court together in the department lounge, wearing matching maternity dresses. Peter would go to parties with the baby in a backpack, just like Dave Herbert. Then Peter stood up and did an imitation of Dave dancing like a spastic robot, with little baby Hannah's head whiplashing back and forth. Everyone laughed until tears streamed down their cheeks. Everyone except Josie.

A few days later, Peter said, "I suppose we should get married. We don't want The Sequel to be illegitimate."

Finally, Josie got angry. "I'm sick of being treated like a joke. I'm sick of you treating this baby like a joke." They had been sitting at the kitchen table having breakfast, but now she was on her feet, hands on her hips, hyperventilating over Peter's coffee. "And you don't have to marry me either," she added. Oddly enough, all her speculations about having a baby with Peter had never included marriage, maybe because marriage was something you had to decide to do and plan in advance. So far, everything in their relationship—from living together to getting pregnant—had simply . . . happened.

He hung his head and turned his palms up helplessly. "I'm nothing but an asshole," he said. "An *immature* asshole." Peter was an expert at self-recrimination, which made it hard for her to stay very mad at him. "This baby scares me to death, and the only way I can deal with it is by making dumb jokes. I'll be better." He reached his arms around Josie's waist, rubbed his bristly cheek against her slightly rounded stomach, and kissed it. "And besides, I always thought we should get married, baby or no baby." She closed her eyes and stroked his hair, but couldn't banish the image of his arm launching through space while he said, "Eighteen months max, and I'm out of here."

Josie called Louise to ask her opinion about marrying Peter, which curiously seemed like a more incautious act than bearing his child. Louise was the only person she knew—unlike her mother, or Stedman, or of course herself—who was impervious to Peter's charms. "So," Josie said, trying to sound lighthearted, "do you think I'm making the biggest mistake of my life?"

There was a pause. "No," said Louise doubtfully.

"But you always said he was unreliable. You *do* think I'm making a mistake, right?" Josie didn't know why she was badgering Louise into saying yes, because she suspected she would marry Peter anyway, no matter what Louise said.

"In the beginning, I was sure Peter was going to dump you. But he hasn't yet, so maybe he's changed."

Josie took this as Louise's blessing. "So will you be my maid of honor?"

"Oh, Josie, I can't," Louise said, for once not sounding sensible. In fact she was tearful. "My doctor says I'm already half effaced, and I can't travel."

Josie wasn't sure what "effaced" meant, but she couldn't help thinking it meant affronted.

Peter and Josie planned their wedding at the Penguin Café. The ceremony would be performed by the department secretary, Rosemary, who moonlighted as a justice of the peace. Stedman would host the reception at his house and hire a disc jockey as a wedding present. Monica offered to make her famous chocolate mousse cake and bought two plastic penguins to put on top. They wouldn't invite any relatives. "We'll just send them telegrams," Peter said grandly, although no one was sure if you could send people telegrams anymore. And then they would take a wedding trip to Pittsfield, and retrace Melville's footsteps.

Josie ended up telling Eleanor anyway, and then Eleanor wrote Grif. *I think you should know that our Josie has decided to get married.* She tactfully left out the part about the baby.

Grif immediately called to throw a monkey wrench into their plans. "I always dreamed of giving you away in the Trask homestead," he said in a wounded voice. "And you coming down the staircase in your mother's wedding dress." Of course, this was nothing but his typical bluster. He hadn't stepped foot in the Trask homestead in nearly twenty years, not since the day he packed up his Mustang and left for Coral Gables. Eleanor's wedding dress had gotten so mildewed in the leaky attic that it had been thrown away years ago. Her father and Terry never attended any function where they might run into Eleanor; they had even skipped Josie's graduation from Dartmouth.

Nevertheless, Eleanor took Grif's side. "It's so important to your father," she said. "And he has offered to pay for the reception." Which was a first. Everyone at the Penguin Café thought the Trask homestead sounded like a fun place for a party, and so it was decided.

Even Ruth Stadler was coming from California for the wedding. "Maybe we shouldn't mention to Mom that you're pregnant," said Peter.

"Why? So she won't think I entrapped her baby boy?" Surging hormones were making Josie waspish. Terry and Eleanor standing side by side at the foot of the staircase was going to be bad enough. But the specter of Ruth, in her perfectly tailored suit and hair swept up in a chignon, her judgmental gaze fixed on Josie's abdomen, was almost too much to bear.

"I never said that."

By now, four months pregnant, Josie couldn't have fitted into her mother's wedding dress even if it had survived. She and Monica, her fill-in maid of honor, had found a Mexican wedding dress with an empire waist that wasn't too bad at a novelty import shop. But when she slipped into the dress an hour before the wedding, she discovered that she had expanded. Her breasts, blue-veined and swollen, bulged over the top. She'd washed her hair that morning and it hung past her shoulders, a thick, frizzy mess. Instead of wearing a veil, she'd had a wreath of flowers made for her hair, but the cut-rate florist delivered something considerably bigger than what she had in mind. She inspected herself in the full-length mirror—the exploding hair under the Christmas-sized wreath, her round doughy face, and the wedding dress straining at the seams. "I look like Heidi," she wailed to Monica. "All I need is a goat."

Monica was not prone to histrionics. She pushed up a billowy sleeve and checked her watch. "Fifty minutes. Just enough time for a salvage job." She set her hands on Josie's shoulders and pushed her down into a chair, then stood back, arms crossed, and assessed the damage. She raised Josie's hands to the light and examined them, her brow furrowing. "Honestly, Josie. Your nails. I guess we better start there." Josie curled her fingers up into fists, embarrassed. She'd scrubbed at her nails with a duck-shaped brush that morning, and she didn't think they looked so bad. But obviously, she didn't know about such things.

Monica opened up a suitcase-sized makeup bag and set it at Josie's feet, its gaping mouth spewing out oddly shaped brushes and tiny tubes in shiny black plastic. Monica selected an emery board and some stainless-steel implements and started carving away at Josie's fingernails. Then she spread a bath towel across Josie's lap, fanned out her fingers, and painted on some tawny polish.

"Don't budge," Monica ordered, unpinning the wreath and pitching it on the bed. She gathered Josie's hair like a horsetail and started brushing it in long strokes. Josie closed her eyes and tipped back her head. "That's right," said Monica, sounding almost maternal. "Breathe deeply, relax. It'll be good for the baby." She twisted the sides of Josie's hair prettily and pinned it back. Then she attacked the wreath with a pair of manicure scissors, sending carnations and stems flying all over the floor.

"You sure you know what you're doing?" said Josie.

"Trust me." The wreath, slimmed down to a few feathery ferns and white ribbons, nestled down between the ropes of twisted hair. "Do this," Monica said, opening her mouth wide and tightening her lips over her teeth. She straddled a chair in front of Josie and narrowed her almond eyes as she traced along Josie's lips with a lipstick brush. "Of course, my makeup is all wrong for you. My undertones are peach, and you're a pink. Great skin texture. You're lucky." She handed Josie a Kleenex. "Blot."

Josie obediently made a dark coral circle on the Kleenex. "How do you know about this stuff?"

"My mother took me to the cosmetics consultant at Gump's when I was fourteen. I'm not even going to ask what your mother taught you."

The extent of Eleanor's makeup drawer was a withered Revlon "Fire and Ice" lipstick and a Coty compact with most of the powder scooped out. The only feminine instruction she had provided was a black-and-white brochure about menstruation, which she handed Josie when she was twelve, along with a sanitary belt and a box of Kotex. If Josie had a girl, she would have to do better; maybe she should make Monica a godmother.

Monica finished off with a dusting of blush and a few strokes of mascara. "Done," she proclaimed. She stepped back, surveyed, and then as a final gesture slipped off her own dangly pearl earrings and fastened them on Josie. "Something borrowed."

She swiveled Josie around to face the mirror, and the transformation was admittedly spectacular. She looked round but beautiful, her hair cascading artfully across her cleavage.

There was a gentle tap on the door, and Grif poked his head in. "Ready?"

Grif had blown into town the day before and had immediately taken charge of the wedding plans. (Without Terry, to everyone's relief.) Josie had found him in the kitchen that morning wearing Eleanor's apron and rubber gloves, polishing silver-plate platters and ice buckets he'd unearthed in the pantry. She had to admit it was fun having him around; Grif always enjoyed a good party.

He sidestepped in and looked at Josie's image in the mirror. "Well, now. Here's the buxom bride."

Without turning, Josie studied her father's reflection. He clasped his hands in front and drew himself up proudly, straightening his fancy charcoal-brown suit coat like a human coat hanger. His hair had gone pure white since she had seen him last, two years ago, but he still had it parted in the middle and brushed back like the Fitzgeraldesque college boy. Twenty years of shady real estate dealings, under indictment twice for possible fraud, hadn't left a mark on him. He still was Congressman Trask, no matter what.

"Listen, Dad," she said, spinning around to face him. "Do you think you can not be a sexist for six hours?"

"I meant that as a compliment."

"You're pathetic." She said this with a smile; she didn't feel like picking a fight. "Why can't you say the standard father-of-the-bride stuff?"

He paused, ruminating. Grif was always mystified by what his daughters expected of him. "You look beautiful, Josie. Just like your mother on our wedding day." He stepped forward and held both of her hands in his. Warm, her father's hands were always wonderfully warm. "I'm proud of you. And I think Peter is a fine fellow."

Despite herself, Grif's coerced compliment brought a little rush of pleasure. "That's better." She gave the wreath a final pat, picked up her bouquet, and slipped her arm through his. Through the open door, she could hear voices congregating at the foot of the stairs, and felt the heat rush into her face.

"Even if he did get my daughter knocked up," Grif added.

At the top of the stairs, Josie paused, and the crowd at the bottom parted to form a chute just wide enough for her and Grif to pass through. She looked over the sea of faces and the only one she could spot, almost as a prophecy, was little baby Hannah's. She was sitting on her father's shoulders, her patent-leather party shoes bobbing up and down, her wispy brown hair pulled up on top of her head and fastened with a pink satin rose, her mouth open in anticipation.

Josie marched forward, her eyes fixed on Rosemary, who was wearing a long purple dress that made her look like a high priestess. And when Rosemary asked her if she took Peter Stadler to be her husband, she said "I will" slowly, pausing between the two words so she could imagine three quick beats of the baby's heart. She turned to Peter, who was staring over Rosemary's shoulder, out the window toward the back field, and felt certain that he was thinking of their baby too. Stedman held out his hand, the rings nestled down in his fleshy palm, and then the knot of guests broke into applause, as if they were watching street jugglers.

Josie and Peter turned, linked arms, and processed through the living room and dining room and kept on going until they somehow ended up in the dark pantry, alone. Through the glass-fronted cupboards, she could see enough Spode for a hundred and tomatoes put up in mason jars back in the fifties. For the first time, she raised her eyes past his shirt to her husband's face. He was wearing a goofy grin, as if he was about to burst out laughing, and his enlarged pupils were shiny black.

"What are you on?" she asked, and then regretted that her first words to him as his wife were an accusation.

Air rushed out as if he had been holding his breath. "Stedman brought some dope back from Antigua. We smoked a joint in his car while you were getting dressed." He saw her disapproving expression. "He's got plenty more, if you want some."

"I'm pregnant. Remember?"

The reception was a typical Trask affair—bad food, good booze and plenty of it. Eleanor had ordered party platters from the local supermarket—rolls of cold cuts and cubes of cheese, each speared with cellophane-tipped toothpicks. (When Grif complained about the chintzy fare, she waved the supermarket flyer in his face. "But they're deluxe platters. See? Fresh fruit, crudités, and gourmet breads.") At Grif's insistence, they had a full bar with mixers and a professional bartender borrowed from the Bull Run. The graduate students, used to Budweiser and Gallo, went a little wild, ordering piña coladas and Bloody Marys garnished with leafy celery stalks. Peter and Stedman appropriated a bottle of Chivas, which they drank out of tiny Dixie cups from the bathroom dispenser. Stedman opened up the ancient record player cabinet and put on a stack of Eleanor's big band 78s. Before long, all the living room furniture was pushed against the walls, and everyone started swinging so violently that the needle bounced across the records.

As the June afternoon faded to dusk, Eleanor and Grif started to dance slowly, Grif bending over so he could talk softly in her ear. Josie, dancing with Dave Herbert, watched with shame as Grif's hand slid up and down along the back of Eleanor's slippery rayon dress. Josie could tell by the slight stagger in their fox-trot that they were both drunk, and she glanced around to see if anyone else was watching. Someone was—Ruth Stadler, perched on the arm of a sofa now pushed deep into the corner, her shapely legs crossed, a suede pump dangling off an upturned foot. And then, as if by telepathy, her eyes lifted from Grif and Eleanor and swept around the room to Josie. They stared at one another without expression or gesture, the only two sober people in the room.

By eleven, when the party platters were stripped down to a pile of toothpicks and the bartender had left, Grif decided that it was time for Josie and Peter to depart for Pittsfield, where they were spending the night at the Melville Inn. The guests all gathered in the driveway to watch the happy couple climb into their car. Peter pirouetted gracefully around on one foot, waving the car keys. "Good-bye. Good-bye, my friends. Thank you for sharing this great moment with us."

Josie stood on tiptoe and snatched the keys out of his hand. "I'm driving," she hissed.

She bent over the steering wheel, squinting ahead into the darkness, while Peter reclined his seat back and rested a hand over his forehead as if he were in anguish. When they got to the inn, he was able to rouse himself long enough to walk up to their room and collapse, still dressed, across the bed. Just before he fell asleep, he reached across to Josie in the darkness, patted her hip, and said, "Good night, wife." She turned her back to him and, like the heroine of a bad romance novel, cried herself to sleep on her wedding night.

The next morning, with the help of a handful of aspirin, Peter revived. Even though he kept fingering his wedding ring as if it were a wart, he was his usual gregarious self over blueberry pancakes. His recap of the wedding low points actually made Josie laugh—his mother's toast, which sounded as if she were at a funeral ("I always dreaded the day I would lose Peter . . ."); Debbie Herbert's dress, which looked like a tropical-print rain poncho; Eleanor and Grif dancing together (he'd noticed too); Stedman and Monica (already on the outs) conspicuously not dancing together.

They had planned to spend the day climbing Mount Graylock, and even though she didn't feel up to it, Peter insisted. He made her wait in the car while he went into a gourmet store for a picnic lunch. When the gravelly trail turned steep, Josie sank onto a rock, overcome by pregnancy fatigue. "Let's go back and take a nap," she pleaded.

He took her elbow and tugged her back onto her feet. "Come on. I'll help you. It's not much farther." He put his arm tightly around her waist and half-carried her the rest of the way. At the top, he spent a few moments searching for the perfect spot for their picnic. "Here," he said, pointing to a flat, mossy rock shaded by a stunted spruce. "You sit. I'll wait on you." He squatted down in front of her and unpacked sandwiches wrapped in white butcher paper. "Curried chicken salad, or ham and Boursin?"

For the first time since before the wedding, she actually felt hungry. Peter stayed hunkered down, balancing on the balls of his feet, and watched her lick curried mayonnaise off her fingers. He was wearing shorts for the first time that summer, and his wiry legs were stark white. Behind him stretched a panorama of the Berkshires, the trees iridescent green with new leaves, the glassy black of a faraway lake. Somewhere, down there, was Arrowhead, Melville's house. Melville had climbed this mountain with Hawthorne, as devoted to Hawthorne as a lover, later turning as bitter as a lover spurned, burning all his letters. Josie wondered if they brought a picnic with them—a loaf of bread and farm cheese wrapped in burlap. If they sat on this very rock. Did Melville secretly watch Hawthorne's handsome face, with its brown curls and pale eyes as he studied the vista, and try to guess his thoughts? Was he searching for a gesture, a word, that Hawthorne loved him back, even a little?

Peter unzipped the side pocket of his pack, took out a small white box tied with a gold cord, and tossed it into her lap.

"What's this?"

"A wedding present."

She pulled the cord slowly, wishing he hadn't bothered. Peter wasn't very good at presents. Usually he gave her some weird CD or a volume of literary theory that he wanted for himself. Their first December together, when they celebrated a day midway between Hanukkah and Christmas, she had to work hard not to look disappointed when he presented her with an electric pencil sharpener. She unfolded a wad of tissue paper and pulled out a gold locket on a chain. It was old and dented, with *Josephine* engraved diagonally across its oval face, the script letters nearly rubbed smooth.

"You like it?" He sounded dubious.

"Yes." She dangled it off her fingers and swung it in the sunlight, considering whether this was quite enough to make up for his bad-boy behavior during the wedding.

"The lady in that antique store on Fox Point said you would. I was going to get you this book of Tennyson but then I saw the locket and mentioned your name was Josephine. She insisted I buy it. She kept knocking the price down until I surrendered." He shrugged as if to say he was used to getting bossed around by women.

"Well, she was right."

"You're supposed to put pictures inside."

"I know." One of Peter and one of the baby, but she kept this sac-charine thought to herself. She beckoned to him with the hand that held the locket. "Come here. Now I'll give you your wedding pre-sent." He sat down on the mossy spot next to her. She slid an arm around his shoulders and lowered his head into her lap. "Close your eyes."

He obeyed. "What are you going to do to me?" He tensed and grabbed hold of her hands as if she were going to start tickling him.

"Relax. This won't hurt." She smoothed his straight hair off his forehead, and then recited Longfellow's "My Lost Youth." She spoke slowly, her voice deep and rich as it carried out across the void.

> A boy's will is the wind's will,
> And the thoughts of youth are long, long thoughts.

On the last line, Peter opened his eyes and stared up at her face, his hand reaching up to trace a finger along her cheek, and she bent down to kiss the boy she had married.

chapter *9*

*The most important thing for a successful marriage is for a husband to do what
he likes best and does well. The wife's satisfaction will follow.*
— JACQUELINE KENNEDY

And this is the young lady who is supposed to be sleeping with my husband.
— JACQUELINE KENNEDY,
during a tour she was giving of the White House

❦

Henry is making supper. He takes a fistful of aqua-green play-dough,
pounds it onto the enamel kitchen table, and then rolls it flat with a
toy rolling pin. Six tubs of play-dough in rainbow colors made by
Allison that morning line the windowsill by the table. Josie didn't
even know you could make your own play-dough. "Oh, gosh, it's
easy," Allison said. "All you need is food dye and a vial of alum."

He lays the dough on a hard-boiled-egg slicer and lowers the wire
screen, which slices it into six strips "Your french fries are ready," he
calls out. Josie watches his fingers as they set the strips on an aluminum pie plate—still fat and dimpled, like a baby's. He jumps
down and carries the pie plate out to Eleanor, who is sitting on the
porch.

Josie reaches into a tub absently and scoops out a lump of yellow.
Some kids need cookie cutters and rolling pins, but she's always preferred the simplicity of snakes. She places a ball of dough under her
palm and rolls it back and forth, watching hypnotically as the snake
grows longer and thinner. Just before it breaks in two, she coils it on
a pie tin and begins another snake. By the time Henry comes back,

she's made a stack. "S'ghetti," he says, delighted. He squashes his french fries together and starts rolling snakes too. "Your s'ghetti's ready," he yells toward the porch.

Josie is getting used to these cozy evenings at home—Eleanor enjoying her cocktail hour, Josie playing with Henry, Fred cooking dinner. Fred, a dish towel tucked in his pants, is bending in front of the open oven door, squeezing the rubber bulb of a turkey baster over a roast chicken. "The Ayer meat market had free-range chickens. Can you believe it?" His brow furrows. "Cooking up kind of scrawny, though."

"So, Fred, how was your day?" Josie asks.

He shakes his head. "That jerk Petrie was on my case again." Petrie is Fred's boss at the McDonald's Distribution Center, and Fred complains about him almost every day.

"What did he do this time?" She remembers Grif's paean to the cocktail hour—a time to describe the events of the day, to reflect upon your life. Now she's finally doing it—without booze, and without Peter.

"I was filling out inventory sheets for the cold-meat storage, and then Petrie comes and takes my clipboard and double-checks everything. And I'm the only guy he does that to, like I can't be trusted." His face is turned toward the sink, but Josie can see the anger in the squareness of his shoulders and the muscles of his neck.

"Can't you get another job?"

He looks at her darkly. "I was lucky to find this job."

"Sounds rough. I'm sorry," she says, but her sympathy feels presumptuous. Eleanor is right; she has no idea what it would be like to be distrusted by everyone.

"How's it going with those Kennedys?"

She lets out a sigh. "Not so great. I'm researching Jackie's courtship with JFK, and I just don't get it."

The chicken, scrawny as predicted, is out of the oven and resting on the cutting board while Fred thickens a pan of gravy on the stove. "What's to get?"

"I don't understand why Jackie fell for JFK. She was so private. What attracted her to this extroverted, public man?"

He turns around, smiling as if she's a small child who's said something foolish. "Oh, come on, Josie. We're talking about Jack Kennedy."

"So?"

"This is a man everyone was in love with. Girls, men. My grand-mother goes out and buys her first TV at the age of ninety so she could watch the convention. When I was his driver, I would have done anything for him. He had this charm no one could resist."

"But was that a reason to marry him?"

Fred empties the pan into a china gravy boat. "Look, she was just like anyone else. She wanted to marry the guy every other woman wanted."

This strikes Josie as oddly original. Jackie—just like anyone else? Fred's the one who doesn't get it. Jackie *wasn't* like anyone else—ever; that's the Jackie mystique. Could she have been motivated by something so common as wanting to hook the world's most eligible bachelor?

The phone rings and Henry runs to answer it; Peter's nightly calls usually come around dinnertime. "Hello," he says, listens, and then grins at the receiver. He thinks smiling is holding up his end of a phone call.

"Who is it? Ask them if they want to talk to Grammy," she says, bending down to him. Now Henry starts to laugh; it must be Peter. Only Peter can make him laugh like that, with his head tipped so far back he almost falls over. "Is it Daddy? Say bye-bye, Daddy."

"Bye-bye, Daddy." Henry hands the phone to Josie and runs back to his play-dough.

"Bye-bye, buddy. I love you," Peter says to Josie.

"He's gone."

"Oh," says Peter, surprised. He's only been gone two weeks, but he seems to have already forgotten what it's like to converse with a three-year-old. "You'll talk to me, won't you?"

"Of course I'll talk to you." He sounds uncharacteristically low. "What's the matter?" she asks.

"Classes start tomorrow, and I'm pulling together my lecture for Introduction to American Literature, and I'm afraid I'm going to bomb."

"Oh, come on. Remember the Brown Course Guide?" The

course guide had said, "Peter Stadler is a pop-culture guru and his seminar on the sixties is a don't miss."

"This is different. This is eighty students, and I'm talking about *The Scarlet Letter*, not 'Dobie Gillis.'" He sounds nervous, but she's seen this happen before. Before a lecture, he would lick his lips, flip through his note cards, pace the floor, and she would think he was going to clutch. And then he would step on stage and transform. No need for note cards or a water glass; adrenaline would carry him along brilliantly for forty minutes. And if he didn't know something, he would just wing it. Not like Josie, who spent days and days preparing her meticulous lectures on American poetry, who wouldn't cite a single date or fact without checking it first.

"You'll dazzle them," she says emphatically. His students will probably never notice that he doesn't know when Hawthorne attended Bowdoin College or the historical sources for *The Scarlet Letter.*

"Well, I need your help with my syllabus of secondary sources." She rattles off a dozen titles, and he copies it all down, saying, "Yup . . . right . . . got it . . . that's a good one."

Fred is carrying the platter of chicken to the dining room, beautifully carved and garnished with parsley sprigs, and Josie starts to sign off.

"Wait," Peter says. "There's something else. Monica called today all freaked out. Seems she's having problems with some creepy guy in the apartment next door. She says he sits outside her window and follows her around, and she's decided she has to move out." He sighs as if this a long, tiresome story, and in a way it is. Monica has always been paranoid about urban crime. In Providence, she fretted about rapists climbing up her fire escape, and once had Peter come over in the dead of night to check out a mysterious clanking sound. "She's made a proposal which you're going to hate."

"Yes?" Josie gives the word three syllables.

"She says if she can stay here for the summer, she'll pay me what she would have paid for her apartment—nine hundred fifty dollars. The money would be great, but I know how you feel about Monica."

"I've never said anything about Monica." Fred, making decorative swirls on the top of the mashed potatoes with a spatula, shoots her a curious look.

"You didn't have to." His voice takes on an exasperated tone. "Anyway, I told her I would check with you. So, yes or no?"

"That's not fair," she says, aggrieved. "Don't dump this in my lap. You're the one who's going to be her housemate. What do you want, Peter?" Fred has turned his back and is conspicuously busy rinsing dishes.

"What do I want?" He sighs, as if this were a profound question. "Look, she's put me on the spot. She's being stalked, or at least she thinks she's being stalked, and she's scared. So what am I going to say? Too bad? I don't see how I can say no."

Peter has a point; they are all still allegedly friends. He can't turn her down without admitting the rift, admitting Josie's jealousy. Through the doorway into the dining room, Josie can see Fred pulling out Eleanor's chair. She watches as Eleanor steps in front and lowers herself down without turning to check, confident that Fred has scooted the chair in behind her.

"I won't see her that much," he adds. "I'll be teaching at night."

Josie thinks of Louise, her eyebrows knitted over her sensible brown eyes, saying, "When are you going to stop worrying about Monica?" Right now, Josie thinks. I can spend the rest of the summer, the rest of my married life worrying about Monica. Or I can sit down without checking to see if Peter's pushed the chair in. "I understand," she says, feeling strangely elated. "I know how Monica gets these notions in her head. *A girl's will is the wind's will.*"

"What?" he says, and then laughs, remembering.

"NOT EUNICE, not Jean, not Pat, not even that Joan, and she's not a Kennedy anymore," Fiona huffs. Things are not going as she hoped with her interviews. So far not a single Kennedy or Kennedy hanger-on has responded to her letters and phone calls. "I called Ted Kennedy's office fifteen times and I never got past the secretary. It's not as if I'm one of his constituents complaining about a parking ticket. Doesn't he know who I am?" She sounds offended.

"Mmm," Josie says sympathetically. He probably does know who she is, that's the problem. After the hatchet job she did on Pablo, Vivien, and Elizabeth, who would talk to Fiona Jones except one of Jackie's enemies? It seems surprising that after twenty years of chasing celebrities for interviews Fiona hasn't developed a thicker hide, but Josie doesn't feel it's her place to point this out.

Fiona lists the indignities she's suffered in the pursuit of Jackie. The dowager at the Maidstone Club who looked aghast and retreated into her cabana when Fiona mentioned the Bouviers. The time Fiona approached Arthur Schlesinger at a book party with some Jackie questions and got glared at disdainfully while he chewed a canapé. Having Lee Radziwill Ross's cleaning lady hang up when she offered money—*quite a bit of money*—for some inside dirt. Tracking Evelyn Lincoln down in some retirement home with a lot of cheerful wallpaper, and finding out she doesn't remember who Jackie is anymore.

"So Josie, I think it's time for you to get going on the good stuff."

Good stuff? She'd been probing the good stuff already—childhood trauma, love and marriage—hadn't she? "What did you have in mind?"

"JFK's infidelities," Fiona proclaims. Josie can hear a thick shuffling of papers, as if Fiona were flipping through notes as long as the Manhattan Yellow Pages. Were JFK's indiscretions that vast? "What was his compulsion to screw every woman in sight? And how could Jackie have put up with it? I want you to make a concordance of all his different women."

Josie wishes there were some way she could disqualify herself. I am incapable of understanding infidelity, she would say. Look at my father, who carried out an affair right under my nose. Look at my husband whom I have just given permission to cohabit with another woman. I'll probably decide that JFK was a faithful husband after all. "I'll do the best I can," she says meekly.

"Good girl."

THE NEXT DAY at the library, Josie is relieved to find Roger's usual desk empty. That's right, he had said something about spending the day at Widener. At least she won't have to admit to a fellow academic that she's making a quantitative analysis of JFK's bimbos. But "bimbo" is a term used for the modern presidency; Clinton has bimbos. What did JFK have—chicks, broads, girlfriends, dates? Girlfriends, she decides. A juvenile word for juvenile behavior.

Was Terry Grif's girlfriend? The word seems too innocent for the activities of those two. Leslie called her his fuckfriend. Not at the time, of course, at least not to seven-year-old Josie. But later, when Josie was a teenager, Leslie seemed to think it was her sisterly duty to inform Josie about what had really gone on in their parents' marriage. She went about it grimly, as though it were an unpleasant chore that someone had to do. The first time she brought it up, Josie was having a bath. Normally, the family respected bathroom privacy, but Leslie had barged into the bathroom they shared and instead of backing out the moment she saw Josie in the tub, she sat right down on the closed toilet seat for a chat. Maybe this is what happened in college dormitories; Leslie was twenty-three and full of sophisticated behavior that Josie admired. At first Josie was embarrassed, but then she looked down at her breasts, already larger than Leslie's, and felt a little prideful. This was the first summer that boys had been interested in her, and she was starting to realize the significance of things like breast size.

But Leslie didn't seem interested, in fact didn't even cast as much as an appraising glance in Josie's direction. She stared at a spot above the sink and finally Josie realized that she was studying her own reflection in the medicine cabinet mirror. She started to tell Josie about the summer they did *Meet Me in Saint Louis*, about the things she had witnessed—catching Grif and Terry kissing in the wardrobe room, watching him slide his hand up Terry's miniskirt at the cast party and pat her ass. "You realize that Mom was plastered all summer, don't you? Remember when we would come home after the play and find her passed out in the living room?"

Of course it had never occurred to Josie that her mother had been drunk; it had never even occurred to her that her mother had acted strangely. "When do you think Terry became Dad's girlfriend? Was it that summer, or was it when she ran his campaign?" This struck Josie as a very perceptive, even sophisticated, thing to ask.

"Girlfriend?" said Leslie. Her face twisted into an unpleasant sneer, an expression that Josie had seen often enough to dread. "I think the proper word is 'fuckfriend.'" She said it slowly, drawing out the *k* sound in the middle, and watched Josie's shocked expression with pleasure.

At first, Josie tries to use the computer but eventually retreats to index cards—one for each girlfriend. She makes two stacks—one of for-sures, and one of maybes. The for-sure list runs the gamut from a gangster moll to Georgetown socialites, with a good number of White House secretaries (in the days before sexual harassment), stewardesses, and campaign volunteers. Josie puts many more in the maybe pile because she can't really quite believe all of these women were his "girlfriends"—Angie Dickinson, Jayne Mansfield, Marilyn Monroe, Princess Elizabeth of Yugoslavia, and Other Men's Wives. JFK would have thought about married women this way. The highest compliment he could pay to another man was to try to screw his wife.

Poor Jackie, she thinks. This is the first time she's ever felt much empathy for Jackie. How could she have put up with him? The tales are almost unbelievable—nude swimming parties in the White House pool, naked blondes romping around the White House elevators, kinky threesomes at the Carlisle Hotel, JFK slipping out of the inauguration ball for a quickie with Another Man's Wife, Jackie finding strange women's underwear in her bed. Jackie dealt with it by being tactfully gone a lot—riding horses in Virginia, cultural visits abroad. But even when she was home, they had a curious Old World marriage. Separate bedrooms, although hers had twin beds like a kid's so she could have sleep-overs.

Even Grif wasn't this bad; not that the junior congressman from Massachusetts could have attracted women as JFK did. But Josie doubts that he ever would have behaved so poorly, would have treated Eleanor so shabbily. Having a charitable thought about Grif is so novel that she almost feels nostalgic. Maybe he wasn't so bad after all. At least he didn't subject Eleanor to years of humiliation; one searing summer of shame and degradation, but then it was over. And in the beginning, it would seem that they loved one another, lusted for one another, started the marriage with romantic illusions—more than Jack and Jackie ever had.

Josie shuffles back through her cards and stops on one with the heading "Pam Turnure."

Pam Turnure

— *Georgetown debutante, looked and talked like Jackie.*

1958— *Hired as secretary in JFK's senatorial office, starts having affair with him.*

— *Leonard and Florence Kater, her Catholic landlords, make secret tapes of JFK doing it in her apartment and take photographs of him making late-night visits, try to get them published by newspapers.*

1960— *JFK persuades Jackie to hire Pam as her press secretary.*

1962— *Becomes Jackie's research assistant for White House restoration.*

1964— *Stays as Jackie's assistant to help with correspondence after assassination, conducts oral histories for John F. Kennedy library.*

1964— *Pam Turnure marries, Jackie hosts wedding reception in her apartment.*

That's so weird, Josie thinks. Why would a woman hire her husband's girlfriend? Maybe it was a pragmatic choice; she knew that if she hired Pam, JFK would eventually become bored and move on—which he did. Perhaps it was a sadistic impulse—she could rub it in daily that Pam was nothing more than an employee, that Jackie was the one who got the adulation of the world. But perhaps it was something even more complicated—the irresistible, almost sexual, pull one feels toward a rival. The way Josie sometimes felt when she was around Monica.

Josie tries to imagine these two women working side by side in the White House basement, peeking under dusty drop cloths, unearthing strange objects wrapped in brown paper and twine. One day as they were sorting through a tangle of brass andirons, the conversation took a dark turn.

JACKIE: That's the way he is. I should be used to it by now.

PAM: I know. But he treated me even worse.

JACKIE: No. You're the lucky one. He didn't marry you.

The two women, their faces eerily similar, now streaked with soot and sweat, stared at one another in the shadowy gloom of a 20-watt bulb. A small moment of truth that need only have happened once for them to be friends forever.

Josie suspects that Jackie must have hoped, secretly, that JFK would eventually change his ways. Maybe if they had a few more children, maybe when he was no longer President, when he was older and his back really started to act up, he would be . . . better.

Would Jackie ever have gotten sick of his screwing around and said, "Enough"? Was there a betrayal that she couldn't ignore or forgive? Josie can't imagine what that could be; he'd already done plenty of unforgivable things. Like the time Jackie delivered a still-born baby girl while JFK cruised around the Mediterranean with a bunch of babes in bikinis and couldn't be bothered to cut his vacation short. But maybe if JFK had lived, if one day a teenaged Caroline had flopped down on a couch and said contemptuously, "So where's Dad? Out with one of his girlfriends?" Jackie would have called it quits.

At least Peter isn't unfaithful, Josie thinks, waving the index card in front of her face as if it were a fan, at least not like that. She stops. *At least not like that.* Well, then, how is he unfaithful?

She stands up, marches to the elevator, glides through the gift shop with its postcards of Jackie and Jack, smiling at one another tenderly, outside into the summer glare, the heat thick with highway fumes and rotten seaweed, and the *Victura*. She shuts her eyes and mentally fills out the index cards of Peter's infidelities.

Flirts with Students

Rebecca Howe, student in Peter's senior seminar on the sixties, develops passion for Anne Sexton and Peter Stadler. He invites her to dinner at our apartment on my birthday. Spends all evening deeply engaged in conversation with her about suicidal women poets.

Stacey Klein, whose senior thesis Peter supervised, sends him fat letters from Washington, where she's going to law school. He takes letters into his office and reads them secretly. Never leaves them lying around. When I ask what she's writing about, he says, "Nothing much."

Hangs Out with Buddies

Plays basketball with Stedman every Sunday afternoon.
  Usually doesn't come home until after midnight. Never
  bothers to call and tell me he won't be home for dinner.
Goes to American Studies conference with Stedman in San
  Francisco. I can't go because Henry is still nursing. He
  alludes cryptically to sushi bars and wild cocktail parties in
  hotel suites. Every time conference is mentioned for months
  afterward, Stedman and Peter grin guiltily.

His Dissertation Comes First

After Henry is born, Peter implies that his dissertation is more
  important than mine. Insists that he has to work Saturday
  and Sunday while I take care of Henry.
"I'd watch him," he says, "if you were really getting any work
  done."
"Monica's ahead of schedule," he says. "She never lets anything
  slow her down."
Says, "I don't know why you can't just sit down and write it.
  Why do you let yourself get hung up by every picky detail?"
Says, "Maybe you should just dump Ada."

And So Does His Book

When he gets book contract, immediately calls Stedman, Ruth,
  and Monica.
Dedicates book to Ruth.
Author's Acknowledgment says, "The author would like to
  thank Stedman Rollins and Monica Glass, who provided
  insight, inspiration, and humor every step along the way;
  and to thank my wife, Josephine Trask, who put up with my
  bad moods and who found every split infinitive and
  dangling participle."

Of course, this summer has already provided a few more entries
for the index—"Visits Louise with Monica," "Shares House with
Monica." She stands up, disgusted with herself. Who couldn't com-

pile an index card of offenses against one's spouse? Peter probably has a few long-held grievances against her, although she can't imagine what they are. But he probably doesn't hold them very dearly; despite his many faults, he never holds grudges. Wasn't that the secret of a good marriage—never keeping a running list to be thrown back in a moment of rage? Even though Josie has always kept a list, she nursed it privately; it was never intended for later ammunition, or to be shared with Louise or some other sympathetic woman friend. She always defended Peter publicly to his few detractors, those other graduate students who found him glib, or self-serving, or simply better at playing the graduate school game than they were.

So why, thinks Josie, does she have a need to nurture and revisit these old betrayals? Because, she concludes, he is unfaithful, sort of. He will always flirt with other women, woo other academics, and constantly be on the make in some way or other. And he will let her know he finds other women superior in certain ways—more driven, more hip, less dogged. Her list making is a way of preparing herself for the next time he does it.

Back inside, Josie makes a detour through the museum and stops to meditate on the exhibition case of Jackie artifacts—a place setting of gilt china with the presidential seal and gold-plated flatware, photographs of Jackie lugging furniture around for the televised White House tour, a red-beaded gown on a headless mannequin. Two women have their faces pressed against the Plexiglas case. "How could anyone fit into that, especially after two kids." "Imagine her dry-cleaning bills. Dry cleaning beadwork is very expensive, you know."

Did Jackie keep mental lists of all those betrayals and moments of humiliation—the unexplained absences, the furtive looks Jack would exchange with his latest bosomy blonde? No, Josie decides, that wasn't Jackie's strategy. She made herself too regal to notice, above it all. She probably didn't even keep private lists. If anything, she kept a file of his rare moments of consideration and kindness, so she could replay it like soothing music when the going got rough.

> *Men are such a combination of good and evil.*
> — JACQUELINE KENNEDY

A hard thump on the door startles Josie awake. "Phone call, Josie," says Fred.

She glances over at the clock and panics. Who could be calling at six-thirty in the morning? "Do you know who it is?"

"Dunno. Some girl," says Fred, his footsteps retreating down the hall.

It's Monica, she thinks as she pulls a sweater over her nightshirt, calling to say that something has happened to Peter. But what could happen to Peter in the middle of the night? The stalker, of course. Tracking Monica to Berkeley, crawling through an open window, taking vengeance on his rival.

"Mrs. Stadler?" a tiny voice says.

"Allison?" Josie says, so relieved she sinks onto a kitchen chair.

"I don't think I can come today. I have a migraine. I always get them when I have my period."

"Oh, I have a friend who gets those," says Josie sympathetically. The friend, in fact, is Monica, but they went away after she went on birth control pills. Josie considers mentioning this but decides she better not. Allison could be some sort of born-again type, and might be offended. "No problem. Hope you feel better, and see you tomorrow," she adds pointedly.

At breakfast, Josie runs through the list of things she planned to do at the library that day—finish the infidelity index, begin reading through the oral histories. And she had promised Roger Denby she'd bring the lunch today. She wonders if he'll wait mournfully by the *Victura* all afternoon, or if he'll give up and buy lunch at the snack bar. He'll buy lunch, she decides. He can live without her, just like Peter.

Henry pushes his Cheerios around the bowl, pretending they are motorboats. He makes putt-putt noises with his tongue, showering the table with drops of milk. "Stop making a mess," she says sharply, mopping up the milk with her napkin. He looks up wounded, picks up his spoon, and shovels in a mouthful of cereal in an obedient way that makes her feel ashamed.

"Hey, guess what?" she says in a coaxing voice. "You and I are going on an adventure today. Where do you want to go with Mommy?"

"To the circus," he says, the hurt expression vanishing. "See elephants standing on balls."

"Honey, I don't think there is a circus around here."

He looks thoughtful. "Get on a rocket ship. Go to the moon."

She smiles to let him know he's made a joke. "We can't go on a rocket ship, silly. Only astronauts can go on rocket ships." One of her child-care books said this is how you should talk to a three-year-old—elaborate on what your child says to expand his worldview. But whenever she does this, she feels stupid and suspects that Henry thinks so too.

"Watch TV," he says finally.

"I know," she says brightly. "Let's go to Whalom Park." Whalom Park was an ancient amusement park the next town over and the only thing within a ten-mile radius that could honestly be called an adventure, even for a three-year-old. Josie worked there the summer she turned fifteen, and she can still remember the smell of the Fryolaters, the hiss of the hydraulic brakes on the Tilt-A-Whirl. Henry studies her skeptically. "It has a merry-go-round, and a train and a clown. It's fun like a circus."

He jumps down and runs toward the back door. "See elephants standing on balls."

An hour later, Josie is sitting next to the fire truck ride in Tot Land. Miniature airplanes, motorcycles, boats, rocket ships, and teacups spin around under canvas pagodas. Past the low wooden corral surrounding Tot Land looms the white scaffolding of the Comet, the neon octopus arms of the Tilt-A-Whirl.

Even though she bought an All Rides/All Day pass for Henry, he refuses to budge off "Fire Alert!" She waves every time he circles by, but he doesn't look up. His fire truck has a steering wheel and a big silver bell attached to a string, and it takes all his concentration to steer and clang at the same time. She perches against the exit gate and gazes dotingly at his grave little profile. What she loves most about Henry's face is his nose. Right now it's a cute little kid nose, but there is enough of a bump in the middle so she can tell it's going to be big, like Peter's. Peter once told her that when he was twelve, his nose and feet grew to full size and nothing else, and she likes to imagine Henry at that stage. With skinny arms and legs poking out of an oversized T-shirt, shaggy hair hanging below a baseball cap, and a mouth full of braces. She's already decided what he'll be like—he'll play the saxophone, and read science fiction, and memorize baseball statistics, and draw weird cartoons, and he won't be a good student, at least not yet, but when Josie tries to get on his case about his homework, he'll make jokes and they will both end up laughing.

The ride stops, and the attendant, a teenage girl, unbuckles Henry's seat belt. "Go to your mommy," she says, pointing over at Josie.

"Go again," he says, pointing at the fire truck. The girl looks over at Josie for permission.

Josie shrugs. "Fine with me." The girl rebuckles him, pushes the control switch, and the fire truck lurches forward. He's the only kid on the ride, in fact he seems to be the only kid in Tot Land—a typical Wednesday morning at Whalom Park. The attendant settles back on a stool next to the control panel, swinging a freckled leg. She inspects her hands with their long glittery nails and silver rings, and adjusts the yard-long brown ponytail poking through the hole of her

Whalom Park baseball cap. She sinks down in a bored slump and then slides a surreptitious look toward the Comet, the roller-coaster in the adult section of the park.

That's the way it was the summer Josie worked here—the girls were assigned to Tot Land and the ice cream parlor, the boys were assigned to the big rides. The boys who worked on the Comet were the oldest—high school seniors—and had godlike status with the girls. They got to wear chamois work gloves, and when they snapped the metal safety bars into place over the Comet's round cushiony seats, their biceps flexed impressively. The head of the Comet team, Kevin Moran—Fitchburg High hockey star and allegedly a hot prospect for the Providence Bruins—was the heartthrob of Tot Land.

The next time the fire truck stops, Josie walks over and unbuckles him herself. "Come on. It's time for lunch." She prepares herself for a fight, but he hops down and grabs her hand. On the way past the fun house, Henry stops to inspect himself in front of the funny mirrors. He doesn't get that it's supposed to be a joke, and he stoops down low so he can see himself where it's undistorted. The mural above the fun-house door of Aladdin rubbing a lamp, the trash barrels decorated to look like open-mouthed clowns, the red pennant flying over on the bumper-car shed, the word "Comet" spelled out on a wooden sign in licking red flames—all unchanged since the summer she worked here fifteen years ago.

Henry decides on curly fries for lunch and insists that they sit at the picnic table next to the Comet so he can watch the little train climb up the wooden trestle. He dips a six-inch curly fry in a mound of ketchup and then dangles it in front of his face, puzzled by what to do next. Finally, he lays his head down on the table and lowers the fry into his mouth. Someone dressed in a panda bear costume stops, stoops over him, and waves a paw.

The first day Josie worked at Whalom Park, she sat under a tree during her lunch break and read *The Old Curiosity Shop*, and after that was pegged by her coworkers in Tot Land as a nerd. But two weeks later the girl who dressed up like Alice in Wonderland was fired for smoking on the job, and the manager cruised through Tot Land looking for a replacement. The girls wore their hair pulled back in hair bands and smiled coyly, but in a scene right out of a chorus girl movie, he picked Josie. Dressed up like Alice—with a pinafore that made her look ridiculously voluptuous, her blond hair hanging down her back, her rouged cheeks, her eyelids shadowed with spangly blue—Josie suddenly attracted the attention of the Tilt-A-Whirl and Boomerang boys. She didn't read under a tree at lunchtime anymore; instead she hung out with the boys in the parking lot behind the bumper-car shed. She sat on a concrete bumper so she wouldn't get her Alice costume dirty, and watched the boys smoke and make dumb jokes. And then one day Kevin Moran strolled over and asked if she would like to watch him play pickup hockey after work. As far as the Tot Land girls were concerned, this was a public declaration of love.

Every night that summer, when the park closed at ten, Josie climbed into Kevin Moran's Toyota pickup truck, drove to the Fitchburg Ice Dome, and watched him play hockey until midnight. She sat on the top bleacher, shivering and rubbing her bare legs, hypnotized by the echoes in the empty rink—the smack of sticks against the puck, blades cutting into ice, the grunts the boys made as they shoved each other into the boards. Afterward, Kevin and his teammates—fellow high school stars who also vaguely aspired to the Bruins—sat on the bleachers and split a few six-packs while Josie, still shivering and still in her Alice makeup, watched. And then he drove her home.

It wasn't until years later, when Josie joined a women's group in college and had her consciousness raised about date rape, that she realized Something Bad could have happened with Kevin Moran. But all they did was kiss while he slid his hand under her sweatshirt; and then he deposited her back home, disheveled and smelling like a sweaty hockey jersey. It's possible that things didn't go any further because he still had his hockey equipment on, including those padded pants with the suspenders, or that he was too worn out from slamming guys into the boards. Even more puzzling than Kevin's behavior was Eleanor's. How could she have allowed her fifteen-year-old daughter to stay out until one in the morning with someone who was years older in every way? Someone with arms as thick as

Josie's waist and a beard so heavy he shaved twice a day? But Eleanor, who was pathologically incapable of thinking ill of anyone, told Josie she thought Kevin had good manners. Which he did.

Josie searches through the crowd for Alice in Wonderland's blue pinafore, feeling wistful for that girl who wanted nothing more from life than Kevin Moran's salty, bristly kisses. And then later in bed, alone, three more chapters of *The Old Curiosity Shop*. What would that fifteen-year-old girl think of Josie now—married but still living at home, with a husband on the other side of the country cohabitating, Platonically or otherwise, with another woman? Josie sees the giant panda, a clown, a dragon, but no Alice in Wonderland. Whalom Park must have laid her off.

"Wake up, Mommy," Henry says. Josie looks across at him, startled. The cardboard boat of fries is empty except for a few smears of ketchup.

"I am awake," she says defensively.

"No," he says, shaking his head solemnly. "You were sleeping." He makes an imitation of her face—head drooping to one side, eyes open in a blank stare, mouth hanging loose. She wonders if that's the way she really looked—vacant, lost to the world, lost to her child. Behind her, she hears the chain slipping over metal gears as the Comet slowly climbs to the top of the first dip. It's a sound she heard a hundred times a day for an entire summer, and without turning around she knows the split second when the screams will begin.

Later, as they cross the parking lot, Josie glances nostalgically toward the throng of teenagers lounging behind the bumper-car shed. Squinting through the glare of the afternoon sun, she looks again, harder this time, at a girl in a short skirt who is sitting on one of the boys' laps. Laughing, the girl leans back, swings her long hair behind a shoulder, and tries to grab something out of his hands. Josie is sure this time; the girl is Allison.

OF COURSE, Eleanor has always been too trusting, Josie thinks on the drive back from Whalom Park. That's her problem. She trusted Grif, she trusted Kevin Moran, now she's trusting Fred. Maybe Eleanor trusts people because she lacks self-esteem. That's the sort of thing Leslie would say.

When she pulls into the driveway, Josie inspects the garden for Eleanor's tiny figure on hands and knees, weeding the arugula that Fred insisted she plant. Not there. Josie unbuckles Henry, who is slurping the remains of a soggy Sno-Kone, a wide circle around his mouth stained cherry-red like a clown's. With his sticky hand in hers, she walks through the kitchen, pokes her head out on the porch, circles through the living room and up the front stairs. "Mom?" She peers into Eleanor's bedroom—the four-poster with its yellowed coverlet, a pile of old *National Geographic* magazines stacked on the bookshelf along the wall, a jar of Pond's cold cream on the bureau. Not one single thing different than it was twenty years ago. The skin on Josie's arm starts to prickle. Why does she live like this? Josie corrects herself. Why does she *not live?*

"Come on," Henry begs, tugging her arm toward their room and his toys. He unglues his hand and starts lining up his Matchbox cars to form a huge serpent slithering across the length of the room. Josie heads toward the bathroom to wash off the red handprint he's left on her arm, and then pauses, staring down the back hall at Fred's bedroom door. Why not? she thinks. This is the first time she's been left alone in the house; she may never get another chance.

She knocks on the closed door. "Fred? Are you in there?" She waits, the sweat trickling under her arms, listening to Henry.

"Fire, fire, fire," he yells.

She pulls the knob toward her hard and turns it slowly so it won't make a sound. As the door swings silently open, she prepares herself for one of those scenes in a scary movie—weapons strewn around, pornographic posters of children, plates of rotten food. But the room looks just like—Leslie's room. Which is hardly surprising, after all, since it used to be Leslie's room. Her china horses and Baryshnikov posters are gone, but there are the curtains and bedspread covered in matching violet nosegays. Despite the feminine touch, the room is as bare as a monk's—the lavender bedspread pulled so tightly she could bounce quarters on it, a Bible and rosary on the wicker bedside table, a pair of pants folded crisply over the back of a chair. A double frame on the bureau holds two color snapshots. Josie bends over and studies them—both of a bride and a groom, their arms linked, smiling at the camera. The brides are small, dark, pretty—

clearly sisters, clearly Fred's daughters. The dresses have a late-seventies look—puffed sleeves, wide-brimmed hats draped with organdy. Was Fred there, or did they send him the pictures in jail? Wish you could have joined us, Dad.

A yellow legal pad and a mug with two Bic pens sit on top of Leslie's squat student desk. Josie sinks down on the desk chair, the inside of her mouth turning sour and sticky, and pulls open the squeaky top drawer. A single manila folder. Josie cocks her head and reads what's written on the tab—"Eleanor." With shaking hands, she lifts the folder out, sets it on the desk, and opens it. The top item is a sheet of yellow legal paper with a list of something written in blue ballpoint. She takes it out and looks closer: IBM, 500 sh. @ 32; Am Tel., 200 sh. @ 20; Ford Motor, 500 sh. @ 5; Quaker Oats, 500 sh. @ 3. She skips down the list to Elgin Watch, 200 sh. @ 9. A penciled note at the bottom in what she assumes to be Fred's handwriting says "all sold—6.18.94." The other item in the folder is a multi-page typed inventory bound with a metal clasp. The figures appear in a column marked "Appraised Value."

> *Hepplewhite sideboard, ca. 1830, French foot, original*
>   *brass pulls . . . $5,200*
> *Hepplewhite dining table, ca. 1845, pedestal base, 3*
>   *leaves, rosewood inlay . . . $8,300*

The inventory reads like a guided tour of the Trask homestead listing every antique, room by room, including the books, the family portraits, the Spode and silver in the pantry. The final entry is:

> *Early American Pencil Post bed, ca. 1780, very fine,*
>   *tiger maple . . . $4,200*

She combs through the inventory for the name of the appraiser or a date, but the front page is missing, as if all identification had been removed on purpose.

Down the hall, Henry's high voice calls, "Mommy. Where are you?"

Josie jumps up, banging her knee on the pulled-out drawer,

quickly jams the inventory and yellow sheet back in the folder, and drops it in the drawer. She pauses at the doorway, double-checks that every sign of trespass is erased—drawer closed, chair pushed back—and then silently releases the knob.

"I'm in the bathroom," she answers.

*Mummy thinks the trouble with me is that I don't play bridge with my
bridesmaids.*   — JACQUELINE KENNEDY

Josie doesn't say a thing at cocktails, or over dinner, or afterward
when they are having coffee in the living room. She wills her face to
stay as flat as a doll's, her eyes fixed in a china-blue stare, her mouth
pulled up in a frozen half-smile. Fred must not know that she knows,
or even suspects. She compliments him on the halibut in lemon-
and-dill sauce, she describes Henry's first visit to Whalom Park for
Eleanor. "Remember that boy Kevin Moran?" she says.

Eleanor looks up from her crossword, ruminating. "Oh, yes. The
hockey player with the lovely manners. What do you suppose ever
became of him?"

"I wonder." Did he ever make it onto the Providence Bruins?
Josie hopes so. She imagines him now, heavier but still black Irish
handsome, the sole proprietor of his father's travel agency in Fitchburg. She pictures a framed color portrait of Kevin in his Providence
Bruins uniform, stick back mid-slapshot, hanging next to the glossy
travel posters of white sand beaches and bullfights. If a customer
asked, he'd say modestly, "Oh, I played with the pros for a while."

Later, when she's alone in her bedroom, she ponders whom she
should tell about her discovery. How she wishes she could slip down

the hallway to Eleanor's bedroom, and blurt out the truth. "You won't believe what I've found in Fred's room," she'd whisper urgently, holding Eleanor's soft spotty hands in hers. "Let's run for it." And then the police would come and eradicate the Fred problem, neatly, invisibly, the way an exterminator gets rid of carpenter ants nesting under the front stoop.

But Eleanor would consider the only crime to be Josie's. "You went through Fred's things?" she would say, her mouth sinking down with disappointment. And then she would turn her back and refuse to hear another word of tainted testimony. That's the way it was when they were children. Leslie would find an irrefutable piece of evidence in Josie's room—the paint set borrowed without asking, her best sweater—and all Eleanor would say was, "Not another word. You had no right to go into her room without permission."

The person Josie most wants to talk to is Peter, who would find the whole situation ominous and hilarious at the same time. But it's only six in California, and if she calls now there's a good chance that he's still teaching and she'll end up talking to Monica instead. Josie is not in any mood to deal with Monica, who would probably consider snooping through Fred's drawers both foolish and paranoid. (Not that Monica is above snooping, or paranoia about crime, for that matter, only she would set her sights higher than an ex-convict boarder.)

Josie considers calling Leslie, but then decides that's as out of the question as telling Eleanor. Leslie would be on the first plane from Phoenix and would barge in, spoiling for a confrontation. She would confront Fred, confront Eleanor, and by nightfall Eleanor and Fred would have sneaked off together and eloped.

Lying on her bed, listening to Henry's breathing grow raspy as he falls into deeper sleep, Josie suddenly has a startling urge to call Roger Denby. She can picture his face, listening intently—the ridge between his eyebrows folding deeper, his lips rubbing against each other. He would offer an opinion the same way he spoke about McGeorge Bundy, as if the burden of judgment were almost too heavy to bear. But she doesn't have Roger's phone number; even though they've broken bread together they haven't progressed to that level of intimacy. All she knows is that he's subletting an apartment somewhere in Cambridge for the summer. Ah, of course, Josie thinks, her panic slipping away. *I will tell him tomorrow, out by the Victura.*

"Headache all gone?" Josie says when Allison strides in the next morning, pink-cheeked and bright-eyed. Before she can answer, Josie is out the door, swinging a paper bag with two meat-loaf sandwiches and a tub of pesto salad. She hasn't got the energy to deal with Allison's lie; she can only handle one deceit at a time. On the way down Route 2 to Boston, she rehearses her conversation with Roger in a whisper. The story about Fred doesn't make any sense unless she provides some background on Eleanor—the childhood in Elgin, the marriage to Grif, the years as a congressman's wife, Grif's affair with Mrs. Mascone, her life as an impoverished divorcée. By the time Josie has gotten through an abbreviated version, it's thirty miles later and she's already on Morrissey Boulevard. That's the problem with asking strangers for advice—having to synopsize your family history first. After six years, Josie and Peter have finally gotten to the stage where they don't have to provide footnotes anymore. When she says "Crowley Players," she doesn't have to explain the suffering, the loneliness, the betrayal those two words signify. How can she start all over again with someone else? She'll call Peter after all, she decides, as soon as she gets to the library.

Suddenly a mustard brick building looms up on the right-hand side of Morrissey Boulevard, with "Boston Globe" written in gigantic aluminum script across the front. "The *Globe!*" Josie shouts, veering in front of a UPS truck and across two lanes, and screeching into the parking lot. Why hadn't she thought of this before? She walks into a large marbled atrium that looks a little like a shopping mall with escalators escalating silently to somewhere. She'd been half-expecting a newsroom with clacking typewriters and some burly city editor shouting orders from a glassed-in cubicle. She studies something called "The Cornerstone of the *Globe*," which is engraved in marble behind the security desk, searching for clues about what she should do next.

My aim has been to make the Globe *a cheerful, attractive, and useful newspaper that would enter the home as a kindly helpful friend of the family. My ideal for the* Globe *has always been that it should help men, women, and children get some of the sunshine of life, to be better and happier because of the* Boston Globe.

—*Gen. Charles H. Taylor, Founder*

No "All the news that's fit to print" stuff. A newspaper that's like a plump maiden aunt, doling out recipes and sensible advice. That's just what I need, Josie thinks, stepping up to the security desk. "Morgue, please," she says.

"What?" says a woman in a security uniform, looking baffled.

Isn't that what they call it in those newspaper movies? Doesn't the city editor always tell the cub reporter to check something out in the morgue? "The library?" Josie tries, which wins her a smile and directions. She walks past a chiseled marble map of New England with symbols for local industries—leaping fish around Cape Cod, potatoes in Maine. If the map were up-to-date, it would replace the factory gear next to Fitchburg with a half-abandoned shopping center.

The library is located at the end of a long corridor, past a whirring printing press, and down a spiral staircase. The reference librarian apologetically informs her that this is an in-house library for staff only. "Occasionally we make exceptions for scholars," she says. "For example, if you were doing a book on the Kennedys."

"What a coincidence," says Josie. Seated at a mammoth computer terminal, she searches four different newspaper indexes and finds only a single reference under "Rizzo, Frederick." The article she pulls up is from a 1981 *Worcester Telegram* about the appointment of a new building inspector. She studies a smudgy picture, mentally removes a mustache and adds ten years. Nope, wrong guy. She leans back and sighs, discouraged. If only she knew the name of his restaurant, or the dates of his trial. She scrolls back through the Rizzos. There are quite a lot of them; hard to believe that there are so many newsworthy Rizzos. *William, Vincent, Salvatore, Raymond, Peter, Joseph, Joseph, Frances, Eva, Carmen, Armand, Alfred, A.J.* She almost misses it. Alfred; Fred is also a nickname for Alfred. The index cites a cluster of articles in 1988 and 1989. She pulls up the earliest article from the *Boston Globe* business section.

March 19, 1988.

Mama Rizzo's Declares Bankruptcy

*Saugus—The Mama Rizzo's Italian restaurant and pasta shop
located in Revere and Saugus declared bankruptcy yesterday.
Owners Alfred Rizzo and Frances Terrasi, both of Revere, issued
a statement that the chain will reorganize under Chapter 11.
They blamed the chain's financial problems on rising interest
rates and the recession in the Route 1 area. Mama Rizzo's
employs 38 people.*

Well, that doesn't seem so bad, Josie thinks, almost disappointed.
Not something to get sent to jail for. The next is a short article in the
Boston Globe metro section.

October 7, 1988.

3-Alarm Blaze Destroys Saugus Restaurant

*Saugus—A three-alarm fire reported at 4:18 Thursday night gut-
ted the Mama Rizzo's Italian restaurant on Route 1 in Saugus.
According to owner Alfred Rizzo of Revere, the Mama Rizzo's
chain is currently being reorganized under Chapter 11. Saugus
fire chief Victor Sliwa said the cause for the blaze is as yet unde-
termined and is under investigation. No injuries were reported.*

Josie can't help feeling a twinge of sympathy for poor Fred. First
bankruptcy and now this—the guy seems to have nothing but rotten
luck. The next article is on the front page of the *Globe's* metro section.

October 31, 1988.

Revere Man Arrested in Saugus Blaze

*Revere—Alfred Rizzo, 55, of Revere, was arrested yesterday in
connection with the October 6 fire that destroyed the Mama
Rizzo's restaurant on Route 1 in Saugus. Rizzo is the owner of
the Mama Rizzo's Italian restaurant and pasta shop, which
declared bankruptcy in March. According to Saugus fire chief
Victor Sliwa, a container of incendiary fluids was discovered in
the trunk of Rizzo's car. Two witnesses identified Rizzo's vehicle*

*in the vicinity of the Saugus restaurant shortly before the Octo-
ber 6 fire.*

A year later, a short article on the last page of the metro section
reported that Alfred Rizzo had been convicted on one count of arson
and one count of insurance fraud and had been given the maximum
sentence of six to eight years incarceration. The *Revere Sun* gave
more coverage to the troubles of a local boy and ran a feature story
after his arrest tracing his rise and fall. A storefront pasta shop that
overexpanded into a restaurant. Then came the outside business
partners, mounting debts, cost cutting that resulted in slipping quality and alienated customers, bankruptcy, the bank foreclosure on
Fred's Colonial-style house on Tamarack Circle.

"Fred is a good man," said his wife, Sylvia Rizzo. "He would
never hurt anyone. He won't even use bug spray."

"Mr. Rizzo willfully and wantonly attempted to commit insurance fraud," said Essex County prosecutor Joseph X. Flynn.

The librarian prints out copies of the articles on filmy paper,
which Josie folds and tucks in the back of a folder marked "JBKO;
Gynecological Problems." Back in her car, she forces herself to sit
on the sunbaked vinyl seat without flinching, to breathe in the oven-
hot air and wrap her fingers around the scorching steering wheel.
She needs to think about fire. The cars parked on either side have
huge accordion fans unfolded across the dashboard to keep the interior nice and shady. Where does one buy such a thing? She wouldn't
even know what to ask for.

Fred is an arsonist, Fred is an arsonist. The phrase rolls over and
over in her mind, like a punctured beer can in the surf, as she
searches for clues to unlock its meaning. In a way, she's relieved—
arsonist seems better than an embezzler or a con man who bilked little old ladies out of their life savings. She considers how Fred could
possibly commit insurance fraud with the Trask homestead, and
doesn't see how he could get title to Eleanor's property, even in
some felonious way.

What does it all mean? she thinks, pulling out onto Morrissey
Boulevard. And then it comes to her, not as a thought but as an

image—in sharp-edged, brilliant colors, like a psychic's vision. The Trask homestead with smoky orange flames licking out through the fanlight and the cupola. Each room is stripped bare, empty and on fire. At the stoplight, Josie makes a U-turn and heads west toward home.

One by one the clues fall into place until it becomes perfectly, perfectly clear. He plans to empty the house and then torch it. She remembers the way the Crowley Playhouse looked the day after the fire—a mound of steaming ash and charred timber. Who would be able to tell that the Hepplewhite sideboard and the Trask silver were missing in such a wreckage? He could do it one day while she was at the library and Eleanor was tagging clothes at the church, or visiting inmates at the prison. It would be so easy, Josie thinks, almost smiling as she weaves around the Concord Rotary.

The checkout girl at Kmart stares at the contents of Josie's cart— a case of smoke detectors, six packages of D-batteries, an electric drill, two fire extinguishers, a chain-link escape ladder. "Is it, like, Fire Prevention Week or something?" she asks.

By the time Eleanor comes home from tagging clothes, Josie has finished with the downstairs and is in the upstairs hallway in front of the fanlight. Eleanor stands at the bottom of the ladder and looks up at her, waiting for the whir of the electric drill to stop. Plaster dust sifts down over her white eyebrows and ruddy cheeks, but she doesn't step to one side or reach up to brush it away. Finally, Josie lifts her finger off the red plastic trigger.

"May I ask what you're doing?" For the first time that Josie can remember, her mother's voice sounds weak and quavery like an old woman's.

Josie stands on tiptoes and screws the smoke detector in with a few vigorous turns of the screwdriver. This is her fifth one, and she's finally figured out a technique. (The first one she screwed in immediately fell down, bringing along a chunk of plaster the size of a dinner plate.) "There was an article in the *Globe* today about a Victorian in Athol that burned to the ground in half an hour." She's pretty sure she's safe with this lie; Eleanor usually sticks to the national news in the front section.

Eleanor watches a few moments more as Josie tightens the last screw, climbs down, and brushes the plaster dust off her pants. "I suppose you're right. This place is a firetrap. I probably should have put up smoke detectors long ago." She heads toward the stairs.

"Maybe we shouldn't mention these to Fred."

Eleanor pauses halfway down the stairs and looks at Josie through the fancy turned balusters. "Why not?"

"Aren't you required by law to have smoke detectors if you have tenants? You don't want to admit to Fred you're just getting them now." Amazing. When she opened her mouth she had no idea what she was going to say, and then a completely plausible lie flowed out like divine inspiration.

Eleanor shrugs and sinks from view.

Josie attaches the final smoke detector to the ceiling of her closet, a final ruse she's dreamed up to foil Fred. He might deactivate all the rest of the smoke detectors, but he'll never know this one is even there. Then she goes through the house with a dustpan and brush and sweeps up every last paint chip. As she carries the stepladder across the lawn toward the barn, Eleanor calls out from the porch. "Josie?"

She lets the ladder clatter onto the grass. Suddenly she feels a tired ache spread over her shoulders and up her neck. She's not used to all this physical exertion; in fact this is the first time she's ever done anything more complicated with tools than nailing in a picture hook. For some reason leaky faucets and wobbly table legs were always considered Peter's domain, even though he wasn't much better with a wrench than she was. "What?" she says, not very pleasantly.

"Could you come up here for a minute? I think we need to have a talk."

Josie slouches toward the porch like a child who's about to get scolded—Eleanor is obviously going to accuse her of some injustice to Fred. Eleanor is sitting on the wicker couch with Rascal's sausage body stretched across her lap, her hairless belly turned upward, inviting to be scratched. There are two iced teas on a tray; she's been lying in wait. Josie flops down in the armchair facing Eleanor's, throws her feet up on the wicker coffee table (always strictly forbidden), and crosses her arms. "Yes?"

"Josie." Eleanor knits her hands together and props them on top of Rascal. Her voice is slow and deliberate as if she's reciting a practiced speech. "I'm worried about you."

Josie's mouth pulls tight, and she has to suppress the urge to laugh. If she let herself go, it would be one of those hysterical laughs that goes on and on until it ends in sobs. "*You're* worried about *me?*"

"Why, yes. Does that surprise you?" Eleanor sits up straighter, as if she's emboldened by this newfound assertiveness. "I don't understand what you're doing here. Spending the day at Whalom Park. Installing smoke detectors. Doing all this silly research on Jackie Kennedy instead of finishing your Ph.D. You need to go back home to your husband."

Josie slaps her feet on the floor and slides to the edge of her seat, balancing as if at any second she'll jump up and stomp off. Don't lose it, she warns herself. "My silly research, as you call it, is a job. In fact, I'm earning a lot more this summer than Peter is. I resent being treated as if I'm some helpless female that needs a husband to protect me. I think I'm capable of taking care of myself." She leans back, winded.

But Eleanor, for once, is not willing to accept pat answers. She shakes her head. "No. I think you're using this job as an excuse to avoid your problems with Peter. That's the way it seems to us."

"Us?"

"Fred and me."

"You've been discussing me with your tenant?"

"Fred is much more than a tenant. I'm surprised you haven't realized that by now. Fred has suffered many hardships in his life and is a very wise man." She makes serving time in jail sound as if it were an ennobling ordeal—like surviving a bone marrow transplant or being lost in the wilderness with three matches and a Swiss Army knife.

Josie stares at Eleanor's face, as earnest as if she were giving a Bible reading in church, and speculates whether she knows about the arson of Mama Rizzo's. Probably, and it hasn't affected her good opinion, in fact may even have bolstered it. She's brainwashed, Josie concludes. If she had to choose between Fred and me, she would choose him, may already have chosen him. Careful, she thinks, be careful. She must not understand that I am his enemy. "I appreciate Fred's concern, but I don't think he knows me well enough to have an opinion about my marriage." The tone of her voice is remarkably reasonable.

"All right. Don't listen to Fred. Listen to me. I presume I know you well enough to have an opinion." She rushes ahead, not waiting for an answer. "You cannot ignore problems and hope that they will go away. That's the mistake I made in my own marriage. It's taken me twenty years to figure that out. I should have fought harder."

Josie can hardly believe her ears. Eleanor, who never fought for anything in her entire life, whose guiding principle was pacifism, or passivity, or maybe both. Eleanor proclaiming to be a woman warrior is as implausible as Adelle Davis wolfing down a box of Ho-Hos, a Greenpeacer clubbing baby seals. Josie glances over at Eleanor's iced tea, all gone now except for a few sprigs of mint, and wonders if it was spiked with something. "Do you think you could have made any difference?" she asks.

Eleanor pauses, wipes the back of her hand across her forehead as if she's erasing some lurid memory. "That summer when I knew your father and Terry were having an affair, I thought the best thing to do was say nothing and pretend I didn't see." The word "affair" gives Josie a jolt. Obviously Eleanor knew, obviously Josie and Leslie knew she knew, but they have never discussed the brutal truth of that summer. "I don't know if I could have stopped them. But I should have tried. I owed it to you girls to try."

That's right, Josie thinks bitterly, too bad you couldn't have been more like Jackie, who never allowed her kids to get shortchanged, forgotten. But Eleanor looks so stricken that Josie repents her hard thoughts. It was all Grif's fault anyway, and Eleanor's kidding herself if she thinks she could have stopped him from screwing Terry, from leaving them. "What's the point in dwelling on this now, Mom? You're just torturing yourself. We turned out okay."

"I need to dwell on it. That's what Fred has taught me. I need to take responsibility for the mistakes I've made. That's the only way I can change myself."

Josie's skin turns sweaty with irritation. The audacity of Fred—the arsonist, the insurance defrauder, the convicted felon—telling

Eleanor to take responsibility for her mistakes. Josie cannot remain silent any longer; she inhales sharply, is about to let go and tell all, when Eleanor surges ahead.

"And I'm not sure you *have* turned out okay." Her defiant tone reminds Josie of her friend Sarah when they used to play something called the "honesty game" in sixth grade. The point was to tell each other the absolute truth, the things only your real friends would have the guts to say. "Everyone knows your mother bought those sneakers at Sears. You jiggle when you play field hockey and you should wear a bra." These are the things that Sarah told Josie; Josie can't remember what she said to Sarah, but it couldn't have been so mean. By seventh grade, they weren't friends anymore.

"Really?"

"Look at Leslie with that awful Simon."

This is the first time Josie has ever heard Eleanor make a negative comment about Leslie's husband, Simon. Leslie had married her college psychology professor, who was Eleanor's age and who treated all of them as if they were dim-witted students. Usually, Josie loves a good complaint session about Simon and all his patronizing ways, but not now—Eleanor's mood is too dangerous. "Leslie seems happy enough," Josie says halfheartedly.

"And look at you. You're so smart and you're so pretty, but you seem to think so little of yourself." Eleanor's voice has grown distant, as if she has forgotten her audience and is musing aloud to herself. It doesn't seem to occur to her that anything she's saying might hurt Josie's feelings. Her eyes have left Josie's face and are staring past her shoulder toward the back field.

Josie turns around to see what's captured her interest. A goshawk is making lazy circles over a stand of spruce; Eleanor has been keeping a bird-watching life list ever since she was eight and is always distracted by an unusual sighting. "Is that what Fred told you? That I have a self-esteem problem?"

"No. I thought of that by myself." Eleanor drops her eyes sheepishly and starts stroking Rascal.

"I think someone could say the same thing about you." Allison's cute metallic-blue hatchback pulls up the driveway, and Josie can hear Henry. Hell-Low. Hell-Low.

"I guess I wasn't much of a role model to my girls." She sounds as if she were talking to a disinterested third party—a psychiatrist . . . or Fred. Maybe she really is drunk.

Josie stands up. "Look, Mom, this conversation is doing nothing but make us both feel shitty." She waits for the disapproving frown Eleanor makes when she hears her daughters use bad language, but her face remains impassive. "I'm planning to get back to Peter just as soon as I can. In the meantime, I'd appreciate it if you wouldn't discuss my shortcomings with Fred."

"Well, of course I won't," says Eleanor, looking relieved that this heart-to-heart is over. She readjusts Rascal and picks up her latest mystery—*The Umpire's Last Out*. The cover has black silhouettes of baseball equipment—a mitt, a bat, and a catcher's mask.

Without a backward glance, Josie slams out the screen door, picks up the ladder, and circles fast around the back of the house. Fred will be home any minute, and she doesn't think she can face his brimming bags of groceries, his jolly pleasantries about the day. Henry is by the barn with his shorts pulled down around his ankles, peeing on Eleanor's hostas while Allison watches approvingly. He hasn't had an accident since Allison started, which fills Josie with self-reproach. "Successful toilet learning," the child development book says, "depends on consistent and positive coaching."

"Good job. Guess what? We're going out to dinner."

"To Donald's?" he says, brightening. He's developed a passion for McDonald's ever since they started handing out vehicles shaped like McDonald products. He already has a Chicken McNugget van and a Big Mac helicopter and covets the Large Fries motorboat.

"No way. We're going to take a picnic to the playground." She might have relented if Allison weren't standing there, who has undoubtedly learned the sodium levels and fat content of a Happy Meal in her child development classes.

The playground is behind the stuccoed, green-shuttered elementary school where Josie went through fourth grade. The big-paned windows are decorated with construction-paper Easter bunnies and baskets—now all faded into sickly pastels. She didn't think kids were allowed to make holiday cutouts anymore, especially of religious holidays; they probably aren't anywhere else but Crowley. The playground is vintage fifties—everything made of iron pipes and chain link sunk into poured concrete—and still so hot at dusk that the air shimmers over the slide. No friendly tire swings or spongy wood chips here. It even has the crude merry-go-round that they used to get spinning so fast that it launched kids in every direction onto the concrete slab. Josie remembers how they came staggering in from recess with bleeding shins and elbows and headed straight for the nurse's office.

She reclines against the seesaw as if it were a beach chair. The raw danger of the place seems to have ignited some atavistic streak in Henry, who's climbed to the pinnacle of the jungle gym—a circle of metal pipe shaped like a crow's nest.

"Look at me, Mommy." He raises both his arms into the sky.

"That's not safe. Hold on with both hands, or you'll have to come down." She sits up to show him she means business.

"Okay." He clambers down and runs over to the swings, where he drapes himself over a sling seat and donkey-kicks his legs.

She replays the conversation with Eleanor and tries to analyze it dispassionately. Fred is definitely trying to get rid of Josie, which she decides is a good sign. He's probably waiting for her to leave before he carries out his plan to torch the homestead. She'll stay until she can figure out some way to expose his scheme and get rid of him. After that, she needs to get Eleanor deprogrammed and functioning normally again, and finish up with Jackie. How long will that take? Three weeks, a month max, and I'm outta here, she thinks, her hand slicing through the air like a rocket.

Then the rest of Eleanor's words ooze in around the neat edges of her analytical grid. *You should go back to your husband. An excuse to avoid your problems. I should have fought harder. So little of yourself.* Was Eleanor worrying in a general way—one needs to work hard at one's marriage? Sensible advice, of course; one shouldn't become complacent. Or was this a specific warning? Watch out. Monica's going to run off with Peter, like Terry ran off with Grif. Don't be like me; don't sit by and let it happen.

Josie finds Eleanor's concern curiously shocking. She's used to having her private fears about Monica pooh-poohed by Louise, like that little lump your doctor dismisses year after year as nothing but a cyst. You're not prepared for the day he sends you straight to the hospital for a biopsy. And coming from Eleanor, of all people, who waved away every childish torment. You'll pass the test; you'll get into Dartmouth; your baby will be perfect—don't worry. Is she really worried now, or are these Fred's words seeping from her lips?

Henry reaches up toward the high end of the seesaw. "Let me on!"

She straddles the board near the center, and lowers the end down to him. "Alley-oop," she says, and sends him flying up. Henry is dangling six feet above hardtop, clutching a pipe handle that is half unscrewed. "Down we go," she says nervously, lowering it slowly until his navy Keds scrape.

"No! Up," he says, pushing his legs straight to make his end go back up.

"Want to know how this works? Even though I'm much bigger than you are, I weigh the same as you when I sit in the middle and you sit at the end. That's because this"—she pats the splintery green plank—"is something called a *lever.*"

Ruth Stadler maintains that young children, at least *very bright* young children (and is there any doubt that Peter Stadler's child is very bright?), can grasp complex concepts if they are *clearly* explained. Last time Ruth visited, when Henry was two, Josie overheard her saying, "See how the poem has fourteen lines. It's called a *sonnet.* Say *sonnet.*"

"Funny," says Henry, swinging his sneakers as Josie eases him back up.

"Hey, Henry?"

"What?" he sings.

"I'll fight hard for you. Okay?"

He grins blankly. It occurs to her that the word "fight" is as strange as "lever." "Funny."

AT ELEVEN, after Eleanor and Fred have retired to their rooms and Henry is sound asleep, Josie sneaks out to call Peter from a pay phone. She's decided calling from the kitchen phone is too risky; her voice, even in whispers, might echo up the back stairs to Fred's room. She coasts the car down the driveway and doesn't turn on the lights until she's around the common and half a mile down Longley

Road. The closest pay phone is outside the Red Cock package store on 2A. She stands under the buzzing orange vapor light so the lone store clerk can see her through the window festooned with neon beer signs. She stretches the receiver as far as it will go on its steel cable and waves it at him. See? I'm making a phone call. Please call the police if some trucker drags me off.

As she feeds in the coin and dials, she imagines how Peter's voice will sound when the operator asks him if he will accept a collect call. "*Yes, I will.*" Deep and eager, with a touch of longing. Ever since Monica moved in, their conversations have been filled with tenderness. "When are you going to be finished? I *miss* you," he says, as if to encompass all the ways a person can be missed. When she asks about Monica, he sounds beleaguered and helpless. "Thank you," he says, "for being so understanding about *that.*"

The voice that accepts is not eager or deep; it is cool and female. "Josie?"

"Monica?"

"So how are you?" The voice is intimate now, the way it used to be when they went to the Penguin Café for cappuccino after class.

"Oh . . . fine. Is Peter there?" The store clerk walks around the counter, locks the front door, and flips the sign to "Closed."

"No. I expect him soon, though."

The clerk is now pushing a vacuum cleaner around, his head bent so low that his bald spot gleams under the harsh fluorescent light. Oh, God, Josie thinks. She has *expectations* of him, they discuss their schedules in the morning over croissants and Blue Mountain coffee from some fancy Berkeley gourmet shop. Josie wishes she could hang up.

"So tell me about your research? How's it going?"

"Great, really great." Josie tries to sound hearty. "I'm almost done."

"Wow. That was fast." Josie tries to detect a hint of disappointment, but Monica sounds genuinely glad. "So, tell me. What kind of sources have you been using?" These are the kinds of questions they used to ask one another in the study group they formed with the other women graduate students. At least these are the kinds of questions Monica asked.

Have you checked for documentary sources? Where? How about the census, case histories from social welfare organizations? Afterward everyone secretly complained about her patronizing attitude, unwilling to admit that Monica knew what she was talking about and her advice was sometimes helpful. Irritating, but helpful.

"Mostly secondary sources," says Josie, trying not to sound defensive. "Jackie didn't leave much of a paper trail, you know." Suddenly the lights inside the Red Cock snap off except for a plastic Massachusetts Lottery sign that casts a comforting blue glow like a nightlight. The salesclerk has disappeared. Josie hears a back door slam and the roar of a distant engine.

"Have you considered checking . . ."

"Listen, Monica, I'm not interested in having a discussion about my research methods. I'm calling from a pay phone outside a liquor store, and I need to go." As if to prove her point, a ten-wheeler roars by.

"Oh," she says, disconcerted. "Why are you calling from a pay phone at—what is it there—midnight?"

Josie considers telling the truth—because my mother's tenant is an arsonist and I'm afraid he's plotting to burn her house down—about as plausible as being stalked by your neighbor. "Good-bye," she says. As she scurries back to the car and pushes down the buttons, she realizes she forgot to leave a message. *Tell Peter it's urgent.*

She parks the car at the Unitarian church, steals silently across the common, settles against the cool granite base of the Civil War Statue for a cigarette before she goes back to the house. After her encounter with Monica, she needs one. She squints at a tantalizing shape leaping back and forth in front of Fred's still-lit, unshaded window but then realizes it's nothing but a leafy magnolia branch bobbing in the wind. Josie doesn't remember ever sitting in the middle of the common at night before, and is struck by the massive outline of the Trask homestead, as impregnable as an ocean liner on a tranquil sea. Hard to believe that danger lurks inside.

She looks up and studies the summer sky—an old habit left over from her days as a nature counselor at a Y camp on Lake Fairlee in Vermont. She had taken the job seriously, had spent the spring before she started poring over nature books, memorizing tree barks and animal tracks, and even took a course on star watching at the

Hayden Planetarium. Later she discovered they didn't expect her to know anything about nature, and had made her nature counselor because she wasn't good at anything else like swimming or sailing or crafts.

She thinks about the row of little brown cabins rimming the shore, the loon calls echoing across the water at night. She was assigned to the older girls, the thirteen-year-olds, who at first were disappointed that they hadn't gotten one of those counselors with racy underwear who tell dirty jokes and describe the first time they went all the way. During afternoon rest, Josie insisted on reading out loud to them; not the Stephen King book they clamored for, but *Pride and Prejudice*. At first they were restless, but after a couple of days they settled down. Then they started begging during dinnertime discussions to know if Elizabeth would marry Mr. Darcy or Mr. Wickham; that's when Josie decided she would become a teacher.

Once when they were visiting Ruth at her cabin in the Sierras, Josie had tried to teach Peter the constellations. Huddled together with an unzipped sleeping bag wrapped around their shoulders, she had held his finger up to the sky and traced a line with it along the bowl of the Big Dipper out to the North Star. "I don't see it," he said.

"It's dim; don't look for a bright star." It was hard to single anything out of the dazzling mountain sky. It would have been easier in Providence with its night sky polluted by a hundred Wal-Mart vapor lamps.

"Oh, right," he said doubtfully. The natural world was a mystery to Peter; the only camps he'd been sent to in the summer were enrichment camps for gifted children where they taught things like chess and the binary system.

Still holding his index finger, she drew Ursa Major's head and paws, the W of Cassiopeia, the square of Pegasus, but she suspected Peter wasn't really paying attention. He wrapped the sleeping bag more tightly around them and burrowed his head against her shoulder. "I see," he said. "Yes, I see it now."

chapter | 2

During a trip to Greece, Jackie met a man named Aristotle Onassis. Most people called him Ari. Ari owned a big shipping company in Greece. He was very rich. He lived on his own private island called Skorpios. Ari was 23 years older than Jackie. He was short and had a big belly. Sometimes his clothes were rumpled. But Jackie liked him.

— Meet Jacqueline Kennedy Onassis, A Bullseye Biography

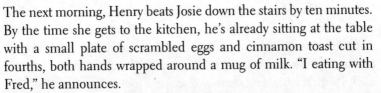

The next morning, Henry beats Josie down the stairs by ten minutes. By the time she gets to the kitchen, he's already sitting at the table with a small plate of scrambled eggs and cinnamon toast cut in fourths, both hands wrapped around a mug of milk. "I eating with Fred," he announces.

"I see." She turns to Fred. "You didn't have to do that," she says. "I would have made him breakfast."

Fred is sitting next to Henry and is writing something into a small spiral notebook with the stub of a pencil. "I know," he says without looking up.

God, what's he up to now? she thinks as she pours coffee from the old glass Chemex coffeepot on the stove. She makes a mental note to get Eleanor an electric coffeemaker for Christmas, that is if the house hasn't been reduced to cinders by then.

By the time she sits down with a piece of toast, she already feels wrung out and wonders if she can deal with this crazy situation for another month. For a delicious moment, she pictures going upstairs, packing her bags and cartons, and leaving with no more of a good-bye than a scrawled note on the kitchen table—*You're right, Mom,*

I'm going back to my husband. Eleanor, as Leslie would say, owns the Fred problem.

"All done," says Henry, jumping down.

Fred pulls a six-inch ruler from his back pocket and draws three neat columns on a blank page. He pushes his reading glasses down his nose, examines a page of the newspaper, and then copies down some figures in a cramped print. Josie assumes he's checking stock prices (the latest figures on Eleanor's portfolio?) but then sneaks a peek and realizes it's the sports section. She can't help herself. "What are you doing, Fred?"

"Oh, sorry," he says, looking up with a start. "Didn't mean to be so rude. I keep statistics on all my favorite baseball players. And then, if a player leaves the Red Sox for another team, I still keep his stats. Here's my page on the Eck, and here's Boggs." He flips to the front of the book and shows her a page with "Wade Boggs" written across the top in an elegant, almost Old World script. A red line divides the page with the notation "To Yankees, 6/1990."

"Interesting," she says, in the same tone she uses when Peter tells her about the latest trades on the Giants. Once again, she finds herself scrutinizing Fred's tidy person—the thick gray hair sharply parted, the polo shirt that looks as if it had been starched and ironed.

"I used to keep these little books when I was a kid. And then I took it up again a few years ago when I had a lot of time on my hands," he says, and then pauses, lifting his eyes from the notebook to her face. "When I was incarcerated," he adds deliberately.

This is the first time he has ever mentioned the fact that he was in jail. Josie feels a pang of shame for him, and glances away, back to his book as if there were still more she wanted to learn about Wade Boggs. His small hand holds the pencil poised above "Runs Batted In," his neat fingernail ends lining up like a column of commas. She imagines Fred in his room at night on the edge of his monastic bed, manicuring his nails. Maybe he even had one of those manicure sets for men as her father used to, in a zip case of pebbled leather with clippers in different sizes for fingernails and toenails, and stainless-steel implements for trimming and pushing down cuticles. The underside of his nails is chalky white, as if he used one of those manicure pencils.

JFK did that. Teddy White wrote that Kennedy kept a manicurist pencil in his suit pocket and spruced up his nails on the campaign plane right before each stop. Who taught these men such fastidious habits—their Catholic mothers? She doesn't think Ruth ever instructed Peter (Josie's only yardstick for typical male behavior) about nail care; he just cut them to the quick every once in a while and that was that.

Fred tucks the ruler back inside his book, binds it closed with a rubber band, and slips it in his back pocket. "Off to the salt mines," he says, heading toward the back door. He pauses by the pantry where Henry is stacking Tupperware. "Bye, Henry. Have a good day."

"Bye, Fred. Good day."

Josie watches through the kitchen window as Fred crosses the driveway, climbs in Eleanor's car, pulls the seat belt across, and slowly backs down the drive. Suddenly the scenario she constructed yesterday seems hysterical. In fact, all of her behavior of the last forty-eight hours seems slightly deranged—no wonder Eleanor's worried. She thinks of Fred's doting expression as he watched Henry eat his cinnamon toast, the courtly way he offered Eleanor his crooked arm after dinner to help her up from her chair. Either the man is completely harmless, wouldn't even use bug spray, or is so devious that it's beyond her comprehension. What she needs is an expert on deviant human behavior, someone who can plumb to the bottom of the human soul and see the darkness that lurks therein.

"So what makes you think that this is a problem?" says Leslie on the phone, unconvinced. She is already in her office and using her neutral, psychologist tone—probably the same way she asks patients why they think the FBI has implanted transmitters in their fillings.

Josie runs through it again—Eleanor's bank card, the file folder in Fred's drawer, his criminal record—and then reads the articles into the receiver, saying "Willfully and wantonly" in the kind of deep, foreboding tone that they use on true-life crime shows.

"Oh, come on. Just because the guy is an arsonist doesn't mean he's planning to burn our house down." Her voice is unconcerned, as if it wouldn't be a big deal even if her family was incinerated. "Don't you think you're overreacting?"

"You haven't seen the way she acts around him. It's spooky."

"All right, I'll come." It comes out like a sigh, and Josie can hear the pages of her Week-At-A-Glance flipping. "But I can't make it for a couple of weeks. That's when I've scheduled my vacation with my patients. Simon and I have to plan our schedules months in advance, you know." We've got *real* jobs, *real* responsibilities, she implies.

Josie hangs up and stares down at the filmy photocopies spread across Eleanor's bed, feeling betrayed—some hard-core evidence; all they did was make her look foolish. She had planned to call Peter next and give him the same dramatization, but now decides not to risk it. He might laugh at her, or accuse her of being paranoid, or aimless, as Eleanor did. I don't understand what you're doing there, he'd say. Aren't you supposed to be working? Even worse, she might get Monica instead and be subjected to a detailed inventory of his plans for the day. He's teaching until noon, and then he has afternoon office hours but I'm expecting him home for an early supper. It's been so hot, we'll just have a big salad Niçoise on the deck with a bottle of Pinot Grigio, and some of that good crusty bread from the bakery on Telegraph. You know the one. Oh, that's right, you haven't been here yet. I keep forgetting.

If Peter wants to talk to me, he'll just have to call, Josie thinks. Suddenly it occurs to her that his nightly phone calls had been dwindling lately to once every two or three days. He always made the excuse that he was working late at the library. How long will it take for him to notice that he hasn't spoken to his wife in a while—a few days, a week?

But then there is the Fred problem; she ought at least to let him know, shouldn't she? On a blank sheet, she writes the heading "Found in Fred Rizzo's desk drawer in the house of Eleanor Trask, Crowley Center, on July 23, 1994" and writes a description of the stocks and furniture inventories. Then she gathers up the photocopies, sticks on a Post-it note that says "Peter—FYI," and stuffs the whole bundle in a manila envelope. She imagines him sitting alone on his narrow cot in Berkeley (for some reason it's a cot even though she knows perfectly well he's sleeping in their platform bed from Providence) opening the envelope. Her eyes tear up as she thinks about his stricken face half illuminated in a slant of western light, his eyes lifting from the page to stare out the window across the bay. Josie and Henry may be in danger, he will think. Why didn't I call sooner? Oh, why, why, why? A wave of tenderness washes over her and she adds "I will always love you—J." at the bottom of the Post-it note.

FIONA'S SPIRITS have brightened now that they are wrapping up Camelot and moving on to Ari. For starters, she's found some people who are actually willing to leak some Jackie dirt—a stewardess on Olympic Airways and one of Ari's former henchmen. "You see," says Fiona in an accusatory tone, "Europeans don't have this sick reverence for the Kennedys like you Americans. They see Jackie for what she was—an absolute zero."

"If that's what you think, then why are you bothering to write a book about her?" says Josie testily.

There is a pause. "All right, I admit zero is a bit extreme. It's just that you Americans seem to feel it's your patriotic duty to buy into the Jackie myth lock, stock, and barrel—the artistic, sensitive woman who cherished her privacy, who lived life her own way. Blah, blah, blah. No one gets treated like that in England, not even the Queen Mum."

"What's this 'you Americans' stuff? You don't see me groveling in front of the Jackie shrine."

"So what *do* you think, Josie?" Her voice has turned hushed and coaxing, like Eleanor's used to be when she padded into Josie's darkened bedroom to kiss her good night and talk about the day.

Well, now, that's a good question. Here she's been doing research on Jackie for six weeks, and she's never asked herself the obvious— now what do I think of her? If anything, Josie feels she knows less about Jackie than when she started; the more she delves, the less she understands. As one contradictory fact piles on another (she married for love/she married for money; she was generous/she was a tightwad), Jackie seems to be slowly fading away, leaving only a Cheshire-cat smile. "I think," says Josie slowly, "that she did the best she could. She just muddled along like anybody else."

"Nothing like muddling along with a millionaire and a billionaire." Fiona lets out one of her short laughs, a sort of cynical cough. "You're such a romantic girl."

FIONA MAY think the post-Camelot Jackie is easier, but Josie doesn't. Back at her desk at the Kennedy Library, she flips through her notes on Jackie's marriage to Aristotle Onassis, and they read like one of those cute quizzes printed in the backs of ladies' magazines.

1. *Jackie married Ari because:*
    a. *She suffered from post-traumatic stress syndrome after the death of Robert Kennedy*
    b. *She had become increasingly concerned about the physical safety of her children*
    c. *She wanted to be out from under the Kennedys' thumb*
    d. *Ari had checks appeal!*
    e. *All of the above*
2. *During their first year of marriage, Ari gave Jackie:*
    a. *A heart-shaped ruby-and-diamond engagement ring worth $1.25 million*
    b. *A solid gold belt adorned with lions*
    c. *Sapphire-and-diamond earrings shaped like the* Apollo 2 *to celebrate the moon walk*
    d. *All of the above*
3. *During their first year of marriage, Jackie gave Ari:*
    a. *A bookplate with a pen-and-ink sketch of the* Christina *for his book collection*
    b. *365 new silk neckties (bought in a single shopping trip at a men's store in Palm Beach)*
    c. *All of the above*
4. *Ari gave John-John and Caroline:*
    a. *A jukebox*
    b. *A speedboat*
    c. *A mini-Jeep*
    d. *Shetland ponies*
    e. *All of the above*
5. *Jackie's mother thought Ari was:*
    a. *Short, ugly, and charming*

b. *Short, ugly, and vulgar, with poor table manners*

c. *A bum because he had dumped Lee*

6. *Rose Kennedy's opinion:*

a. *Strongly opposed Jackie marrying a divorced man*

b. *Thought Ari was charming and fun*

7. *Which of the following are true quotations about the Jackie-Ari marriage:*

a. *They go up the street together holding hands, dancing, playing like kids. It looked to me as if they were very much in love.*

b. *Ari wanted to show the world that he could buy anything or anybody.*

c. *He should have married Maria Callas. He told his friends that his greatest folly was that ego trip of marrying that silly Jackie Kennedy. The person Onassis wanted to marry he couldn't. We all know who that was—Queen Elizabeth. So he settled for Jackie.*

d. *I have no idea why she married him. I mean, to me, he was so unattractive—about five feet tall—and I thought he was just not very pleasant.*

e. *You can't ask a woman with a touch of vulgarity to spend the rest of her life over a corpse.*

f. *I find Ari charming, kind, and considerate. I think Jackie made an excellent choice.*

g. *All of the above*

Answers: 1—e; 2—d; 3—c; 4—e; 5—b; 6—b; 7—g

Josie opens a gray file box of periodicals on JBKO from the Ari years and flips through a stack of yellowed clippings and magazine articles. Back in June when she started her Jackie research, she pored over the advertisements (Elsie the cow, smokers with black eyes), the upbeat articles ("Philadelphia Housing Project Gives New Hope to Poor Families") in *Look* and *The Saturday Evening Post*, but now she avoids them. It's the pictures she finds so depressing—those greenish-yellow people looking with adoration at their white plastic shoes with the big gold buckles, at the new breakfast nook with the black gingham curtains and the table fashioned from a whiskey barrel. They stand jauntily with a hip-huggered hip jutting out, unaware that twenty years later their with-it clothes will seem laughable.

At the back of the box, she finds a reprint from something called *The Southwest Methodist Quarterly* by one Dr. A. J. Samuels. The article, "Jacqueline Kennedy Onassis—A Modern Day Ariadne?" proposes that an explanation for Jackie and Ari's marriage can be found in Greek mythology. Josie has come to find these long-winded academic articles about the Kennedys oddly restful. She doesn't bother to read them from start to finish to get the gist of the argument, but instead lets her eyes surf through the waves of tiny print, pulling out sentences at random.

And did not Jacqueline Kennedy find herself like Ariadne deserted on a lonely island, and did not Aristotle Onassis come like Dionysus to dry her tears, give her drink from his cup, and crown her as his bride?

Through her marriage to Onassis, Jacqueline Kennedy was no longer uxorious as she had been with John F. Kennedy (if indeed there was some female version of uxorious, which there is not), and was finally able to enter into a marriage, like Ariadne, as the object of adoration and not the adorer.

Josie tries to think if there is, indeed, some female version for *uxorious*, and decides that there wouldn't be. Women were supposed to be foolishly submissive and fond of their husbands—it was the natural state of things, not a character flaw. She has to admit that Dr. A. J. Samuels (described in the contributors' notes as a world-renowned authority on the role of women in Greek mythology) might be on to something and writes on the top of an index card "Jackie uxorious of JFK?" Of course she was—packing his suitcases, filling up the freezer with quarts of his favorite fish chowder in case he had a midnight craving, using the bit of money she inherited from Black Jack to buy him a white Jaguar (which he decided was bad for his Democratic image and traded in for a Buick). And she certainly was not uxorious (unuxorious?) of old Ari—no fish chowder in the freezer for you, buddy boy. Jackie had shed uxorious for luxurious.

* * *

"JOSIE?" he whispers.

She opens her eyes and sees the silhouette of a face above hers. "Oh, Peter," she moans, "you've come back." She reaches her arm up around his neck, and pulls him down with all her strength toward her parted lips.

His lips brush lightly against hers but then he struggles and pulls back, leaving her arm outstretched into the air. "Well, actually, no," the voice says. "It's me. Roger Denby."

Josie jumps up, blinking and whirling around in the harsh light to get her bearings—the gray water, the lush patch of lawn, the looming wall of glass and steel, the little wooden sloop. God, she's been snoozing next to the *Victura* again. She checks her watch—two-forty!—and sees her arm is bright pink and starting to freckle.

"Oh, dear." She manages a rueful laugh while she peels a sweaty piece of hair off her forehead, and then runs a finger along her upper lip as if it were still indented with Peter's . . . or Roger's. "I must have fallen asleep."

Roger has taken off his glasses and is polishing them with a pocket handkerchief. She must have smudged them when she grabbed him. He slips the glasses back on and furtively blots a dab of saliva off his chin before he slips the handkerchief back in his pocket. "All my fault," he says. "I shouldn't have startled you. I just wanted to give you something." He picks two gray boxes up off the lawn and offers them to her as if they were a precious gift.

The edges of the boxes say "Strathmore 50% Bond," and Josie wonders why in the world Roger is giving her two boxes of typing paper. "Why, thank you," she says uncertainly.

"It's the manuscript for my book—*McGeorge Bundy and American Foreign Policy, 1960–1968*. You probably don't remember that you offered to look it over." He looks down sadly at his manuscript, as if it were a child that had been picked on by the class bully and left in tears.

"Of course I remember." She grabs the boxes out of his hands in what she hopes is an eager way, but then nearly drops them—they're heavier than she expected. "Wow, looks long."

"Not as long as it used to be. I cut it drastically and got it under six hundred pages." Roger sits down on the indented spot she's left in the grass and lights a cigarette. "But a couple hundred of those pages are footnotes and the index, so you can just skip those."

"Oh, no. I love footnotes. But I'm not sure how helpful I'm going to be. American foreign policy isn't exactly my field." She sits down next to him, takes a cigarette, and lets him light it. (Jackie did that. At parties, she would hand her gold lighter and cigarette case to the nearest man whenever she felt like smoking.) Josie wishes she could go inside and get back to work, but she needs to explain that kiss, needs to explain why she was writhing on the Kennedy Library lawn with sexual longing. She glances back at the wall of library office windows behind them and wonders if any archivists were peering out at the moment she lunged for Roger and he wrestled away.

"I don't want a specialist—that's just the point. I think my book needs a little less Roger Denby and a little more Fiona Jones." He reaches into his shirt pocket and pulls out a three-pack of yellow Post-it notes. "If you have any ideas on how I can liven things up, jot me a note."

"Sure. If anything, you know, jumps out at me." They sit in silence for a few moments, staring out across the water. A tugboat chugs along in the distance and lets out a long, low blast of its horn, and a gull perched on a stanchion takes off with a start. One of Henry's favorite books is *Scuffy—the Tugboat*, about a toy boat with hubris. Discontent seems to be a prevailing theme in children's books, and in the end the dissatisfied duck/elephant/clown always learns that there is no place like home and settles happily back into the same old rut. Be complacent—what kind of life lesson was that?

With his head still turned toward the water, he clears his throat. "It must be hard being away from your husband all summer. You must miss him."

A faint blush has spread over his sallow cheeks and she has to resist an impulse to lean over and kiss him with gratitude. "I do. I miss him a lot. I'm afraid I'm uxorious."

His head swivels toward her, blush gone, professional curiosity back. "I beg your pardon?"

"If there was a feminine version of 'uxorious,' which there isn't."

He still looks baffled. "In plain English, my problem is I love my husband too much."

"Why is that a problem? I'm sure your husband feels the same way."

She shakes her head, and straightens her legs so her sandals crunch in the gravel under the *Victura*. "Nope. In fact, this summer he's living with another woman." Just saying this out loud gives her a tiny thrill of self-pity.

Roger, bless his heart, lets out a gasp. "He's what?"

"Yes. He's living with this woman we went to graduate school with." *This woman we went to graduate school with* — so much more dangerous sounding than "a friend of ours from graduate school" or "my maid of honor." "He says she's being stalked or something and has no place to stay." She shakes her head skeptically, all the while thinking, Why am I doing this? Why am I making Peter into a swine?

"He has no right to treat you that way." Roger says this so softly she looks up and finds his eyes narrowed with indignation.

"When I call him up, I have to speak to her. Last night she gave me the third degree about my research. She seemed to think I wasn't using enough primary sources." Am I doing this to justify kissing Roger somehow, so that he'll think I'm too distraught to be responsible for my own behavior?

"I wish there was something I could do to help." He reaches over and gives the top of her shoulder a gentle squeeze, and even though it's right on her sunburn, a shiver of pleasure runs down her spine. The only other male who's touched her in the last month is Henry.

"Thanks, but it's not your problem. I'll handle it, somehow. If I could, I'd go to California and confront him." Confront! Is Leslie channeling through me? "But my mother is falling to pieces, and Fiona Jones is on my back to find some good stuff on Jackie Kennedy . . ." She lets her voice trail off and ends with a soft sigh. Or am I trying out the worst-case scenario like a dress in a store, twirling in front of the three-way mirror to see how it looks from all angles?

"What about you?" Josie says, relieved to change the subject from her own sad state of affairs. "Are you uxorious?" She studies Roger's sweet face, and thinks he must have found someone to love after the brutal, unappreciative Gretchen.

He turns his head back to the water, and she wonders if maybe he didn't hear her, then sees a muscle tighten and jerk along his cheek. "Well, according to the woman I was living with for the last seven years, not uxorious enough. She said that she didn't feel adored, so she packed up and moved out in June. At first I got mad, I told her I didn't know what she was talking about, that mature adults don't need to be adored. But this summer I decided she was right. I didn't love her enough. We got along and we had a good time together, but I didn't adore her." He swings his gaze onto Josie's face, and leaves it there until she turns away, embarrassed. She stands up, tucks her wrinkled tank top into her blue jeans, bends down to tighten the strap of one sandal. It's hard to believe that she could be the object of anyone's adoration, but that penetrating look of Roger's was supposed to mean something, wasn't it?

"I'd at least like to take you out to dinner to thank you for reading my book," he says, with an unmistakably wistful tone. They start to stroll toward the serpentine stairs leading up to the library, their shoulders bumping together. At the first step, they both simultaneously stop and spin around to look back at the two gray boxes they've left orphaned in the middle of the lawn, downwind of the *Victura*.

THAT NIGHT, Josie takes Henry to the Leominster Mall to see *The Lion King*. All those dusky elephants and wildebeests dropping to their knees to worship the blond, male lion cub strike her as ominous, but no one else in the theater seems to mind the racist (or is it speciesist?) overtones. The upturned faces in the glow of the movie screen are as joyous as a Third Reich pep rally. She leans over to Henry, who is standing on his seat and flapping his arms like a bird. "Like it?" she whispers.

"Funny monkey," he says.

Later at Friendly's, she tries to enlighten Henry, who is now trying to eat something called a Clown Head Sundae, which consists of a scoop of ice cream with M&M eyes and wearing a cone hat. Her women's study group at Brown used to have earnest discussions about educating the young, and since Josie was the only one with a child, and a male child to boot, things usually digressed to how she should raise Henry. Teach him from infancy that women are not objects, show him how advertisements victimize women. It wasn't until Henry was in day care that she realized how infinitely superior the two-year-old girl was to the basic grunt-and-point pee-on-your-self-and-let-it-dry boy.

"Don't you think that Simba's friend Nala is the one who should be king? She's smart and brave and she didn't run away like Simba did."

Henry sucks on an M&M thoughtfully, spits it into his hand, and shows it to Josie. "Look. MM is all white."

Josie decides she better go back to basics. "Are you a little boy or a little girl?"

"I'm a little boy."

"Right. Now, is Mommy a boy or a girl?"

Henry smashes the cone with his spoon and presses it into an ooze of ice cream. "Mommy is a mommy."

She sighs. "Close enough, I guess."

By the time they get home, Eleanor and Fred have already gone upstairs, leaving the kitchen with a single counter light on and the dishwasher humming. Josie spots a slip of paper on the table with a ragged edge—clearly a page torn from Fred's spiral notebook. She tiptoes over, her heart racing, in hopes that he's accidentally left some damning clue, but it's a note for her, written in Fred's formal hand.

Friday, July 23

Dear Josie,

Your husband (Peter Stadler) called while you were out. He is spending the weekend with your friend at his mother's cabin. He says you can call him there and to give Henry a kiss for him.

Sincerely Yours,
Fred Rizzo

chapter 13

I always called her "Belle Mere"—and I still call her that.
— JACQUELINE KENNEDY ONASSIS

Jackie has often quoted the words in the biblical Book of Ruth in which Ruth declares to her mother-in-law Naomi: "Whither thou goest, I will go." And I too feel that the bonds of loving understanding between Jackie and me are just as strong as those between Ruth and Naomi.
— ROSE KENNEDY

❦

To: Fiona Jones
From: Josephine Trask
Re: JBKO and Rose—an annotated version

Rose: *She was invited to spend a few days at our Palm Beach house. I wasn't there myself at the time. Soon afterwards, however, I received a thank-you letter. It was signed "Jackie." I thought it was from a boy, and how extraordinary for a boy to write such a letter.*

Jackie: *The first time I met her was about a year, a little more than a year, before I married Jack, when I came that summer for the weekend. I remember that she was terribly sweet to me. For instance, I had a sort of special dress to wear to dinner—I was more dressed up than his sisters were, and so Jack teased me about it, in an affectionate way, but he said something like, "Where do you think you're going?" She said, "Oh, don't be mean to her, dear. She looks lovely."*

Langdon Marvin: *It was no secret that they deplored one another. Jackie constantly poked fun at Rose. She found hilarious Rose's habits of pinning little notes to her clothes to remind herself of some* *chore or task she had to perform. And Rose was just as amused by Jackie's trick of running the water faucet whenever she went to the bathroom to drown out the sound of her bodily functions.*

Rose: *Jackie is a rather quiet and shy person and soft-spoken — at least in comparison with most of our brood — and there may have been doubts about her among one or another of Jack's brothers or sisters or cousins at first, but that marvelous poem [about JFK by Jackie] immediately resolved them.*

Jackie: *We spent every Christmas and Easter vacation with them, until the White House. We spent the first four summers with them at Hyannis Port. During Jack's convalescence from the operations we spent the whole time with them in Florida, and I had every meal with them. And I think it's so sickening when you hear those mother-in-law jokes on the radio. . . . And then this woman, my mother-in-law, she just bent over backwards not to interfere.*

Mary B. Gallagher *[JBKO's personal secretary]: She was so different from Jackie, who spent her time closeted in her bedroom, even having meals served there. I sensed that this seemed rather strange to the senior Mrs. Kennedy — that her daughter-in-law should stay secluded and not participate more — and I suspected that the two women did not understand each other too well.*

The climax came one particular moment when Mrs. Rose Kennedy stopped by my desk. "Do you know if Jackie is getting out of bed today? . . . Well, you might remind her that we're having some important guests for lunch. It would be nice if she joined us."

I immediately went to relay the message to Jackie, but she took it gaily. She imitated her mother-in-law's manner of speech and sing-songed, "You might remind her . . ."

The luncheon guests arrived and departed without any sight of Jackie. In my own opinion, things were never the same between Jackie and her mother-in-law after that.

Rose: *I warned [Jackie] in the beginning. There would be rumors. There would be letters, anonymous letters.*

Frank Saunders *[Rose Kennedy's chauffeur]: She was determined to be on the best-dressed-women list with daughter-in-law Jacqueline, and she had trunks of dresses shipped back from Paris. Perhaps she secretly envied Jacqueline Kennedy's extravagant spending sprees,* *although I doubt she could understand them. She was afraid to spend her husband's money.*

Mary B. Gallagher: *To her credit, Mrs. Rose Kennedy always included Jackie in the family notes and reminders of religious days and anniversaries she would mail to each Kennedy wife. She even sent reminders to Jackie concerning memorial masses for Jackie's own father.*

Rose *[note to J. B. West, White House usher]: When the President used the house in Palm Beach late last spring, after we had gone, a lot of dirty dishes, pots and pans, and linens were left strewn about the kitchen.*

J. B. West: *She came to the White House more often when her daughter-in-law was away than when she was in residence. She acted as hostess for her son at official functions during those times.*

Rose *[after the death of Patrick Bouvier Kennedy]: She shouldn't have been doing all that water-skiing.*

Jackie: *When I married Ari, she of all people was the one who encouraged me. Who said, "He's a good man." And, "Don't worry, dear." She's been extraordinarily generous. Here I was, I was married to her son and I have his children, but she was the one who was saying, if this is what you think is best, go ahead.*

Rose: *She's just going to have to learn how to manage within a budget. Mr. Kennedy's office cannot pay for every whim of Jacqueline's, you know.*

Jackie: *If I ever feel sorry for myself, which is a most fatal thing, I think of her. I've seen her cry just twice, a little bit. Once was at Hyannis Port, when I came into her room, her husband was ill, and Jack was gone, and Bobby had been killed . . . and the other time was on the ship after her husband died, and we were standing on the deck at the rail together, and we were talking about something . . . just something that reminded her. And her voice began to sort of break and she had to stop. Then she took my hand and squeezed it and said, "Nobody's ever going to feel sorry for me," and she put her chin up. And I thought, God, what a thoroughbred.*

Rudolf Nureyev: *I asked Caroline, "Why in God's name did you name your baby Rose?" and she said, "I didn't name her. My mother did."*

* * *

TWO DAYS AFTER Henry was born, Ruth Stadler announced that she was coming to Providence for a couple of weeks to help out. When Peter came to the hospital to tell Josie the good news, she was trying to interest Henry in nursing, plunging her nipple into his tiny mouth while he struggled to push himself away. She pulled the johnny down over her breast, wrapped Henry back up in a flannel blanket, and set him down in the Plexiglas bassinet under the "I'm A Boy!" sign. "No," she said. "She can't. Call her back and say thank you, but we don't need any help."

"But we do need help. That's what Deb Herbert says. She says he's going to keep us awake all night and we're both going to be exhausted. She says you won't be able to do anything except nurse and sleep, and I'll have to do all the cooking and the laundry and walk the baby around in a Snugli for hours until he stops crying. And when I'm teaching and have office hours, you'll be all alone." He reached into the bassinet and tried to wrap the blanket tight, the way the nurses did, like a cocoon, with only Henry's face and tufts of black hair poking out. He clumsily tucked Henry's arms in under the blanket but somehow managed to make his head jerk back in the process and he started to cry—a mewling, kittenish sound. Peter shot her a panicked look as if to say See, we can't do this all by ourselves.

He's scared, she thought, and he wants his mother. As if to contradict him, she picked Henry up, expertly rewrapped the blanket, and quieted him down with a few jiggles. "No, Peter. I can handle it."

In her early days with Peter, Josie had thought that she would form a natural bond with his mother because they had so much in common—Peter, academics. She'd imagined that Ruth might become a mentor, or even a surrogate mother—the kind of high-powered professional mother that she always wished Eleanor had been. She even had the improbable expectation that Ruth might find her *more* serious than Peter; her field was Early American literature, after all, not television. But their in-law relationship evolved into the kind described in Ann Landers.

Dear Ann Landers,
My problem is my mother-in-law. On the surface "Ruth" is

very cordial, but I know she doesn't think I'm good enough for her son (she is a widow, and he is her only child). When my husband and I are with her, she directs all of her conversation toward him. Even though "Peter" and I are both in graduate school, she refuses to treat me as his equal. As far as "Ruth" is concerned, I am invisible.

What can I do to improve our relationship? Don't tell me to talk to "Peter." He says "Ruth" is very fond of me, and that I'm just being silly.

She'd already caved in to Ruth about the baby's name. For some reason, they had been so certain that it was a girl (or at least Josie had been certain, because Peter had wanted a girl and because the only other baby they knew was a girl), that they hadn't given any thought to a boy's name until he was born. Christopher, Josie had suggested. "Jews don't name their kids Christopher," said Peter. Finally they agreed on Nathaniel, a rock-ribbed New England name. But the next day, Peter said, "How about Henry, after my father, you know?" "Is that your mother's idea?" Josie asked. "No, not really." But Henry was a geek's name, the head of the chess club, the kid in the outfield. "Henry is important to me," he said cryptically. So Henry it was, and she had to admit that Henry suited this brown, scrunched-up, funny-looking thing with the spiky hair whom she already adored.

"I think," he said, looking sheepishly toward the window, "it's too late to tell her no." Then he confessed that Ruth already had her ticket, was all packed, had a cab ordered to take her to the airport at 7 A.M. He thought it would make Josie happy that she wanted to come at all. "You always say she doesn't like you," he said. "Now you can spend some time together, it'll be fun." The notion that help was on the way gave him new confidence, and he took Henry back and held him against his shoulder, thumping his back softly.

Maybe he was right, she decided. Maybe things with Ruth would change now that they finally had something in common—their sons. "Well, at least clean up the apartment," she said.

"You know Mom. She doesn't care about that kind of thing." Peter was always under the illusion that his mother didn't care about niceties such as whether he ever called her up or remembered her birthday.

"Clean it anyway. I mean it. The refrigerator, the bathtub; vacuum under the bed."

Two hours after Josie got home from the hospital, as she lay sprawled across the bed littered with diapers, and boxes of wipes, and Kotex, and a heap of pink baby clothes handed down from Hannah Herbert, she heard a cab pull up and Ruth's high heels clacking up the stairs. Josie was wearing only a flannel shirt (unbuttoned) and kneesocks, and she quickly scooted her white flabby legs under the covers.

"Hello. Anyone home?"

"I'm in here. Peter's at the grocery store." Josie peered over the edge of the bed at Henry, huddled up and asleep in a carry-cot on the floor, and wondered if Ruth would be disappointed by her first grandchild. He looked much scrawnier now that he was dressed in a terry-cloth stretchy (pink, unfortunately) and out of the hospital bassinet.

Ruth poked her head in. "Where is he?" she whispered, slipping off her heels, and tiptoed across the floor in her stockinged feet toward the carry-cot. She was in her college professor outfit, the one she always wore except when she was at the Donner Lake cabin—a tailored suit with a nipped-in waist and a short skirt, and her hair twisted up into a chignon. Her hair was still chestnut brown, although Josie assumed she dyed it, and her brown, freckly skin looked young, not soft and loose around the jowls like Eleanor's. She knelt her slim legs down on the floor by the carry-cot and sat for a time studying Henry, and then reached out with a finger and stroked the back of his fisted hand, the black spears of hair. "He's beautiful. He looks just like Peter did when he was a tiny baby." And when she looked up at Josie, her round brown eyes were moist. "Why's he wearing pink?"

"We borrowed clothes from friends who have a little girl."

"Well, he looks ridiculous." Josie had to agree with her on that one. "We'll buy him some new outfits tomorrow. My treat." Her eyes narrowed on Josie's face. "You look terrible. I don't know why they didn't let you stay in the hospital longer. I got to stay for a week with

Peter. Now, you go to sleep and I'll give the baby his bottle when he wakes up."

"I'm nursing," said Josie, slipping down farther under the covers. "But maybe I will have a nap."

Suddenly the lower door slammed open, and Peter yelled up the stairs. "Mom? Josie? We're back." There was a thunderous procession of footsteps up the stairs, and in marched Peter with a case of beer, Stedman with a jug of Gallo, the department secretary Rosemary with a bouquet of flowers, and the Herberts with little baby Hannah. They formed a circle around the carry-cot. "Ohhh," they said in unison while little Hannah bent over and poked the cot with her foot. Henry turned his head and let out an indignant bleat, his face turning red and his eyes shutting tighter. "Ohhh," everyone said again.

Peter scooped him up and nestled him in his arms, swaying back and forth on his black high-tops. "Isn't he cute?" he said, turning Henry outward so the crowd could have a look. "You're so cute." He gazed at him dotingly and then planted a wet smack on Henry's forehead. Josie didn't think she'd ever heard Peter call anything cute before. She glanced over toward Ruth, who was watching Peter with the same silly expression—he's so cute. Henry had quieted for an instant, but it was only to catch his breath so he could switch to a fierce wail. "He's probably hungry," Peter explained. "Josie needs to feed him."

She took the baby and waited for everyone to leave, but clearly they were settling in for a long visit. Stedman stole one nervous glance at Henry, opened a beer, and then busied himself checking out the books stacked next to Peter's side of the bed. Rosemary and Deb were sitting on the bed inspecting the baby clothes, and Hannah had pulled out a Kotex and was using it as a doll bed for her Barbie. They were all probably used to Debbie Herbert, who would nurse anytime and anywhere, including during her oral exams. But Josie wasn't about to let anyone watch her nurse Henry, which was more like a wrestling match than a Madonna-and-child scene. She held him against her shirt and let him grope, hoping they'd get the hint.

Finally, Ruth clapped her hands and they fell silent. "All right. Everyone out. Let's give Josie some privacy." They all filed through the door with their flowers and beer, Hannah with her doll bed, and headed down the hall toward the kitchen. Henry settled in for a half-hearted nurse that could take an hour, and she listened to the party get under way, with Stedman's big booming laugh followed by Peter's. She was hungry and wished that someone would bring her something—toast, cereal, she wasn't picky. She looked down at her breasts, as stiff as warheads poking through the Velcro flaps of Deb Herbert's hand-me-down nursing bra. A few weeks before, she and Peter had been sorting through the grocery bags of baby supplies lent them by the Herberts and she had pulled out the nursing bra. They had stared in mute horror at the yards of nylon and elastic straps before she let it drop back with a shudder. Now it fit like a glove.

An hour later, there was a soft knock at the door and Ruth walked in carrying a cookie sheet doubling as a tray (Josie and Peter didn't own anything so practical as a tray). "I bet you thought we forgot you. Here's your dinner," she said in the kind of bright voice one used for invalid grandparents. "I sent out for some Chinese." For some reason, Josie had imagined Ruth's offer to help out included cooking, but she was just as inept in the kitchen as Eleanor. The only difference was that she preferred takeout to Stouffer's. She rested the tray on the bed—greasy strips of eggplant in chili sauce on top of a mound of rice, a glass of milk, and a bunch of daisies in a coffee mug. "Peter said this was your favorite dish."

Henry had fallen asleep again and Ruth gently peeled him loose. "I'll hold him. You eat. So lightweight, he feels like nothing. You always forget how little newborns are." It was a little unclear who always forgot; Josie never knew how a newborn felt. She re-Velcroed the bra flaps, buttoned up her shirt, and slid the tray onto her lap. Louise, who had her baby six months ago, said that one of the strangest things about nursing was strutting half naked around people you barely knew. "There I am with the UPS man," she said, "and I look down and my boob's hanging out."

Josie felt about as intimate with Ruth as she did with the UPS man, which was not to say she didn't know Ruth well. Over the years, Peter had told her the Ruth stories—that's what he called them, as if she were a legend, and in a way she was. Her father was a Polish immigrant tailor who specialized in custom-made suits for

Hollywood moguls back in the big-studio days. Peter painted this image of his grandfather grandly (he was good at American archetypes) — kneeling down on a floor littered with film clippings in front of Irving Thalberg, with his chalk and tape measure, and pins in his mouth. Little Ruth, who started at the age of six doing fine sewing after school in her father's shop — buttonholes, tacking down linings, all the parts of a suit that should properly be done by hand but aren't anymore. (She made her own suits — in the early days because she couldn't afford to buy them, and now because she couldn't find any suits as well made as her own. Last summer when she came for a visit, she offered to teach Josie tailoring. "But what would I make?" Josie asked. "Suits for Peter," she said.)

Ruth set Henry back in the cot and turned her scrutiny to Josie, who was trying to eat the eggplant without splattering drops of chili oil onto the sheets. "So tell me," Ruth said, lowering her voice discreetly, "how do you think Peter's handling all this disruption." She cocked her head toward Henry.

Josie thought tenderly about his panic in the hospital. She and Ruth could laugh about it now. You know how men are around babies — so helpless. "He was a little scared at first . . ." She stopped when she saw Ruth's forehead furrow with disapproval.

"Well, I'm not surprised. He's way behind on his dissertation. I thought he'd be done with Chapter Six by now, but he said he spent the last two weeks painting a room for the baby and an office for you." She shook her head mournfully.

"I didn't ask him to paint my office," said Josie, taking on the defensive tone she always seemed to use around Ruth. "It was a surprise."

Ruth didn't appear to have heard her. "Poor Peter. I don't know how he's going to keep going." She stooped down and picked up Henry's carry-cot by its blue canvas handles. "Why don't you have your nap now. I'll bring him back when he's hungry. Don't worry about a thing."

Josie slid down under the cool sheets (Peter, as instructed, had changed them) and wrapped the pillow around her head so she couldn't hear the soft murmur of Peter and Ruth talking in the kitchen. Was he telling her that it had been his idea to fix up Josie's office? Or was he saying, "You're right Mom, I've made the biggest mistake of my life."

She tried to arrange her wounded body in such a way that nothing hurt, and mused that this was all the product of unbridled lust. Well, that would certainly never happen again, even after they waited the requisite month. Because the baby would be wailing, and if he wasn't, all three of them would be dead asleep. If they did have sex again, it would probably feel the way it was supposed to in the nineteenth century—like a dry, hot tearing. No wonder those Puritans felt that childbirth was divine retribution for carnal sin. I am being punished, Josie thought, for something.

If she hadn't been so sleepy, she would have buried her head in the pillow and had a good noiseless cry. Eleanor had warned her about the baby blues. That was just like her mother, to call up six hours after she had this beautiful, perfect baby, when she couldn't even sleep because she was so excited, and issue some dreary warning. "Do you mean postpartum depression?" Josie asked. "No, I mean the baby blues. My doctor told me that the first thing I should do when I got home from the hospital was make myself a cocktail—a double."

In the middle of the night, the breast milk spiked with spicy eggplant sent Henry into paroxysms, his distended belly and jerking legs reminding her of the bloated sheep in *Far from the Madding Crowd*. She and Peter took turns holding him stomach-down across their knees and patting his back. "Boy, Deb Herbert was right," Peter said. "It's a good thing Mom's here."

Even though no one actually invited her, Monica managed to stay for dinner every night during Ruth's visit. She said she wanted to help out, but the real reason was that Stedman had finally broken up with her for good. The night Henry was born, he had moved his stuff (the complete works of Roland Barthes in hardcover, a leather bomber jacket, a Water Pik for his bad gums, and a basketball) out of her apartment and back into his house, which he had been renting to a sorority. Even though he hadn't come right out and admitted that Josie and Peter's baby was making him nervous about commitment, the timing was suspicious. But Monica was very sweet with Henry. She changed his diapers, always being careful not to stab him accidentally with one of her long fingernails, and bought him a few boyish blue outfits decorated with footballs and anchors. She arranged to have the weekly meeting of the women's history study group held in Josie's bedroom so she wouldn't miss hearing the latest progress on everyone's dissertation.

After the women all left, Josie crept down the hallway past Ruth's sleeping form on the living room couch to her new office, turned on the gooseneck lamp, sat down in front of the student's desk. Maybe she could do a quick rewrite of Chapter Four, sharpen it up. The books and manuscripts for her dissertation sat piled in two cartons on the floor, and she picked a sheet of paper off the top one—a photocopy of the Whittier letter that Josie had found so long ago in the basement of the Crowley Library. *My Dear Miss Silsbee . . . I feel you have a powerful and original poetic voice. . . .* In Chapter Four, "The Birth of a Poet," Josie had called this letter "the watershed event of Silsbee's career." She reread it and felt herself slipping into another attack of the "baby blues."

Suddenly there was a soft knock on the door. "Josie?" Ruth whispered.

Josie wondered how long she had been standing there eavesdropping on her shuffling and unpacking. Josie swung the door open, feeling shamefaced, as if she'd been caught in the act of doing something naughty. "Thought this might be a good time to do a little work on my dissertation," she explained to Ruth's shadowy form still in the hallway.

Ruth stepped into the pool of light from the gooseneck lamp. She was wearing a quilted robe in peacock satin, and her hair was unpinned and hung past her shoulders. Josie had only seen her a few times before with her hair down, when they went swimming at Donner Lake, and the effect was slightly grotesque—like a wrinkled teenager. Ruth crossed her slippery satin arms across her chest. "Go to bed," she whispered urgently. "This can wait, forever if it has to. Your job now is to take care of Henry."

"You went back to work right after you had Peter," Josie whispered back. She wanted to show Ruth how tenacious she could be.

"Your baby and your husband are much more important than some article no one is ever going to read." Josie wasn't sure whose articles Ruth was talking about. Her own maybe, those translations of Descartes she made two weeks postpartum so she wouldn't slip behind on her publications.

Josie was ready to give up anyway and obeyed, trudging back down the hall toward her bed, too tired even to feel resentful. She slipped in next to Peter, slid her arms around him, and pressed herself long against the warmth of his back. She wished he were awake so she could reassure him. She would say, "Don't worry, Henry won't change your life that much," even though she didn't believe it.

The next night at dinner (takeout enchilada platters—Ruth couldn't quite get the hang of bland food), Monica held forth on her dissertation on the evolution of birth control in the United States. She'd unearthed some oral histories of unwed mothers made by a social worker in the 1920s. "All on crumbling yellow paper, covered with coal dust," she crowed, scooping up refried beans with a taco chip. "I don't think anyone had ever looked at them before me." Monica always got a fierce look in her eye when she talked about beating out other scholars, getting the edge on something publishable. She leaned toward the wine bottle and refilled her glass, shaking out the last drop with an aggressive flourish.

"I think your subject is extremely interesting. You can't imagine what women's lives were like before there was reliable birth control and legalized abortion." Ruth pushed back her chair and adjusted the shirt cuffs below her suit jacket. They should show two inches, she had once told Josie—no more, no less. "I had to have an illegal abortion myself. I had just been hired as an instructor and I would have lost my job if I had a baby. And we couldn't have afforded a baby then anyway. Harry was still in law school."

Monica frowned with compassion. "How traumatic that must have been, Dr. Stadler."

"It was. I'll spare you the gruesome details."

"Do you think . . ." Monica folded her hands docilely as if she were keeping her eagerness under wraps. ". . . do you think I could talk to you sometime if it wouldn't be too upsetting? There aren't many oral histories of women who had illegal abortions." Peter, walking behind her with a stack of Styrofoam containers, glanced over at Josie and rolled his eyes.

"Of course. It was very difficult being a woman in academics in the 1950s. I don't think you girls understand the sacrifices we had to make."

"You paved the way for Josie and me. We are in your debt," said Monica.

Ruth looked pleased. "I'd be glad to look over your manuscript when you're finished."

"Thank you, Dr. Stadler. That's so generous."

"Please, call me Ruth," she said, now straightening the collar of her silk blouse.

"All right, then." Eyes downcast shyly. "Ruth."

FOR THE NEXT three days, Josie carries Fred's note, folded and refolded so it is the size of a postage stamp, around in her pocket. At least twice a day, she flattens it out, stands in the light of a window, and studies it as if it were written in code. *He is spending the weekend with your friend at his mother's cabin.* Did Peter say "her friend," "my friend," or "our friend"? she wonders. She could ask Fred to reconstruct Peter's exact wording, but that would invite him to have another whispered conference with Eleanor over the state of Josie's marriage. Peter would have said "our friend," she decides. Was Ruth at the cabin? Of course — she was always at Donner Lake in July and August. Peter probably thought Josie would be reassured that his mother was there as chaperone. That's why he called beforehand, to let her know he isn't trying to hide anything.

How can he be so stupid? she thinks. How can he not understand that Ruth's being there makes the betrayal so much worse? She imagines Ruth and Monica sitting side by side in canvas sling chairs on the redwood deck, watching the sun sink behind the Sierras, leaving nothing but a streaky glow. Ruth turning to Monica and saying, "Tell me all about that fascinating dissertation of yours."

When the note finally starts to tear along the folds, Josie mends it with two pieces of Scotch tape. She plans to keep it for later; although she's not sure what kind of later — later when they have a blowout, or later when everything's patched up? She'll put it in the shoe box where she keeps all of Peter's letters and notes, not that he has ever had much opportunity to write her until this summer. So far, Peter's written communication has consisted of funny postcards

to Henry. "*Here is a big skyscraper that Daddy saw in Chicago.*"
"*Have you ever seen such a big bunny? Me neither!*" "*Here is the big
library where Daddy is spending all summer missing you.*" Josie has
sent Peter a few real letters written at the Kennedy Library when she
is supposed to be working, but every time she turns mushy, she imagines the letter being left unfolded on the kitchen counter for Monica
to read, and restrains herself.

Peter has never sent me a single love letter, she thinks bitterly.
Jackie had the same complaint about JFK. Ari tried to make it up to
her, used to leave her little notes and presents on her breakfast tray,
tried to show he had at least something up on old number one. Maurice probably wrote her love letters too—he looked like the type.
Josie knew a few love letter writers at Dartmouth—slightly built,
ardent boys who surreptitiously slipped poems into her *Moby Dick*.
The ones she wanted love letters from were too busy hot-waxing
their skis or getting laid. Roger Denby probably writes love letters,
she thinks; nice ones too.

When the phone rings on Monday night, she doesn't look up
from her book. She is having after-dinner coffee in the living room
with Fred and Eleanor, and the three of them sit motionless, listening to the rings echoing down the hall from the kitchen. Finally,
Eleanor stands up. "Well, I guess I'll get it." She comes back a
minute later. "It's Peter," she says quietly, as if she's delivering bad
news. So Fred has told her about the message after all.

Josie walks slowly and loudly toward the phone so he will hear
her footsteps approaching. "Yes."

"*Have* you lost your mind? *Have* you?" His voice is high and
almost hysterical.

"Excuse me?" she says. God, I sound like Terry when she's in one
of her you-must-have-the-wrong-number moods.

"This package you sent me. Don't tell me you've forgotten."

"Oh," she says and then pauses for a moment, because she *has*
forgotten. Oh, right, the package with the clippings and the Post-it
note that says *FYI, I will always love you*—*J.* "You mean you opened
it?" For some reason, she imagined that he wouldn't bother to open
it, that he'd throw it in the pile of unread catalogs and magazines
that accumulated on the floor next to his desk.

"Well, of course I opened it. I thought it was a long letter from you, and instead I find all these crazy clippings about an Italian restaurant that's burned down and a list of things found in Fred Rizzo's desk. I think you've been reading too many assassination books."

"I haven't read a single assassination book." Now she's huffy.

"Okay, but why a letter? Why didn't you just call me up so we could talk about this?" His voice is normal now, her old Peter, and she wishes that they could do something so simple—talk about it.

"I tried to call you. But I got Monica instead, and she interrogated me about my research methods."

"She what?"

"She wanted to know what primary source materials I was using."

"She's so obnoxious," he says fondly. Back at Brown, he frequently played the role of Monica's sole defender. She can't help it, he'd say, that's just the way she is. Then his tone turns serious. "What about this Fred guy? Do you really think he's dangerous?"

"Maybe. Hard to say."

"You can't talk?"

"Right."

"Maybe you and Henry should move out. Seriously. You can go stay with Stedman in Providence."

"Did I tell you Leslie's coming next week?"

"Calling in the cavalry, huh?"

"You've got it."

Eleanor pops in with the tray of coffee cups and sets it noiselessly on the kitchen table. "We're going upstairs now," she whispers. "So you can have some privacy." She heads toward the door, then stops, turns, and gives her a thumbs-up as if to say "Be brave."

Josie waits for the footsteps to make their way up the stairs and down the front hall toward Eleanor's bedroom. "How was your weekend?" she says coolly.

"Oh, great." He sounds nervous. "Mom's in good shape. She missed Henry, and you too."

I bet, she thinks. "Did Monica have fun?"

"I guess. I missed you too. I saw all these little kids fishing, and I thought how much Henry would love it. And maybe you and I could have gone camping by ourselves for a couple of days. You know."

He's resorting to desperate tactics, she thinks. Back before Henry, they used to go on three-day camping trips in the Sierras, where they spent a good portion of the time in their tent. Peter was unschooled in outdoor sex until Josie came along. Is that what they taught you in the Dartmouth Outing Club? he asked.

"Your mother probably enjoyed seeing Monica again. They always seemed to hit it off."

"I don't know, Josie."

"What did you eat?"

"One night we grilled chicken breasts with this fresh tarragon marinade."

"Monica was always very creative with marinades."

"Stop it, all right? How else was I going to get to Mom's if Monica didn't drive me in her car? I'm sorry if that pisses you off."

"It does piss me off." There is silence on the other end, and she listens to the phone lines thrum. It does piss me off—just saying those words clears her sinuses, like a brisk walk on a winter day. Why hadn't she ever said that to him before? she wonders. Because she could never quite bring herself to play the jealous, wounded wife— even though that's how she felt more frequently than she cared to admit.

"We didn't sleep together, if that's what you're worrying about." His voice has taken on the hard edge of someone unjustly accused.

"Peter, sleeping together is almost beside the point. First you drive out west together, you visit Doug and Louise together. Then you're living together, and now you're spending the weekend at your mother's. It's like you've got a surrogate wife, and I'm supposed to sit here in Crowley and say isn't that wonderful."

"It's not like I planned this out in advance, Josie. All this stuff with Monica just happened. You should have told me if it upset you so much."

"Why do I have to tell you that spending the weekend together with your mother upsets me? Why can't you figure that out all by yourself?" She realizes her voice is getting louder and louder, and she hears Eleanor's bedroom door tactfully close.

"What do you want me to do? Kick her out?" he says, aggrieved.

She almost says, No, no, of course not. But then she thinks of

Eleanor on the porch, her lips pressed into a grim line, saying, "I should have fought harder." "Yes."

There is a pause, and she wonders where Peter is standing in this unseen house—their bedroom maybe? She pictures an unmade bed, the window open with crickets chirping outside, his suitcase from the weekend on the floor spilling out a wet bathing suit, black high-tops, his book. What is he reading? She doesn't even know. "All right," he says in a way that isn't angry or even resigned. In fact, he almost sounds glad. "The next time you talk to me, she will be gone." Before Josie can say thank you, or I think it's for the best, or even before she can change her mind, he hangs up.

At the top of the landing, she stops. The Palladian window at the head of the stairs is open, and the linen curtains, the ones Eleanor brought back from Bermuda with the scenes of cottages and palm trees, flap softly in the breeze. In the distance comes the sound of metal trash cans thumping and rolling—the raccoons have knocked them over again and strewn garbage across the back lawn. And then, from behind Eleanor's door, as close as a secret whispered in her ear, a long, soft sigh.

"Uxorious?" Fiona sniffs. "No, no, no. Won't do at all. The biggest word my readers know is 'liposuction.' By the way, you don't think . . ."

"Nope," says Josie, running a hand over the slope of her own pudgy upper thigh. "Just the eye tuck in '79, and the full face-lift in '89. Check my 'Beauty Routines and Plastic Surgery' memo."

"Oh, of course. You have to understand, Josie, that you can never make your readers feel stupid." Fiona says this as if she were giving advice to an aspiring celebrity biographer. "People read my books because they want to feel smart. When they see what a hash these famous people have made of their lives, they feel superior. I may be a poor fat slob, they say, but at least I'm still married and I don't pop pills. My books can be very uplifting. So you save 'uxorious' for your little poet."

Fiona always refers to Ada as "your little poet," as if she and Josie were somehow related. But Fiona, she wants to say, I can't use "uxorious" for Ada Silsbee because she was never married, never thought about any man besides her clergyman brother and that gout-ridden old Quaker, Whittier. Oh, if only Ada had been uxorious, or libidinous, or devious, or any other "ous" word besides conscientious and industrious.

"And it won't be long now before you can get right back to Adelaide or whatever the hell her name is. And back to that husband of yours. Is he still roomies with your maid of honor?" She doesn't wait for an answer. "All I need now are memos on Lee, Maurice, and Black Jack's blue balls. You haven't forgotten about them, have you?"

WHICH SOUNDS more academic, Josie wonders, scrotum or testicle? She tries it both ways. "I am doing research on a Wall Street financier who may have had a dermatological condition that discolored his scrotum. That discolored his testicles." Scrotum, she decides.

She hasn't spoken to Kitty Taggert in eight years, not since they sat next to one another at graduation. Josie had forgotten all about her until she read in the class notes section of the *Dartmouth Alumni Magazine* that Kitty had been appointed a Fellow in Dermatology at the University of Colorado and given birth to a daughter. My, my, my. Josie hasn't sent anything in to class notes yet, because if she did, it would have to be self-deprecating and ironic.

> *Josie Trask '87 is still working on her dissertation and still trying to toilet-train her three-year-old son, Henry. If you're in Providence for the Dartmouth–Brown game, drop by!*

Of course, now she could do a new version.

> *Josie Trask '87 is a lowly researcher for Fiona Jones's latest not-worth-the-paper-it's-printed-on biography on Jackie O. At Dartmouth, Josie won the Edward Matthews English Prize and the Richard Eberhart Poetry Prize. Sic Transit Gloria Mundi, or what? If you're ever in Crowley Center visiting friends at MCI-Crowley, drop by!*

The secretary says Dr. Taggert is with a patient. "But if you're an old college friend, I'll get her."

"No, please," says Josie, but she's already on hold. I can't believe I am doing this, she thinks. Some poor teenager with bad skin has to sit and wait while I ask some pointless question about Black Jack's blue balls. For the first time, Josie wonders how JFK got that piece of information. Did he see them? Surely not. Did Jackie tell him? Surely not.

"Josie! What a surprise!" At least Kitty remembers her and doesn't sound as if she's in a rush. They swap personal information. Kitty's husband is a fellow dermatologist, her ten-month-old daughter is already trying to walk and has a vocabulary of twenty words. Josie speculates on what dermatologists do when they're alone together. Inspect each other's moles, discuss a cure for baldness?

"I always thought you'd be a full professor of English by now. I remember you sitting on your bed at Woodward Hall reciting Emily Dickinson."

Sitting cross-legged in her flannel nightshirt and sweat socks, she would read out loud from her Untermeyer's, because she couldn't bear to read it silently. "*Futile—the Winds/—To a Heart in port—/ Done with the Compass—/Done with the Chart!*" Josie feels her cheeks get hot; she hadn't realized that anyone else was listening. "Yeah. Well. Turns out Emily Dickinson isn't a very marketable skill." Then she hears herself saying, "I'm doing research on my dissertation, and I discovered this reference about John Greenleaf Whittier's skin. It was a strange dark color. Apparently his scrotum had a bluish cast." Bluish cast—that sounds like something that might go in someone's dissertation on Early American literature, doesn't it?

"Really?" Kitty's medical curiosity is piqued. "Mmm. Could be a lot of things. Hemosiderosis from iron poisoning. Argyria from silver poisoning. Silver salts were an old-fashioned remedy for venereal disease. That could have given him a blue-slate appearance. Or it could be from racial pigmentation."

"What?"

"You know. Maybe he was part black. Then again, maybe he just had dark skin and sat in the sun too much."

Josie tries to make this vague medical speculation sound as good as possible in her memo.

According to Dr. Katherine Taggert, a dermatology expert at the University of Colorado, there are several possible causes for the increased and unusual pigmentation of John V. Bouvier's skin.

Maybe Fiona won't notice that all the expert said was "maybe he had something, and then again maybe he didn't."

A few days later, Fiona calls. "Dynamite," she pronounces. "TNT in a FedEx envelope."

"What is?" says Josie, dread rising.

"Black Jack being treated for venereal disease. And being part black. Of course, it all makes sense. The terrible secret that Jackie was trying to hide."

"Fiona, there is no proof that he had anything. He probably just sat under a sun lamp too long."

"But your expert said that it *could* be true, right?"

"Right," Josie admits reluctantly. Fiona should have been a federal prosecutor; she was good at making people incriminate themselves.

"And they did call him Black Jack, right?"

"I think you're being too literal. Black was a metaphor. Black as in black-eyed, blackguard, black sheep, black-hearted, the Black and Tans." She's talking faster and faster, as if she's on one of those "Beat the Clock" game shows.

"Black as in black," Fiona concludes.

chapter 14

> *Nothing could ever come between us.*
> — JACQUELINE KENNEDY ONASSIS

> *I recall her listing colors and what she was going to do in this room and how she would furnish that room. I remember Lee Radziwill saying, "Oh, how I envy you." And she kept on saying it.*
> — FRANK SAUNDERS, Kennedy family chauffeur

> *Lee was always the pretty one. I guess I was supposed to be the smart one.*
> — JACQUELINE KENNEDY ONASSIS

To: *Fiona Jones*
From: *Josephine Trask*
Re: *Jackie and Lee*

Whom did Daddy love the most? *Jackie. Black Jack was in love with Jackie, courted her like a suitor, bragged about her good grades and horse show blue ribbons shamelessly. He bragged about Lee's good looks too ("Will you look at those eyes and sexy lips?" he said to his Bouvier relatives over Sunday dinner), but Jackie was number one, whom he referred to as "all things holy." Both sisters married men many years older.*

Whom did Mommy love the most? *Neither. Janet was hypercritical and argued frequently with both Jackie and Lee. After she married Hugh Auchincloss, she had two more children as well as three stepchildren to contend with, and two huge houses to run, and didn't give them much attention. "No matter what Jackie and I did, it was never good enough," Lee said. Although Janet said,* *inexplicably, at the end of her life that Lee had always been her favorite child.*

Who was smarter? Jackie was an academic superstar at Chapin and Farmington, and Lee, an average student, always had her teachers asking, "Why can't you be like your sister?"

Who was prettier? As a child, Lee was pudgy and plain, but later slimmed down. Which sister was the prettiest was always a matter of personal opinion. Jackie was tall with striking dark looks, but was cold and aloof, and somewhat ungainly. Lee was smaller, more feminine, sweeter-looking.

Who dressed better? Both were snappy dressers. Lee copied Jackie's Camelot look. Later, Lee dressed with more flair and dare — dramatic colors, bare breasts. She also put herself into hock trying to keep in the latest couture outfits.

Who was sexier? Lee. From the moment fourteen-year-old Lee in a strapless dress upstaged Jackie at her own deb party, Lee was considered the sexy one. Of all the things that have been said about Jackie, no one ever called her sexy.

Whom did the boys like more?

JFK: Married Jackie but thought Lee was cute and sexy. Lee played hostess in the White House when Jackie was indisposed. Jackie said, "Lee is so dippy about Jack it's sickening."

Stas Radziwill: Married Lee but became extremely attached to Jackie. He felt protective of her, and they stayed close friends after his divorce from Lee, in fact closer than Jackie and Lee.

Aristotle Onassis: Started having an affair with Lee in 1963, but after the assassination moved on to Jackie, a much bigger catch. When Lee learned that Jackie planned to marry Onassis, she screamed, "How could she do this to me?"

Rudolph Nureyev: Lee was in love with him, even though she knew he was gay, but he was much more smitten with Jackie and courted her favor.

Who was a better mother? Jackie. Everyone seems to agree that Jackie was a selfless and devoted mother, and that Lee was too self-centered and alcoholic to be much of a parent. As a teenager, her daughter Tina had such a poor relationship with Lee that she

*lived for weeks at a time with her Aunt Jackie, which Lee bitterly
resented.*

Who had a better personality? *Lee was more spontaneous and fun,
but she was also more insecure and unstable than Jackie. Both
preferred the company of men and had few female friends. Plenty
of disparaging things have been said about both of them — avari-
cious, snobbish, capricious, entitled, cold, mean-spirited, imperious, shallow, phony, hypocritical, manipulative . . .*

JOSIE AND HENRY are waiting at the gate when Leslie gets off the
plane from Phoenix. Josie considered waiting in the car outside by
the baggage claim, but suspected Leslie might be offended, so she
had parked and carried Henry for what seemed like miles all the way
down to the gate, which was the last one, of course. She spots Leslie
before Leslie sees her. Tall, lean, long purposeful strides, dressed in
crumpled earth-tone linens, swinging hair expertly highlighted so it
looks as if it had spent the summer at the beach. Almost beautiful,
except for her scowling expression, which is not directed at anyone
or anything but at the world in general. Leslie's expression in repose
is a grimace and people usually assume she's pissed off. When she
sees Josie she flashes her broad smile and waves a bronzed arm but
then, as she waits in line for the rest of the passengers to file through
the narrow gate, the scowl sneaks back.

Josie picks Henry up onto one hip, and he wraps his arms tightly
around her neck. "There's your Aunt Leslie," she says, pointing
toward the throng, but his eyes are fixed out the huge windows
where a jet is taxiing down the runway. She smoothes his dark hair
back behind the pink rim of an ear and kisses his round cushiony
cheek. Leslie hasn't seen him since he was a baby, and Josie is
already worrying if she'll think he's gorgeous, and if she'll bother to
say so.

Leslie walks over to them and stoops down to give Josie a peck on
the cheek. Leslie is a good four inches taller than Josie's five feet
five, a fact that surprises her anew every time they meet, which these
days is about once every two years. When she was a kid, she always
assumed that she'd catch up to Leslie, but then one day she realized

that she would always be, chronologically and literally, the little sister.

Leslie rests an uncertain hand on Henry's forearm. He peels his eyes away from the baggage truck unloading the plane, stares down at her hand, and then smiles. "Hi," she says uncertainly, as if it were a question. "He sure has gotten bigger since the last time I saw him. He looks just like Peter, doesn't he?"

"That's what everyone says." Josie has come to find this observation vaguely insulting—as if she had nothing to do with Henry except provide an incubation chamber for Peter's genes. She waits for additional comments—he is so beautiful, I don't know how you do it, I envy you—but Leslie has already swung her overnight bag onto her shoulder and is heading toward the concourse.

"This is all I brought," she says, pausing so Josie and Henry can catch up, and pats her leather bag, which is the size of a briefcase. "So we can go straight to the car."

"I thought you were staying a week." Josie's heart starts to sink. This is going to be one of Leslie's classic forty-eight-hour visits—just long enough to stir up a lot of trouble and then leave the mess for Josie to deal with. Simon rarely let her get away for longer. After a day, he usually called with some pressing reason for her to hurry back—his enlarged prostate, a crisis with the receptionist in their office. Once it was because he'd discovered fleas on their miniature schnauzer and claimed he was too busy to take him to the vet for a flea bath. "Simon says I have to come back," she would announce as if it were a biblical prophecy.

"We'll see. I might have to leave early. Simon says he's not sure he can handle my patients if more than one of them has a crisis while I'm gone." This was the kind of tantalizing remark that Leslie liked to make about her patients. If Josie asked for details about what kind of multiple crises could happen in a single week, she would plead professional discretion. So instead Josie speculates silently—a rash of suicide threats, or maybe the eating-disorder support group that Leslie ran would all simultaneously start bingeing and purging in the waiting room. Josie likes to think of Simon having to deal with a smelly mess all by himself while Leslie is gone.

Stuck in a traffic jam in the Callahan Tunnel, Josie tries to bring Leslie up-to-date about the Eleanor situation. "And now I'm almost certain she's sleeping with him."

Leslie turns toward Josie, her face orange in the murky tunnel lights. "Really? How do you know that?"

"Well, I think I heard them . . . ah . . ." Josie searches for the appropriate word. If it were anyone else besides Eleanor she would say fucking. ". . . making love in Mom's room." She replays that soft sigh in her mind—deep, filled with satisfaction, as if a long-hoped-for wish had finally come true. What else could it have been?

"Have you actually seen him go into her room?" Leslie is always skeptical of Josie's opinions—but that's what you *think*, she would say, you don't know for certain. Peter says that's because she's a shrink, but Josie knows better. It's the primordial stew of sibling relationships—no matter what you accomplish, your sibling will always see you as a five-year-old who can't tie her own shoes. Peter, the only child, doesn't get it.

"No."

"Well, maybe she was just masturbating."

Josie checks in her rearview mirror to see if Henry is paying attention to this new word, but he is slouched sideways in his car seat, asleep. She looks again, so she can admire his face, which is always so perfect when he's asleep. "Mom? Get serious."

Leslie glances over, her mouth pulled to one side in a superior smile. "You get serious."

Josie wonders why the idea of Eleanor masturbating is so much more unpalatable than having an arsonist as a lover. Maybe because she never imagined that Eleanor had desires—sexual or otherwise, except of course for the nightly cocktail.

Josie is about to launch into more explanations about Fred, about Eleanor's drinking, and then feels overwhelmed by the futility of it all. Why bother—she won't believe me anyway. Now they're threading their way along Storrow Drive, and Josie can only take her eyes off the road long enough for a quick peek at Leslie, who has her face turned out the window toward the bikers and joggers bobbing by the Charles River. The belt (hip western, with snakeskin and silver) of Leslie's pants nips in tight, without any fleshy folds around the waist.

This surprises her; Leslie's middle had thickened considerably in the last few years.

"You've lost weight," Josie says.

Leslie turns, her face inscrutable behind sunglasses except for a pleased smile. "About ten pounds. Feels great." She gives her stomach a pat, as if it were a small child that had behaved well. Then she scrutinizes Josie's hips. "Looks like you've lost some too."

"As my friend Monica would say, stress is dietetic." She tells her about Fiona Jones, carefully steering clear of Peter and what she's come to think of as the Monica situation.

"You know I used to have a Jackie obsession," says Leslie, actually laughing.

"When?" says Josie skeptically. It is hard to imagine Leslie ever doing anything as schoolgirlish as Jackie worship.

"When I was about nine I made scrapbooks about the Kennedys and Dad's career in Congress. You were too little to remember."

Josie has to pause for a moment; these glimpses of Leslie's childhood always come as a shock. She forgets that Leslie is so much older, that she had a whole childhood back when they lived in Washington that Josie knows nothing about—favorite toys, mean teachers, best friends. She tries to imagine nine-year-old Leslie—a chubby girl with a pixie haircut and big front teeth—cutting pictures out of old *Life* magazines with blunt scissors and gluing them in a scrapbook with white paste. Suddenly it occurs to her that she could get some mileage out of those scrapbooks with Fiona Jones. "You don't still have them, do you?"

"I don't know. I haven't seen them in years. Mom probably threw them away."

"Mom never throws anything away."

As they circle around the Crowley common, they see a black plume of smoke rising up in the rear of the Trask homestead. They exchange frantic glances, and Josie accelerates, roaring up the driveway and screeching to a halt just inches from the rear of Eleanor's car. Eleanor and Fred look up with a start. They are standing side by side next to a rusty Weber grill, which has been dragged out of the barn and perched by the kitchen steps, and Fred is squirting charcoal lighter on a smoldering heap of briquettes. He smiles over at them through the shimmering waves of smoke and flame, his white teeth demonic. Eleanor frowns and walks toward them, wiping her hands on a butcher's apron. "My goodness. Slow down. You could have hit us."

"Sorry, Mom," says Josie, not sounding sorry at all.

Leslie steps out of the car, pauses dramatically with an arm resting on top of the car door, and surveys the grounds. She smiles appreciatively at Eleanor's yellow daylilies running along the barn, and then sweeps her gaze up the back of the house to the eight-sided cupola, its tiny paned windows turned a brilliant orange in the setting sun. "It's so good to be home. I'd forgotten how beautiful New England is in the summer." She sniffs deeply. "Mmm. All those green smells."

All Josie can smell is the residue of charcoal lighter and smoke. In the car, Leslie had told her that she planned to use a "non-confrontational approach" with Fred and Eleanor, but Josie hopes she doesn't lay it on too thick.

"Mother," Leslie says simply, opening her arms and gathering Eleanor to her breast. Eleanor's eyes over Leslie's shoulder shoot Josie a puzzled look. With her arm still draped around Eleanor's tiny shoulders, Leslie turns to Fred and offers her hand. "Fred. Mom's told me all about you."

"I've heard all about you too," says Fred, waving a long-handled barbecue fork toward her, then pointing it at a platter of uncooked meat, bloody and flayed open. "I had them butterfly this lamb at the Ayer Meat Market, just for you."

Josie wonders what Eleanor has told him about Leslie. Her mother was mostly baffled by Leslie's constant faultfinding. ("Fault-finding" was Eleanor's term; Leslie called it having a dialogue.) "I don't know what I've done to your sister that's so bad, do you?" she sometimes says to Josie.

Henry lumbers by with a dented wheelbarrow, his sneakers smacking against the flagstone path. "Beep, beep. Choo, choo."

"Isn't he cute?" Leslie says to Eleanor. "You must dote on him."

"Yes," says Eleanor cautiously. "But I think your decision not to have children is very wise." Simon insisted on having a vasectomy before they were married, and Leslie was adamant that children wouldn't fit into their "lifestyle."

Josie waits for Leslie to find some hidden slight ("You are always comparing us to Peter and Josie," she'd say), but she seems to take this as a perfectly reasonable remark. "Sometimes I wonder, Mom. I see Henry and he's so adorable, I think I'm missing out."

"You *are* missing out," Fred announces over the sizzle of lamb fat. "There's no other joy in the world like kids." He squints at Leslie through the clouds of smoke. "You still look pretty young. Bet there's still time to have a couple."

Leslie gives him a good-natured smile. "Think so, Fred?"

Later, when Josie is setting the table, Eleanor silently beckons her into the pantry and closes the door. "Don't you think Leslie is acting strangely?" she whispers.

"What do you mean?" Josie whispers back.

"Well, she's being so . . . pleasant."

"Isn't that good?"

"I'm not sure," Eleanor says doubtfully. She looks down at the cocktail she's mixing and then pours in another jigger of gin.

"Careful with those, Mom," says Josie, tapping the side of the glass. She suddenly realizes that this is the first time she has made a direct reference to Eleanor's drinking.

"Oh, I will be. Just need something to steady my nerves."

Once again, Fred has outdone himself—lamb, baby potatoes freshly dug from the garden, minted peas, a silver vase of strawflowers that he has cut and arranged. He has opened two bottles of Merlot. "The man at Red Cock package said these were just the thing for lamb. I have to take his word because I don't drink," he explains to Leslie.

Josie waits for Leslie to cross-examine Fred on his drinking history. Are you in recovery? Do you attend a weekly meeting? No? Why not?

Leslie smacks her lips and dabs off the faint traces of a red mustache with her napkin. "Your man was right." She reaches across the table with her fork and spears another chunk of charred lamb. "Can't seem to stop myself. Simon won't let me serve red meat anymore."

Eleanor glances timidly over at Leslie. Josie has been monitoring her drinks and she is not, as promised, being careful—this is her second martini and second glass of wine. "Don't you think Fred is a treasure?" It comes out in a breathless gush.

"I certainly do. So Fred, tell me about yourself. Where did you learn to cook like this?"

Fred is circling around the table refilling their wineglasses, although he conspicuously skips Eleanor's. "From my Italian mama," he says jovially.

"More milk, Fred," says Henry, banging a Lion King mug on the table. Even he has developed a taste for Fred's cooking.

"Have you ever considered opening a restaurant?" Leslie's face is as sweet and innocent as Henry's when he pockets another kid's Matchbox car.

"Well, in fact I used to run a restaurant, but you know what? Running a restaurant is harder than it looks. You work like a dog and don't make a penny."

"Poor Fred had an awful experience with his restaurant," Eleanor says sympathetically. She's speaking too loudly now, and swallowing her words. Then her hand darts up to her mouth as if she realizes she's let the cat out of the bag.

"Well, that was a long time ago, thank goodness. Now all I have to do is punch a time card and wheel around cartons of hamburger patties. The life of Riley." He expertly carves off the last of the lamb and carries the platter around the table. He reminds Josie of the maids Grif used to hire the few times they had a dinner party, with black uniforms and white scallop-edged aprons. "Oh, for heaven's sakes, Grif, who are we trying to fool?" Eleanor would say, unimpressed by his highfalutin ways. "It's the way things are done," Grif would reply. What he meant, of course, was it's the way things were done—back when his father, a big-shot Boston lawyer, ran the homestead with a cook, a maid, and a full-time gardener.

"From the way you were talking about kids, I'm guessing you must have children," says Leslie. She's pushed her chair away from the table and has her hands crossed in front of her stomach, which is not looking as flat as it did that afternoon.

Josie marvels at the smooth way Leslie drops this question, as if it were a natural evolution from the McDonald's Distribution Center. Josie's been wanting to ask Fred about his kids ever since she saw the photograph on his bureau, but couldn't think of a way without his guessing that she'd been snooping. You probably learn that as a psychologist, she thinks, how to ask nosy questions as if it's your business.

"I've got two daughters, real beauties. They're both married and I've got five grandchildren now. Can you believe that? Me a grandfather, and I'm only sixty-one."

"Do you see them very much?" Leslie asks, and Josie feels a stab of empathy for him. You know he doesn't, she thinks. Why don't you lay off?

Fred's jaw sags, and he drops his eyes to the platter of lamb, as if someone had offered it to him as a substitute for his family. Suddenly he looks small and gray, much older than sixty-one. "Not much lately," he says, and before Leslie can ask, "Why not?" he's picked up the platter and is backing his shoulders through the swinging door into the kitchen.

Eleanor jumps up as if she's about to run after him but the move is too sudden. Her chair topples backward and she lurches forward into the table, gripping the edge so she doesn't fall over.

"Here, Mom. Let me help you," says Leslie, scooting around the table on her long thin legs and sliding her arms under Eleanor's armpits. Gently, she guides her mother toward the living room couch.

Later that night, after they finally get Eleanor upstairs to her bedroom with Fred's help, Josie lies in bed, wide-eyed and guilty. This was what she wanted Leslie to see, Eleanor and Fred at their worst, but now that it's happened she can't help feeling complicit. She turns over on her side so she can see Henry's little slumbering shape on the trundle bed, sleeping with his mouth open just like Peter. All day she's kept her worries about Peter locked away, as if she feared that Leslie could somehow read her mind, and now they come leaping out like goblins in the darkness. She hasn't spoken to him since that fateful phone conversation ten days ago. Occasionally she scribbles out long, passionate messages—*Nothing is more important to me than our marriage and Henry. I love you. I miss you. I cannot wait for this horrible summer to be over and for us to be together again—*

and then crumples them into the wastebasket. She's issued the ultimatum and now all she can do is wait.

The bedroom door swings open, and Josie can make out a form standing in the shadows. "Josie?" Leslie whispers.

Josie sits up in bed. "What is it?"

Leslie creeps across the floor and settles on the end of the bed. "I just wanted to tell you that you were right. The situation is much more serious than I thought. I'm glad I came." She's wearing a V-necked mint-colored sleep shirt and lacy black leggings—the kind of outfit the Victoria's Secret model lounges around in. Is this the way she dresses for Simon? He, undoubtedly, has strong opinions about her nighttime attire.

"You really think so?" She pulls her legs up so Leslie can stretch out and get comfortable. When was the last time Leslie sat on the end of her bed and they whispered in the darkness? Not for a long, long time, maybe not since the old Crowley Player days. It's possible that they never did anything so sisterly, that her memory is playing tricks on her because she wishes it were true.

"Absolutely. Mom's drinking is worse than I've ever seen it. She's out of control."

"Tonight was particularly bad." Josie doesn't have the nerve to tell Leslie that her visit has driven Eleanor to hit the bottle harder than usual.

"Don't make excuses for her. She was drunk on her ass. And that Fred—colluding with his fancy wine. He's sleazy. You know, I admit I didn't believe you at first."

"Really?" Josie says without a touch of irony. "So what do you think we should do?"

"There's only one thing we can do," she pronounces. "Get rid of him."

"Are you sure? We may be wrong about Fred. Mom really likes him."

"Trust me," Leslie whispers, and with that her mint-green body tiptoes back across the room and vanishes as quickly as an oversized Peter Pan.

*   *   *

THE NEXT morning Leslie has them all up and organized by eight-thirty. She'd read in *The Crowley Crier* that today is toxic-waste day at the dump, and she's decided that they should clean out the barn. "Look at this stuff, Mom," she says, waving a disdainful hand toward shelves of old paint cans and bags of fertilizer. "Don't you realize they could spontaneously combust and burn the house to the ground in a flash?" She snaps her fingers dramatically.

"That's what your sister keeps saying. I probably haven't given enough thought to fire safety," Eleanor says meekly.

Leslie divides them into three work groups: Fred and Eleanor will load old tools into the trunk of Eleanor's Pontiac for scrap metal recycling; she and Josie will handle the toxic wastes (she implies that Eleanor and Fred are not to be trusted with combustibles); and Henry will empty the dirt out of the old flowerpots and stack them. Josie watches Fred wheel and drag her childhood by: the old push mower her father had sometimes used (although usually he hired someone else to cut the lawn); a pair of stilts; the rake (now handle-less) they used for fall leaves; an aluminum Hula Hoop; the red Schwinn she got for her eighth birthday (Grif's parting gift). Eleanor questions every item. "Are you sure we should get rid of this? We could get some new tires and a seat for that bike. Henry would love it."

"No!" they all say in unison.

The whole exercise makes Josie feel liberated, like having a good, cleansing cry, and the momentum picks up. Eleanor starts throwing what seem like perfectly functional garden tools into the heap while Fred whistles "Heaven, I'm in Heaven . . ." By ten, the trunk is filled with rusty skeletons and Leslie dispatches Fred, Eleanor, and Henry to the dump. The car creaks and groans down the driveway, scrapes bottom, and then cruises around the green with a clunky rattle.

Leslie is bending over the paint cans, pounding the tops down with the hammer. "We don't want anything to spill in the back of your car."

Josie looks over at her, dressed now in shorts and a tank top, and studies her upper thighs, which don't look flabby or puckery even though she's squatting down. "You really do look good, you know.

Have you been exercising?" Peter has always chided Josie about not exercising more, and she'd planned to start jogging when she got to California. Now her exercise future seems as up in the air as everything else.

"StairMaster," Leslie says, smacking her haunch, which obediently does not jiggle. "It must be because I'm pushing forty."

"All you need now is to have an affair." The moment she says it, she realizes it's true. So that's why she's acting so strangely, so nice.

Leslie stands up and gives Josie a lewd smile, then grabs her wrist and pulls her toward the hammock. "Let's talk."

Josie hangs back and lets herself be yanked along by one arm like a child. She's not sure she can stomach hearing about Leslie's affair—the lies she's told Simon, the apartment she borrows from a friend for afternoon trysts, the sexual rapture. "Best sex I've ever had, never knew it could be this great; I think about it, I want it, constantly." Leslie stretches herself out on the hammock with her arms behind her head in what could only be described as a postcoital position, and Josie props herself primly on one edge. She pulls out a cigarette.

"You're smoking," Leslie says with a disapproving frown. "Give me one." She lights it awkwardly, takes a big drag, and grins. "So what do you want to know?"

"I don't want to know anything. You're the one who wanted to talk. Maybe you shouldn't tell me."

"Oh," says Leslie, sounding disappointed, and toys with her cigarette.

Josie feels a pang of guilt—obviously Leslie is busting to tell her every lurid detail. "So, you're having an affair?" she says dully.

"Yes! Could you guess? Is it obvious?"

Josie studies Leslie's face and tries to figure out why it *is* so obvious. Maybe it's the way the skin over her cheeks shines, or her musky smell. "No. Who's the man?"

"It's"—she bites her lip and drops her eyes coquettishly—"the guy who cleans our pool."

"Oh." Josie can't think of anything else to say, and feels almost ashamed for Leslie—the horny housewife and the Roto-Rooter man.

"He's not a regular pool guy, you know. He's doesn't wear a nylon jumpsuit and skim leaves out with a sieve. He's sort of a visionary."

"A pool visionary?"

"Yes, in a way. He owns this environmental pool company called Whole Earth Pool. No chemicals, all-natural filtration system. Chlorine aggravates Simon's eczema. So Ralph designed this whole new cleaning system for our pool and then kept coming back every week to check out the bacteria levels and things just . . . developed."

Josie tries to picture this. Was Leslie coincidentally sunbathing by the pool in plunging black spandex each time he dropped by? Did they have conversations about the pool filled with sexual innuendos: I think my filter needs to be unclogged; let me check your chemical level with my dipstick. Leslie is waiting for her reaction. What does she want her to be—shocked, titillated, disapproving? "Well, I suppose that's nice if it makes you happy."

"It does," Leslie says emphatically.

"Does Simon know?"

She lets out a derisive snort. "Are you kidding? If he found out, he'd probably head straight to the hospital for a triple bypass." This is the first time Josie has heard her refer to Simon irreverently.

"So why do you think you're doing this?" This is the kind of question Leslie would ask her. In the world according to Leslie, no one does anything merely for fun; there is always some ugly truth lurking underneath, being denied. "Have you and Simon been having problems?" Josie has to work hard to make this sound like a serious question. Who wouldn't have problems with Simon—that overbearing, pompous, know-it-all jerk?

"Well, yes, in a way." Leslie lowers her arms and sits up in the hammock; this is clearly not as much fun as gabbing about Ralph, the visionary pool guy. "You know about Simon's problems with his inflamed prostate."

"I guess so." Josie has always been a little unclear about prostate problems. Grif had a prostate operation a few years ago after referring darkly to "unpleasant symptoms." In Simon's case, his prostate seems to be one of his many ailments, along with his shingles and carpal tunnel syndrome, which he uses as an excuse to keep Leslie home.

"Well, lately he's been having problems with, you know . . ." Leslie's rolling a hand over and over, and Josie bobs her head along, still not sure what she's driving at. " . . . impotence."

"Oh," says Josie, once again at a loss for words. This is not a problem she's encountered before, certainly not with Peter, who always
seemed to have plenty of youthful gusto for sex. "How long is lately?"

"Maybe the last five years."

"Is this an occasional problem or a frequent problem?"

Leslie reaches for Josie's cigarettes and lights another. "I would
have to say frequent."

"Well, then"—Josie reaches out and gives Leslie's knee a maternal pat, which seems like an absurd gesture considering what they're
talking about—"no wonder you're having an affair." She and Peter
have speculated about Leslie and Simon's sex life for years. Peter
used to do an imitation of Simon's postcoital behavior. "Thank you,
my dear," he would say, kissing Josie on the cheek, "that was
extremely pleasant." Now that she knows the truth, which is much
bleaker than anything they ever imagined, it seems sad rather than
funny.

"So what about you? Have you ever had an affair?" Leslie gives
her a conspirational nudge with one knee.

"Sorry to be so boring," Josie says. "Every time I meet a possible
candidate, he never seems quite as . . . inspiring as Peter." She's
thinking of Roger Denby as she says this. His handsome face behind
those horn-rims. The same long, thin frame as Peter—only for some
reason Peter's is sexy, and Roger's is bony and undernourished. Sex
appeal—as intangible as the rhythm of a walk, the curve of an eyebrow, the lilt of a voice.

"Peter is an unusually attractive male." Leslie has said this before,
but she usually implied that it was a character flaw. When Josie was
about to get married, she said, "Oh, sure, he's handsome, just like
Dad." Suddenly Eleanor's Pontiac comes bouncing up the drive,
and Leslie scrambles off the hammock as if she's about to be caught
in the act. "He's the type that women want to have affairs with."

Josie's not sure if this is a pointed comment or a lucky guess.
"Right, except I married him," she says gloomily. "So what are you
going to do with this Ralph? Where's it heading?"

"You know what?" says Dr. Leslie T. Calderwood, Ph.D., who
once accused Josie of leading an unexamined life. "I've decided I'm
just not going to think about it too much."

*   *   *

BY THE NEXT afternoon, they've worked through the barn and the basement and are now tackling the stifling attic. Their numbers are diminished to two—Eleanor has pulled a muscle in her back and has taken to the porch, Fred is at work, and Henry has gotten bored with the whole production and is over at Allison's. Leslie and Josie are stripped down to their bathing suits (Leslie in plunging black spandex and Josie in a gingham bikini bought during one of those Florida vacations), with their hair pinned up on top of their heads. Every hour or so they go down to the lawn and hose off the rivers of sweat, as they did when they were kids. They've managed to wedge open the two tiny windows and have set up an electric fan in one with the futile hope of getting a cross-breeze stirring.

"God, what is that smell?" Josie says once again. All the musty odors of the homestead seem to be concentrated up here, and she's sure they're going to find something decomposing in one of the cartons they're sorting through, stacked four-deep everywhere. They've already found a few shriveled bat carcasses under the eaves with little pulled-up hands and grimacing teeth, which Leslie is able to sweep up into the dustpan without even a shudder. In summer, bats were always insinuating themselves under the eaves, and swooping down the hallways, until Eleanor dispatched them with her old wooden Dunlop.

Leslie cuts the tape on a box marked "L. & J. Winter clothes— 1972" and pulls out a gray flannel jumper, now a Swiss cheese of moth holes, a red tartan kilt with a matching tam. "Remember these?" she says bitterly.

Josie peers in at a navy cardigan and yellowed blouse with a Peter Pan collar. "Mmm," she says. They've never been able to joke about the clothes from the church rummage sale they had to wear after Grif left. Eleanor picked out good-quality, sensible clothes with labels from Saks and The Scottish Wool Shop that were twenty years out of date. If she bought something newer, there was always the risk that the former owner might recognize it at school, which happened more than once for both of them. Without another word, Leslie tapes the box shut and drags it over to the discard pile.

Some of the boxes are more fun: Grif's college papers ("C+:

Found your analysis of *Othello* to be somewhat rambling and vague"); Grandmother Fahnstock's collection of painted teacups. All the while they're having whispered consultations. First, there's Fred and what to do about him. For the last two nights, Leslie has stayed up late with him, and has coaxed a few tidbits out of him. (Leslie is quite proud that she's gotten him to open up, but it sounds to Josie as if he was perfectly willing to confess everything she wanted to know.) He has told her about the two daughters—Renee and Sylvia—who felt humiliated by his arrest and never forgave him. "Not that I was such a great father," he said, "because I was a drunk." And about his wife, Sylvia senior, who divorced him while he was in prison and married his younger brother. "The funny thing is I always thought they had a thing for one another, since we were first married. I just gave them a handy excuse." Fred was less forthcoming about the Mama Rizzo's arson.

"Did he say he did it?" Josie asks. She still secretly hopes that he's innocent and has a perfectly plausible explanation for his arrest— that he was framed by his shady business partners, or that it was set by a disgruntled employee and he was actually trying to put the fire out.

"He didn't say he did it, but he didn't say he didn't do it, which I find significant," says Leslie in an authoritative voice. She's worked with women prisoners in Arizona, who always say they didn't do it, that they've been set up. Leslie has figured out her strategy for getting rid of Fred—she's simply going to tell him it's in Eleanor's best interest that he leave.

"And you think that will work?" says Josie doubtfully. She'd expected something a little more ingenious: a threatening letter from a lawyer; contacting his parole officer; at the very least enlisting the help of Allen Railsback, the minister who got Eleanor involved in doing good deeds at MCI Crowley in the first place.

"He says Mom's the most important person in his life. Really, that's what he said. So if he means it, he'll do what we ask. It's kind of a test. And if he refuses, we call the cops."

Josie thinks this logic seems flawed—he would only leave if he really did care about Eleanor, and would refuse to go if he was a scumbag. So if they get him to leave, that means he should really stay. The whole conversation about Fred, along with the blast-furnace heat and the moldy smell, makes Josie's head spin, and she decides to leave it up to Leslie, the expert on criminal behavior, after all.

Leslie also fills in more of the details about Ralph Cavanaugh — that he wears a small gold hoop earring, has a blond ponytail streaked with gray, drives a brown Isuzu, was married for ten years but doesn't have kids. That he is also long and lean — like Peter and Roger Denby — but definitely seems to possess the Peter intangible. That sometimes they meet in the afternoon in a country and western bar and slow-dance to the jukebox.

"Well, at least you won't run into Simon," Josie says. Simon disapproves of anything except classical music.

"He thinks I'm beautiful," says Leslie in an incredulous way that Josie finds touching. She looks over at Leslie's freckled shoulders glistening with sweat, the smudges of dirt on her cheeks, the tendrils of hair that have broken free of the topknot and are curling down her neck. She is beautiful, at least when she's not scowling, but Simon has probably never bothered to tell her that. "And he thinks I'm fun."

Josie almost laughs out loud, but then she realizes that for the last two days they've been having fun together, for the first time that she can remember.

As they sort through a steamer trunk of old sheets, so mildewed and frayed that even Eleanor doesn't use them, Josie finds herself confessing her dark fears about Peter. "I haven't spoken to him in almost two weeks," she says. "It's so weird. We've been apart for two months and it's like we're not even together anymore. Peter never chose to spend his life with me, it just ended up that way," she says. "I went to his apartment for coffee once and I never left, like a stray cat. He married me because of Henry. That's the only thing that ties us together."

"The only thing?" says Leslie, who's stopped sorting linens and has settled her bare legs onto the dusty floor so she can fix her concerned shrink look on Josie.

"Well, what else is there?"

"Oh, I don't know. What about shared interests? You know — all that American Literature stuff."

Josie shakes her head skeptically. Leslie never understood exactly

what Peter and Josie were studying in graduate school; didn't com-
prehend that they dwelled in different centuries.

"All right," Leslie says, seeing that Josie is unconvinced. "What
about love?"

"I love him. I don't know if he loves me."

"Do you think you're so unlovable?"

Josie shrugs and busies herself refolding a stack of sheets. She
feels pitiful, the way she usually does when she asks Louise for
advice, as if she's begging for flattery.

"You're smart—much smarter than I am. You're a wonderful
mother. You're good company. You've got a great body. What more
could Peter want?"

"I don't know." But she does know—he could want someone who
was brilliant about all that pop-culture stuff—Jackie Susann, Jackie
Kennedy, Jackie Collins—who thought the age of Jackie mattered.
Someone who wasn't going to be a weird misfit in California, who
didn't have old poems rattling around her head. Someone who
hadn't grown up in a house like this.

"It seems like you two have a lot to talk through," says Leslie the
marriage counselor.

"But we can't, not until he's evicted Monica."

"Look, Josie, don't get into some stupid standoff. If you want to
talk to Peter, call him up."

"But what if Monica answers?"

"You say, 'Hi, Monica. Can I speak to Peter?' "

Leslie slams the trunk shut, drags it over to the discard pile, and
then drags a big square carton off the top of the next stack. The lid is
labeled "Leslie's Desk" in Eleanor's loopy script, and the inside
looks like a jumbled drawer—rusty paper clips, dried-up Scotch
tape, ballpoint pens. "God, look at this junk. Didn't she ever throw
anything away?" Leslie starts shoveling handfuls into a plastic
garbage bag, tossing in bundles of letters without a second glance.

"Isn't there anything you want to save?"

"My letters from Frankie Derby? I don't think so."

Josie doesn't say anything when Leslie drops in two Concord
Academy yearbooks. Leslie had to transfer from Concord to Ayer
High School the year Grif left because he said he couldn't afford the

tuition anymore—another subject, like their clothes, that's too painful to talk about.

At the very bottom, Leslie unearths two oversized scrapbooks and heaves them across the floor. "Here you go. Send these to Fiona Jones."

Josie kneels down and spends a few minutes examining these artifacts, which feel as ancient and foreign as a papyrus manuscript sealed up in a clay jar. The covers are padded burgundy leatherette tied together with silky cords; the pages are pulpy beige construction paper, so brittle that they crumble when she turns them. On the flyleaf of the first scrapbook, nine-year-old Leslie had printed in aquamarine ink: "Griffon L. Trask, United States Congress, Massachusetts, 3rd District, 1958–1964." The scrapbook is a chronological record of Grif's congressional career starting with a 1957 newspaper clipping announcing his candidacy (FITCHBURG LAWYER TOSSES HAT INTO RING FOR O'BRIEN SEAT) and ending with a clipping on his defeat in '64 (VASKIAN BESTS TRASK), and in between congressional memorabilia: a letter from Eisenhower congratulating Grif on his election; a photograph of Grif speaking on the floor of the House (Josie wonders how many times Grif actually gave a speech—her impression is that he spent most of the time going to Georgetown cocktail parties); a campaign photo of Eleanor pinning a "Trask for Congress" campaign button on Leslie; the program from JFK's funeral. Each object has a tidy and completely superfluous peacock-blue label: "Letter from President Eisenhower," "Photograph of Congressman Trask," "Campaign button."

"Why did you make these?" Josie says finally, feeling as if she's asking a prying question, more invasive than anything she's asked about Ralph Cavanaugh.

"It was a social studies project for fourth grade." Leslie has stopped shoveling out the box and is squatting down in the dust, watching Josie turn the pages from a six-foot distance, as if she can't bear to get too close. "We were studying the different branches of government. It was the first year we were back in Crowley, and I wanted to impress everyone that my father had been a congressman and had gotten a letter from Eisenhower. And then I made the scrapbook about the Kennedys because I wanted them to think we were friends with the Kennedy family." She exhales sharply through her nose, as if to say, "Isn't that pathetic."

She walks over and flips the Kennedy scrapbook to the last page. "See. This was the grand finale." A piece of powder-blue stationery with rectangular yellow stains where the Scotch tape has shriveled up and fallen off; the spidery handwriting as familiar to Josie as her own.

November 17, 1957

Dear Mrs. Trask,

Thank you so much for the dear stuffed lamb for Caroline. It looks very cunning sitting on her toy shelf. Jack and I were so touched by your thoughtfulness.

Sincerely,

Jacqueline B. Kennedy

Josie knows from the tell-all memoir by Jackie's secretary that Jackie batted out these notes by the hundreds, that most of the baby presents for Caroline and John were sent straight to the Salvation Army.

"I found this old letter to Mom and I thought a real letter from Jackie would make the other girls like me," says Leslie, her voice sharp with scorn. Is it scorn for those cruel girls, or for herself? "Nineteen sixty-six was a bad year," she concludes.

The year 1966 was part of the Trask family lore, the worst year of their lives. Moving back to the tumbledown homestead with its leaky roof and sputtering furnace, Grif trying in vain to restart his law practice, Leslie having a hard time "adjusting" to Crowley Elementary after the Potomac School. "The only good thing that happened," Eleanor used to say, "was that we had a brand-new baby." But Leslie didn't think so, Josie muses. I was probably the last straw. She made these scrapbooks so someone would pay some attention to her, and probably all they accomplished was to make everyone hate her more. And then there was her baby sister, who was always so agreeable, so uncritical; who was Mommy and Daddy's favorite from day one. No wonder she always hated me, thinks Josie, understanding for the very first time.

Leslie is still staring down at the Jackie letter, as if in a trance.

Josie considers going over and wrapping her arms around her shoulders. She imagines their thin, slick arms rubbing together—awkward, uncomforting—and decides not to. They've never been huggers; the closest they ever got was a peck on the cheek. Josie stands up and slips the scrapbooks under her arm. She wants to hide them away in her room before Leslie can change her mind and shred them page by page. She reaches down and tucks one of Leslie's sweaty tendrils back under a bobby pin. "Let's go have a beer and a cigarette," she says.

THE FIRST GLOOMY glow of dawn is filtering below the shade, and the birds have started their morning riot, when Leslie wakes her. Not with a word but with a touch, smoothing the hair off her forehead. She opens her eyes slowly, unstartled. Leslie is sitting next to her on the bed, studying her in a sad way. *Is she sad for me or herself?* Josie wonders.

"I wanted to say good-bye. My cab's here."

As predicted, Simon has summoned her home after three days. He called yesterday just as Josie and Leslie had settled on the porch with bottles of Corona (Leslie's new favorite—because of Ralph?) and cigarettes. The computer system, with patient medical and billing records, had crashed. Leslie knew he was hopeless when it came to computers, didn't she? Yes, of course, said Leslie, but Josie was glad to hear the sarcastic edge in her voice as she promised to be back in time to fix his dinner.

Josie sits up in bed and hugs her knees. She feels inexplicably sad too, the way she used to when Leslie would go away—to camp, to college—and leave her behind, the little kid at home with Eleanor. "How'd it go with Fred?" she says. Leslie had stayed up late with Fred last night talking, presumably telling him to leave.

"Good, I think. He says he'd been planning to leave anyway. He doesn't like his job here, and he's got a cousin who owns a restaurant on the Cape. He says he'll hire Fred as the assistant chef." Leslie raises her eyebrows skeptically. Who knows, who cares if it's true, just so long as he goes.

"I guess that's for the best," says Josie, trying not to think about how Eleanor will take this news.

"It is," she says. The cab honks, and Leslie stands up. "And promise me you'll call Peter."

Josie lies back down and shuts her eyes, listening to the hard slap of Leslie's leather-soled flats on the stairs, the screen door slam, the cab with a cracked muffler backing down the drive. She's not willing to think of Eleanor yet, how old and tired her face will look when Fred tells her he is leaving. Has he told her already? Has she spent the night in his arms, weeping? Instead she tries to imagine Leslie walking through the airport, stopping at the newsstand for a *New York Times* and gum, fastening her seat belt, ordering a Corona. Maybe she's arranged for Ralph Cavanaugh to pick her up at the airport—she told Simon she wouldn't be home until dinnertime, after all—and they'll spend the afternoon at an airport hotel. But Josie pictures them instead at the country and western bar—a low stucco building in the middle of a sunbaked parking lot. Inside, it will be cool and quiet except for the hum of an air conditioner, the blinds pulled down so only a few bars of white hot light seep through. They will drink Coronas in silence, and then Ralph will drop a few quarters in the jukebox, and they will stand together, and he will slide his arms around her waist, hooking his thumbs over her snakeskin belt so his hands can hang limp, and she will turn her head to one side and nestle one of her sharp cheekbones into his shoulder, while his ponytail rubs back and forth along the side of her neck, tickling her ear.

chapter 5

He's a decent man with an abundance of common sense.
—JACQUELINE KENNEDY ONASSIS

◈

Josie examines Eleanor's face closely over breakfast. She is peering through her half-moon reading glasses at an article on pruning lilacs in the home section of the *Boston Globe*. It's a cool morning, with the first bit of fall snap, and she's wearing a quilted robe in cranberry-red flannel which Josie gave her for Christmas a few years ago. The color is becoming, Josie decides; it makes her cheeks look pinker, a nice contrast with her white hair. Eleanor puts down the paper and smiles at Josie, a beautiful, straight-toothed smile. No, she definitely doesn't know about Fred yet.

"I think Leslie's visit went very well, didn't you? I wish she could have stayed longer." This is a switch; Eleanor usually heaved a sigh of relief after one of Leslie's blitzkrieg visits.

"Yeah," says Josie. "Leslie looked good, didn't she?" She considers telling her about Ralph Cavanaugh, thinking it might give Eleanor an evil thrill; she's always felt patronized by Simon. But mostly it would make Eleanor worry, might even give her insomnia. And then she'd let slip some flat-footed comment (I hope you're not spending *too* much time around the pool), and Leslie would know that Josie had spilled the beans. Nope, forget it. Mothers can't handle affairs.

"She and Fred really seemed to hit it off. I'm glad you girls like him so much." As she says this, her blue eyes, which at times can look milky, turn translucent like cobalt glass. She gazes over Josie's shoulder out the back window toward her weeded vegetable garden, the cleaned-out garage, the trash cans that the raccoons for once did not tip over during the night. All is right with her world.

Josie stands up and picks Henry's sneakers off the floor. "Got to run. I'm spending the day at the Boston Public Library." She bends down and kisses the top of Eleanor's head, right at the crest of her pink part, and inhales Breck shampoo. Do they still make Breck shampoo?

At the Boston Public Library, in the vaulted, echoing reference room, Josie scrolls through the computer guides with a kind of masochistic pleasure. The entries under "Maurice Tempelsman" list dozens of books and periodical articles. Good, it will take her all day, especially with the library's surly runners, who are either losing call slips or taking a break. She files a dozen requests for books on the African diamond industry and sits down at a long table with green-shaded reading lamps under a spot marked "178" to wait, for once not impatient.

Half an hour later, a boy with half his head shaved head dumps three books on the diamond cartel in front of her with a sneer. For two hours, she tries to understand what kind of man would make a fortune as a middleman in industrial diamonds and uranium; would become the confidant of African potentates. What is even more mysterious to Josie is why Jackie would choose him. If one assumes that Jackie could have had almost any man she wanted to be her consort, any of those proper Groton-Yale WASP men that she had grown up with, why did she pick Tempelsman — a married man, an Orthodox Jew? Josie studies the magazine pictures of him taken right before Jackie's death. A portly man in a trench coat, putting his arms tenderly around Jackie, who, even when deathly ill, looms taller. He reminds Josie of . . . Fred.

Maybe handsome first husbands are a youthful habit you out-grow — like frosted eyeshadow and short skirts. Even if JFK had lived, Jackie might have cast him off eventually for the comfort and devotion of a Maurice Tempelsman. Someone who loved you when you were old and tired out, someone whom you didn't have to impress.

Jackie's Camelot years were a single relentless effort to be impressive—with her clothing, her entertaining, her interior decorating, her knowledge about the arts, her mothering. The memoirs by her secretary and Evelyn Lincoln expose the massive effort it cost Jackie to be perfect. Planning her wardrobe two seasons in advance, reviewing sketches and fabric samples, arranging fittings. The memos to White House staff about every detail—how the rooms should be dusted, how tea sandwiches should be prepared, what kind of food should be served to John and Caroline—so that JFK could blow through at any time, look around him, and see nothing but perfect order and beauty. What a relief it would be to give that all up.

Josie thinks of her favorite photograph of Jack and Jackie—they are sitting at an empty banquet table at the end of a formal White House dinner. He is leaning back in his chair, his elbow on the table, his hand holding a cigar, gazing out ahead. His mouth is open and he is speaking. And she is leaning toward him, over the empty seat between them, in a strapless dress, her hair swept up in a French twist so you can see the graceful curve of her back and neck. Her long white gloves are thrown over the back of her chair. She is the perfect wife, sixties-style—beautiful and adoring.

Josie spends the afternoon in the periodical room ferreting through old *Forbes* magazines ("De Beers: Can a Cartel Be Forever?" or "Maurice Tempelsman's African Connections") and whirring through microfilms of the *Wall Street Journal*. By five, she has a splitting headache, and a stabbing pain darts down the side of her neck and one shoulder. She drives home feeling virtuous, a penitent who's been through self-mortification.

She tries to imagine what kind of scenario there will be with Fred and Eleanor when she gets home. Maybe the deed is done. He's come back from his job, told Eleanor he is leaving, she has had a sinking spell of tears, but by the time Josie gets home at seven the crisis will have passed over like an afternoon shower. Or maybe he has no intention of leaving and will tell Eleanor her daughters are trying to get rid of him. Then what? Oh, fine, Josie thinks, let him stay. Let him stay, and let me get away.

She finds Eleanor on the porch, alone, not reading or doing a crossword puzzle, but sitting motionless. Josie can't make out her expression because she's sitting in a chair that's pushed deep in one corner, a chair no one ever sits in because one leg is loose, and her whole body is cloaked in shadow. "Mom?"

"I'm here."

Her voice is drained and flat, but at least it doesn't sound as if she's been crying. Josie doesn't think she can handle Eleanor's crying. She's only seen her mother cry a few times, and then it was always for other people's grief—a bad biopsy, a bad husband—never for herself. "Is anything the matter?" Josie asks. I am an awful person. How could I have done this?

"Fred is leaving. That's all."

"What did he say?" Please don't let her know the truth. Josie kneels down on the floor in front of her, clasps Eleanor's soft, wrinkly hands in her own, and looks up at her. Her eyes are staring, her hands are cold and clammy. Oh God, Josie thinks, she's already starting to die.

"His cousin is going to give him a job at his restaurant on the Cape. He says he needs to get away from here and get his life going again." Her voice is matter-of-fact.

Josie starts rubbing her hands, trying to warm them up. "I'm sorry. I'm so sorry. I know how much you're going to miss him."

"I never knew how lonely I was until Fred moved in. I'd forgotten what it was like to have someone to talk to every day. Someone to tell everyday little things. I think it's going to rain. Isn't it terrible about O. J. Simpson. I need to fix that hole in the screen door." The voice is still detached and objective, as if she were talking about somebody else.

Josie's eyes fill with hot tears and she wipes them against Eleanor's hands. "Maybe we can get Fred to change his mind. Where is he?"

"He went to his AA meeting. No, he's right. He needs to get away from here, where everyone knows he just got out of MCI. He has to quit that awful job. It's time for him to leave, and I'm happy for him." Eleanor looks down sadly at her, and wipes the tears off Josie's cheeks with the back of her hand. "I'll be all right."

Josie searches for something to say, some comforting words. "Henry and I could stay through the fall." Suddenly this seems like a plausible idea. Henry could go to the nursery school in the church basement; Josie could get a job in the Crowley Library, or be a substitute teacher in the high school. On the weekends, she could work on Ada Silsbee. Maybe this is what is meant to happen—she will never live in that house in the Berkeley Hills, she will stay here.

"You think that's what I want? For you to end up like me?" She shakes her head and smiles bravely.

AN HOUR LATER, they've both managed to pull themselves together. Josie makes a decent pasta dish out of the gourmet treats Fred has left in the refrigerator (sun-dried tomatoes, Gaeta olives, extra-large capers, fresh basil), plunks Henry with his bottle and blanket in front of *Beauty and the Beast*, sets two places in the dining room, lights the candles, opens a bottle of Chianti. She pours out two glasses and clinks hers against Eleanor's.

"To us."

"To changes," says Eleanor. She then describes the article on pruning lilacs that she read this morning. "You may have noticed how leggy the lilacs out front have gotten. I've decided I'm going to cut them all the way back."

"Good idea."

"Yes," says Eleanor, gazing deeply at her red-streaked wineglass. "Sometimes you have to hack things down to the nub."

They lapse into silence, and Josie can feel Eleanor's dark mood seeping back to the surface. "Hey, guess what? Leslie's got a boyfriend."

Eleanor looks up, startled. "What?"

"Yeah. She told me all about it. She's having a fling with the guy who cleans their pool. That's why she was looking so good."

Eleanor opens her mouth to say something and then starts laughing silently, with her shoulders shaking. She waves her hand in front of her face as if she's trying to make herself stop. "I suppose it's not funny."

"Yes, it is."

"I was just thinking about Simon. What he would say if he knew Leslie was having an affair with . . ." She starts laughing again, even harder.

". . . the pool guy." Josie starts laughing too. It's all ridiculous—Ralph Cavanaugh, and Fred Rizzo, and Fiona Jones, and Monica Glass. And Eleanor, and she herself. Two months ago her life was normal. What has happened?

"Oh, my," says Eleanor, dabbing at her eyes with the corner of a large white napkin. "I suppose it's very wicked of us to make fun of Simon."

"Probably," says Josie and they grin at each other.

The back door slams and Fred calls out, "Hello."

"We're in here, dear," Eleanor yells, sounding mercifully chipper.

Fred pokes his head through the swinging door. "Hi, girls." He casts an appraising glance toward Eleanor. "Looks like you two are having a good time. What's so funny?" He walks behind her chair and rests his hand on her shoulder, bends over and brushes his chin for an instant along the top of her head.

"Oh, nothing. Just mother-daughter talk," Eleanor says.

Without turning around, she reaches up and strokes his hand. It's an oddly intimate gesture, more intimate than a kiss. Josie wonders why they feel they can be publicly demonstrative now that Fred is leaving.

Fred sits down, refills Eleanor's plate with a helping of pasta, and eats it himself. "You're lucky to have such great girls, Eleanor."

AT MIDNIGHT, Josie creeps down the dark hallway. She pauses at the top of the stairs and listens for voices, or sighs, or sobs, but there is nothing but the faint hum of traffic far away on Route 2. You can hear it sometimes late at night if the weather is about to change. She has never understood how sound travels, just one of many things she doesn't understand and probably never will—electromagnetic fields, supply-side economics, plate tectonics. And probably the day will come, sooner than she thinks, that Henry will expect her to explain such things, and then what will she do? Recite Longfellow?

She pads down the stairs, slowly enough so the treads don't squeak. Moonlight streams through the fanlight over the front door, and Josie steps into the brilliant arch illuminated across the floor. She stretches out her arms, fans out her fingers and admires them—as perfect as alabaster, all freckles and moles erased. Then she strolls through the rest of the downstairs rooms and studies them as if she were seeing them for the first, or last, time—the wheat sheaves sculpted into the doorframes, the lion-claw feet of the sofas and tables, coiled as if any moment they would spring across the floor. In the ghostly light, the homestead is restored to its former grandeur; the poor caretaking of the last generation is wiped away.

In the kitchen, she pulls a chair over to the wall phone and dials by moonlight. She doesn't dare break the mood by turning on the overhead; maybe the Trask spirits (although she's never felt they were particularly benevolent) will be her guardian angels. As the phone rings, she recites lines from one of her crumpled-up letters— *I love you, I miss you, nothing is more important to me than our marriage.* Monica answers.

Just do what Leslie told you to, Josie reminds herself. "Hi, Monica, it's Josie. Can I speak to Peter?"

"No," she says. "He's at some faculty party." Then silence—no helpful details, no how are you doing. The voice is icy and formal, the way it used to be with Stedman after they had broken up.

"Could you please tell him I called?" Josie says in a slightly pleading way. Don't be mad at me. Move out, disappear, but let's still be friendly.

"Fine," Monica snaps, and then a click.

Josie stares at the purring receiver and tries to figure out what just happened. Monica may still be at Peter's, but she's pissed off about something, and at least she didn't go to the faculty party as Peter's date.

She hangs up the phone and then, with a shiver of premonition, looks up. There, standing motionless in the shadow of the back stairs, is Fred—watching her.

She jumps back, sending the aluminum kitchen chair skidding across the linoleum. "What?" she calls out, loud enough so Eleanor might hear in the front of the house. She can't really bring herself to scream. "What do you want?"

He reaches over to the wall and switches on the overhead light, a coiled neon tube that flickers and then flashes on, as bright as a klieg light. She blinks and squints over at Fred. He's still dressed in the same white polo shirt and khakis, but his expression is grim. "Sorry to startle you," he says. The voice is low, barely above a whisper, but fierce. "We need to talk."

Josie edges backward toward the swinging door to the dining room. Why is he sneaking up on her in the middle of the night? "About what?"

"About this." He raises his hand, and there is the white folder from his desk drawer. From across the room, Josie can read the word "Eleanor" in black marker on the file tab. His voice is still low, and ominous.

"What about this?" She puts her hand up on the swinging door and positions her feet for a sprint start. The high school track coach used to berate her on her sprint starts. Why didn't I pay better attention?

He starts walking toward her. "It's about your mother's finances. I wanted to review some figures with you." He sits down at the kitchen table, puts on his reading glasses, and pulls the list of stocks and the furniture appraisal out of the folder and spreads them out on the table.

Josie changes her expression, from fear to mere wariness, but doesn't budge from the door. "I'm listening," she says.

He looks over at her, perplexed. "You can't see much from over there." He pulls out the chair next to him. "Have a seat."

She hesitates, then slowly crosses the kitchen and sits down, not in the proffered chair but two chairs down. "What's in that folder?" she asks in a voice that strikes her as remarkably sincere. Could he really not know she'd been snooping, or is this some elaborate charade? She glances back toward the door and decides she could still get a head start if he lunged at her. She sticks one leg out for her sprint start.

"This is some financial information your mother gave me a couple of months ago. You don't know this, but she's been really concerned about her finances. Her money is starting to run out. She didn't want to tell you girls because she didn't want to worry you." He shakes his head reproachfully.

Who's he disgusted with, Eleanor or me? Josie wonders.

"So you have to promise me you won't tell your mother what I'm about to tell you. Okay? Josie, are you listening?"

She's staring stupidly at the documents on the table. Why hadn't she thought to question Eleanor's financial situation before this? *Why was I so incurious?* she thinks. *I just assumed she'd muddle along the way she always had.* Josie raises her eyes to Fred's. "Yes, I'm listening."

"Okay," he says, studying her face skeptically for a moment. "Now, here's the list of your mother's stock portfolio two months ago. These were basically the same stocks she inherited from her mother in 1967. Mostly blue chips—General Motors, General Electric, Bell Telephone. Very conservative, not much growth. They're only giving her an income of about ten thousand a year. Her only other income is alimony from your father, and that's dropped to six thousand."

"Yes," says Josie in her crisp, academic voice, feeling inexcusably stupid and irresponsible. She didn't know anything about Eleanor's stocks, or even about how much alimony Grif paid her. Could Eleanor live on $16,000 a year? She hardly spent anything. Of course not—that would barely cover taxes and utilities on this house.

"So she's been spending principal—about eight thousand dollars a year. And at that rate, her money will be all gone in about ten years."

Josie nods, unable even to say yes anymore. She's remembering all the money she's borrowed from Eleanor over the last five years— one hundred here and three hundred there. Eleanor always sent the check with a note saying, *Now don't worry about paying this back.* And Josie didn't worry.

"So here's what I've done." He pulls out another list from his folder, one that hadn't been there a month ago, and a copy of the *Morningstar Newsletter.* "I've sold some of her stocks and switched them into Fidelity Mutual Funds. See? Their highest-rated funds. Some of them are earning as much as twenty percent." He opens up the newsletter and points out the performance ratings of Fidelity funds highlighted in yellow. "So that's helping, but she still needs to do more."

"Such as what?" *All right, here it comes,* Josie thinks. *He's going to propose some wild investment scheme. A real estate trust, a time-sharing condo.*

He folds his hands on top of the folder, his white nails lining up neatly, and gazes at her earnestly over the top of his glasses. "She needs to sell this house and most of the furniture in it. Some of these antiques are worth a lot. I figure she could bank as much as two hundred thousand and move to a much smaller place."

Josie almost laughs out loud. "Is that all? Then why doesn't she do it?"

"Because she thinks you and Leslie would mind. She says the house has been in the family for two hundred years and she doesn't have the right to sell it. She wants to save the furniture for you and Leslie to have in your own homes."

It's not my fault, she thinks, it's Grif's fault. He's the one that saddled her with this fucking albatross, he's the one who's not paying her enough alimony. She's going to end up like Jackie's aunt, Edie Beale, in a wreck condemned by the board of health, eating cat food. Only I can't bail her out. "I hate this place," Josie explodes. "I want her to get rid of it. Tell her that."

"You have to tell her that."

"All right. I will. Tomorrow." To show her good faith, she moves her sprinting leg in and tucks it under the table. "How do you know so much about financial planning, Fred?"

"I subscribed to *Money* magazine when I was incarcerated." He shrugs. "I know it sounds crazy. I figure out how to handle money after I pissed away every cent I ever had."

"I've misjudged you, Fred. I wish you would change your mind and stay. My mother really . . ." Josie considers all the proper WASP terms of endearment—is fond of, cares for. "My mother really loves you."

"And I love her."

He says it so sweetly and plainly that Josie's heart jumps, as if someone had said it to her. And then, incredibly, she feels a pang of envy. When was the last time someone said he loved her? Peter said it, again and again, before he left for California, but it almost felt like a teenager begging for permission to use the family car. *If I say I love you, will you let me go, will you stop being mad at me?* And Henry said it all the time, whispered it wetly in her ear, his breath smelling like pancake syrup. But that didn't count, did it?

"But I have to get out of here. I have to get away from MCI. I have to quit my job. I plan to keep seeing her after I move to the Cape, if that's all right with you."

"Are you asking my permission to date my mother?"

"I guess I am." He neatly stacks all the papers and slips them back in the file marked "Eleanor."

But history made him what he was . . . this lonely sick boy.
All the time he was in bed this little boy was reading history . . .
Marlborough . . . the Knights of the Round Table. If history made
Jack that way, made him see heroes, then maybe other boys will see.

— JACQUELINE KENNEDY

The next day, Saturday, nothing goes as planned. Before Josie can talk to Eleanor about selling the homestead, she has gone off with Allen Railsback to spend the day at MCI. On Saturdays, they take care of the children during visiting hours, so the prisoners can have a chance to talk privately with their significant others. "Prison is such a frightening place for children," says Eleanor, heading out the door as straight-backed and noble as a missionary plunging into the bush. Josie hopes she might have a chance to have another heart-to-heart with Fred about Eleanor, but he's gone too — off to the Cape to talk to his cousin about the chef job and find a place to live. Even Henry has plans for the day that don't include her — he's going to the Fort Devens Air Show with Allison.

Josie wanders around the house in Peter's Stanford T-shirt and white socks, wondering how she's going to spend the rest of the day. There's her Maurice Tempelsman memo to write up, and maybe she could mine Leslie's scrapbooks for a memo on Jackie's portrayal in popular ladies' magazines. She finds herself sitting on Eleanor's unmade bed, dialing Peter again, but this time there is no answer.

Where could Peter and Monica be at seven-thirty in the morning? Best not to think too much about that one.

She's sitting in front of her computer, staring at a stack of micro-film printouts about industrial diamonds, when the phone rings. She runs back down the hall, throws herself across the bed, grabs the phone on the fourth ring. Peter was in the shower, of course. She pictures him stepping out, water drops beading on his naked body, hastily throwing a towel around himself. "Hi, Peter," she says breath-lessly.

"Josie?" a man says.

"Roger?" This is the second time she's mistaken him for Peter; the poor guy is going to get a complex. Or think that she's delusional, that she wanders around calling strangers Peter and trying to kiss them.

"I missed you at the library. I was afraid you'd gone back to Cali-fornia."

"I missed you too," she says passionately. She hasn't seen Roger since she tried to wrestle him to the ground two weeks ago, and sud-denly she realizes she hasn't had anyone to talk to about Jackie.

"I was wondering if you had a chance to look over my manu-script."

"I'm about halfway through it," she lies, trying to remember where she left it. Was it still in the trunk of her car? "It's very inter-esting. You've created a very complex portrait of McGeorge Bundy."

"Really?" His voice rises boyishly. "That makes me happy, that you liked it. Do you think we could get together sometime to talk about it?"

"Sure."

"I don't suppose tonight would work, would it? I have something I want to give you."

"Tonight would be perfect," she says. After she hangs up, she stretches out on Eleanor's bed and thinks, I'm going out to dinner in Harvard Square. I'm going to leave Eleanor, and Fred, and Henry, and have a conversation with an adult. I'm going to get drunk on margaritas, and watch street jugglers. I'm going to go to a bookstore and splurge on expensive quality paperbacks. I'll put it on my charge card and I won't feel guilty. Then, still dressed in a T-shirt and anklets, she runs down to her car, finds the two boxes of *McGeorge Bundy and American Foreign Policy, 1960–1968* in the trunk, picks them up with such a surge of relief that she actually kisses one of the boxes, right over the Strathmore label. She lugs the boxes upstairs, trying to figure out how fast she has to edit if she's going to get it finished by six. Eighty pages an hour, she figures—doable, very, very doable.

I have something I want to give you. He had sounded excited as he said that. What could Roger Denby possibly want to give her? A recommendation, the galley proofs of *McGeorge Bundy and American Foreign Policy,* a love letter, a poem he had written especially for her—there were a lot of possibilities.

Roger's book, thank God, turns out to be much better than she expected. Its long multi-claused sentences dash forward and duck back elegantly, like a contra dance. *Bundy was a man of mathematical intelligence and Yankee flint, raised on violent lawn sports and in Groton cubicles; a man with an exacting, analytical mind who knew how to be charming at parties.* The description reminds her oddly of Roger himself, even though she doesn't think he was probably very good at violent lawn sports or charming at parties. But he was full of contradictions like McGeorge Bundy—New England formal and down-at-the-heels academic, analytical and self-doubting, athletic and stumbling over a tree root. Endearing and thoughtful with his sandwiches and iced tea and cigarettes.

Peter was never thoughtful. Once, when he had forgotten their anniversary, she had said, "That's all right. You don't do thoughtful." He could be kind in small ways—such as getting up early with Henry on weekends so that she could sleep late, or bringing her a cup of coffee when he made himself one; spontaneous acts of kindness, nothing that required any planning. And he was always lustful for her, not in a generic lusty way, but in a specific way, for her and her body, which felt like a small kindness. But when he was away from her, she suspected that he never thought of her, at least not in a thoughtful way. He didn't see a sweater in a store window or read a book review and think, oh, Josie would like that, not the way she did.

She works hard at editing Roger's book; she wants to impress him.

Maybe he has an editing job for her, maybe Ruth Stadler was right—she should become a book editor. She brackets out academic jargon such as "arguably" and "pedagogically" and spruces up his lead sentences. She has to admit that she's learned a thing or two about writing from Fiona this summer. Not about good writing, exactly, but how to hold a reader's interest. How to tell a story to make her (Fiona's readers are all women) feel as if she's eavesdropping on a conversation at the next table in a restaurant—holding her breath and trying not to clank the silverware so she doesn't miss a word.

She edited Peter's book too, but his writing was like A.M. radio, full of hyperbole and commercial breaks. *In Jennifer North, the sexpot starlet who commits suicide rather than succumb to a mastectomy, Jacqueline Susann has created a camp doppelgänger to the beheaded heroine of our era—Jayne Mansfield.* Her role as his editor was to hold him back, rein him in, protect him from his own self-indulgence. Sort of like her role as his wife.

By five-thirty, she's finished. She steps back and admires the six-inch-high manuscript on her desk, yellow Post-it notes fluttering from its edges like those pennants they used to have at gas stations. Then she takes a long soaking bath and puts on her one good summer dress—a retro orchid-print sundress from a trendy store in Providence (picked out, alas, by Monica), with wide straps and a heart-shaped neck that shows a lot of cleavage. Peter calls it her killer dress. Take that, Peter, she thinks as she slips into a pair of skimpy sandals, brushes on mascara (a makeup sample also, alas, from Monica), and spritzes herself with Eleanor's Shalimar. *I'm going out on a date.*

"Sure it's okay for me to go out?" she asks Eleanor, who's sitting in one of the boudoir chairs reading *Curious George* to Henry. *George wondered if he could flap his arms and fly like a bird. He was very curious. Splash!*

"Of course. You deserve a night out. You work so hard." She looks up and inspects Josie's image in the mirror. "You look lovely, but don't you think that outfit is a bit revealing for the city? I wouldn't want you and your girlfriend to get into any trouble."

Josie has only told her that she's having dinner with a friend from the library, and Eleanor has drawn her own conclusions. In her Smith worldview, two unescorted women could get a lot of unwanted attention from strange men, especially if one was dressed provocatively. Eleanor opens a bureau drawer and pulls out a navy cashmere cardigan that smells of mothballs. "Here, wear this. I got it in Bermuda on my honeymoon." She waits while Josie slips it on, then fastens the pearl buttons one by one up to Josie's chin and pats her shoulder. "There, now. Much better."

Josie parks by the Loeb Theater and then strolls down Brattle toward the Harvest Restaurant, which Roger promises has a festive terrace. A boy and a girl, both wearing spandex bicycle shorts, are sitting on the curb sipping foamy coffee drinks. It's only been two months since she's been around other students, but they seem miraculously young and vibrant. What wouldn't seem vibrant after two months in Crowley—home of the old and the incarcerated?

She sees Roger leaning against a skinny maple tree, reading the *New York Review of Books*. She strips off the cardigan and tosses it jauntily over a bare shoulder. "Hi," she says, dropping her tote bag with Roger's manuscript on the sidewalk with a thud.

He lowers the paper, and smiles tentatively. Then he looks her over, up and down, and literally does a double take. "Wow! You look great." He leans over shyly and gives her a peck on the cheek, and she leans over and gives him one back.

"You look good too." And he does. He's not wearing his glasses, and has replaced his usual khakis for some pleated linen pants that she feels sure must have been picked out by his unadored woman friend. He's even shed his library pallor for a tan, and the end of his nose is slightly sunburned. Clark Kent into Superman.

He smiles, showing a lot of white teeth that contrast nicely with his tan. "Went sailing in Maine for a week."

As they walk into the Harvest, she speculates about whom Roger went sailing with. His old girlfriend, perhaps? Maybe in the last two weeks he's decided he adored her after all, and they had a blissful reunion on the deck of a tossing sailboat. She finds this notion irritating, but she's not exactly sure why. Does she want Roger to be unattached, or is she just jealous that his love life is less bereft than hers? They sit down on metal chairs perched unsteadily on a wavy brick terrace. A squirrel on a shedding ailanthus chatters at them—pastoral beauty, Cambridge-style. "Who did you go sailing with?" she asks.

"My brother and his wife. Our family has a place in Seal Harbor."

Seal Harbor conjures up all sorts of rugged images—surf crashing against giant boulders, the smell of salt and decaying shellfish, the sting of freezing cold water against bare flesh. Roger at the helm of a graceful sloop, expertly weaving through a chain of tiny islands. She takes a deep sip of her margarita, and then licks the coarse salt off the rim of her glass. She tries to think of something intelligent to say about sailing off the coast of Maine. "Yum."

"What?"

"My drink. It's good."

"So's mine." He raises his martini (straight up with an olive) and clinks it against hers. "How are things going with Jackie?" he says, staring deeply into her face after a quick glance toward the top of her dress.

"Fine. I'm working on Maurice Tempelsman." What does she mean, working on? She sounds like a dentist.

"Maurice Tempelsman," he says thoughtfully, propping his elbow on the table and leaning toward her. "He really is very interesting."

"You think so?" she says eagerly. Roger, bless his heart. How she's missed him over the last two weeks, her Jackie confidant. "I'm trying to figure out what she saw in him."

Roger polishes off his drink and orders seconds for both of them. The waiter deposits their appetizers—a plate of tiny sushi and a calamari salad. "He was urbane, sophisticated," he says, lowering a calamari into his mouth by one tentacle.

"But he invested in African diamonds. He supported apartheid. How could JFK's widow be involved with someone so politically incorrect?" she asks.

"We're talking about the widow of Aristotle Onassis too, you know. I don't think being politically correct was part of Jackie's agenda. He was fun. He helped her invest her money so she became even richer. He loved her."

She could never talk to Peter about Jackie—not like this. He tended to regard her abstractly—what did the bouffant hairdo and the sleeveless dress signify? He didn't consider her a real person with regular human motives for doing anything. When she asked him, "But why did she marry JFK?" he said, "How should I know?" Peter's opinion on Jackie seems somewhat beside the point, now that she hasn't talked to him in two weeks. "Do you think love is enough?" she asks.

"I don't want to talk about Maurice Tempelsman, Josie. I want to talk about you. How are things going with your husband? I've been really worried about you."

She drags a piece of sushi through a pile of wasabi, pops it in her mouth, and waits while the tingle spreads out through her sinuses. "I'm not sure. He told me he was going to evict the woman he's been living with. That was two weeks ago, and I haven't spoken to him since." As she says this, she realizes how irretrievable her marriage sounds. "So maybe she's not living there anymore." Maybe she's moved out since last night. "Everything is probably fine."

Suddenly Roger's hand snakes across the table, between the sushi plate and the dish of teriyaki sauce, grabs hers, and holds it tightly against the rim of her butter plate. "I think your husband is a fool."

She looks down at their entwined hands, at her wedding ring being set lopsided by Roger's fingers. She and Peter had bought the cheapest wedding bands that they could find, and now hers is all dented and misshapen. But the patina is so rich. She loves her wedding ring.

"Look, Josie, maybe you shouldn't go back to your husband, not after the way he's been treating you. There are other options. I could probably help you get a job at Rutgers next year. Teaching freshman comp. Or you could be my research assistant. It wouldn't be much, but it could tide you over."

I've flirted with him, I've confessed my marital problems, she thinks. I've even tried to find out if he's patched things up with his old girlfriend. But now that he's obediently pledging his devotion, I'm not sure. Suddenly the waiter appears with their baby lamb chops and grilled salmon, and their hands fly apart like teenagers caught in the act. She waits until the meals have been set down and explained by their waiter, prophetically named Peter.

"That's a wonderful offer, but I don't know what's happening with my marriage." Why do I always refer to Peter as an institution when I'm talking to Roger Denby? "We have a child. We have to work things out, if we can." Great words, Josie. Eleanor would approve, Ann Landers would approve. But what does Peter think? Does Henry mean anything to him? He loves him, of course, but would he change his behavior because of his love for Henry? Would he not come on to Monica, or Rebecca, that undergraduate who had the hots for him, because he loved Henry? And if I love Henry so much, why am I here? I should be in California, working on my marriage. I don't know, she thinks in despair, piling green peppercorns on a wedge of salmon. I don't know.

"Josie?" says Roger.

"What?"

"You suddenly seemed very far away."

She stares over at him, his sunburned nose fading in the dusky night. "But if things don't work out, maybe I'll take you up on your offer." She tries to imagine herself living in some shabby yellow brick apartment building in New Brunswick, New Jersey, stepping into a library carrel in September as Roger Denby's research assistant. A scenario as remote and strange as living in a cedar house in the Berkeley Hills. "Now let's talk about McGeorge Bundy," she says, holding up the tote bag with his manuscript.

He reaches over and fills her wineglass. "All right," he says and grins boyishly, like Clark Kent. Who was much cuter than Superman, Josie always thought. What was Lois Lane's problem, anyway? She flatters Roger shamelessly about his book, which really is clever (in fact, she suspects he gave it to her so she could see how good it was, not for her editorial comments), and he laughs in an embarrassed way.

"But you need a new title. Something catchier," she concludes.

"Academic books don't have catchy titles."

"Who says? You wanted a little more Fiona Jones, right? This book is about McGeorge Bundy's failure. First for pursuing a wrong-headed policy in Vietnam, and then for not denouncing it when he realized it was a failure. So how about"—she makes a flourish with her hand—"*McGeorge Bundy and the Broken Promise.*"

Roger repeats the title slowly to himself and smiles. He pushes back a piece of sandy hair that has flopped down over his eyes, which seem quite blue in the flickering mustard glow of the bug candle.

After dinner, Josie has a double espresso to sober up for the drive home.

"Remember that I told you I had something to give you," Roger says, reaching into his briefcase.

"Oh, right," she says, having forgotten.

"You told me that time at the library that Fiona Jones was on your case and that your research for her was forcing you to stay here."

"That time at the library" is Roger's tactful way of referring to the time she kissed him. I would have said anything, she thinks, I wasn't responsible for my actions. "I guess I did tell you that."

"So I found something that might help you." He holds up a large manila envelope that has "For Josie" written in an urgent-looking hand across the front.

He hands it to her, and she hefts it, trying to guess what it could be. It seems to hold a few papers, practically weightless. She looks over at him and cocks her head to one side.

"It's Teddy White's original notes for the Camelot interview."

"The library gave you the notes for the Camelot interview?" she says, annoyed. The reference librarian had been adamant that the Camelot interview was closed until May 1995—a full year after the death of Mrs. Onassis. No exceptions, she had told Josie (who had been bludgeoned by Fiona into asking for special permission), for *anyone.* So why did Roger Denby get special treatment? Because he was a full professor, because he was on the Emily Smith DeForest Fellowship, because he was writing obsequious things about the Kennedy Administration (not true, actually, but maybe they thought he was), because the reference librarian thought he was cute? It wasn't fair.

He shakes his head. "They're not from the Kennedy Library. I found them in Teddy White's papers at Harvard, stuck away in a file marked 'Miscellaneous and Unidentified Notes.' They were in two envelopes that White had labeled 'Sent to Kennedy Library' and 'Not Sent to Kennedy Library.' He had terrible handwriting, and the archivist probably couldn't read it. White donated most of the notes and drafts to the Kennedy Library in 1968, with the stipulation that they remain closed until a year after Jackie's Kennedy's death. But . . ."

Josie is leaning over the table toward him, as close as she dares without setting her hair on fire in the candle. He gives her a teasing smile because he knows that he's telling the story as if it were a conversation eavesdropped from the next table, knows that he's got her hooked. She's being careful not to clank her silverware.

"But he kept copies for himself, which ended up at Harvard. And it seems that White didn't send everything to the Kennedy Library. Some of the things that Jackie told him were so personal that he decided they should never be made public. He kept those, and hid them away. Until now. I had Xeroxes made of everything in both envelopes. So you have the official Camelot interview and the unofficial Camelot interview."

"What do the notes say? Tell me."

"Believe it or not, I didn't read them. I wanted to give you the first crack." He's sitting back in his seat now, the mischievous smile gone. The story is over.

She glances down at the manila envelope, her hands actually trembling. Roger Denby has just handed her the future. An article, maybe even a book, something to make a professional name with. Forget Fiona Jones. This is mine, she thinks. "I don't know what to say."

"Don't say anything. I wanted to help you. And if it helps you finish up your job, and get back to your husband, then so be it. I'm happy for you."

I'm happy for you. That's what Eleanor had said about Fred Rizzo's leaving. Could I ever be that generous? If Peter said, "I've found the woman I want to be with," would I say, "I'm happy for you"? Of course not.

Roger walks her back to her car. The effects of two margaritas and two glasses of wine have worn off. In fact, she feels hyperalert—the streetlights are buzzing and glaring, the car fumes are extra noxious. It's the adrenaline rush from the Camelot notes, she thinks, hugging them tighter against Eleanor's sweater, which she's now wearing. She opens the passenger door, places the envelope reverently on the seat, and considers for a moment putting the seat belt over it. Then she stands up and turns to face Roger, having a sinking sensation that she will never see him again. "I can't thank you enough."

Suddenly he steps toward her, slips his arms around her waist, bends her over backward, and kisses her. A big openmouthed kiss, his tongue against hers. She closes her eyes, rocks back on her heels, lets her body settle against his arms, and kisses him back. And then, just as suddenly, he sets her upright and steps back again. "Keep that in mind," he says. "In case things don't work out with your husband."

Before she can say anything, before she can feel embarrassed and apologize, or even more likely suggest that they go back to his apartment, he has turned around and is walking away quickly down Brattle Street. She leans against a parking meter with a shiver and reaches up to button Eleanor's sweater. "I will," she whispers.

WHEN SHE GETS home at the stroke of midnight, she finds a note from Eleanor waiting on the kitchen table.

> *Peter called while you were out. Says he*
> *will call back later tonight. Henry was an*
> *angel. Hope you had fun.*
>
> > *Me*

Josie reads it, wads it up in a tight ball, and tosses it across the kitchen into the trash can. Peter was much better at wastebasket basketball; she usually missed. Well, not tonight, she thinks. She's heading up the stairs when the phone rings. Why is he calling so late? she thinks crossly and considers letting it ring. But he'll wake up Eleanor, if he hasn't already, and then Eleanor will come and get her. And won't understand if she refuses to talk to him. "Oh, fine, I'll answer it," she mutters, heading back downstairs to the kitchen.

"Yes."

"Josie?"

"Hi," she says, feeling shy. It's been so long since she's talked to Peter that she marvels at his voice, how deep and resonant it is as he says her name.

"Well, I said I wouldn't call until I did it. So I did it." Now his voice doesn't sound so marvelous, it's sarcastic and pissed off.

"Did what?"

"What do you mean, did what? Got rid of Monica. Like you told me to."

That's not true, she wants to say. I just talked to her last night, she answered the phone at your house as if she lived there. "When did this happen?"

"Today, if you must know. We loaded her stuff into a U-Haul, and she moved into a garden apartment in Piedmont. Where there presumably aren't any stalkers."

His tone lightens up slightly, as if he's trying to make her laugh, but she's past seeing the humor in any of this. "How does Monica feel?"

"Oh, come on, Josie. How do you think she feels? She's been kicked out by people she thought were her two best friends. She's hurt, and angry, and thinks she's being treated unfairly. And frankly I don't blame her."

I'm not sorry, Josie thinks stubbornly. She flirted with Peter, she came on to him, she made me feel like the third party. It's all her fault. "I think it's for the best."

"Well, I'm glad someone's happy."

I'm happy for you. "It doesn't make me happy. I just think it's for the best."

"So where were you tonight? Out on a date with the sandwich guy?"

"His name is Roger Denby. And it wasn't a date. We had dinner together."

"What did you wear?"

This strikes her as a sweet question. "That sundress with the orchids on it."

"Your *killer* dress. You went out to dinner with this guy, this Roger Denby, and you wore your *killer* dress." He sounds more wounded than indignant.

"It's my only summer dress. What am I supposed to wear? Blue jeans? Borrow a dress from my mother?"

"Christ, Josie. We're not that broke." Wounded has given way to contrite. "Buy another dress if you want to. Put it on our Visa card."

"This is not a conversation about my wardrobe. I had a legitimate reason to have dinner with him. I edited his book on McGeorge Bundy, and he wanted to thank me."

"Oh, well. I can certainly tell him from personal experience what a great editor you are. Creative, penetrating, tireless, enthusiastic. How else did he thank you?"

"What's that supposed to mean?" she says with cold fury.

There's a pause. When he starts talking again, his voice is quiet and pleading. Her old Peter. "I'm sorry. I don't know why I'm being such an asshole. It's just that this guy clearly has the hots for you. It's not so innocent."

Well, he's right about that. All the things she told Roger about Peter, that was hardly innocent. Roger offering to help her get a job, giving her the Camelot notes—that wasn't so innocent either. And the kiss. She pictures herself bending over backward, melting into Roger's arms, thrusting her tongue toward his molars. Yes, well.

"I'm not sure I would call your relationships with other women innocent either," she says in a reasonable way. I am giving Peter a dose of his own medicine. *A dose of his own medicine*—God, what a stupid expression. Eleanor said that.

"Maybe." This conversation is going nowhere, proving nothing except how estranged they've grown. "So what's going to happen to us, Josie?" He sounds worn out, and so is she.

"I don't know. We've got a lot to talk about," she says. Peter's classes end next week. He's still planning to come east so they can drive to California together, isn't he? And then they'll have five days together in the car—plenty of time to talk it all through.

"How's Henry?"

"He went to an air show at Fort Devens today. He said the stunt planes could do loopty loops just like Dumbo."

"I miss him. I miss him so much."

There is a catch in his voice, and she wonders if he is weeping.

chapter 17

A talk with Mary Todd Lincoln a week after Lincoln's assassination would not have been nearly as compelling, for Jacqueline Kennedy was a superior wife, a superior person, and wise. But as she began to talk, I realized that I was going to hear more than I wanted to.

—THEODORE H. WHITE

She thought her husband was truly a man of magic, which is a lovely thought in any wife.

—THEODORE H. WHITE

That night, as Josie falls asleep, she purposely does not think about Roger's kiss or Peter's tears; she's afraid either might give her bad dreams. Instead she muses about Jackie and the secrets she told Teddy White. She reaches under the pillow, where she's hidden the manila envelope, and caresses one corner, thinking here lies the answer. The answer to what? The answer to everything.

In the morning, she finds Eleanor on her hands and knees in the garden, pulling up shriveled pea plants. This would be a perfect time to suggest that she sell the homestead, but Josie doesn't have time right now. She's on a mission, an urgent mission to find the truth. "Can you watch Henry this morning? There's some work I need to do for Fiona, or else." She slashes her hand dramatically across her throat.

Eleanor stops pulling plants and sits up, not looking particularly pleased. Why should she? Josie thinks guiltily. She watched kids at MCI all day yesterday, and she had Henry last night. But this is important, she reminds herself.

"All right," says Eleanor, sounding resigned. "Come on, Henry. Come help Grammy in the garden."

Henry runs over with a dripping hose. "I help you," he says. He's cute, Josie tells herself as she walks upstairs, and we won't be here that much longer. Grammy doesn't mind, not really. She closes her bedroom door and locks herself in. The key scrapes and scratches as it throws the bolt, and it occurs to her that this corroded lock may never unlock again. It doesn't matter, she thinks airily, because we're selling this dump.

She sits at her desk and places the manila envelope squarely in front of her. Not yet, she won't open it yet. She remembers her American poetry professor at Dartmouth, an ancient, stoop-shouldered man with funny orthopedic shoes whom the younger faculty laughed at and kept trying to retire. He began the semester by reciting from *Song of Myself*:

> *You shall no longer take things at second or third hand . . .*
> *You shall not look through my eyes either, nor take things*
>   *from me,*
> *You shall listen to all sides and filter them from yourself.*

Yes, she thinks, I shall listen to all sides.

She pulls out a copy of Teddy White's autobiography, *In Search of History*, to brush up on his version of the Camelot interview so she'll be able to figure out what he left out. He tells a good story, a classic Jackie story.

It was a week after the assassination, the day after Thanksgiving, and he was in the dentist's chair in New York City. His ancient mother, who was staying with his family for the holidays, called the dentist's office, frantic. Jacqueline Kennedy wanted him, right away, in Hyannis Port. There was something she needed to tell the world, and he must say it for her.

White called *Life* magazine and told them to hold the presses and then prepared to leave for Hyannis Port. Suddenly his mother, unused to taking phone messages from Jackie Kennedy, keeled over with a heart attack. What should he do—go to the hospital with his mother or drive through a hurricane to Jacqueline Kennedy? What a question! Go to Jackie, of course.

She shooed all relatives and hangers-on away, and sat with him on a small sofa talking in a trancelike monologue from eight until midnight. He jotted down notes about her appearance: *compo-sure . . . beautiful . . . dressed in black trim slacks, beige pullover sweater . . . eyes wider than pools . . . calm voice.* Three subjects ran together—the grisly particulars of JFK's murder, her plans for the future, and how JFK was going to be treated by history.

> —*there'd been the biggest motorcade from the airport. Hot. Wild. Like Mexico. The sun so strong in our faces. I couldn't put on sunglasses. Then we saw this tunnel ahead, I thought it would be cool in the tunnel.*
> —*I could see a piece of his skull coming off. It was flesh-colored, not white . . . I can see this perfectly clean piece detaching itself from his head. Then he slumped in my lap, his blood and brains in my lap.*
> —*the ring was all bloodstained . . . so I put the ring on Jack's finger . . . and then I kissed his hand.*
> —*I saw myself in the mirror, my whole face spattered with blood and hair. I wiped it off with Kleenex. History! I thought, no one really wants me there.*
> —*Caroline asked me what kind of prayer should I say? And I told her, "Either, 'Please, God, take care of Daddy,' or 'Please, God, be nice to Daddy.' "*

Whew, thinks Josie. She's not used to this Jackie; she's used to the buttoned-down Jackie who said things like "Thank you so much for the dear stuffed lamb for Caroline." Now that she feels ready to listen from all sides, she pries open Roger's manila envelope and takes out a pile of smudgy Xeroxes. Is this all? she thinks. It doesn't look promising.

She starts with the thicker pile, much thicker, with a Post-it note from Roger identifying it as "Sent to Kennedy Library." It contains a misspelled letter from White and a typed transcript, messy and uncorrected, of his Camelot notes.

Dearest Jacquie:

Herewith my rough-typed notes of our sad conversation last November. They must remain rough-typed (and I hope you excuse the messy script) for I have never let anyone else see them, not even my secretary or Nancy.

I have left out of my transcript one or two matters so delicate I could not commit to paper, no matter how private.

What could White have left out that was *more* private and delicate than a description of the pink ridges inside JFK's skull? She goes through the transcript and pulls out all the quotes that didn't appear in his autobiography.

—I'm not going to be the widder Kennedy.

—I'm going to live on the Cape, I'm going to be with the Kennedys; Bobby is going to teach Johnny. He's a little boy without a father, a boyish little boy, he'll need a man.

—That was the first thing I thought that night—where will I go? I wanted my old [Georgetown] house back. But then I thought—how can I go back to that bedroom. I said to myself—you must never forget Jack, but you mustn't be morbid.

—Hill threw his coat over Jack's head; and I held his head to throw the coat over it. It wasn't repulsive to me for one moment—nothing was repulsive to me.

—I always remember when Ambassador Kennedy had his stroke, Jack said don't let that happen to me. I thought "I'll take care of him every day of his life. I'll make him happy." But I knew he was dead.

—Doctors are so bossy, they boss you around. I remember his operation at Columbia when I was supposed to be with him, we promised each other, and then they took him away and I didn't see him again for hours and hours and I said: they're never going to keep me away from him again.

—I saw them put him in the coffin . . . he was naked . . . I guess they just put his little body in.

—*This is the closest thing I have to a memory of him—it's a*
  man's wedding ring. He bought it in a hurry in Newport
  when we were married.
—*That baby was so beautiful. You know. Jack's Irish mystique.*
  When we buried him, I asked Jack, "Just give me something
  for Patrick, to remember him," so he found this one. [She
  held out her hand. There was a ring with emerald chips.] So
  I have one for Jack and one for Patrick.

Josie unclips the "Not Sent to Kennedy Library" stack. Three
Xerox pages of Teddy White's handwritten notes. Not full pages, but
fragments, written in a cramped, awkward script that looks like a
twelve-year-old boy's. Josie stares at the scribbles.

—*Jack hd. his girls—knew that—bt. loved me—proud of me.*
—*once thght. I'd leave him—when I younger—*
—*can you imagine? if I had, alone when he died.*
—*Patrick not like first baby—Jack there—didn't have to beg—*
  cried first time.
—*our children—brought us together—more children*
—*begin—couldn't make other happy, but learning, getting*
  better

She drops the notes back on the desk and stares out the window,
tears stinging her eyes. There's nothing here. I thought I was going
to find something important, something that I could publish, and
it's nothing. Gradually her disappointment gives way to anger toward
Roger Denby. How could he have done this to me? How could he
have gotten my hopes up?
She picks the notes up again and wonders why Teddy White
bothered to suppress them. What is she missing? She sits down at
the computer and tries to reconstruct Jackie's monologue from the
notes.

Jack had his girls. I knew that. But he loved me the most, I
knew that too. And he was proud of me. There was a time, when

I was much younger, that I didn't think I could deal with his girls. That I thought I might have to leave. Imagine if I had left him, if he had been all alone when he died.

Jack didn't let me down with Patrick, not the way he did with the first baby. He was there. I didn't have to beg him to come back.

Our children brought us together. And there would have been more children, of course.

In the beginning of our marriage, we didn't know how to make one another happy. But we were learning, we were getting better.

Josie looks away with a shudder, feeling as if she's been caught reading someone's diary. In a way, she is reading someone's diary, isn't she? So this is what Teddy White was covering up—not some immense truth, but a small, ordinary truth. A week after her husband's brains had been spilled in her lap, Jackie admitted that heroic, magical Jack was less than a heroic and magical husband. What strikes Josie as even more touching are the excuses and justifications Jackie made to forgive his betrayals. "Jack had his girls, but he loved me the most. We were learning how to make one another happy, we were getting better." Jackie had nursed the illusion that eventually, if they were together long enough, if they had enough children, her marriage to Jack Kennedy would become a happy one.

Jackie was good at making up stories—the story of the Camelot marriage was like the story of becoming the queen of the circus. But I make up stories about my marriage too, thinks Josie, with happy endings and sad endings. Who knows where the truth lies?

She wonders what Fiona would make of these revelations—probably plenty. In true Fiona Jones–style, she could inflate three pages of scrawled notes into a cover blurb—*The shocking truth of the Camelot Interviews! A week after the assassination, the tearful widow admitted that her marriage was a loveless sham.* Josie imagines Fiona's face (or how she's come to imagine Fiona's face based on the hectoring voice over the phone line) with its ever-present cigarette and half-moon glasses perched halfway down her beaky nose, flipping through the Camelot notes and underlining all the good parts with a red marker. Like the part about the inside of JFK's skull, and seeing his naked body lowered into a coffin. Jack had his girls—possible chapter title?

No, Josie thinks, I can't do it. Fiona's going to have to unearth her own scandals about poor old Jackie; maybe that stewardess from Olympic Airways really does have some dirt (how Jackie left crumpled peanut wrappers all over the floor during transatlantic flights). Josie gathers the Xeroxes up in a crooked stack, stuffs them back in Roger's manila envelope, folds it in two, and dumps it in the wastebasket next to her desk (a squat tin one with Grif and Eleanor's wedding invitation shellacked to the front). How could she have thought Jackie's suppressed Camelot notes could have saved her academic career? She's been spending too much time around Fiona Jones. She stares up at the yellowed photocopy of Ada Silsbee's tintype taped above her desk. Ada gazes off to the right as if something curious has caught her attention, her lips pulled back in a half-smile. "I guess we're stuck with one another," says Josie out loud.

When she deletes Jackie's monologue, the computer flashes back to the main screen with two file folder icons marked "Peter" and "Josie." How odd. She hasn't thought of Peter all morning; she's been able to put that awful phone conversation right out of her mind. She looks at the little Peter file folder and for the first time wonders what's in it. For some reason, it had never occurred to her to snoop through it before. Probably because she assumed that nothing was in it, that he wouldn't leave anything incriminating in the computer his wife was using for the summer. But now all this detective work has gotten her curiosity going. People left incriminating things around to be found, smart people like Teddy White. Even though she has just protected Jackie from the onslaught of Fiona Jones, this was different. This wasn't Jackie, this was Peter.

She clicks on the Peter file, and half expects that it won't open, that she'll need a password. The document list flashes up.

Articles
Book Reviews
C.V.

> *Henry*
> *Job Applic.*
> *Lecture Notes*
> *Letters*
> *1966*
> *Recommendations*

She inspects it, disappointed. What had she expected: "My Secret Diary"; "Love Affairs—Rebecca"; "Love Affairs—Monica"? She considers looking through the letters, but can't quite bring herself to do it, so she clicks on Henry instead.

Jan. 6, 1991

Tonight I became a father. Our baby, our son, was born at 3:26 A.M. He poked his head out, all covered with black hair, and started to cry. I knew before seeing the rest of him that it was a boy. And then Josie pushed him out the rest of the way, and they stretched him out on top of her, and she laughed with joy. It sounds stupid, but I was so amazed that it was a baby, with arms and hands and feet and a mouth. I don't know what I thought was growing in there.

Later, after they had moved us up to a hospital room and Josie had fallen asleep, I sat and held the baby. He had a blanket wrapped around him like a cocoon and had this hat on his head that looked like an elf's. I stared at him for over an hour, while the room turned pink with the sunrise. I tried to figure out who he looked like. His mouth is perfect, like Josie's, but he has kind of a big nose, at least for a baby. Then it hit me—it's the Stadler nose. Not my nose, but Harry Stadler's nose. Suddenly I missed him and wished he could see us—Josie and me and our baby—my family. And then just as I was thinking that, the baby opened his eyes and looked at me. I tried to figure out what color they were but they don't seem to be any color. He looked ancient and wise, and I knew my father was there, watching us.

My family. I have a family. How did such a thing happen me? What did I do to deserve this blessing?

The diary goes on for several pages. A real baby diary with first steps and first words recorded, but Josie has snooped enough for one day. She clicks on File, then walks over to the bedroom door, turns the rusty lock, and sets herself free.

chapter | 8

I'm going to bring up my son. I want him to grow up to be a good boy. I have no better dream for him. I want John John to be a fine young man. He's so interested in planes, maybe he'll be an astronaut or just plain John Kennedy fixing planes on the ground.

—Jacqueline Kennedy

The things you do with your children, you never forget.

—Jacqueline Kennedy

The next afternoon they are busy preparing for Fred's good-bye party. Henry is convinced that this is a birthday party, the only kind of party he knows about, and has insisted that Josie take him to Toys "R" Us to buy decorations. They spend a long time in the party decoration aisle trying to decide on the theme—Aladdin, Sesame Street, or Lion King? Josie personally prefers Aladdin because the rubbery blue genie on the party hat reminds her of Fred. It seems that everyone reminds her of Fred—first Maurice Tempelsman, and now the genie. Will she keep seeing Fred everywhere after he leaves?

"Come on, honey. Make up your mind," she says.

Finally, he wrestles down a huge shrink-wrapped Lion King Party Pak for eight, which includes a tablecloth, plates, cups, napkins, hats, noisemakers, party-favor bags. There are only going to be five for dinner, including Allen Railsback, and she can't see him wearing a Lion King party hat. She glances at the price tag—$10.99. "I don't think we need this big package. Let's put it back, okay?" she says.

Henry sets his lip. "No!"

"Oh, fine." What the hell, it might cheer everyone up. Eleanor had gone around all day looking as if she'd been diagnosed with a terminal illness. Josie throws in two packages of streamers, balloons, and a box of birthday candles. "Let's go."

When they get back, they find Eleanor in the kitchen attempting to roll out a bowling-ball-sized lump of cannelloni dough. She's decided that she's going to make an elaborate feast for Fred, and has gotten food for all his favorite recipes. The kitchen looks like a scene out of "I Love Lucy"—flour is sprinkled across the floor, the pounded veal cutlets are laid out like dead rodents on the kitchen table, a pot of tomato sauce is boiling over on top of the stove. And Eleanor looks like Lucy Ricardo, with a crooked tomato-splattered apron and hair falling down over her sweaty face.

"Christ, Mom. Let me help you."

"No," she says grimly. "I want to do it all by myself. I want Fred to know I'm not helpless."

"Well, look," Josie says, dividing the dough ball into quarters with a knife. "I think it will work better if you try to roll out a smaller piece." She puts one of the dough balls on a sheet of wax paper and rolls out a long thin strip. Not as exquisitely delicate as one of Fred's, but good enough.

"I guess you're right," says Eleanor, sounding utterly without hope.

Henry insists that they set the table for eight people. Together they spread out and center the paper tablecloth and set a party hat, noisemaker, and bag at each place. Henry puts on a party hat and runs around the table with a blower, while Josie hangs a cluster of balloons from the crystal chandelier and drapes twisted streamers over the windows and doors. This was the way Eleanor used to decorate it for their birthday parties. Josie can't actually remember any of her parties, but she has a clear image of the dining room decorated like this, so she must have had birthday parties. She looks over at Henry, who is now on his stomach coloring a large piece of cardboard on which she's written "Good-bye, Fred, and Good Luck!" Will Henry remember anything of this summer? Probably not, and he won't remember this house either, because by next summer it will be gone from their lives.

She stands by the swinging door and studies the room. The bow-front mahogany sideboard with the silver cake basket and crystal decanters, glowing a rich amber in the afternoon sun. The tattered Oriental rug faded to peach and rust. Fred's right, she does mind that Eleanor will sell every remnant of her past. But it is only a slight gnawing, like a hunger pang.

"Oh, hell's bells," Eleanor wails.

Josie pushes through the door into the kitchen. Eleanor has moved on from the cannelloni to making a cake. The kitchen is, if anything, an even bigger disaster—the cake pans and the battered porcelain Mixmaster have been pulled out of the cupboards, slabs of dough are draped all over the counter, there are now two saucepans boiling over on the stove. Eleanor is studying her *Fannie Farmer Cookbook.* She looks up; one cheek is streaked with flour.

Josie bursts out laughing. "Let's go out to dinner. How about take-out Chinese?"

"That isn't funny," says Eleanor, wiping her forehead with a clean corner of her apron and taking a long sip of iced tea. "You don't seem to realize how important this is to me."

"Okay, sorry. What's wrong?"

"I need confectioners' sugar and there aren't enough eggs. I'm going to the store." She unties her apron and heads into the back hall for her pocketbook.

Josie glances around the kitchen—this is worse than a disaster— and takes a quick swig of Eleanor's iced tea. It's spiked with vodka. How could she have been so blind; Eleanor's drunk and it's only four-forty. "Mom, I'll go to the store," she calls out as the back door slams. Josie runs after her, grabbing hold of her shoulders just as she's opening the car door. "I'll go," Josie says, snatching the keys out of her hand. Eleanor stops, looking puzzled. "You go turn off the stove and relax. Keep an eye on Henry. He's coloring a card and he won't bother you. I'll be right back, okay?"

Eleanor pivots slowly around toward the back door, still clutching her pocketbook, pushing back a damp piece of hair. "Oh, all right," she says, opening her pocketbook and handing Josie a ten-dollar bill.

As Josie circles around the common, she sees Allen Railsback pushing a lawn mower in front of the church. Thank God. She'll talk to him when she gets back from the store. He must know something already about Eleanor's drinking. He'll help me, I know he'll help me, she thinks over and over as she drives to Ayer. This fucking place, why do you have to drive five miles to get confectioners' sugar? And something else, what was it? Eggs, right, eggs. Eleanor can move to someplace like Newton, and then she won't have to drive five miles for eggs. So what do I do? I can't go to California with her like this; she will die. We'll do an intervention. Right. Leslie will come back and handle everything. And then Eleanor will join AA and be all better. Perfect.

Josie runs down the aisles looking for the baking-goods section and grabs a box of confectioners' sugar, then dashes over to dairy for eggs, and swings by frozen foods for ice cream. Henry always likes ice cream with his cake—vanilla fudge ripple. By the time she arrives at the express checkout, she's panting like a marathoner.

"In a rush?" the girl asks, flashing her braces.

"Making a birthday cake." She points toward the Trues in the rack of cigarettes behind the salesgirl's head. "Those too," she says, smiles, and slaps down the ten. You know birthday parties, they drive a person to cigarettes, or worse.

On the way back, she thinks of Allen Railsback, willing him to still be there. She pictures how his shirtless body looked as it pushed the orange mower. Stringy arms, ribs showing, a round tuft of blond hair in the middle of his chest. She's glad Peter doesn't have chest hair that looks like that. He has a nice amount of dark, curly chest hair, not so little that he looks like one of those underfed English actors, not so hairy that you feel you're curling up to a gorilla. One of her Dartmouth boyfriends, Stu, was covered with a pelt of hair—not only on his chest but over his shoulders and down his back. Disgusting, but that's not why she broke up with him. What kind of chest hair does Roger Denby have?

Oh, dear, Allen is gone, she thinks as she circles back around the common. But he's left his lawn mower there, in the middle of the lawn. And it's still running, she can hear it. She'll have to tell him that when he comes for dinner. Someone has pulled a car up on the middle of the common, at a crazy angle. He must have been drunk, a drunk driver. She can even hear a woman yelling, a noisy drunk. Well, at least Eleanor wasn't the drunk driver. There's Allen Rails-

back. He's bending down over something in the road. Now he's
standing up and he's waving at her. There's Fred, he's standing up
and waving too. And there's Henry's Lion King party hat, right in the
middle of the road. Why did he leave it there? That bad boy.

She pulls up behind the crooked car, and gets out. The party hat
is on the pavement; she will bend down and pick it up. But then a
gust comes and scoots it away, over toward the Civil War Statue.
There is that screaming woman, a big blond pregnant woman, with
hands in front of her face. She is not screaming as loudly anymore.
Now Allen Railsback stands up and calls her over with his hands,
and his mouth is moving but she can't hear him over this screaming.
Fred is rising up; his mouth is moving too, but she can't hear him
either.

Now here comes another sound, and she can hear it . Beautiful, a
beautiful musical sound. All the other sounds shrink away—the
lawn mower, the screaming pregnant lady, Allen, Fred. It's shrill,
like a small animal that's trapped, coming in gasps. But it is Henry,
and he is crying.

SHE SLAMS THE car door and runs around the crooked car to where
Allen and Fred are standing. She stumbles on the curb, her legs
aren't moving right. Henry is lying on his back in the middle of the
road. So tiny, he looks like a doll, a Henry doll in a cow T-shirt and red
shorts. She falls down on the street, the pavement into her knees. His
face is turned away from her, she can only see the back of his head,
curly dark hair, and then the head moves around and he is looking at
her. He is moving his head, his eyes are open, he can see her.

She grabs hold of his hand, curled up under his chin, stiff but it is
warm. "It's Mommy. I'm here. Henry, it's Mommy."

He gazes at her silently. His eyes are huge—*like big pools*—and
frightened. "Henry, say something to me. It's Mommy. Are you
okay?" Her voice is coming out loud and frantic. Don't sound
scared, you will scare him.

"Okay?" It comes out like a question. And then his mouth opens,
showing tiny teeth with gaps between them, and he moans.

She bends down and kisses his hand, again and again. "Everything will be fine. Mommy's here," she whispers into his hand. Then she rocks back and examines his body for the first time. There are scrapes on his face, his arm is bleeding, and his leg is at a funny angle.

"I called the ambulance." It's Allen Railsback.

"Are you his mother?" The pregnant woman is standing next to her, with her hands in front of her face, as if she can't bear to look. It's not repulsive, Josie thinks. "He just ran in front of me. He came down the hill from that big house and straight into the road. I turned up sharp and jammed on my brakes, but I still bumped him. It wasn't my fault. Really." Then her face reddens and puffs out as she starts to cry.

Josie glances up at the house. The front screen door is still standing open. He ran down the marble path into the road. She traces his course with her eyes. He was heading straight for the Civil War Statue. *Me get the gun, Mommy.* She looks over at the pregnant woman. Of course it wasn't your fault, she thinks crossly, it was my fault. Why are you crying?

She turns back to Henry, bending over him. His eyes are watching her. Why are you so quiet? she thinks. Is he breathing? She leans over and listens to a rasping sound. I will sit him up so he can breathe better.

Allen is holding both her arms, pinning them down by her side. "Don't move him, Josie. Don't."

"Does it hurt, Henry? Talk to Mommy." He is going into shock; aren't you supposed to talk to people so they don't go into shock?

"It hurts." Then he makes a whining sound, as if it is starting to hurt more.

"Good boy. Keep talking to me. The doctor is coming and he'll make you all better."

A blue Crowley police car pulls up, blocking the road, and then the ambulance behind it, pulling up on the common, around the crooked car and her car, and stopping right next to Henry's head. Then a rush of people with beepers and bags, all very busy.

Allen puts his hands under her armpits and pulls her up and away from Henry, over by the Civil War Statue. "We need to stand back."

One of the EMTs comes over, a woman with short blond hair and bright pink lips. I know this person, thinks Josie, I went to high school with her. Annie? Ellie?

"We need some information about your child's medical history. Allergies?" she says, poising a pencil over a clipboard.

Then the policeman comes over to her, looking disapproving. "Are you the boy's mother?"

"Yes."

"Tell me what happened."

"I'm not sure." She can't see Henry, he's surrounded by a swarm of people. Get away, let him breathe. "He ran out of that house"— she points up to the door—"into the road."

"Who was watching the child?"

"My mother." You wouldn't let her drive. But you let her take care of Henry.

"Where is she? I need to speak to her."

Josie waves her hand up toward the house. "She's in there some-place." Making a cake.

Just then Eleanor steps out onto the front stoop and looks down at them quizzically. She's got her apron back on, stained and crooked, and the flour smudge is still on her cheek. "Rascal!" she calls. "Josie, where's Rascal?"

Suddenly Josie starts running toward her, scrambling up the embankment. "It's not Rascal!" she yells. Her voice is louder than it has ever been before—a howl. "It's Henry. Your grandson. You were supposed to be watching him, but you were too *shit-faced.*" Her voice echoes across the common.

She's standing in front of her now, gasping, and Eleanor looks frightened and steps back. Josie pulls back her hand and slaps Eleanor across the face, as hard as she can. She hasn't hit anyone since she was a small child, and it stings her hand, her wrist bends back painfully. She knocks Eleanor sprawling, as easy as knocking down a child. She topples over backward, her skirt flying up so her stocking tops and garters show. Who still wears stockings anymore? Eleanor sits up on her elbow, confused, her mouth hanging open as if she's trying to say something. Josie considers reaching down, grab-bing her arm and pulling her up. But then Fred scurries up the hill, past her, gently raises Eleanor back onto her feet, and brushes down the folds of her skirt. Josie turns and scrambles back down the path, back to Henry.

THEY HAVE HIM on a stretcher now, a plastic oxygen mask over his nose, his neck in a white collar like a clown's. His eyes, bugging out and terrified, sweep over the strange faces. They don't seem to register Josie's, his mother's. "Henry, Mommy's here. I won't leave you again." She touches his arm, his tiny brown arm, strapped down to the stretcher. And now his eyes, with those long eyelashes, are fixed on her face, only her face; he knows her.

The EMT in charge—Mr. Kroeger the fireman?—tells her that he probably has a broken leg, and possibly internal injuries. "It could have been a lot worse. He was lucky." He hands her a bundle of cloth.

Lucky? she thinks as she watches them slide Henry into the back of the ambulance. She stands frozen in the road as the EMTs pile alongside the stretcher, one after another, as if it were a circus car, and winces as they slam the back shut. Then Mr. Kroeger walks around, opens the passenger door, and with a courtly wave of his hand gestures her in. Oh, I get to go too, she thinks. He slips on aviator sunglasses and flicks on the siren. Too bad Henry's not here, she thinks, he would love this. She looks down at the bundle she's been holding; it's Henry's cow T-shirt and red shorts and underpants—all cut into pieces. On the way to the Ayer Hospital, they flash by the Victory Supermarket, where Josie bought the confectioners' sugar. A woman with two children in a shopping cart stops and points at them. I once shopped there, thinks Josie, before.

WHEN THEY PULL up to the hospital, the EMTs whisk Henry's stretcher into the Emergency entrance, and leave her all alone to go in the regular way, into a carpeted waiting room with chairs and piles of magazines. She has to be interviewed by a secretary, who asks her questions like "What's your insurance number?" which she can't answer because her purse and wallet are sitting on the kitchen counter at home.

And then she is supposed to sit in one of those chairs and read magazines and wait. Most of the magazines have Jacqueline Kennedy Onassis on the cover, Jackie the young bride with lustrous eyes and windblown hair. Who doesn't know what was going to happen to her yet, what life had in store. That woman had bad luck, everyone around her had bad luck, now she's giving me bad luck, Josie thinks, flipping all the magazines over. She walks back to the secretary. "What's happening to my son? I need to see him." She sounds husky, like a forties movie star. She must have strained her voice when she screamed at Eleanor.

The woman doesn't even glance up from her computer terminal. "They sent him upstairs for a CAT scan and X rays. The doctor will be with you as soon as the tests are finished." *Doctors are so bossy, they boss you around.*

Ellie/Annie the EMT comes through the swinging door and sits down next to her. "You probably don't remember me. Annie Galvin, but now it's Kelleher. We went to high school together."

"I remember you." You were a cheerleader, Josie thinks, I thought you were a dope. "How's my son?"

"It looks like he's going to be fine, except maybe a broken leg. He was really lucky." Then she furrows her brow in a concerned way. "How are *you* feeling?"

"How am I feeling? My baby was run over because I left him with my mother who was drunk. I feel great. Tip-top." Now her voice is a croak, a loud croak. She seems to be shouting.

Annie pats her upper arm to say that she understands, that anger is a very normal emotion in a situation like this. "You can cry if you want to."

"I don't want to cry."

"It's not your fault. Don't blame yourself."

"Oh? Whose fault is it?" The blame-free nineties. Nothing is ever anyone's fault.

Annie says she has to go home to her twin baby daughters. "Don't worry," she calls out, giving Josie a thumbs-up sign through the plate-glass door.

She considers calling Peter from the chrome pay phone in the corner. Hello, remember that beautiful baby with the Stadler nose? Well, I nearly killed him today, I nearly got him squashed in the road

like a cat. He may only have a broken leg, a bit of a limp for the rest
of his life. Isn't that lucky? Or maybe there are some broken bones
we don't know about yet. A ruptured spleen, a concussion. What
good luck. No, this good news can wait.

An hour later an orthopedic surgeon, a cocky man with hair like a
rooster, ushers her through a warren of halls to a tiny room. "Only a
broken femur after all," he says, flipping X rays up on a light board.
"Here and here. We'll put him under general anesthesia to set the
bone. Then two weeks in traction, and a full body cast for six weeks.
There probably won't be any permanent disability, we'll keep checking to make sure the bones are growing evenly." You wouldn't want
him to have a short leg, would you? She looks at Henry's ghostly
bones against the black. So perfect, so orderly, invisible all this time,
like the inside of JFK's skull. "He was very lucky. You can see him
for a few minutes before he goes to the operating room."

Henry is in a curtained cubicle, on a gurney now instead of a
stretcher, which makes him seem even tinier. The oxygen mask is
gone, but he still has on the white clown collar, naked except for a
diaper. The scrapes on his face and arm are bandaged in white
gauze. His eyes flicker over toward her and he gives her a sleepy
smile. He doesn't seem so scared, a nice nurse is holding one hand.
"Hi," Josie says, feeling oddly shy to have this nurse eavesdropping
on their conversation. "Is my buddy all right?"

"All right," he says hoarsely.

"Do you want something?"

"I'm firsty."

She reaches for a cup by the sink. "He can't have anything to
drink. He's about to have general anesthesia," the nurse says, quite
sharply. Does she think I'm a bad mother because I let him get hit
by a car? Probably.

"I'm firsty," Henry says again, and he licks a sticky tongue over his
dry lips.

She tries to think of some comfort to give him. "Once upon a
time there were three little pigs." He smiles; this is one of his
favorites. He likes the huffing and puffing when the straw house gets
blown down.

*   *   *

An hour later she is in another waiting room, which she likes better—on the third floor at the end of a hallway, with no comfortable chairs, no magazines, and no high school acquaintances offering kind words. By great good fortune, she has her cigarettes in her pocket, and she is hunched over in the most remote corner of this remote waiting room secretly smoking—a sign above her head announces that this act is strictly forbidden anywhere in the hospital. She doesn't care if someone catches her and bawls her out. In fact, it would feel good, she deserves it. *Doctors are so bossy, they boss you around.* When she hears the elevator door close and steps echoing down the hallway toward her, she stubs out the cigarette on the swirly green linoleum.

It's Fred, tiny dapper Fred, holding her purse. She can't bring herself to say hello to him; it's partially his fault. If he hadn't been going away, they wouldn't have been having a party, they wouldn't have needed confectioners' sugar, Eleanor wouldn't have been drunk. She crosses her arms petulantly across her chest, slouches down in her chair, and nods toward him.

He sits down in the chair next to her. "I hear the little guy is going to be all right."

"I'm not so sure about that. His legs might be uneven. That's not all right, is it?" Her voice croaks, but Fred doesn't seem to notice.

"It could have been worse."

"It could have been better. It could have not happened at all."

He says nothing, he stares straight ahead at a shut-off television mounted on the wall. At least he has better sense than Annie, isn't trying to tell her how lucky Henry is. "I brought you your purse." He holds it up. "I put your toothbrush inside, and some cash. Fifty bucks. I thought you might need it if you have to spend the night." That's what Eleanor's mother used to do—give them wallets for Christmas with two-dollar bills inside. It always made the wallets so much sweeter, seem so much more useful with crisp new bills inside, and those novelty coins that you had to get at the bank— Kennedy half-dollars, moon-walk quarters, silver dollars. "I thought about bringing some of your clothes, but . . ."

"You didn't want to go through my drawers?"

He shrugs.

"Thanks, Fred," she says, still sounding like a sullen teenager. She should ask about Eleanor, of course. Find out if she was hurt when Josie slugged her. Is the kitchen strewn with food, the dining room still decorated for the Lion King party? It wasn't Eleanor's fault, but Josie can't help it, she blames her anyway. She was so drunk she didn't know it was Henry. She was worried about her fucking dog.

"Would you like to pray?" Fred says.

Oh, please. The AA prayer, perhaps. Oh, please give me the serenity to accept the things I cannot change, and the courage to change the things that I can change. What can I change? Nothing. Does that mean I have to accept it serenely? "You pray for me, all right?"

He nods and then sits silently, staring at the blank television. Is he praying?

How would I pray for Henry? *That baby was so beautiful.* She thinks suddenly of "Threnody," Emerson's cry of grief after the death of his five-year-old son.

> *The hyacinthine boy, for whom*
> *Morn well might break and April bloom,*
> *The gracious boy, who did adorn*
> *The world whereinto he was born*

"My hyacinthine boy, my gracious boy," she repeats over and over to herself. But "Threnody" is a dirge, not a prayer. Could it bring bad luck? I don't need any more bad luck. She hits her forehead hard with the heel of her hand to knock those words out, and hears the dull thud of bone. Could she knock herself out, could she crack her own skull? She hits herself again.

"Christ, Josie. Cut that out. You'll bruise yourself." He grabs her hand and pins it down on the edge of his seat. His hands are soft and warm, but when she tries to pull her hand back, it feels as if it's shackled in iron. He doesn't look that strong.

My gracious boy, my hyacinthine boy. "Talk to me, Fred."

"About what?"

"About . . ." She tries to think what could hold her interest, drive out these voices. "About Mama Rizzo's."

"Okay," he says, sounding neither offended nor surprised. He lets go of her hand and settles back into the molded plastic chair. "My wife and I started this pasta shop in Revere. Long time ago—1962— when we were first married, and I was just out of the Navy. Who wanted fresh pasta then? Little grandmothers, and that was about it. The younger ones, they wanted supermarket Italian food. Chef Boyardee canned spaghetti. Yech!" He shakes his head. "So it was pretty rough for a long time, and we thought we'd give up. But then, in 1974, suddenly these Beacon Hill types figure out about fresh pasta, and *Boston* magazine names us best pasta shop three years in a row. We had the reviews framed and hung them in our store window. The Beacon Hill types actually drove to Revere to buy Mama Rizzo's tortellini and ravioli, and the lines stretched out into the street."

"Uh-huh," says Josie. I don't want to hear about this, I want to hear about the fire.

"You probably want to hear about the Mama Rizzo's restaurant. Okay. Skip ahead ten years to the eighties. We're doing pretty well. We've bought a new house, we're sending both girls to Salve Regina. Sylvia's happy with the pasta shop, but I want something better because I want to be a big shot. So this guy I grew up with makes me a proposition—let's start a restaurant; he'll put up the money. Sylvia says let's start a little place next door, then all the Beacon Hill types can stay and have dinner. No, I say. Not big enough. I want one of those huge places on Route 1 like the Hilltop Steak House and Weylu's. You know that giant cactus, I'm thinking I want a giant gondola, with 'Mama Rizzo's' spelled out in little red lights." He draws the outline of a gondola with his hand.

The fire, tell me about the fire.

"So we buy an old building that used to be an Arthur Treacher's Fish and Chips, and we fix it up, make it three times bigger. It costs a fortune, so now I'm putting my money in, all the money we'd saved from the pasta shop. Don't worry, I say to Sylvia, we're going to be rich. The place opens, and it's a nightmare. It's too big, like serving food in a football stadium. By the time the dishes get from the kitchen to the table, they're cold. People say they don't want a big pasta restaurant. No. Pasta places are supposed to be little, and cozy.

So we make all these changes, cut the place up into small rooms with red tablecloths and travel posters of Italy. I'm spending all my time there, the jolly owner shaking hands and kissing the girls. I'm really spending most of my time at the bar. I'd always been a lush, but with free booze I went straight into the toilet. And I'm having a thing with one of the waitresses."

The story comes pouring out easily, as if he's told it a hundred times. And he probably has, at AA meetings. Mea culpa, mea culpa. I am such a bad person, I let everyone down. When this is all over, I'm not going to confess to anyone, Josie thinks. I will not be absolved.

Where is Henry now? Is he stretched out on stainless steel with anesthesia dripping into his veins? She tries to imagine what his little leg will look like up in traction. All she can come up with is something out of a cartoon—with pulleys, and ropes, and weights, and a huge plaster cast. And then something awful always happened to those people in traction—the weight got cut so the broken leg went flying up, the bed on wheels got pushed down the stairs. What was so funny about that? She flinches. Should she call Peter? Not yet. She'll wait until she sees Henry, so she can tell him what traction looks like.

"What about the fire, Fred?"

"Oh, that." He stops and studies her face. What is he looking for? Then he continues at the same pace. "After four years, we go out of business. My business partner Marty files for bankruptcy and moves to Florida."

Kind of like Grif, she thinks.

"So now I'm responsible for the whole loan. We lose the house, and Sylvia moves into the apartment above the pasta shop where we started. I'm living with my waitress girlfriend. I'm drunk all the time, and finally she kicks me out. So one night, I have a great idea. I'm going to kill myself and I'll take Mama Rizzo's with me. Then Sylvia and the girls will have the insurance money, and they'll be happy. I get two big gas cans and I go to the restaurant. I have to break in because the bank has boarded it up. I soak all the carpets with gasoline, this expensive red wall-to-wall that I insisted we get. Then I sit down at the bar with a bottle of Seagram's, and drink half of it, until

I almost pass out. You see, I'm going to sit there, and let the place burn down around me. Then I light a roll of paper towels and throw it into a puddle of gasoline. Whoosh. Up it goes, flames all around. Suddenly I think, Oh, no, I don't want to die. So I grab my Seagram's and run like crazy, back out the hole I made. I sit in my car, and drink the rest of it while I'm watching Mama Rizzo's burn down. Then I pass out. That's where the cops find me, in the parking lot. Smart, huh?"

"So you did it?"

"Of course I did it. What did you think? That I was innocent?"

A nurse sticks her head around the corner. "Mrs. Stadler. We're moving your son up to pediatrics." She must be a pediatrics nurse— her lab coat is made of material printed with Mickey and Donald, clip-on teddy bears hang off her stethoscope. Josie stands up to follow her. *Doctors are so bossy, they boss you around . . . and then they took him away and I didn't see him again for hours and hours and I said: they're never going to keep me away from him again.*

"Thanks for waiting with me, Fred. How's Mom doing?" She doesn't really want to know, she's reached her guilt overload for one day. But she has to ask, because what kind of daughter would she be if she didn't?

"She's pretty shaken up, but Allen's with her." He looks relieved to be going.

"Tell her I don't blame her for what happened. It was my fault. And tell her I'm sorry I hit her. Please give her this." Under the buzz of the overhead fluorescent, Josie bends over and gives Fred a kiss on the cheek.

ON THE WAY up in the room-sized elevator, Josie tries to prepare herself mentally for the sight of Henry's twisted body encased in white plaster. How can you prepare yourself for such a vision? Never, nothing can prepare you for this pain, the pain of being a parent. "How's he look?" she asks the nurse.

The nurse seems puzzled, as if this is a strange question. Maybe it's the way Josie's voice sounds, a raspy whine, as if she's been on a three-day binge of booze and cigarettes. "He's all right, if that's what you mean."

Oh, right, thinks Josie. *I should have asked how he was, not how he looked.*

"The procedure went very well. He was such a brave little boy."

When Henry is being brave, he smiles crookedly and breathes sharply through his mouth so he doesn't break into tears. Josie used to think it was so cute that she couldn't help laughing. Now the idea of Henry being brave seems grotesque, obscene; she wants to scream.

The nurse escorts her down the corridor, past a nurses' station covered with cutout paper clowns, past a bulletin board with photographs and cards from former patients—grinning children at the beach, in front of Christmas trees. A couple are bald, but no one seems to have a leg that's shorter than the other. "We're not busy," the nurse says, "so your son has his own room." She pushes open an oversized door and beckons Josie in. "Here he is."

The room has two beds and is dim, like Henry's room at home—back in Providence—with the night-light on. One bed has the side rails up, an IV bottle, a stainless-steel contraption arching over the bed, but no Henry. Oh, yes, there he is, he is in there somewhere. His dark head on a pillow, eyes shut, his curly eyelashes like twin caterpillars, mouth open, snoring softly. His arms lie limp at his side, covered with tape and gauze: for the IV tube, at the crook of his elbow where they drew blood, on the side where he got scraped. How can he sleep like that? He never sleeps like that at home. His poor leg strapped up, but without a cast, his little brown toes curling, perfect, undamaged. Those miraculous toes, the first thing she saw when he was born. She bumps a finger along the top of them. Normally, he would shriek with laughter and jerk his foot away. "What's the matter with him? Why isn't he awake?" Josie asks the nurse in an accusatory way.

"Mrs. Stadler, he is still under the effects of the anesthesia. It will take a while to wear off. And he's been through a trauma; he's exhausted. If you have any concerns, I'll call the doctor for you." *Don't blame me, lady. You're the one who let your kid get hit by a car.*

"All right," says Josie. *I said: they're never going to keep me away from him again.* She's feeling so woozy she pulls a chair over to the bed and lowers her head against the bed rail. From this angle, all she can see is Henry's hospital bracelet. "Henry Stadler; Mother: Josephine Trask, The Common, Crowley Center, Ma." is stamped in smudgy purple ink—his return address, she thinks.

After the nurse leaves, Josie picks up the phone to call Peter. Before she dials, she practices what she will say. Henry has been in an accident, but he's all right. She'll say it quickly in one breath, so he won't have a single second of terror. Henry went out the screen door; it all happened in an instant; it was her fault. She won't mention that Eleanor was drunk, she won't mention Eleanor at all. Because if Peter knew the truth, he might blame Eleanor, and that would be unfair. He will want to come east right away. But she will say no, finish your classes, come in a week. I can handle this by myself.

She calls collect; it's the only way to make a long-distance call from the hospital. What if Monica answers? Grow up, Josie. How can you possibly think that matters now? Besides, she's not going to be there. She's in her new garden apartment in Piedmont hanging pictures. The phone rings five times. "Your party is not answering," an automated voice says.

I know it's not answering, thinks Josie. What do you think I am? Stupid?

"Please try again later."

She checks the wall clock above the bathroom door. It's only five o'clock in California. He has afternoon office hours. It's the last week of the semester, students are lined up along the corridor outside his office—wanting advice about their final papers, wanting extensions and incompletes. He's dressed like a student himself, in shorts and Teva sandals, with his feet up on his desk. He's talking to each one longer than he should, asking them questions about themselves—Where are you from, what's your major, how did you like the course? With each answer he smiles, showing those square teeth, and they will think, what a cool guy. And then he'll give one of his big laughs—ha, ha, ha—and the students waiting in the hallway will all look at one another impatiently and check their watches.

Josie closes her eyes and tries a visualization technique that Stedman once described to her. Peter, she thinks, this is Josie. Go home, I need you. She visualizes him standing up, slinging his book bag over his shoulder. "I have to go now," he says to the waiting students, "please come back tomorrow." He runs down two flights of stairs, steps into the heat and sunshine, slips on his sunglasses, walks down Telegraph. Don't stop for takeout Thai, she thinks, don't stop for coffee, don't stop to browse in the used-book store. She sits him down at the bus stop bench. Here comes number 33, right on time.

Peter, I need you. Something awful has happened to our little boy.

She props her knees up on one of the side rails and dozes off. God, she's exhausted but she can't let herself fall asleep. What if Henry woke up and she wasn't there, waiting. Another nurse in a Mickey-and-Donald coat comes in with a tray. "I ordered you some dinner, Mom," she says.

The nurse checks Henry's pulse, heart, sticks a thing in his ear to check his temperature, feels his diaper to see if he's wet, adjusts the weight on his ankle. She pinches his cheeks and shakes his shoulder. "Come on, Henry. Wake up."

He raises an arm, the arm that's all strapped to the IV, and rubs his eye. His mouth twists and he makes a spluttering cry, the way he does when he wakes up from a nap in a cranky mood. "Hi, darling," Josie says. "Mommy is here." Why did she call him darling? She's never called him that before. He struggles to sit up. When he can't, the cry escalates to a shriek. She gives the nurse a pleading look. Now what do I do?

The nurse pours a drink. "Henry," she says in a soothing tone. "Open your eyes. Here's a drink of water. You are all right." Unbelievably, this works. He opens his eyes, takes a few sips of water through a straw, looks down unalarmed at his leg, smiles dopily at Josie, and falls back asleep, the tears still wet on his cheeks.

She lifts the cover off her supper—a hamburger patty, cottage cheese, fruit cocktail. The diet plate—why do they always order you the diet plate? It tastes almost delicious. She dozes off for an hour and then tries Peter again. Ring and ring and ring and ring . . . "Your party is not answering," says the cheerful female voice, "please try again later." Now, what could he be doing at eight P.M.? she thinks abstractly. Dinner with one of his colleagues, another single man perhaps, and then a movie. What would he see? *Four Weddings and*

a Funeral, Forrest Gump? Peter likes depressing, violent movies that
Josie usually refuses to go to. *Flesh and Bone,* she decides.

She rescues some old newspapers from the trash can in the hallway—the *Boston Globe* and the *Boston Herald*—and reads them
both thoroughly. First, she catches up with the O. J. Simpson case.
Both papers refer to various clues, as if she's supposed to know what
they mean—the bloody glove, the sealed envelope, Nicole's dog
named Kato. She probably should have followed this more closely;
Peter undoubtedly has, although they haven't discussed it. Why not?
she wonders. Her horoscope in the *Globe* says: "Although expenses
are higher than expected, you make excellent progress today." In the
Herald it says: "A nutritious breakfast will help you start the day on
an energetic note." Henry's are: "Be wary of wishful thinking; this is
not a good time to go out on a limb" and "Intuitive prompting
should be heeded." What does it all mean? Perhaps it means nothing. "Today in History" reports that the American Railway Union led
by Eugene Debs called a general strike in sympathy with the Pull-
man workers in 1894, and President Eisenhower joined Queen Elizabeth in opening the Saint Lawrence Seaway in 1959. That's really
quite interesting, Josie thinks.

The nurse wakes Henry at midnight, and Josie spoons in a few
bites of cherry Jell-O, which he seems to like. She's never let him
have Jell-O before because of the artificial colors and flavors. How
could I have ever been worried about such trivial things?

She tries Peter again. When the voice says, "Your party is not
answering," she says into the receiver, "Hi, Peter, it's Josie. Henry got
run over. Thought you might want to know." All right, she thinks,
let's examine the worst-case scenario. He is over at Monica's for dinner. She needs help moving furniture, putting her bed together,
hanging pictures. It's the least he could do, after all, since he evicted
her. I could get her number from information and call. This is an
emergency, after all. Never, she decides.

What if I can't get in touch with him? she thinks in a panic. This
seems like a real possibility; they went for nearly two weeks without
speaking before. Then what will I do? She studies Henry and imagines spending day after day trying to keep him amused while he's in
traction. Suddenly relief spreads through her body and limbs like a

drug. I will read to him, we'll do puzzles and build Legos, I'll draw pictures of trucks and tractors (forgetting for a moment what a terrible artist she is). I can handle it by myself.

She dozes off again, fitfully, having horrible, hallucinatory dreams. A buzzing lawn mower abandoned in the middle of the church lawn. A metallic-blue sedan pulled up cockeyed on the common. Allen standing up, his face ashen. Henry, lying tiny and motionless on the pavement. She wakes up with a start, and when she sees Henry sleeping quietly, she moans with joy. She strokes his warm cheek, puts her face down to his mouth, and counts each soft breath.

When the nurse wakes Henry at three, they get barely a flutter of his eyelids and a yawn before he is off again. It's now 3:26 A.M.; Henry was born at 3:26. A.M. Josie remembers looking up in desperation at the big clock on the birthing-room wall—how time leapt ahead by hours and then seemed to stop dead. A pain would last forever, a whole hour, and then that clock, which came to seem like an enemy, would say that it had only been five minutes.

She falls asleep again in her chair, but this time she has a sweet dream. She is at Horseneck Beach with Peter and Henry. Henry in his lime-green trunks is zigzagging down the beach, with Peter and Josie chasing behind. They each catch an arm, wade into the surf, and swing him out over the waves, the water licking his toes. "Again," he shrieks. "Do it again."

When Josie wakes up, it is dawn. For the first time she can see out the window and get her bearings. A rosy glow spreads over a gravel-covered roof, bounces off an aluminum air-conditioner vent, and then slowly seeps over Henry's face. *I stared at him for over an hour, while the room turned pink with the sunrise.* It's a sign; she picks up the phone and calls Peter. She has no doubt he'll be home, and she anticipates how his voice will sound—worried with a sleepy edge. No answer. Maybe the phone is out of order; why hadn't she thought of that before? She calls the operator and asks her to check the line. "That number is in service," the woman says, letting it ring ten more times.

Josie replaces the receiver carefully and looks down at Henry. The rosy glow has passed away, and now he sleeps in naked daylight where she can see all the bruises—a yellowish one on the side of his face, a small blue one on his elbow, an ugly black one over his thigh. I won't even speculate where Peter is or what he is doing. All I know is that he is not home, and my marriage is over. Something much worse has happened to Henry than getting hit by a car.

She thinks of her basement bedroom in Grif and Terry's Coral Gables house. They had decorated it like a girl's bedroom—with lavender gingham bedspreads and shag carpet—but it always smelled of mildew. Where will Monica put Henry? *I should have fought harder.* She kneels on the floor next to Henry's head, leans her head against the side rail, and, for the first time, cries.

chapter 19

Learning to accept what was unthinkable changes you.
— JACQUELINE KENNEDY

The door opens, and Josie quickly wipes her eyes and nose on the pillowcase. Why can't they ever leave you alone in the hospital? Why can't I have a good cry in peace and quiet?

She glances up, and there, standing in the doorway, is Peter.

She blinks and rubs her eyes, not quite recognizing him. He looks terrible, she thinks, like a street person. He is unshaven and his hair hangs in greasy clumps; his T-shirt (a drab-green one she has never seen) and blue jeans are skewed, as if he'd dressed in the dark. And his face. He is staring at her as if *she* were the one who looked awful. "What is it?" he says, his voice a strangled whisper. "Is he all right?"

"Henry?" she says, standing up. "He's fine." She sounds even more croaky than she did yesterday.

"Then why are you crying?"

As if you didn't know, Josie thinks. "What are you doing here?" She makes her voice cold, indifferent.

Peter is gripping the IV pole by Henry's bed; he doesn't seem to have heard her. He is staring at Henry and all the blood has drained from his face. This is the first time Josie has ever seen that happen, literally, as if someone had pulled a plug. Glistening beads pop up across his forehead, giving off a sharp smell of sweat and fear. He is going to faint, she thinks; she shoves the chair behind him and he falls down into it. She pushes his head down to his knees. His hair is sopping wet, as if he had just stepped out of the shower.

She has seen him faint before, several times, actually—Peter is a fainter. Low blood pressure, the doctor at the Brown infirmary said; he'll live forever if he doesn't faint and crack his head open. You're so irritating, she thinks as she brings a cup of water to his lips. Henry is the one who needs attention, not you. Peter takes the cup and shakes his head like a retriever stepping out of a stream. She stands behind him and rubs his shoulders through his T-shirt, broad but thin, sinew and bone. She'd forgotten how good his shoulders feel.

"Is he unconscious?"

"No," she says in a soothing voice, the one she uses with Henry when he has had a bad dream. "He's sleeping. He had general anesthesia when they set his leg, and he's worn out from the trauma of the accident." Does Peter know about the accident? He must, why else would he be here? But who told him?

Peter has recovered himself. He is sitting up straight, examining Henry. He strokes his hand over his forehead, down a cheek, along his arm. His hand and Henry's are exactly the same ruddy brown. Josie's hand against Henry always looks so white, as if they were different species. Peter starts asking questions cogently, much more cogently than any Josie asked yesterday. Where is his bone broken? Why is he in traction? Are they sure it will heal correctly? Will it affect the growth of that leg? Was he knocked unconscious? Are they sure there will be no brain damage? Why does he have an IV? When will he wake up? Are they sure he will be all right, really sure?

It doesn't matter how concerned he is being about Henry, thinks Josie. Nothing has changed. "I tried to call you," she says in an accusatory way. "But there was no answer."

"You know where I was, don't you?"

"Yes." She stands on the other side of the bed, looking across Henry's body, down at him. Peter is beginning to look familiar again, handsome again, but it doesn't matter anymore. They have gone too far. "I know where you were."

"On the airplane. Coming here. I got to the airport around eight.

The only plane I could get was to Chicago. Then I caught the last plane to Boston, rented a car. Then I got lost finding the hospital."

She pauses as this information sinks in. I am going crazy. Paranoid and crazy. "Right," she says uncertainly. "How did you find out about . . . this."

"Your mother called me."

Considering the shape Eleanor was in, Josie is surprised she could even dial a phone. And she wouldn't have thought Eleanor had the courage to call Peter. "What did she say?"

"What did she say?" He slowly swings his gaze from Henry's face to hers. His face turns pasty again and then he shakes his head hard, as if he were trying to cast something away. "I had just come home from office hours, and I caught it on like the tenth ring. It's Eleanor, but she's speaking very slowly and strangely. 'Peter,' she says, 'something very terrible has happened to Henry.' " He imitates Eleanor's formal pronunciation, the way she presses her lips together and squints when she's concerned.

"She says, in this robot voice, 'Are you sitting down? I think you need to sit down before I tell you.' There's no chair around, so I sink down on the kitchen floor. She is going to tell me Henry is dead, I think. My son is dead." As he says this, Peter lifts his eyes toward the window, and they become completely flat. Yes, I went to that place too, Josie thinks, for just a moment, when I thought he could possibly be dead. This is the first time she has said the word, even silently.

"All the while, she's droning on, in this painfully slow way. About Fred Rizzo leaving, about the good-bye party, about needing eggs for a cake. I don't say, come on, snap it up, get to the point, because I don't want her to get to the point, ever. So I sit and listen. And all the while, I'm looking out the window at the bay, and I think Henry will never see this. When she tells me Henry has a broken leg, I actually start to laugh. Is that all? I say. Eleanor sounds offended. Well, yes, she says. Isn't that enough?"

"Did she tell you she was drunk?"

He nods. "She said that it was all her fault. She sounded pretty desperate, so I told her that I forgave her, and you did too." He shrugs, as if to say, What else could I do?

"I guess that was the right thing to say." She admits this begrudgingly; she is the one who should do the forgiving, not Peter. How can he forgive someone who has hurt their son so easily? They stare at one another across Henry's hoisted-up leg.

"She said you gave her a black eye." He gives her a rueful smile. "Wish I could have seen that."

Did she hit her that hard? Josie hopes she doesn't have to see the soft skin around Eleanor's eye bruised purple. She reaches across the bed for Peter's hand and pulls it awkwardly toward her lips. She means to kiss his knuckles, but instead manages to kiss his wedding ring. "I'm glad you came back."

She lets go, and he pulls it back, examining the ring closely as if she's left something on it—spit perhaps—and then shifting his scrutiny to her face. "Jos-ie," he says, drawing the first syllable out long. No one has called her Jos-ie in two months; she didn't know she had missed it. "You're not making that much sense. Why don't you go to sleep." Sleep, real sleep in a bed. Yes.

He stands up, walks around Henry's bed, puts his hands on her shoulders, and tenderly steers her over to the other hospital bed beside the window. "Go to sleep now," he says.

She sits on the edge of the bed, and he stoops down and unbuckles her sandals, the way he used to when she was nine months pregnant. Her toes are dirty; she should probably wash them before she goes to sleep. She smells too, like Peter, with the acrid smell of fear. What would she have to do if she washed—turn on the water in the corner sink, lather up a washcloth with one of those miniature soap bars? It's all too complicated, she thinks, falling back on the bed.

He tucks the blanket around her and kisses her on the forehead, as if she were Henry. That's right, she thinks, he hasn't really kissed me yet. Just as well; her mouth tastes of cigarettes and reheated coffee. She closes her eyes. "Promise me you won't go anywhere. Promise me you'll be right here when Henry wakes up," she murmurs.

"I promise."

She opens an eye a slit and sees Peter sitting between the two beds, feet propped up and reading a newspaper, like a security guard. She shuts her eye and falls asleep without dreaming.

*　　*　　*

HENRY IS LAUGHING. Loud shrieks of laughter, one after the other, and then a break as he grabs a breath. "Again, Daddy."

"All right. Here comes the big truck down the hill. Oh no, oh no. The brakes have failed and he's going to crash right into the school bus. All the boys and girls are yelling help, help. CRASH."

Josie can hear metal toys spilling onto the hard linoleum floor, and more choked squeals from Henry. She opens her eyes and sits up. Peter has put a hospital table across Henry's lap and set a line of Matchbox cars at one end, waiting to be picked off by the runaway truck. He is playing Henry's favorite game, car crash, which seems like an inappropriate choice, considering. Peter has raised the head of Henry's bed so he can sit up, and now his leg looks even more contorted. Did Peter check with the nurse? He needs to check with the nurse before he does stuff like that; Josie should have instructed him before she went to sleep. She checks Henry's face to see if he's in pain.

"Again, Daddy. Pick up the cars," Henry yells in his bossy tone. He thumps his good leg against the mattress and slaps the table.

She has to admit he doesn't seem as if he's in pain, but Peter shouldn't get him so excited. Peter always gets him hyper; in fact she hasn't seen Henry act like this since Peter left. He was always doing these goofy stunts that Henry seemed to love—putting a paper bag over his head and jumping out of a closet, taking a mouthful of milk and gargling so it slopped down his chin, pretending that Henry was a jacket and trying to put him on. Really. And what did it say about Henry that he thought this was so funny? Was this some kind of dumb humor that only males understood, that was passed down from father to son?

Henry looks over at her and grins triumphantly, clutching onto Peter's wrist with both hands. "*My* daddy. See my daddy?"

"That's right. Daddy's back. We missed him, didn't we?" She walks over to his bed and bends down to kiss his beaming face. Henry's back. We missed him, didn't we?

He turns his eyes back to car crash and pushes her face away. "Go away, Mommy."

"Hey, buddy," says Peter, lining the cars back up. "Don't talk like that. You know we love Mommy. We all love one another, because we're a family." He gives her a pleading look.

Josie goes over to the sink and busies herself brushing her teeth. We're a family—since when? She and Henry are a family and Peter is more like a satellite that orbits by once in a while, the West Coast branch of the Stadler family. Where do you get off, she thinks, coming in here and taking over my child? How can Henry give in so easily to Peter's charms? She studies her face in the mirror—a little pasty but not too haggard—and then grins so she can inspect her teeth. "You shouldn't have raised his bed without checking with the nurse," she says, turning toward him and leaning against the sink. "It might hurt his leg."

"The doctor said it was all right."

"When was the doctor here?"

"When you were asleep. We had a long talk about the break, and the traction. He seemed pretty hopeful that Henry's leg would be completely fine. Did you know he's going to have to be in a complete body cast after he's out of traction?"

Well, why didn't you wake me up? she thinks. You're not qualified to discuss my son's health with his doctor. Because he was letting me sleep, she thinks. A small kindness.

A nurse comes in with a clump of Mylar balloons and a picnic basket. "Somebody sent Henry these, and a gentleman left you this." Each balloon has a smiling teddy bear in a hospital bed and the card says "Dearest Henry, Get well soon. Love, Grandpa." Josie hands it to Peter. "I think these must be for someone else."

He studies it. "Could they be from your father?"

Grif had only seen Henry once, when he was a baby, and sometimes he seemed to forget that Josie even had a child. What's that noise? he would say on the phone when Henry yelled in the background. Of course the balloons are from Grif, Josie thinks, almost fondly. An extravagant, show-off gesture filled with nothing but hot air.

Inside the picnic basket are grilled chicken sandwiches on French bread, a Tupperware container of spinach salad, two pieces of pecan pie, a bottle of white wine (still chilled), and a corkscrew. A note says, "Thought you might be getting sick of hospital food, Love, Eleanor and Fred."

"This is from your mother? I can't believe it," says Peter, taking such a huge bite that mustard smears over his chin. "God, I'm starved."

"It's really from Fred. He's a gourmet cook." She realizes she hasn't told him this before. She hasn't told him any of the Fred and Eleanor saga. Where does she begin?

"I thought you and Leslie had sent Fred Rizzo packing," he says, pulling the wine cork out with a satisfying pop.

"Well, it seems I was wrong about Fred." And then she tells him—about snooping through Fred's drawers, the smoke detectors, the moans from Eleanor's room, Leslie's visit, Ralph Cavanaugh, Eleanor's financial plight, Fred's confession. By now, the only light in the room is the last glimmer of dusk outside the window, and Henry has drifted back to sleep. They've pulled up two chairs to the lowered hospital table, and the effect is oddly romantic. Like the old days, when they used to have supper on their back porch in Providence sitting on aluminum beach chairs and using a cable spool for a table. They looked out at an alley strewn with junked cars and refrigerators, at the porches on the other two-families, at the slit of sunset they could make out between the two neighboring houses, and Josie remembers the joy she felt—the simple joy.

Is this what Fred was thinking when he packed the picnic? That Peter and I needed a romantic little dinner to patch things up, to get reacquainted? He probably did, bless his heart. She takes a sip of wine—her third glass—and sloshes the sweetness over her tongue. Thank God he sent some booze, I needed a drink. Like mother, like daughter.

"Ralph Cavanaugh, huh? So Leslie gets laid, and lo and behold, turns into a normal person."

"I think it's more complicated than that," says Josie defensively. I can't believe it; I'm sticking up for Leslie. "She's really changed."

And then Peter tells her about his summer—about his courses, his students, the political battles of the English Department (the academics hate the writers, the writers hate the academics, the Women's Studies Program hates the men, and the men hate the Women's Studies Program. No one thinks I'm important enough to hate, they treat me like the court jester.) The clothes everyone in California wears (neoprene Rollerblading outfits). Peter's silly stories; they always make her laugh.

She studies his face in the fading light. He looks better than he did this morning, that's for certain. He must have shaved and combed his hair with the bag of complimentary toiletries the nurse handed her last night. Was it only last night, was it only twenty-four hours ago? She examines him suspiciously for changes—the new T-shirt, his hair longer and cut differently over the ears, more deeply tanned than he ever got in the East. She swings her bare foot into his lap, and he runs a finger along the top of her foot, along her ankle-bone, up her calf. "Let's leave the dishes," she says, and he smiles.

"Listen, Josie. I have a confession to make about Monica." The smile fades.

"Yes," she says. She considers moving her foot, but doesn't because now he is massaging it with both hands. Don't freak out; this is what you suspected all along. Look what Jackie had to put up with. This is only one indiscretion; all right, maybe there were more, but you don't have to know about every single one. Think about Henry.

"When I agreed to kick Monica out, I made you think that it was all your fault, that you were being jealous and unreasonable. That was really dishonest of me."

"Yes," she says, steeling herself.

"I wanted to kick Monica out. She was driving me crazy, absolutely *nuts*."

"She was?"

"I couldn't play my music because it gave her headaches. I wasn't allowed to buy scented laundry soap because that gave her headaches too. She said I didn't grind the coffee beans fine enough. I had to take my shoes off before I came into the house, and it's my house."

Josie, whatever her faults, was not persnickety about anything—a quality inherited straight from Eleanor. She never bothered to tell Peter that his REM CD gave her headaches too.

He lists a few more of Monica's bad habits. "She vacuumed every ten minutes. She was always on some sort of diet, and used to recite how many fat grams there were in everything we ate. She even threw away my box of frozen waffles. She made me realize how much I missed you." He smiles over at her sheepishly.

Josie pulls her foot free from his grip and lowers it onto the floor.

"Is that supposed to make me feel better? That the only reason you missed me is because Monica was such an irritating roommate?"

"No, that's not what I'm saying." He looks disconcerted, as if this is not going the way he hoped.

"Then what are you saying?"

"I'm saying that there was never anything between Monica and me, and that the more time I spent with her, the more I missed you." He leans forward so their knees touch. "I never loved anyone but you, Josie."

"Well, it didn't always feel that way." She sits up straight and pulls her knees back, away from his.

"You know what Monica said? She gave me a piece of her mind before she moved out. First, she informed me that I'm an asshole." He raises his eyebrows as if to say, True enough. "And she told me that I flirt with women and lead them on so they'll develop crushes on me. That I don't want to have affairs with them, but I want them to want to have affairs with me. She told me that she feels sorry for you, and that I don't deserve you." He's staring over at her, searching her face for a reaction.

Touché, Monica. "So what do you think?" Josie says neutrally.

"I don't want people to feel sorry for you because you're married to an asshole." He reaches forward, his straight dark hair falling down over his face, and takes both of her hands in his. "I want to deserve you."

She considers for a moment and then squeezes his fingers to say that she forgives him, that she understands. It's like her with Roger Denby; she wanted him to want her. She will tell Peter about Roger, sometime. Maybe he will tell her more about Monica later as well; she's sure there is more to tell. But for now, this is enough. *In the beginning of our marriage, we didn't know how to make one another happy. But we were learning, we were getting better.* Peter's wide square hands wrapped around hers. She'd forgotten how out of place those peasant hands looked on the ends of his long arms. How could she have forgotten so much?

They fall into silence, their glances drifting back to Henry's sleeping head. He seems to have adjusted to being tied down in a bed with his leg pinned up into the air. He accepts it without question, the way he accepts most things—the need to give up diapers and eat vegetables, the need to look both ways and hold a grown-up's hand when he crosses the street—although being three, he sometimes forgets.

"We were very lucky," says Peter.

"Yes, we were."

That night, when she and Peter lie down fully dressed on the spare hospital bed, Josie feels awkward, as if this were a first date winding down to a good-night kiss. And then he touches her in his old comfortable way, runs a hand across a shoulder and down an arm, knits his fingers into hers. They stare at one another in the sickly orange glow of the vapor lights in the hospital parking lot. They haven't kissed yet, she thinks, and he tilts his head toward her, steers her arm around his waist, and gives her a long kiss. The type that married people don't bother with after a while. She's forgotten what an ardent kisser Peter is, much better than Roger Denby. Sorry, Roger, she thinks apologetically.

After a while, she comes up for air. "Don't get too carried away. I forgot to grab my diaphragm when the ambulance came."

"Well, I was thinking," he whispers. "That we should have another kid."

She's about to laugh, but then opens her eyes and sees that he's serious. "When did you come up with that idea? About a minute ago?"

"No, actually I've been thinking it for a while, but I didn't want to say anything, because you hadn't finished your dissertation."

They had always agreed that a second child was out of the question; as impoverished graduate students, they could hardly afford one child. But maybe the unspoken truth was that their marriage seemed so makeshift and temporary that one child was all the weight it could bear. That a second child would be an act of choice, not like their marriage or Henry, which had happened by default.

"So what's different now? I still haven't finished my dissertation." But they both know that, with Henry's accident, everything is different; they will never look at anything the same way again. She slips her hand under the strange green T-shirt—there is that nice chest hair.

"I know what it's like to be an only child. And Leslie's so much older, you might as well be an only child. We don't want Henry to be lonely like we were."

A lot Peter knows about siblings, she thinks, kissing him again. She is wearing a strange green T-shirt too—given to her by Leslie—and he touches it tentatively as if the texture of the cloth, and the skin underneath it, is unexpected.

"So, I figure that there will be at least four years between Henry and a second baby. I don't think it should be any more than that, do you?" He bends down and slides his lips along her neck.

Would it be four years? He was always so much better at math than she was. A little baby sister for Henry, why not? *Our children brought us together. And there would have been more children.* Peter has managed to get rid of his blue jeans somehow in this narrow bed. It's a lucky thing that they have had this family-planning discussion. The night nurse said she wouldn't be back for another hour. Actually, it isn't as hard to take off blue jeans in a hospital bed as one might think. They should probably flip up the side rails. So no one topples out.

THREE WEEKS LATER, Josie clanks down a metal spiral staircase to the basement of the Crowley Public Library. She is doing her last Jackie memo for Fiona Jones.

Fiona was surprisingly understanding about Josie taking two weeks off to stay with Henry in the hospital, and actually got tearful when she first heard about Henry's accident. "My son fell off his bike once and got knocked out," she said. That was all—one of those experiences that bond parents together.

But now that Henry is home from the hospital, Fiona sounds like her old self again. "So how's Harold doing?" she asks. "Tearing around the house, I suppose."

"He's in a body cast from his chest to his ankles, Fiona. He's not running anywhere."

"Well, that's probably much easier. Too bad you can't keep him in a body cast until he's twenty." She doesn't wait for an answer before she switches the subject back to Jackie. "Now, I got your Maurice Tempelsman memo."

"Yes."

"So that's it? You don't have anything more for me?"

Josie can't tell if Fiona's tone is suspicious or irritated; whatever it is, she definitely doesn't sound pleased. "Sorry, but I've been through everything at the Kennedy Library—the oral histories, her White House memos. There wasn't much to find." Why is she apologizing? She did everything Fiona told her to, she's done nothing wrong. Getting a clandestine copy of the Camelot notes was a fluke; she isn't obligated to hand it over.

"Now, how about the closed material at the library? The Manchester interviews, et cetera. You *did* ask about those, correct?"

"Yup. So sorry, they said. It's closed for a hundred years. Those were Mrs. Onassis's final instructions." Josie has an unnerving feeling that Fiona has somehow read her mind. Eleanor was like that, had a sixth sense when Josie was covering something up. "You would never let a friend copy your homework, would you?" she once said on the very afternoon that Josie had done just that.

"All right, then. I'll send you your last check," Fiona says, sounding dispirited. "I guess I'll have to play up the Black Jack angle. You wouldn't be willing to do some final fact checking, would you?"

Josie is almost giddy with relief. "Of course," she gushes. "Anything. Anything for you."

Fiona has given her a list of what she calls "odds and ends" to research—the date when JFK was first diagnosed with Addison's disease, the hospital where Rosemary's lobotomy was performed, the year Janet showed symptoms of Alzheimer's, the birth date of the stillborn girl. At least Josie doesn't have to trek to the Kennedy Library for this pedestrian info; the Crowley Public will do just fine.

The local-history section in the rear basement annex, where Josie found the trunk of Ada Silsbee papers four years ago, is the oddest section of the very odd Ruth Hawkins Memorial Library founded by Ruth Hawkins, a library visionary who invented her own cataloging method and patented cast-iron shelving. When every other library opted for Dewey decimal, she started her own library. The fact that all the Kennedy books are shelved in the local-history section has something to do with the vagaries of the Hawkins system.

Josie pulls a light chain and steps down a long skinny aisle of Hawkins-patent library shelves packed tight. The Kennedy books are easy to spot—they are the only ones new enough to have book jackets covered over with cellophane. She searches for the call number for Nigel Hamilton's *JFK—Reckless Youth*, and finds it shelved between *Massachusetts Regiments at Gettysburg* and *The First Church of Crowley—A Centennial Celebration*. Ah, the eclectic pleasures of the Hawkins system. It always took her forever to find anything at the Crowley Library because she had to browse on either side. Josie has, in fact, already read *Massachusetts Regiments at Gettysburg*—it was the kind of thing she resorted to during those endless summers in Crowley. She pulls down *The First Church of Crowley—A Centennial Celebration*. On the dedication page is a poem in small type.

The Winter Dress

It will not stay! The gown so satin white,
Which falls in folds on Nature's bosom bare
And dances in the winter moonbeam's light,
A raiment such as dainty spirits wear.
                    —By the Reverend Edward Silsbee,
            Rector, First Church of Crowley, 1858–1879

Josie flashes hot with indignation. The poem isn't by Edward Silsbee, it's by his sister, Ada; it was included in her volume *New England Narcissa*. The man not only forced his sister to live as a hermit, he plagiarized her. Josie flips to the section on Silsbee and checks the biographical note. *Silsbee, the only child of Samuel and Rebecca Silsbee of North Adams, Massachusetts, was educated at home and attended Harvard in the Class of 1853.* Worse and worse, Josie thinks; Ada has been eliminated from his official biography. She studies a photograph of the Reverend Silsbee on the next page. He certainly looked like his sister—the same hook nose and jutting chin, the giraffe neck and elongated hands, even the same ring on the little finger of his left hand. Suddenly the hair prickles up on the back of her neck, and she holds the photograph up to the overhead lightbulb, peering closely. No, he doesn't look like Ada Silsbee, he *is* Ada Silsbee. Josie settles weakly on the floor, rereads the biographical note, and studies the photograph for a full minute.

Ada Silsbee was a man? Josie considers all the evidence—no birth or death records, no social life, no correspondence with anyone who had actually ever seen her, the obsessive record keeping about clothing, the excessive use of female body imagery, the elaborately curlicued handwriting. Letting out a soft groan, she stretches out flat on the cold cement floor and pinches the bridge of her nose. What is she going to do with a half-written dissertation about an oppressed woman poet?

But Josie can't help feeling slightly vindicated. She always knew there was something odd about Ada; she didn't make sense as a woman. She makes a lot of sense as a man—a male projection of female behavior, a creativity that could find expression only as a woman. And the lists of dresses and accessories—Josie could have some fun analyzing those, now that she's become so savvy about people's outfits. She jumps to her feet; she has made a true discovery—the first American cross-dresser—no, better yet, the first transcendentalist cross-dresser, an Emersonian man-woman. Ada Silsbee and Josephine Trask have just been rescued from the dustbin of unpublishable dissertations.

Josie ferries *The First Church of Crowley—A Centennial Celebration* over to the Xerox machine. She selects "1" for number of copies, and then impulsively adds a zero. This news deserves ten copies. She has to tell Peter right away (this will fit right into his Jackie worldview); Fiona will have to wait, once again. Josie jogs down the library steps, past the church, across the common, up the front lawn of the homestead, past the "For Sale" sign. She slams in through the front screen door and marches down the hall to the kitchen. "Peter?"

"He's outside with Henry," Eleanor says. She is baking brownies for her AA meeting. In the three weeks since she's joined AA, she's already volunteered to be in charge of refreshments and cleanup. The brownies, however, are from a Duncan Hines mix—she's sworn off cooking along with booze.

Josie cuts through the porch and finds them sitting around the picnic table on the back lawn. Henry is propped up in his body cast between two chairs, solemnly squishing five tubs of play-dough into a mud-colored lump. Peter is tapping out an article on his laptop—

an "About Men" column on a father tending his three-year-old in a body cast.

"Guess what?" she yells, but they can't hear her because Fred is mowing the lawn. She walks over to them, waits for their identical brown faces to look up, and throws the photocopies high into the air. They pause for a heartbeat in the breeze, and then sail down over their heads.

Henry smiles. "Mommy make a mess."

chapter 20

If I get the ball, which way do I run?
—JACQUELINE KENNEDY, at a Kennedy touch football game

◈

They come to a squeaking halt at the Cape Cod rotary clogged with August traffic, and sit wedged between a camper piled with bikes and an Audi with its dark glass windows rolled up. Josie flings back in her seat with disgust. "We drove three thousand miles for this?" she asks petulantly, rolling down the window of their un-air-conditioned car. Even with the window down, the car is heating up to sauna level, and she starts to worry about the baby getting heat stroke. At two months, his temperature regulation is immature and she should probably at least sprinkle him with water and fan him with the road atlas. She turns around to examine both boys asleep in the back seat—Nathaniel in a T-shirt and diaper with his skinny newborn legs pulled up against the sides of his baby bucket, and Henry slumped in one corner. She rests a finger against Nathaniel's stomach and finds it cool and dry like a dog's nose.

Peter smiles and reaches over to pat her knee with a clammy hand. "Don't worry," he says. "We'll have fun." In truth, Peter seems to be looking forward to this vacation more than she is. At dinner parties in Berkeley, he described her family as if it were a tabloid story with some new delicious detail unfolding each week. The folly of Eleanor's new house clearly delighted him.

When Eleanor sold the homestead last winter and reported she was moving to the Cape to be near Fred, Josie sent away for some brochures on retirement communities which offered services for seniors. Then Eleanor called to say that she and Fred had found the perfect place. No, it wasn't a retirement community. "We're not ready for that yet," she said. It was, in fact, an old Boy Scout camp, with a main lodge and several outbuildings. "We'll have our own compound, just like the Kennedys," she said brightly.

Josie didn't even bother to point out the foolishness of this comment—their family, with a divorced mother, two daughters, and a single grandchild (with one on the way) hardly constituted a clan. An abandoned, ramshackle camp was not exactly comparable to a dozen pristine white houses perched above the ocean. "What do you need all that space for?" Josie asked.

"For the kids and grandchildren in the summer," Eleanor replied. "And in the fall and spring, for some of our friends who need a place to stay while they get their feet on the ground."

"Oh . . ." said Josie, her voice trailing.

Eleanor couldn't help providing a few more unsettling details. It wasn't very well winterized, but Fred would fix that. And he'd work on the driveway too, which was nothing but parallel ruts a quarter mile long, so her Pontiac could negotiate it in winter. "I admit it's a little crude," she said, "but that's why we got it so cheaply."

"Well, I hope you can at least see the water," Josie said.

"Oh, no," Eleanor said dismissively, as if such an idea were ridiculous. "I wouldn't want to see the water. I'm an inland girl. The sound and the smell of the ocean is all I can handle."

After five minutes, the traffic unjams, and they drive swiftly past shingled churches, ice cream stands, and bicycle-rental shops. Just when the ocean looms into view, so Josie can see bobbing sailboats and rocky islands in the distance, they take an ominous turn inland, down a dirt road lined with stubby pine trees. Here and there in tiny clearings stand the vacation homes of those who can't afford a water view—one-story bungalows with shutters perforated by cutout shamrocks and crescent moons, lawns jammed with gas grills and motor-boats on trailers. The road narrows down to grassy ruts and then ends at a tall wooden gate, with "Camp Cochise" spelled out in crooked, warped letters. Peter downshifts and starts humming along with joy-ful anticipation. The pine trees close in so tightly that branches scrape along the sides of the car, and then they pull up in front of a log lodge with a porch constructed of tangled birch branches. At the peak of the lodge, on the end of a tilted whitewashed pole, flaps a tattered navy-blue flag with "Cochise" emblazoned in orange letters. One half of the front lawn has been turned into an enormous corn patch, a battalion of silky tassels gleaming in the afternoon light. Eleanor had written in May, *I am planting ten rows of corn so there will be plenty when you visit in August.* The stalks part, and out step Eleanor and Fred, both dressed in baggy denim shorts and canvas sun hats, both with armfuls of corn. "Look!" Eleanor shouts gaily. "Enough to start our own farm stand."

She drops the corn on the grass and rushes over to peer through the back window at the still sleeping Henry and this new grandchild. "He's a baldy just like you were," she whispers. Everything about Eleanor is plumper and rounder than last summer; her bosom and middle now join together in a smooth mound. Fred's high-calorie meals have taken their toll. But her florid face under the brim of her hat is twinkly and merry, and reminds Josie for some reason of Henry's favorite Beatrix Potter character, Mrs. Tiggy-Winkle the hedgehog.

The moment Josie emerges from the car, still sticky and cranky, Eleanor slips her soft arm through hers. "Let me take you for a tour," she says with an eagerness that is touching. She leads Josie up the warped steps, across the tanglewood porch, through a whanging screen door, and into a huge two-story room with a fieldstone fire-place and hand-hewn beams, still decorated with felt camp banners. The smell of pine pitch and dust remind Josie of the Y camp on Lake Fairlee; the odors of summer camps must be ubiquitous. The furnishings are Spartan—a saggy love seat and a morris chair next to the fireplace, a gate-legged table with four chairs by a kitchen alcove. These are the only modest items Eleanor has kept from the homestead, items Josie can hardly remember from the odd corners of the pantry and library. All the grander furnishings—the antiques, the portraits, the leather-bound books, the silver—were sold at auction. Josie tries to imagine Fred and Eleanor's life in this place: Fred cooking a meal on the two-burner stove while she sits in the chair by the fire on a winter's night, how their voices echo under the vaulted ceiling.

Josie prowls around until she finds their bedroom, a small annex jutting off the rear that is just large enough for a double bed (not Eleanor's tiger-maple pencil post) and two tiny nightstands—one with a Bible and rosary, the other with a volume of Unitarian sermons and a Raymond Chandler mystery. She peeks behind a curtain that conceals a closet pole and studies Eleanor's shirtwaist dresses hanging next to Fred's khakis, her loafers on the floor next to his.

Later, Fred escorts them down a spongy moss path through a sunless pine grove to their quarters—a bunkhouse with open screened sides. Some Cochise camper a half century ago had inscribed "Whispering Pines Cabin" with a wood-burning tool on the plank above the door. Behind the bunkhouse sits a shed that Josie guesses must be the outhouse. (The main lodge thankfully has a full bath, which Eleanor says they are welcome to use.) He holds open the screen door and waves them grandly into a gloomy room with four built-in bunks, a table, and a wobbly crib. "Now, I thought Henry might like the top bunk. The other grandchildren loved it."

What other grandchildren? Josie wonders, and then realizes he must mean his own.

"You and Peter can be on the bottom bunks. And the baby can sleep in this crib we found at the take-it-or-leave-it pile at the dump. Here's a table for you to do your writing on, but I'm afraid there's no power for your computers. Here's a flashlight so you can find the outhouse in the middle of the night." He clicks it on and shines the beam over the bunks made up neatly with olive-green army blankets and the log walls carved with campers' initials, and then waits for their reactions.

Peter jumps in. "This is great, Fred. Reminds me of the Scout camp I went to in the Sierras." Peter never went to a Boy Scout camp, but this has the desired effect—Fred bows slightly with modest pleasure.

"Well, I better go get the water boiling for the corn," he says, retreating back down the path.

Josie turns to Peter, prepared to hear him say this is too strange, we can't stay here. She could already see a swarm of ants heading up the side of Nathaniel's baby bucket. Suddenly Henry leaps down off the top bunk, landing on that newly healed leg with such force that both his parents wince, slams out the screen door, and heads down the path at a gallop, his windmilling bare feet leaving a dust cloud in his wake. Peter grins, shrugs, and reaches down to reroute the ants marching toward Nathaniel's bald, blue-veined head.

Three days later, Josie sits with Eleanor on the tanglewood porch shucking a heap of corn. "How are we going to eat it tonight?" she asks lazily. Fred has already come up with several creative variations—fritters, muffins, pudding, chowder.

Eleanor wipes her hands on her shorts. "On the cob, I think. That's the way that Leslie likes it best." At the mention of Leslie, they both fall into a wary silence and stare nervously down the driveway. Leslie called at noon from the New Jersey Turnpike to say she'd be there by dinnertime. Actually she said, "We'll be there by dinnertime," but they didn't dare ask who constituted the "we." There were a lot of possibilities—Simon, Ralph Cavanaugh, her miniature schnauzer, Maurice.

Over the last year, news of Leslie had arrived in frantic bursts, like bulletins from a third-world war zone. "Simon hired a private detective who followed me to a motel." "Simon's kicked me out and had the locks changed on our office." "I've set up a solo practice." "I've found a studio apartment." She never mentioned Ralph directly (maybe she thought her phone was tapped), but Josie assumed that he must be the cause of all this upheaval. The only thing she had told them of her vacation plans was, "I'm coming sometime in August. You'll see me when you see me." At least the old rigid, judgmental Leslie was predictable; who knew what the new Leslie had in store for them.

Josie has just bent down to shake a bunny rattle at Nathaniel in his baby bucket, when she hears a grinding of car gears. It is still way in the distance, but getting closer. The others have heard it too— Eleanor stands up and shades her eyes; Peter, Henry, and Fred step out one by one from the thicket of cornstalks and stand in the hot afternoon sun blinking with expectation. The gears grind again as whatever is coming toward them downshifts, and there is a metallic dragging sound as a fender hits the top of a pothole. It must be kids in a beach buggy, Josie thinks. Who else would drive down this road so recklessly? A dramatic cloud of dust rises, and in the midst, with its wheels spinning in the sand, comes a brown Isuzu. "Mommy, look. It's a brown jeep," Henry reports.

Both doors fly open, there is a pause, and then Leslie and a man with a blond-gray ponytail step out and stand motionless, as if they are forming a tableau for the enjoyment of this gathering of relatives. The first thing Josie notices is the black and the white—the man in a black T-shirt and black jeans and bare feet, and Leslie in a gauzy white dress and bare feet. Leslie raises her sunglasses to the top of her head and then pushes back her long uncoiffed hair, which has been allowed to revert to gray at the temples. Then, in a single defiant gesture, she runs her hand down the rough side of her baggy dress and pulls it tightly against her body so the outline of a very pregnant, prow-shaped stomach shows. About six or seven months along, Josie guesses with an expert eye. A cousin for her boys.

They all turn toward Eleanor in anticipation of some sort of official greeting, but she stands mutely, her brow furrowed with uncertainty. Josie can almost hear her mental churnings. Should she say, "Congratulations, you're pregnant," or would Leslie be somehow offended? Should she say, "You must be Ralph?" But . . . what if it's not Ralph? Peter, who could never stand social awkwardness for very long, strides forward with arms outstretched. "Welcome to Camp Cochise," he says heartily.

Later that night, after lobsters and steamers (eschewed by the man who was Ralph after all, because he is a vegetarian), and homemade strawberry shortcake, and after everyone has retired into their respective cabins, Peter wedges himself into Josie's bunk so they can have a whispered postmortem. "Well, at least he's better than Simon," Josie says, although she's not completely sure. Ralph had a certain New Age charm (he wore a blue jay feather tucked under the elastic of his ponytail), and was attentive to Leslie. And Leslie did look radiant in the candlelight, with her round belly and her chin slightly shiny with lobster butter. But they talked of a new life that seemed just as unyielding as Leslie's old one. Ralph was a Buddhist and never wore animal products, hence the bare feet. They had had it with Phoenix, and were heading to Taos. "We found an adobe ten miles out of town. We've decided we don't need electricity anymore," Leslie announced.

Peter nestles closer, still smelling pleasantly of insect repellent and clam juice. "Do you think Ralph will deliver the baby himself?" he whispers.

"Hmm," Josie says sleepily. It is already midnight, and Nathaniel will be waking up in a couple of hours.

"You wild Trask women. First your mother takes up with an arsonist. Then your sister bolts with a *Dances with Wolves* pool professional. Who do you think you're going to run off with?"

"I wonder," she says, tucking the camp blanket more tightly around both of them. What she doesn't say is that she has already made her choice, recklessly and illogically, just like the other women in her family. And she has chosen the man beside her, even though she may never be certain of his love, and he may never be aware of his ability to hurt her. No safe, predictable man—no Maurice Tempelsman—for her.

When Nathaniel starts to squawk in the dead of night, Josie pulls on her down coat and polar fleece slippers and hunkers down into the sole chair by the writing desk for his feeding. She strokes his bald head as he ferociously sucks, his eyes pinched shut so tightly it looks painful. When they are open, they are wide-set and blue like hers, and stare out at the world with a slightly alarmed expression. The maternity nurse pronounced that bald babies turned out blond, and it only seems fair that Josie has gotten one that looks like her this time. Outside in the darkness she can hear some small creature scrambling through the underbrush; a raccoon is probably pulling the corncobs out of the compost heap again and will leave them strewn across the lawn. The chill night air is heavy with a saltwater mist that bodes poorly for tomorrow's weather. She pictures all of them gathered around a sputtering fire (the picturesque fieldstone fireplace smokes) playing an incomplete set of Chinese checkers that Eleanor has unearthed in the game cupboard.

As Nathaniel starts in on the other side, Josie switches on the flashlight and peruses the shoe box of correspondence she's brought along with her from California and has left untouched for two weeks. She unfolds a letter from Fiona Jones on stationery as stiff and mottled as a dried-up sheepskin.

Dear Josie,
    Enclosed is a copy of Jackie—The Dark Secret *hot off the presses. Isn't the cover something! Had to pay a pretty penny for that photograph. As you requested, I deleted your name from the acknowledgments, although I can't fathom why. The part about Black Jack's racial background was quite a coup, and I think one should take credit where credit is due. Thanks for the birth announcement and the pic. Cute little buggers. Hope all is well with your poet . . . and your husband.*

Cheers,
Fiona

Josie had tried to read *Jackie—The Dark Secret* so she could at least send Fiona a congratulatory note, but was disappointed to find a biography like all the others she had read; even the allegations about Black Jack sounded unremarkable. She searched in vain for something from her research memos—the homely details of Jackie's life that she had found so interesting—but all she found were the lists of affairs or alleged affairs, the tragedies one after another. Jackie writ large, a life without nuances.

Next Josie pulls out a postcard from Monica (inexplicably, of Hillary Clinton) that accompanied a baby present for Nathaniel (an educational mobile of human faces drawn in black and white lines that made him cry). It was pointedly addressed only to Josie and said: "Apparently babies only see in black and white. Monica."

She called last fall, when Josie finally made it to Berkeley, and suggested the two of them meet for coffee at a remote café three miles from campus so "we can have some privacy." Josie had expected Monica to be sporting her usual healthy California look, but now that she was actually living in California, she had opted for a new image—a black linen sheath, ballet slippers, an angled haircut and sloppy black eyeliner that made her look waifish and exotic like a French cabaret singer. She sighed loudly, dropped three sugar cubes in her cappuccino, and said in a confiding voice, "I think I owe you the truth about what really happened between Peter and me."

Josie fished the tea bag out of her Red Zinger (she was already pregnant), and fixed those smudgy almond eyes with a level gaze. "I already know the truth."

Monica considered this for a moment and then seemed relieved, as if she had been spared some unpleasant chore. "Well, I'm glad he was honest with you," she said. And then, after another moment of consideration, said, "Tell me how your dissertation is going."

Josie had hoped she would ask; in fact, this had been the real reason she had agreed to meet Monica in the first place. She told the story slowly, allowing Monica's attention to flicker away. "Well, you know how stuck I was. Peter was so fed up with me. Everything I'd written was pretty uninspired."

"Uh-huh," said Monica, impatiently agreeing.

"So one day, last August, I was in the basement of the Crowley Library . . ." She stopped and waited until Monica's eyes drifted back, and then she told her the rest. How Josie reexamined Ada Silsbee's writings and diaries and realized they documented the secret life of a cross-dresser. "There it had been, the whole time, under my nose, and I hadn't seen." How Irene Horton had called Josie's discovery "truly significant," how Peter's publisher was interested in considering her dissertation, how *Ms.* had asked her to submit an article on cross-dressing in early America.

Monica gave her an appraising look, as if she were seeing her for the first time, checked her over from the tips of her Birkenstocks and rag-wool socks, up her leggings, to her baggy sweatshirt, and announced, "I'm jealous." And then it was like the old days when they were in the Brown women's history study group, and they discussed the recent studies of cross-dressing, and Monica rattled off the title of an obscure article by a German post-structuralist, which Josie jotted down on a paper napkin. Afterward when they parted Josie couldn't say that they were exactly friends, but at least she could recall why Monica had once been a friend.

Monica's note also includes her new address at a two-year women's college in New Jersey, where she has finally landed a tenure-track job, but Josie won't write her, because what could she say that wouldn't seem like gloating? My marriage is reborn, thanks to you; my children are beautiful; my dissertation is finished; I've been hired as an instructor in English.

Next she pulls out a letter from Roger Denby typed on his Rutgers stationery, another piece of unfinished business. She hadn't talked to him again after their date in Harvard Square. He had called her once in Crowley, but she was still at the hospital with Henry, and he had spoken to Peter instead. "He was pretty unfriendly," Peter said later. "Almost hostile, really. What did you say about me, anyway?" She was tempted to say something lame like he's just being protective, he thinks of me as his kid sister. But that would only make Peter roll his eyes, so she didn't offer any explanation. Last spring, she sent Roger Nathaniel's birth announcement, along with a note about her research, which she hoped would serve as sufficient follow-up to their last conversation. He wrote back a few weeks later:

Dear Josie,

Enclosed are the galley proofs of McGeorge Bundy and the Broken Promise. *As you can see, I made all the changes you suggested (including the title), and many of my colleagues have been highly complimentary. I have listed you under Special Acknowledgments on page vii.*

Congratulations on completing your dissertation. Your discovery about Ada Silsbee sounds very exciting and I will be looking for your book in a year or two. When the time comes, I would be glad to send your CV to the head of the English Department. (I promised myself I wouldn't say that.)

And further congratulations on the birth of your son. You certainly have two handsome boys. I think the older one must favor your husband more. I hope your new baby will take after his lovely mother.

While I am saying things I probably shouldn't, I was back at

*the Kennedy Library this spring. Even though I knew you
wouldn't be there, I brought two sandwiches anyway. I sat
outside, next to the* Victura, *and ate them both, thinking of
you.*

Your Friend,
Roger

Nathaniel has finally finished and drifted back to sleep. She tucks
him into the crook of her left arm, covers him over with the flap of
her parka, adjusts the flashlight so it shines onto a tablet of paper,
and writes:

Dear Roger,
    Thank you for the book. I think M.B.A.T.B.P. *is a page-
turner, but I thought that the first time I read it. You give me
much more credit than I deserve.*
    *I will never forget your kindness to me last summer. As Jackie
once said (about Aristotle Onassis, but that doesn't matter),
"He rescued me at a time when my life was engulfed in
shadows."*

Love always,
Josie

She pauses, chews thoughtfully on the end of her ballpoint, listens to the shuddering breaths of the three sleeping souls around
her, and then adds:

    *P.S. A friend of ours from graduate school, Monica Glass, is
moving to your area, and I am enclosing her address. She is
somewhat high-strung, but I think you may find her interesting.*